“FAST-MOVING [illegible] and laughs . . . Moore k[illegible] pages turning and the blood running. Sad, introspective vampires in powdered wigs need not apply.” —*Page Horrific*

“*BLOOD RED* DOES WHAT ALL THE BEST VAMPIRE NOVELS DO; it . . . digs for blood beneath the skin.”
—Rick Kleffel, *The Agony Column*

“OFFERS PLENTY OF . . . HORROR CHILLS leavened with flashes of humor.” —*Publishers Weekly*

“THE COMPARISONS TO VINTAGE STEPHEN KING ARE JUSTIFIED. Brutal and scary, *Blood Red* has restored my faith, not only in the vampire subgenre, but in horror as a whole.” —Kealan Patrick Burke

“THERE IS SO MUCH TO ENJOY ABOUT *BLOOD RED*. Moore is powerfully descriptive.”
—Baryon-online.com

“MOORE HAS WOVEN TOGETHER THE BEST THREADS OF VAMPIRE LORE with lust, power, and brutality . . . Grab this treat, turn off the phone and enjoy a refreshingly inventive take on the vampire tale.”
—Monsters and Critics.com

continued . . .

BLOOD RED

James A. Moore

BERKLEY BOOKS, NEW YORK

THE BERKLEY PUBLISHING GROUP
Published by the Penguin Group
Penguin Group (USA) Inc.
375 Hudson Street, New York, New York 10014, USA
Penguin Group (Canada), 90 Eglinton Avenue East, Suite 700, Toronto, Ontario M4P 2Y3, Canada
(a division of Pearson Penguin Canada Inc.)
Penguin Books Ltd., 80 Strand, London WC2R 0RL, England
Penguin Books Ireland, 25 St. Stephen's Green, Dublin 2, Ireland (a division of Penguin Books Ltd.)
Penguin Group (Australia), 250 Camberwell Road, Camberwell, Victoria 3124, Australia
(a division of Pearson Australia Group Pty. Ltd.)
Penguin Books India Pvt. Ltd., 11 Community Centre, Panchsheel Park, New Delhi—110 017, India
Penguin Group (NZ), 67 Apollo Drive, Rosedale, North Shore 0745, Auckland, New Zealand
(a division of Pearson New Zealand Ltd.)
Penguin Books (South Africa) (Pty.) Ltd., 24 Sturdee Avenue, Rosebank, Johannesburg 2196,
South Africa

Penguin Books Ltd., Registered Offices: 80 Strand, London WC2R 0RL, England

This is a work of fiction. Names, characters, places, and incidents either are the product of the author's imagination or are used fictitiously, and any resemblance to actual persons, living or dead, business establishments, events, or locales is entirely coincidental. The publisher does not have any control over and does not assume any responsibility for author or third-party websites or their content.

BLOOD RED

A Berkley Book / published by arrangement with the author

PRINTING HISTORY
Earthling Publications hardcover edition / October 2005
Berkley mass-market edition / September 2007

Copyright © 2005 by James A. Moore.
Introduction copyright © 2005 by Simon Clark.
Cover design by Tony Greco.
Interior text design by Laura K. Corless.

ISBN: 978-0-425-21759-7

BERKLEY®
Berkley Books are published by The Berkley Publishing Group,
a division of Penguin Group (USA) Inc.,
375 Hudson Street, New York, New York 10014.
BERKLEY® is a registered trademark of Penguin Group (USA) Inc.
The "B" design is a trademark belonging to Penguin Group (USA) Inc.

PRINTED IN THE UNITED STATES OF AMERICA

10 9 8 7 6 5 4 3 2 1

ACKNOWLEDGMENTS

No book is written alone and truer words have never been spoken. The author would like to thank Paul Miller for his insights, kind words of encouragement, and enthusiasm. Thanks also to my wife, Bonnie, for her amazing patience and love. You have always been and remain my heart and soul. Thanks also to Kelly Perry, one of the finest editors I have ever had the pleasure of working with. Under incredible time constraints, Kelly kept me on track and made *Blood Red* five times the book it would have been otherwise. For those reasons and a thousand others, this book is dedicated with awe and admiration to the people listed above. Thank you, more than I can say with mere words, thank you.

—James A. Moore

QUOTH THE RAVEN

AN INTRODUCTION BY SIMON CLARK

"Stone the crows." A figure of speech uttered in exclamation. "A murder of crows." A collective noun for a gathering of crows. There are more, including the evocative "a story-telling of crows."

These devourers of corpse meat are found pretty much across the planet. There are over a hundred different species of the crow family, including the carrion, hooded, and American crows, plus rooks, jays, choughs, jackdaws, and Poe's iconic raven. Some are big and ominous-looking; as dark as black holes in the sky. Several of the species are small. One is even white.

Crows can be metaphor for the horror story. In the best tradition of Hitchcock's *The Birds,* crows tend not to arrive in a single battalion. A murder of crows assembles in ones or twos. You don't notice them infiltrating your neighborhood until suddenly you realize your house, or that children's climbing frame, is full of the black-feathered daemonic creatures. For me, the best horror stories are like that. The horror begins with a gradual accumulation of off-key details at near-subliminal level in an otherwise harmonious environment. The reader outside the book—and the hero inside the covers—doesn't realize that anything is seriously amiss until it's too late.

That's why horror is subversive. It infiltrates the reader's mind before it launches its attack. Sit with friends and discuss favorite horror movies and stories. A goodly bunch of those mentioned will feature an everyday, safe environment. Or what should be a safe environment. The home for instance. How many horror stories begin with the hero and family moving house to a new home only to find they hear footsteps on the stairs at the dead of night, or the lavatory inexplicably flushing? Psychologists will admit that the home and the self are inextricably linked. So the notion of your house being invaded or haunted by a ghost is, in effect, a metaphor for an invasion or haunting of one's mind. And one thing our culture teaches us is this: what should be our one safe place in the world—our home—is hideously vulnerable to supernatural attack. As children, didn't we fear the monster under the bed? Ghosts are already in the woodwork. Vampires, zombies, and assorted ghouls soon find a way across the threshold (heck, even those starlings in *The Birds* . . . remember the gush of our feathered friends down the chimney?). And it doesn't matter whether you're playwright-turned-caretaker in a swanky mountain hotel or a man of God. They're coming to get you.

Case in point: in 1715, the Reverend Samuel Wesley, father of John Wesley, one of the founders of the Methodist Church, experienced a poltergeist infestation at their home, the Epworth Rectory in England. At night he and his family were alarmed to hear groans and weird howling from the attic, accompanied by frenzied banging. Frequently, he was woken at night by what sounded like torrents of coins cascading onto the floor and the crash of breaking bottles. But when he investigated, he found nothing visibly amiss. Members of the household glimpsed a strange figure in white. His children eventually called the specter Old Jeffrey. See, no one's safe.

Nor are the inhabitants of the peacefully affluent Black Stone Bay, Rhode Island, in *Blood Red*. Oh, they think they're in no danger, but just as the crows settle unnoticed one by one on their houses, a sinister infiltration has already begun in Black Stone Bay.

In this novel of James A. Moore's you're going to encounter crows aplenty, and that's as much of the plot as I'm giving away. Of course, I can let other things slip . . . Quick! While the publisher's out of the room! Come close and listen:

Blood Red is a beautifully written horror novel. The easy-going loquacious style is deceptive. Take it from me: anything that reads so well, with such attention to detail, is damnably hard to write. This prose style is the product of years of hard work, of staying home with the blinds shut when everyone else is out having fun in the sunshine. James A. Moore has paid his dues, honed his craft, and now the delight is all yours in reading a powerful and witty story, which opens in the elegantly tantalizing way that is the mark of exceptional talent. Pun intended but there's a rich vein of humor here as well as horror. Despite the carnage of the climax, the ending is genuinely poignant, too. And as you read, you're forgiven if you exclaim more than once "Stone the crows!" It's a kind of book that unveils surprise after surprise.

Simon Clark
Doncaster, England
July 2005

BLOOD
RED

CHAPTER 1

I

There are those who have and those who do not. The majority of Black Stone Bay, Rhode Island, had it in abundance. Along the shoreline that looked out over the Atlantic Ocean, a long run of mansions stood at attention or sprawled across their massive lawns, regarding the world with blind glass eyes that hid treasures most people would have thought excessive in the extreme. In the summertime, the bay ran thick with yachts and luxury sailboats, with a few smaller speedboats just to add a little balance.

The land could easily have accommodated a hundred times as many houses, but most of the people in town would never allow that to happen. A few had tried to change the minds of the people in power. They had all failed.

Of course, not everyone in the town was disgustingly wealthy; it just looked that way to the uninitiated. Someone had to serve those who ruled and it would hardly be convenient if the hired help had to drive for several hours to get to work. The flow of tourists that poured into Black Stone Bay to see the sights, eat at the numerous restaurants, and blow their money was as large as would be anticipated in any town that had ample seaside views and spacious hotels. That was to be expected, during the summer at least, and sometimes even in the fall, when the leaves changed.

And they needed servants, too; local help that could be hired at a reasonable rate. The town had a lot of blue-collar laborers; it just knew how to hide them from plain sight.

All in all, Black Stone Bay was relaxed and tended to stay that way. The people—whether inordinately wealthy or merely well-off—lived their lives from day to day with the usual numbers of problems and solutions. Certainly the people attending the two universities had their own concerns.

Neither the Winslow Harper University of Arts and Sciences nor the Sacred Dominion University were known for allowing anyone to stay in their programs without being exceptional. The student bodies paid dearly for the privilege of attending and they worked hard or they lost their money. Both of the schools were Ivy League caliber—or "Potted Ivy" as the locals called them with tongues firmly planted in cheeks—and both were acknowledged for their excellence on a yearly basis. All in all, however, the people were comfortable with their positions in life; maybe not always happy, but comfortable.

Mary Margaret Preston, or Maggie if she knew a person well enough, could have told anyone who asked all about the people of Black Stone Bay; she'd lived there all her life. The young lady in question actually attended Winslow Harper and was in the top five percent of her class. Like most of the students, she worked her ass off to keep those grades. Unlike the vast majority, she also worked a job to pay her way. Maggie had more sense than to work at a restaurant, a bank, or in any number of jobs that would have left her financially strapped and worried about paying the outrageous tuition fees. She had managed to find employment that let her choose her hours and paid well enough that she seldom felt financially desperate.

Maggie was a prostitute. Not a hooker. Hookers don't make the sort of money Maggie did. She had no illusions about the work. It was a job, and it paid well. There were risks, to be sure, but most forms of employment have risks. And in the long run it was a means to an end.

Maggie had always been careful. She came from a large family—was the baby, in fact—and was the first member of the clan to ever actually make it to college. She might want children in the future, but they weren't on her current agenda and she didn't intend to add them to her roster of things she had to do. Also, the list of diseases she wanted nothing to do with was large, and a good number of them were sexually transmitted.

Protection was worn or nothing happened. She had Tom to make sure of that. A ridiculous portion of her money went to Thomas Alexander Pardue—Monkey Boy to Maggie, but never to his face—to ensure that he picked the right sort of clients for her. Failure to pay his exorbitant rates could also result in a few tragic encounters with Tom's fists or even a knife blade. Maggie tried not to dwell on that part of their arrangement. He'd done things to a few of the girls over the years and she knew he'd do it again if he didn't get his way.

In exchange for his fees, he got her a clientele that could afford to pay handsomely for her services and worried about getting caught with her as surely as she worried about her career choice being exposed. The thing about getting a good education from a superior school was that the university had an ethics committee. If she was busted and they found out, she could lose her place at the school and her standing in the society she wanted to join.

Of course she'd been of professional use to most of the committee, so that wasn't really too much of a problem, but she liked to keep up appearances.

Maggie knew the score. She was a good student and she was a call girl. The two worked well for her. Both were temporary. She liked sex, but she wasn't a raving nymphomaniac. She also looked at actual relationships as something entirely different from the work she did. For the present time she did not date, had no desire to date, and would not let herself fall for anyone. Not even the dozen or so very powerful men who'd offered to make her life incredibly comfortable. She was doing just fine without their help, and saw no reason to give up her chosen lifestyle.

Monkey Boy knew the score too, though he kept trying to break the rules. Sometimes she had to let him succeed. She was still recovering from his latest need to show her who was the boss.

She could always tell when he was in that mood. He'd start by offering her drugs that she refused. Sometimes he'd insist, and she would take them, but not nearly as often as he wanted. In most cases she was able to handle the matter with a fake-out. Sleight of hand was a useful skill and one she'd learned from her uncle, who was an amateur magician. Uncle Albert was a sweet old man, and not nearly as warped as most of her family thought he was. He was just . . . eccentric in the extreme.

Now and then, as with earlier tonight, Tom insisted on "sampling the wares." That was his way of saying he wanted to get laid. The thing about it was that Tom only felt it proper that the girls protest first, the better to have an excuse for knocking them around a little. He was smart enough not to leave marks, but it hurt when he decided to do his thing. She was also pretty sure the only way the creep could get off was if the girl he was using struggled and complained.

The good news was that he didn't make demands too often, at least not of her. Maggie made too much money for him to slap her around a lot, and he wasn't as horny as he was greedy. She was also smart enough not to get hooked on the shit he served to some of the girls. They were the ones that he took advantage of whenever he wanted. Once they wanted another fix, they would do whatever he told them to do. She didn't play that game. He knew it, she knew it. He just needed to feel big from time to time and that meant doing what he insisted was his right.

Some day she was going to pay someone to kill the bastard, but for now he served a necessary purpose for getting her what she needed. It was all about the future, you see. Maggie focused on what she wanted in the future to the exclusion of almost everything else. It helped smooth out the rough spots, like Monkey Boy.

So she was a little sore, yes, but that was all right. She had a new client tonight, one that was promising to be very lucrative, too. He was also a rarity, because he wanted her to come to his house.

His house, as if the black stone mansion on the Point could be called a house. Maggie drove her Ford Focus up to the gates of the palatial estate and didn't even have to wait for long. The automated iron barrier slid out of her way smoothly as she reached it, and she moved further into the place.

She let a low whistle out past her full lips and admired the architecture. "Damn. I want one of these." Most of the houses on the cliff walk were accessible; meaning that people could, if they were polite about it, actually move over the lawns and see the exteriors of the homes without any difficulty.

This place was not like most of the homes; it had more in common with a medieval fortress, with its heavy black stone walls around the actual perimeter and a main building made of the same dark granite that earned the town its name. The house had been there for as long as she could remember, but this was the first time she had ever seen it close up. It was stunning, to say the least. From what she'd heard when she was younger, there were something like 80 rooms in the place if you counted the extensions for the servants' quarters. That the lawns were flawless was a given, the hedges just so, and the ancient trees on the property were at least as old as the United States of America in most cases.

She didn't have much time to actually look the entire place over before the door to the massive structure opened. Not one to ignore an obvious hint, she shut down her car and climbed out, ready to meet her new client.

He stepped through the door and smiled at her, a man of average height, reasonable build, and dark hair. There was nothing overly impressive about his features, but he carried himself like a king, with confidence and a casual acceptance of his authority over all around him.

He wasn't like most of the guys she dealt with. Half of them came off as cocky; the others came off as nervous or just plain horny. Very few of them ever seemed relaxed about the situation.

"You would be Maggie, yes?" His voice was deep, but the words were softly spoken.

"That's me." She smiled as she spoke, not bothering with false pretenses or putting any seductive tones in her way of talking. For all she knew the man she was looking at was the butler.

He did not move to greet her, but stood within the threshold of the front door and waited for her to come to him. Even that was a bit of a change from the norm. Half the time the men she dealt with practically rolled out the carpet for her. She didn't mind, but she noticed. It was important to understand what was expected of a client, especially one who was still an unknown quantity.

"Come in, please." He stepped back and left her room to get past him without trouble. She looked around, letting herself take in the décor and the furnishings with a quick glance. It was all very nice. Most of the furnishings were museum quality and laid out with a meticulous eye for design and there were around a hundred places where people could be hiding. She didn't like that part at all. Just because the man was supposed to be safe didn't mean she was willing to assume the situation was what it was supposed to be. Tom had made mistakes before and girls had been hurt. Maggie had no desire to become a statistic.

The furnishings had obviously been laid out some time ago. Everything was spotless, but the rugs over the hardwood floors hadn't been set down recently and the furniture on top of the expensive rugs pressed down on areas that had become accustomed to bearing their weight.

Maggie waited until the door was closed before she looked the man over more carefully. His age could have been late thirties to early sixties. He had that sort of face; lots of character lines, but not a lot of wrinkles. Nice clothes, but obviously not meant for power lunches or the like. This was him being casual. That was okay. She preferred that.

She took her time studying him, knowing full well that she was being studied in return. She looked in the mirror every day and knew what he was seeing. Her hair was dark and naturally curly, but she made sure to add a touch of gel to keep it in control. Her face was almost heart-shaped: wide, high cheekbones and large dark eyes above a nose that was straight with a slight upward tilt. Her mouth was generous but just missed being pouty, and her chin was strong. She had an athletic figure from several years of gymnastics and dance that her father insisted would make her a better woman in her adult years, and she'd made it a point to keep herself in shape. She was also, to use Monkey Boy's favorite term, built like a brick shithouse. Today she was dressed in a white cream blouse and dark blue jeans. She looked good. She knew it. It came with the territory. After half a minute of looking her over from head to toe, he moved closer and took her hand.

"I hope you don't mind if we eat first. I like to get to know people." He had an accent, and she was normally very good with deciphering the way people spoke, but she couldn't for the life of her decide where he came from.

"We do whatever you want to do. And thank you, you have a lovely home." The words were calculated. First she made sure he understood that this was business and then she complimented his choice in domiciles. If he wanted to pay her rates and have dinner, that was fine. If he wanted her to perform her services, that was okay too. If he wanted her to move in tomorrow and marry him the week after, that was no longer an option. This way, he at least understood where she was coming from.

She walked with her host into the dining hall—she couldn't justifiably call it a room—and took the seat he offered her. The food laid out before her was the sort normally found only in the finest restaurants. That was okay. To her way of reckoning she'd certainly earned a nice meal.

Before she could settle in comfortably, he was next to her, sitting to her right, and he watched as she took small bites of the food placed before her. The lobster was fresh and cooked to perfection. So was everything else.

He did not speak as she ate, but merely watched her. A lot of people might have been nervous, but not Maggie. She'd been in far stranger situations and, if the man got off by observing her eating habits, that was his prerogative.

When the meal was finished, he poured two brandies and they sat in what she assumed was his study. The books along the walls were not, as she had seen in several places, set there for decoration. It was obvious that either the man in front of her or someone else in the house read, and often.

"Now then, on to business." He spoke calmly, not seeming the least bit in a rush to get anything done. Considering what he was paying, that was perfectly fair. He had paid for the night, which meant that until she left the house in the morning, she was his to do with as he pleased, barring anything that she disagreed to.

He rose from his seat and walked behind her, placing his hands on her shoulders as he leaned down to whisper in her ear. Maggie held her breath, wanting to hear exactly what the man had to say. "I have a few unusual requests to make of you, Maggie . . ."

She listened. Half an hour later she left his home puzzled, but glad to accommodate the man who was paying her so well.

II

It only took Kelli Entwhistle a few moments to realize she'd been duped. The silence in the house was enough to make her know that Teddy was up to something. And who would get the blame if he did something stupid? Why, that would be her, of course. They almost always blamed the babysitter when a kid managed to get himself into grief.

She put down the dishrag and walked out of the kitchen, looking around quickly with practiced eyes. Teddy Lister was a master at Hide and Seek. The problem seemed to be he never wanted to tell her when he was in the mood to play. At ten years of age, the little shit was practically an accomplished escape artist. She would have been pissed about it, too, but he was a damned cute little munchkin.

Bedrooms were empty. So were the rest of the rooms. One quick look at the attic door—where she had planted a very small piece of tape on the carpet to let her know if anyone went up the flight of wooden stairs—told her that Teddy had not gone that way either. That only left one other option worth considering.

Kelly grabbed her coat from off the chair where she'd draped it when she got to the Lister house, and slipped it on even as she reached for the back door's crystal knob.

Before actually leaving the building, she listened and, sure enough, she heard Teddy's voice and that of his best friend and number one accomplice in all things annoying, the equally cute and infuriating Avery Tripp.

She opened the door very, very carefully, letting the light spill out onto the back patio. It was well after sunset and the two boys were not supposed to be outside. One of the two was not even supposed to be at the house at all, but she had grown accustomed to that part of the equation. Avery Tripp was like a cabbage soup dinner: he kept coming back and stinking the place up when you least expected it. Mostly she meant the comparison in a good way.

The two of them were halfway down the stairs and, whatever they were doing, it had them far too engrossed to notice their babysitter sneaking closer. She made it all the way to the top step before a creaking board gave her away.

"Just what are you doing out here?" Kelli put as much venom as she could into the words, just to see how far they would jump. Avery flinched. Teddy let out a yelp and tried desperately to hide the magazine in his hands. Both boys had wide eyes and terrified expressions.

Rather than waiting for an explanation, Kelli walked down the four steps to where they were and grabbed the magazine from the trembling hands of her charge.

They managed to blush, even in the near darkness. Avery dropped a flashlight from his hand and all three of them watched it bounce and roll into the yard.

"Ohgodshe'sgonnafreak." It was one word, and came from Avery's lips in a high-speed whisper.

Teddy said what he always said when he got busted. "Avery made me do it."

Kelli looked at the cover of the *Penthouse Magazine* the

boys had been looking through and smiled. She knew they had to be up to something, especially when it was too quiet in the house.

"*Penthouse*? Where did you guys get a dirty magazine?" Kelli looked at Avery as she spoke, knowing full well he'd brought it with him.

Avery shrugged and looked at the ground for several seconds before he finally looked back at her. "I brought it."

"How much trouble are you going to be in if I tell your mom about this, Avery?"

She couldn't have gotten a better reaction if she'd pumped a million volts into his rear end. "Oh, jeez, Kelli . . . please don't tell on me." He was sweating now, worried, and that meant she had him exactly where she wanted him.

"You get your little butt home right now, Avery, and maybe I won't have to."

Teddy was the one who started to protest, but one look from her while she waved the magazine was enough to make him shut up. After a few moments of hemming and hawing, she gathered the two boys together and walked Avery back to his house three blocks over.

Three blocks doesn't sound like a long walk, but when it came to handling Avery and Teddy, it was closer to three miles. They were boys, and they were energetic boys at that.

Avery looked pale and worried the entire time, and for the first time in the months she had known the kid, he was quiet. When they reached the walkway leading to his front door, Kelli put a hand on his shoulder.

"You okay, Avery?"

He swallowed hard and nodded his response.

"Are you sure?" He looked like he was going to faint dead away and that made her a little worried. He looked at her with brown eyes that threatened tears and nodded again, his throat bobbing up and down.

Finally, she reached into her jacket and pulled out the *Penthouse,* wrapped in a bag from the comic store she knew the two boys frequented. "Well, you go put this back where it belongs,

Avery, okay?" She hadn't been sure about whether or not to let him have the magazine back until just that moment.

"Y-you're not gonna tell?" She shook her head. He looked like an angel in that moment; relieved, happy, and much more relaxed.

"But you know what?"

Avery shook his head.

"You don't pull that sort of stuff; you can't get in trouble for it."

He rolled his eyes and nodded. The kid's whole body got into the *aww, shucks, ma'am* expression whenever he made it.

"Get inside before you get yourself in serious trouble, Avery, and stay home for the rest of the night, okay?"

"Thanks, Kelli. You're the best." He probably would have yelled it to the world like he normally did, but it was dark out and he was supposed to be inside. Sometimes Kelli wanted to swat him, but mostly he was okay.

"Just be good, Avery. Good night." She and Teddy stood there and waited until the boy had gone inside, carefully opening the front door and closing it silently. Then they turned around and headed back to Teddy's house.

"So you're not telling?" Teddy's voice held a mild note of terror blended with hope.

"Nope."

"Why not?" He let himself smile. Teddy was a cute kid, especially when he smiled. "I mean, thanks, but, why not?"

"Well, I could tell if you really want me to . . ."

"No! No, that's okay."

Kelli ran her fingers through her hair and readjusted her glasses. The night was getting cold fast and she wanted them back at the house before Teddy's parents came home.

"I was your age once, Teddy." A shiver ran down her neck and between her shoulder blades. Kelli looked around to see if she could figure out why. It wasn't the cold night, there was something else. The road was well lit and she could see all of the houses along the Cliffside Drive with ease. There were no menacing figures lurking in the shadows that she could see, and even the dog that normally went into fits whenever they walked this part of the neighborhood was silent. But there was something, damn it, and it wouldn't let her relax. She kept looking around, hoping her instincts were just confused.

"So, no punishment? I'm just making sure I have this right."

She smiled and patted the top of his blond-haired head. "No punishment, this time."

"This time?"

"Yeah. Next time I might take it out twice as hard on you, so you learn to behave and we can be friends."

"We are friends, Kelli." He frowned and looked up at her. "Aren't we?"

"Of course we are, silly." She stopped moving and looked up at a faint hint of movement.

And saw them looking back down. The telephone wires above them crossed the street at an angle, and as she looked up, Kelli saw dozens of black shapes resting on the thick cables.

Crows. They covered every inch of the telephone line, all of them silent and watching from above. Now and then one of them would shuffle a foot in one direction or the other, but aside from that motion, there was nothing.

"Whoa." Kelli liked crows. She thought they were beautiful birds, but at the moment they were messing with her mind. Crows were noisy birds, always noisy as far as she could tell. There had seldom been a time when she saw them gathered together that they weren't cawing away at each other or filling the air with that mocking laughter of theirs, but right now they were silent.

Kelli took two more steps, her eyes locked on the black shapes above her, and watched in turn as they tracked her, their heads lowered between their shoulders.

"Let's get home, Teddy. I have to finish the dishes."

Teddy looked up and saw where she was staring. "Yeah, Kelli. Okay." He sounded almost as nervous as she felt.

The birds never moved from their perches. But she felt them staring at her the entire way back to the house. She could tell they were there, because even though the first group never moved, she saw the rest of them on her way home. Hundreds of them nestled on nearly every available branch and rooftop.

III

Brian Freemont watched the little red Tercel rip past his hiding spot and checked the speed. Half a second later he was pulling out onto the main road and hitting the flashers. Nailing the occasional college student in the act was what made his life good.

The car pulled over after only a few yards, and he pulled to the side of the road almost immediately behind it. The dashboard computer was active and he typed in the license plate numbers while he kept the driver waiting. Danielle Hopkins, twenty-two years of age and a college student.

He climbed out of his patrol car and walked over to the driver's side door, one hand resting on the butt of his revolver. The girl in the driver's seat looked his way, her pretty face a study in ruined nerves.

"Going a bit fast, weren't you?" He kept his voice casual.

"I'm sorry. I was in a hurry. I have finals tomorrow." She was chewing on her bottom lip. She had every reason to be worried. He had given her record a quick once-over and she was very, very close to losing her license. Like, one or two tickets away from having to take a cab instead of driving.

"Finals? Those are a few weeks off yet, aren't they?" She looked around nervously. "Tell you what, why don't you give me your license, registration, and proof of insurance?"

Her hands were shaking as she reached into her purse and then into her glove compartment. They were shaking more than he would have expected from someone who was just getting another speeding ticket. He kept his eyes on the contents of her purse, looking for telltale signs that there was more going on than just a case of the jitters.

He saw the edge of a bag filled with white powder and allowed himself a very small smile. "You wouldn't be carrying any illegal substances, would you, Ms. Hopkins?"

"What?" She was positively twitchy. "No, I don't do drugs, officer."

"Why don't you step out of the car for me?" He was enjoying this already. The girl was sweating, and it was in the low fifties temperature-wise. Just to add to her discomfort, he reached into the car and cut off the engine, removing the keys.

She was on the verge of tears by the time she climbed out of her vehicle. He held out his hand for the purse, and she actually started crying by the time he pulled out the baggie with the cocaine inside it. Not enough to make a felony, but definitely enough to cause her a world of grief.

She didn't cry quietly. She let out soft, high-pitched whines from her throat. Freemont looked down at her and shook his head like a teacher who'd found someone passing notes.

"You do know this is an illegal substance, don't you?"

"Yes. I'm sorry. I forgot it was in there."

"Oh, no reason to apologize to me," he smiled as he spoke. "You should be saving all of that for your parents. I bet they're going to be very disappointed in their little girl." He found a second bag; this one with a decent amount of what he guessed was marijuana inside it. He dug in again, pulling out a pocket knife that was just past the legal length.

Brian held the bag up and watched the girl break down even more, savoring every noise she made. He gave her a few minutes to soak in the full impact of how fucked up her life had become with the simple act of speeding, and then he gave her back her purse.

"Are you taking me to jail?" Oh, her voice was so tiny, smaller than the squeak of a mouse. He looked her over for the first time, taking in the details of her tear-streaked face and her body. She was short, moderately heavyset with long blond hair and the sort of face that looked good when she cried.

"Well, now, it is my job. I'm supposed to arrest the bad people who break all the laws . . ." He made his voice stern, just for her, but couldn't quite keep the smile off his face.

She broke down again and this time he put a hand on her shoulder, patting lightly.

"My dad's gonna kill me. My dad's gonna skin me alive." Her voice broke and the words were slurred by tears.

"Well, you knew the risks when you started carrying illegal drugs and walking around with concealed weapons." A little sterner now, more edge to the tones he spoke with because, of course, she had to understand the full gravity of the situation. "Long as you don't have a record, they'll probably let you off with a warning, but I do have to carry out my duties." Her arm trembled beneath his hand.

"You do have a clean record, don't you?" Oh, that one did it. She was crying into her hands, her whole body shaking. He made his face as neutral as he could.

Then he reached for the handcuffs. "Come on then, we'll get this taken care of. You'll be with your folks in no time."

"No! Wait, please?"

He kept silent. It had to be her idea.

"Could we work something out?" Her voice was still shaking and ruined, but she had a little edge of strength coming back. No, not strength; resolve.

"Work something out? What did you have in mind?" He sounded doubtful himself now. It was important to make sure they thought it up all on their own.

Danielle Hopkins, her pretty face still red from crying, reached out with her hand and stroked the front of his pants. The contact got his attention as quickly as it always did.

"Say it. Tell me what you want to work out." His voice was still stern, his demeanor as professional as possible when he considered where her fingers were massaging.

"We could . . . you know . . . and you could forget this happened?" Oh, and she sounded so desperately hopeful when she said it.

Brian reached for the front pocket of his shirt, his fingers patting the package of condoms he kept there. He wasn't stupid enough to get caught in the act. And he wasn't going to leave around any DNA evidence that could cause him grief later.

"I think maybe we could work something out, Danielle."

And was that hope he saw in her eyes? Yes, yes it was. Because, really, it had to be better rolling in the back seat of a squad car with him than it would be riding in the back alone and heading for a holding cell.

It worked damned near every time.

Sometimes it was good to be a cop. He let his hand slide under her jacket, under her blouse, to feel one of her full breasts. Her hand started tugging at his zipper as he guided her away from the road and into a small copse of trees.

It was dark, no one would see what they did, but they would both remember for very different reasons.

IV

Benjamin Kirby watched through his window as the sun started to rise. It was his morning ritual. The girl from his Lit class would be coming home any minute, and he wanted to see her. He always wanted to see her, because, of course, she was beautiful.

Mary Margaret Preston; even thinking her name made his insides feel electrified. She'd been stuck in his mind ever since freshman year, when he tutored her in calculus. She'd been funny, intelligent, and friendly. She'd also treated him like a human being, instead of like a door mat. So, naturally, he'd fallen for her in a big way. He'd fallen bad enough that he moved into the same apartment complex as her, just so he could see her from time to time.

Coffee. Coffee was his friend, and one that he abused regularly. He was abusing it right now, actually. Or he would be as soon as he refilled his cup.

He didn't always wait up to see her. He wasn't completely obsessed; just mostly.

Ben poured another cup of coffee and set his term paper aside. He turned off the lights in his apartment and waited near the window. He wanted to see the look on her face when she saw the package.

It wasn't much. Just a poem he knew she liked, done on vellum with his best calligraphy and a few small illustrations that suited the piece.

> *She walks in beauty, like the night*
> *Of cloudless climes and starry skies;*
> *And all that's best of dark and bright*
> *Meet in her aspect and her eyes:*
> *Thus mellow'd to that tender light*
> *Which heaven to gaudy day denies.*
> *One shade the more, one ray the less,*
> *Had half impair'd the nameless grace*
> *Which waves in every raven tress,*
> *Or softly lightens o'er her face;*
> *Where thoughts serenely sweet express*
> *How pure, how dear their dwelling-place.*
> *And on that cheek, and o'er that brow,*
> *So soft, so calm, yet eloquent,*
> *The smiles that win, the tints that glow,*
> *But tell of days in goodness spent,*
> *A mind at peace with all below,*
> *A heart whose love is innocent!*
>
> —*Lord Byron*

Lord Byron. Ben sighed and waited, and at last was rewarded for his patience. Even after a full night out, she looked like heaven to him. He held his breath as she came into view, afraid to even exhale for fear she would somehow see him in his darkened living room.

Margaret walked over to her door and had it opened before she saw the small rolled paper tube. She looked around; her pretty face set in a puzzled frown and then unrolled the poem.

It was nothing overly elegant. He'd kept it simple in design because, frankly, he didn't know if she liked the extra scroll work and decorations. Better to err on the side of caution than to give her something she couldn't use or would have no desire to look at.

He studied her, memorized the minutiae of her features, her dark curls, every aspect of her expression. And he smiled with her when she looked at the poem.

It was stupid to be in love with a woman who probably didn't even remember his name. He hated himself for it.

But he was in love. He had no doubt of that at all in his mind.

He would do anything for her. Anything.

And one day, he would get up the nerve to tell her that.

But for now, he watched and he savored the few moments a day when he could see her outside of the classroom.

Ben watched Margaret walk through her front door, a tired, happy expression on her face. He left the coffee on the window sill and got ready to take his shower. Classes started all too soon and he had to be ready.

The night was ending in Black Stone Bay. The day to come would be far more eventful than Ben Kirby could ever have imagined. Before it was done, his entire life would be changed radically.

CHAPTER 2

The morning newspaper focused mostly on the disappearance of two college kids. Somehow Matthew William Casey and Louis Harold Blake had managed to vanish without a trace, leaving their cars and everything they owned behind. Several people claimed that the two students were into drugs, and the reporters dug deeply enough to find out that both had been accused of rape by a fellow student before the charges were dropped the year before. Aside from that, little was known.

Maggie knew more. Or at least she thought she did. The pictures of the two of them on the front page of the paper woke her up as surely as a good cup of coffee would have, but without the fun of actually getting her morning caffeine jolt.

All she remembered about that night was running from the two of them and then watching them get devoured by the shadows. She still had to blame Lance Brewster for her faded memories of the near rape she'd survived. This was almost sad, because, really, he hadn't been a bad client until that night. Now he was on her shit list, and so far his two phone calls had gone unanswered.

She set down the paper and walked over to her trusty Mr.

Coffee. It had done exactly what she'd programmed it to do and brewed a nice pot of black ambrosia while she was showering. "My one true love," she said to herself as she added two sugars and a dollop of heavy cream. She could do without a lot of things in her life, but coffee? She'd sooner have her teeth pulled without benefit of Novocain.

She dressed while she drank, pulling on her school clothes and making sure she looked right for the day ahead. Only two classes today, which was especially good because she had a client to satisfy.

Jason Soulis was paying her very good money, and for a change of pace Tom would have no part of what she earned. She didn't think of it as stealing from him. He hadn't worked as her agent in this case; he'd only hooked her up with the man who was acting as her agent.

She looked over the single sheet of paper that Soulis had given her the night before and shook her head, puzzled by his selection of men she was supposed to seduce. Most of them she had never met, but three names in particular stuck out. They were men she had seen regularly for several years, but never in a professional capacity.

She would be done with her classes by noon, and after that she could mark off at least one of the men on the list if she played her cards right.

After she was done dressing, and packing away her outfit for after school, she took the poem someone had sent her and taped it to the wall next to her mirror. She'd always loved that poem.

And then it was a quick breakfast and out the door, smiling to herself as she started the day. Maggie started her car and drove toward the campus, unaware of the crows that watched from the trees that lined her path to Winslow Harper University.

II

The early October air was refreshing. Kelli had a little time for herself and did what she almost always did when she could catch a few spare minutes. It was reading time, and today she was having fun with the latest Janet Evanovich novel. The woman could write circles around most of the writers she'd run across, and Stephanie Plum was her secret hero. She wanted to be just like Stephanie when she grew up. Well, except maybe for the whole bounty hunter thing. She didn't think most escaped convicts would be terrified by her.

Her Mountain Dew called seductively and she answered, drinking down half the bottle before coming up for air. Across the street from her, the sprawling black mansion caught the light of the sun on its windows and shot blinding flashes at her face. Kelli used her book to deflect the beams, savoring the quiet.

Two minutes later the silence was shattered by the phone ringing.

"Damn it . . ." She carefully set the book down and walked back into the house, lamenting that she was too damned stupid to remember to grab the portable on her way outside.

"Hello?" She snapped the phone out of its cradle before the third ring had finished.

Bill Lister was on the other end. "Kelli? Hi."

"Hi, Mr. Lister." She tried to make her heart behave itself. Every time she heard his deep voice, her hormones went apeshit on her. She'd been working for the Listers since she was sixteen, and in the five years since she'd started in their employ, the man of the house had always been a perfect gentleman. Still, part of her kept dreaming that sometime soon he might decide to change his ways. Bad thoughts, but she never acted on the fantasy, so it couldn't really be a sin, could it?

"Listen, Michelle and I are going to be going out tonight. I just wanted to give you a heads-up. We probably won't be home until after midnight. I know it's short notice, but is there any chance you can stay with Teddy tonight?" His words were rushed and apologetic. They always were, at least when he was asking for a favor.

Kelli was supposed to have her weeknights free, the better to handle her homework, but at least half of the time her employers found ways to keep themselves busy. The good news was that Teddy was normally pretty well behaved. The great news was that the Listers almost always gave her a nice tip for taking the extra time.

"Ummm . . . yeah, it's all right." She smiled at the wall, imagining what it would be like to go dancing with Bill Lister. A nice, slow dance; nothing too flashy, just a good excuse to be held in his arms.

"You're a lifesaver, Kelli. Seriously. I forgot all about having a dinner date with one of Michelle's clients, and there's just no way we could cancel at this point."

"Oh, you know I don't mind. Teddy's my little sweetie."

"Well, thank you just the same. You're the best, Kelli."

She hung up after she heard the sound of the call disconnecting, her mind on everything she'd have to get done during the day, with an occasional excursion into taboo territory to imagine what it would be like to have Bill Lister as her lover.

Kelli saw motion across the street, over at the Miles house, just as she was settling back down on the porch. The house was hidden from most of the world, but not from where she was sitting. Albert Miles had packed a few bags and beaten a hasty retreat, which was also sort of depressing, because he was normally her number one distraction on long days. The old man played a killer game of chess.

Almost as if the new tenant had timed it, Kelli saw the front door of the house open and a man step out into the early morning sun, his hand blocking the glare from hitting his face.

The stranger had dark hair, pale skin, and a casual stride that still seemed to eat the distance between the front of his driveway and the front door. He didn't walk in a straight line, but instead moved from tree to tree in the yard, as if he wanted to examine each of them closely. His hands touched each trunk, almost like he needed to feel the texture of the ancient oaks and rare specimens to make sure what he felt was solid and real. He walked like she thought a sleepwalker should.

He walked in shadows whenever possible.

Eventually, and really rather quickly, he made it to the front gate to pick up the newspaper. She almost moved her hand up to wave, then thought better of it.

He turned his head slightly and looked at her from across the street, his face impassive and attractive in a strange way. He was handsome, but alien, with features that were different from the ones she had been raised around.

He smiled. It was a close-mouthed twist of his lips, and his right eyebrow lifted slightly as if preparing to ask a question. The man gave a quick, casual wave of his hand and then, after he had reached for the newspaper at his feet, he bowed in an almost mockingly formal way before turning and heading back the way he had come, once again touching each tree and keeping to the early-morning shade whenever possible.

Kelli watched him go, attracted to the man for no reason she could easily place a finger on. He was handsome, yes, but not overwhelmingly so.

Still, for most of the day before it was time for her to go pick up Teddy from the Sacred Hearts private school, she kept thinking about his little smile and wishing she could remember the color of his eyes.

III

Avery Tripp leaned back in his chair, at ease with his place in the world. The school day was over halfway done and that was a good thing. He hated school work, but he loved the people around him. Avery tended, through no fault of his own, to like people. He also had a strong fondness for anything that could get him into trouble. That was what his mother said, anyway.

Mr. Stark, his Sociology teacher, would have agreed completely. William Stark didn't seem to mind too much, however. He still gave Avery good marks for conduct, even after that embarrassing incident with the smoke bombs Avery had slipped under his car's hood. Man, the smoke had been everywhere.

Just thinking about it made Avery smile.

Teddy Lister was sitting next to him, just as he did every day. He and Teddy were best buds, and Avery couldn't imagine a cooler person in the whole world, except maybe for Teddy's nanny. Kelli had won big bonus points in his eyes when she hadn't narced them out about the magazine. That, and she was about the coolest grown-up he had ever met. And pretty. Very pretty. He'd have paid good money to see her in one of his father's dirty magazines.

Avery frowned and shook his head. No. On second thought, he didn't want to see her that way. She was too cool to be exposed and naked like that. Maybe in the *Sports Illustrated* Swimsuit Issue instead. He was only ten, but Avery could already appreciate the idea of letting his imagination paint in some of the finer details.

Teddy yawned next to him and shook his head in an effort to stay awake. Mr. Stark looked over in their direction, doubtless trying to see if Avery was up to no good. It was like a game between them: Avery would try to get away with something, anything, and Stark would try to catch him before he could do anything too drastic, like blow up the school.

Neither of them would have admitted it, but he bet Stark enjoyed the game just as much as he did. Good, clean fun; and it was free, too.

Teddy started to snore, very lightly, and Avery tapped him in the ribs with an elbow. Teddy'd been acting weird all day. He was pale and so tired he looked like he could just nod off. Of course he had just nodded off, thus, the snoring.

His best friend grunted and woke up, but he didn't look at all happy about it, "Watch the elbow."

"Then wake up, monkey."

"I'm not a monkey." What was the word Kelli was always using? Petulant. Teddy was being petulant.

"You're being petulant. Wake up."

"Did you boys need to share a few secrets with the rest of us?" Stark stood up from his desk and looked in their direction. He was in a good mood today, which was a blessing. Avery could tell he was in a good mood, because he was actually smiling as he asked the question. All around the room several of the girls were looking at the teacher with moo-cow eyes. All of the students had to wear their little uniforms, blazers and slacks for the boys, blazers and skirts for the girls, but

Mr. Stark was the only teacher who was always dressed up for teaching; charcoal gray suit and a lighter gray shirt with a dark red tie. He sort of looked like he belonged in an ad from one of the *GQ* magazines his father set in front of his stack of *Penthouses*.

"No, sir." Avery spoke and Teddy did, too. They weren't stupid enough to ignore a question they knew good and well was directed at them.

"Good. Just making sure, because if you're feeling the need to talk, we could always just finish this quiz tomorrow and let you come on up here and read your reports now, instead." Stark was still smiling. That was a big, big plus.

"Well, I finished my test, sir." Avery held up the page to make sure the man could see that he had, in fact, finished all of the questions. Next to him, Teddy started actually filling in answers, his hand moving with the desperate speed of someone who had just realized he'd forgotten there was a test to take.

Stark grinned. It was a wide, friendly smile that was obviously amused.

"Of course you did, Avery. Well, open your book and start reading at page 72. And read quietly this time."

Avery nodded and followed orders. All around him, the other kids were still working on their papers: everyone except Jayce Thornton, who had also finished and was now making goo-goo eyes at the teacher. She was his only competition for the top of the class. She'd probably win, too, because she was smart enough not to do things like super-gluing the teacher's desk drawers shut. That little escapade had actually managed to make Stark's smile go away. He'd been sent to the offices on that day, and had spent two hours explaining the reasons for his actions to Sister Celeste. Two hours of his life with one of the scariest women God had ever put on the face of the earth had convinced Avery to behave himself. He'd vowed never to do anything that stupid again, and while he hadn't managed to keep the vow, he had certainly meant to.

He shot one last look at Jayce, and saw her staring at Mr. Stark. He wanted to be Mr. Stark when he grew up, or at least to look good enough to make girls like Jayce think he was something special.

When Jayce's head turned in his direction, he looked down hastily. Girls were his Kryptonite. He couldn't talk to them. They made his face all hot and his tongue as confused as Teddy looked working on question number seven.

Avery lifted the edge of his test and let Teddy copy. His friend smiled gratefully and wrote down the answer.

Avery hoped his bud wasn't coming down with something. He didn't want to get sick and he didn't want Teddy getting sick, either. Halloween was coming around soon enough and it wouldn't be any fun hitting houses with toilet paper if they were too ill to enjoy themselves.

Avery thought of Mr. Stark's house and wondered if he should set some eggs aside. How long did it take for an egg to get really, really stinky? He didn't know, but he was willing to find out.

IV

Danni Hopkins spent the entire class looking like her family had just been murdered. It seemed like everything had the girl on the edge of tears. Maggie didn't know the girl all that well, but she hoped everything was all right. Danni seemed like a decent enough girl, even if she was a little too bubbly for Maggie's tastes.

As soon as the class was dismissed, Danni Hopkins ran from the room, her face collapsing. Several of the girls in the room went after her, either to help or to see if there was going to be anything good to gossip about.

Maggie wasn't among them. She had other things she needed to take care of. Ten minutes after Danni had a nervous breakdown she was on her way to the Sacred Hearts Cathedral, a small church with a grandiose name. She slipped her short skirt on over her jeans and then removed the latter with practiced ease.

She had no idea why Jason Soulis wanted her to do what he'd hired her for, but with what he was paying she'd already decided she could worry about her conscience later.

Know Thy Enemy. Someone had said that once, but she couldn't remember who. Patrick Flannery was not her enemy, but he was her target for the afternoon. He would, she suspected, be the easiest of her prey to capture.

The notion brought a smile to her face. Stalking priests: her father would have an absolute coronary if he knew about this. Even more than he would if he knew what she did to pay her bills and keep herself at Winslow Harper.

The interior of the church was semi-dark and very solemn. As always, she was in awe of the place. Not just because it was the House of God, but because it was a beautiful structure. Everything about the building spoke of quiet dignity and strength, from the stone walls to the large carved Christ on the crucifix that adorned the wall above the pulpit. The stained-glass windows caught the sun as it shone down but muted the intensity of the light and painted it in primary colors as it fell to the marble floor.

Father Patrick Flannery was the only living soul in the church when she got there. She knew he would be. She'd been attending the church for most of her life and often stopped by after school.

He saw her and smiled, and aside from that, left her in peace. Maggie never came to the church to speak with anyone unless it was time for her confession. She had told the man many of her sins, but she had never once mentioned her line of work. She would wait on that particular confession until after she had graduated from the university. The reason was simple enough: she knew what she did was considered a sin, but as far as she was concerned it was a minor sin at worst. Mary Magdalene had been forgiven and she knew that she would be, too, when the time came. But it wasn't time yet. Part of contrition might require that she stop, and she wasn't ready for that, not yet. She had to follow through with her plans, and if that meant keeping a few secrets from her family and from the priests that she saw regularly, she could accept that.

Father Flannery was in his late thirties, if she had to hazard a guess. She could still remember when he first showed up at the church, back when she was a freshman at Sacred Hearts. He was stocky, but not fat, with hair that couldn't decide if it wanted to be red, brown, or blond, and a wide, Irish face. He looked like he should have been playing college football back then and these days he looked like he should have been sitting in a pub, talking about the good old days when he played college football.

He was friendly, but slightly distant for the most part. He never let himself get too close to any of his parishioners, save in a professional capacity, and Maggie thought she knew why.

Father Flannery was a little afraid of losing his self-control. He was good about hiding it, good about not making his desires blatantly obvious, but she knew how he felt. She had known since the first time she'd seen his eyes on her legs and her breasts during Mass. She'd known in the way he avoided looking her in the eyes, and in the simple little gestures he made when he saw her. His hands fluttered like birds, and his jaw clenched and unclenched with astonishing regularity when he was around women he found attractive.

And she doubted that it was coincidence that he was almost always the priest who handled confessions for the children at Sacred Hearts. Oh, it might be that he was simply forced to deal with their confessions as the youngest priest at the church and the one who got stuck with the least likeable tasks, but she doubted it. Even if that were the case, he was certainly the most attentive.

He was not a pedophile. She had no doubt of that in her mind. He had probably never broken his vows, either, because he was still as nervous as a virgin whenever he was around a woman.

But he thought about it. He thought about it a lot.

Father Flannery made himself busy, dusting the pews and generally moving about as she lit a candle and then settled herself down for a quick prayer, asking the Lord for forgiveness. She had to do this. She needed the money.

If she wanted to be completely honest with herself, she was looking forward to the challenge.

V

Danni didn't tell anyone. She didn't dare. The bastard had taken all of the evidence from her purse and carefully slipped it into an evidence bag. Then he'd sealed the bag in front of her and meticulously written on the date.

"No one has to see this, ever, Danielle. We made a deal, and I intend to keep it. But you'd do well to keep your end of the bargain. Do we understand each other?" He'd tried to sound all calm and authoritative, but he'd failed. He'd been gloating.

He hadn't exactly raped her. It had been consensual, mostly, but he'd been gloating, savoring her discomfort, and she knew in her heart that, for him, half the fun had been knowing she didn't enjoy herself. It was a power trip, just like they always said rape was.

Either way it was a violation, and she hated him for it. She was just glad he'd used condoms, because the idea of any part of him near her or in her was enough to make her want to cry again. And just as soon as she thought it, the notion became reality and the damned tears started all over.

It was Ben that finally got her to talk.

Ben Kirby was a quiet, sweet, funny boy who always made her feel better when she was down. He wasn't a lover and had never tried to even date her, but he was a friend when she needed one.

And God, she needed one so badly.

Ben always seemed to know when to come by, when to crack one of his stupid little jokes, or even when to just offer a shoulder to lean on. He'd found her out in the park behind the university, sitting on a bench, and doing her best not to fall apart again. Several birds were in the area, all of them whoring for pieces of bread. She didn't have any, but Ben did. He sat down next to her on the bench and said nothing for at least five minutes. He just tore off little pieces of white bread and threw them to the gathering crowd of pigeons, seagulls, and crows. After a few minutes he started giving some of the birds nicknames, pointing them out to her as they pulled different stunts, making up gossip about the lives of the damned birds and making her laugh.

It was silly and it was futile, and she laughed just the same, enjoying every second of the show until he ran out of bread.

When the birds had finally taken a hint and gone off to seek new people with more treats, Ben looked her in the eyes and smiled sadly. He almost always smiled that way, like there was something missing from his life and he knew what it was but could do nothing at all about it.

"Want to tell me what happened?"

"I can't, Ben."

He nodded. "Okay. That's cool." He patted his shoulder and gave her a puppy-dog expression that was so over-the-top pathetic that she laughed again, and then settled her head on the offered shoulder.

They sat that way for almost half an hour, until she was sure his arm must have fallen asleep. "I won't judge you, Danni. You know that, right?"

"Yeah," she sniffed and nodded against his Winslow Harper University sweatshirt. "Yeah, I know. It's just. I did something stupid."

"Did you hurt anyone?" It was a simple enough question. She shook her head.

"Then it couldn't have been too stupid."

"Well, it was up there."

"Look, just don't . . . don't be too hard on yourself. If it was something you did, don't do it again, and if it was something someone else did to you, you can always call the cops."

The last part was meant as a joke, of course. She knew that

because he always said it when he was cheering her up. But she broke down right then and there, and the next thing she knew he was holding her against him, rocking her like a baby. She told him everything.

Ben sat silently and listened. He nodded from time to time, but otherwise, he said nothing at all until she had finished crying herself numb. She rested her head against his chest and he wiped at her tears, missing a few but getting most of the trails off her face.

Then he leaned down and kissed her temple with the same sort of affection her father had always shown her when she screwed up colossally.

"So, I'll get it all back."

"What?" She sat up fast, the world getting fuzzy for a second as she looked at his face. Ben was looking across the park, his eyes tracking a couple of crows talking smack to each other in a language that only crows know.

"I'll get it back." He said the words so calmly, so matter-of-factly, that she could almost believe he meant them.

"No, Ben." She shook her head, visions of what Brian Freemont would do to a kid the size of Ben dancing in her mind. "He'd tear you in half."

Ben got a strange little smile on his face and shook his head. "I didn't say how I'd get it back."

"Ben, I mean it. He'd probably kill you as soon as he'd look at you."

Ben finally looked her way and shot her a quick wink. "Just shows what you know, Danni." He stood up and stretched, his narrow waist exposed to the cold air as his shirt lifted.

"Ben, seriously. Thanks for everything, thanks for being here and listening, but I don't want you to get hurt."

That little smile again and then he was walking, looking over his shoulder for a second to shoot her another wink. "I'll get it back."

He seemed so calm and that was what scared her. Ben was maybe too calm; the sort of calm that always precedes the worst storms.

VI

Maggie leaned forward, her forehead resting against the interior door of the confessional, her eyes half closed as she stifled a moan. Father Flannery sat behind her, his hands on her waist, barely moving. He gasped and then rested his head between her shoulders. His skin felt like warm marble as she moved, slowly, gently rocking back and forth, making the moment last as long as she could. There was something almost sweetly innocent about the man she seduced and wickedly delicious about the act they were engaged in. For the first time in a very long while, she felt something more than merely physically active.

His teeth scraped the back of her neck, and his breaths lashed at her skin. His hands were actually trembling, his fingers clutching at her sides as she continued to slowly increase the tempo of their dance.

Just on the other side of the vestibule door, she could hear people moving, and through the small crack that separated the door from its jamb, she could make out three parishioners walking down the main aisle of the church, heading for the pulpit.

Flannery's body was almost perfectly rigid under her, and she knew he heard them, too. Despite the gravity of the situation, or maybe because of it, she felt a smile playing at her lips as she moved his hand from her waist until she could nibble on his index finger. His other hand moved of its own will and cupped her breast through the simple white blouse, so reminiscent of the uniforms she'd worn back at Sacred Hearts.

He said a small blasphemy as she pushed herself back against his body and started moving faster, in short, tight circles over him. Getting him into the confessional for a different sort of activity had been amazingly easy. One look, three sentences, and a condom in her hand, and he had been putty.

She just hadn't expected to enjoy this anywhere near as much as she was. Forbidden fruit was sweet, after all.

His teeth clamped down harder and for the first time he started moving in reaction to every motion she offered. His actions were frantic and she knew he was about to come.

Maggie bit down harder on the priest's finger, sucking at the skin caught between her teeth as he bucked beneath her, whimpering and sweating and maybe dying a little.

She bit harder still as she climaxed, the feelings hitting her hard and with completely unexpected intensity. The skin between her teeth broke and the flavor of his blood danced across her tongue. He mumbled another blasphemy into her neck and she managed to hold back her own sounds through sheer force of will.

It was almost twenty more minutes before the church was empty and they could safely leave the confessional. He came at least twice more in that time and Maggie gave up trying to count hers.

She left the church a short while later, her body still echoing the pleasures she'd just had. She wore a smile for the rest of the day and into the night.

CHAPTER 3

No town ever truly sleeps. No matter what size, no matter where it's located, no town ever truly knows rest. There are always a few souls who can't manage a good eight hours, or whose jobs force them to stay up through the most insane schedules. Throw a college campus or two into the equation and, just like that, you can guarantee that the town will probably have insomnia.

Father Michael Harris suffered from insomnia most nights. He had since he was a young man, and he doubted that would ever change, at least not without the occasional dose of medicinal brandy.

There was too much going on in his world. He needed a vacation and knew good and well that he wasn't likely to get one. Of course, he was supposed to actually request one from time to time, but he just never trusted that everything would get done if he wasn't there to double-check all the details.

Take the day he'd just spent as a perfect example. Father Donald Wilson was his superior, but despite a good heart, the man just wasn't capable of accomplishing anything in a timely fashion. The only exception was his sermons. Don was one of the best when it came to writing a rousing speech, and he could bring tears to the eyes of an unrelenting sinner. But once you got past that stage of the day, he was effectively useless. So who do you suppose had handled the details for the upcoming pumpkin sales? Who else? He had.

Normally he could have counted on at least a little help from Patrick Flannery, but the lad had been distracted throughout the day, as shaken and twitchy as a cat at a dog show. Mike Harris had tried several times to get the younger priest to open up to him, but it wasn't meant to be.

So he prescribed himself a small snifter of brandy and settled in to read a few pages of the latest by Ed McBain. It might not have been a brand-new book, but it was new to him.

It was after midnight before he finally managed to get to sleep.

He didn't know just how much later it was when he discovered he wasn't alone. The warm mouth covering his penis was the first hint.

Mike sat up fast, gasping, his hands reaching for the source of what was happening to him, and gasped again when the young woman at the edge of his bed looked in his direction and smiled around the prize she'd captured between her lips.

There was a second when he was almost certain that she would bite down and he froze, petrified by the very notion. Then she slowly drew her head back and freed him.

"What are you doing?" His voice was a harsh whisper, not because he was scared of being heard, but because he was having the damnedest time catching his breath.

The moon's light was shining into the Spartan room, and he watched as she slowly stood up, looking down on him in his vulnerable position.

Her face was familiar, but the dark curls of her hair obscured her features almost as much as the darkness that left her partially hidden from his view. And he was also having trouble looking away from the naked body that the moon was revealing to him.

He was not at all accustomed to seeing beautiful young

women in his bedroom. The entire concept was unsettling to him. When he had been younger, he'd been tempted on several occasions, but he'd never given in to the idea of breaking his vows. Oh, there had been many a cold shower, and Mike Harris had certainly entertained all the thoughts that a heterosexual male is bound to have when he sees an attractive member of the opposite sex, but he'd used prayer and faith to keep him from deviating from the course he'd chosen to take.

He swallowed and felt his skin flush. "I said, what are you doing?" His voice was a little stronger when he spoke again, but not nearly as confident as he wanted it to be.

She moved forward, and much as he wanted to flinch away from her, Mike simply stared. His throat was dry and his pulse was thudding along merrily at his temples.

Margaret Preston leaned in closer, and he was shocked to recognize the girl he'd seen in church every Sunday for the last fifteen years.

"Maggie? What are you doing here?" His voice shook and part of the tremble was caused by fear, but there was definitely a healthy dose of lust in there as well.

Maggie lifted one delicate hand and placed a finger against her lips. "Shhhh. I think I made that obvious, Father Harris." The voice of the young woman in front of him didn't jibe with the voice he knew from years of Sunday School and the confessional. It wasn't a child's tones that she spoke with, though he had always thought of her as a child.

"Maggie, please, just get your clothes on and go home. If you'd like, we can discuss this in the morning."

She climbed up onto the bed, her face once again lost in the shadows of the room, her body highlighted by the moonlight that painted her in shades of blue and silver.

"No, Father Harris, we won't talk about this in the morning. We won't talk about it ever. It's our little secret." Her left leg lifted and moved over his body, settling on the other side of his hips. A woman less than half his age was kneeling over him in the bed he had never shared with another soul, and he was both terrified and elated by the idea.

Her weight settled over his body, hardly a burden at all as she leaned in closer to his face, her dark eyes staring into his own.

"Maggie, please . . ." Was he begging? Oh, yes he was. He was definitely begging, because as much as he wanted to cast her away from the bed and scold her for her foolish notions, his body was reacting to her presence and his willpower seemed to have fled into the shadows.

Her hands lifted up to her shoulders, getting lost in her thick dark hair for a moment before they slowly ran down her torso, hiding and then revealing different parts of her perfection before she reached out and touched him. The contact was electrifying and paralyzing.

He wanted her to go away, wanted desperately for her to leave him alone again in the darkness of his one private place in the entire world.

He wanted her to stay, to fulfill the promises he saw in her smile, and the silken touch of her fingers, and the warm kiss she placed on his neck as she leaned over him.

In the end, only one of his wishes was fulfilled. But she was truthful, at least. It was their secret. No one ever had to know.

II

Ben didn't go to sleep at all that night. He had other things he wanted to do. No, other things he needed to do.

He sat in front of his window and read the words on his laptop's monitor, studying details that he shouldn't have had access to, and making notes in a spiral-bound notebook.

From time to time he yawned, stretched, and took a break to get another cup of coffee, but after each of his short breaks he went back to his computer and searched for more information on his target.

Brian Freemont had three bank accounts, two mortgages, a car that he could barely afford, and a wife, Angela, who was pregnant. Amazing the things you could learn about someone if you knew how to crack a few security codes.

He jotted down the account numbers as he learned them, and made sure to note which bank each of them belonged to. He did the same with all of the credit card numbers, and the mortgages, and he made sure to get the Social Security number for his new obsession. There were phone numbers to consider, both the home phone and the cell. He made a point of copying down all of the numbers that had been called and that had called the Freemont residence.

Every time he started getting tired, he thought of Danni Hopkins crying into his shirt and woke right back up. It was easy to do. Danni was a good person, even if she liked to party a little, and he hated the idea that Brian Freemont might change the rules and decide that Danni needed to pay a second time for his silence. Or a third, or a fourth.

Maybe it was the coffee, but the notion of Brian Freemont walking around with anything that could be used to coerce Danni a second time made his jaws clench together.

By three in the morning, he was ready to begin. Ben took one of the seven pay-as-you-go cell phones that he had purchased earlier in the day and activated as he ate dinner, and he plugged his modem into the jack provided. He worked with the speed and precision of a surgeon and began cutting away pieces of Brian Freemont's life.

He was done less than an hour later. He carefully wiped down the cell phone and wrapped it in a paper bag before slipping it into his jacket pocket. Then he stepped out of the apartment, looking for a random trashcan and a decent meal.

The good news for him was that there were several diners open, even in the darkest part of the night. He found one without too much difficulty and sat down in one of the booths that were supposed to be reserved for two or more people.

The waitress, Sally, didn't seem to care that he was breaking the rules, and neither did he. She promised him that the sausage and mushroom omelet was a work of art and he trusted her.

He hadn't even finished a third of the very early breakfast when Margaret Preston came into the place.

Sally looked at the girl and smiled. "Hey, hon, how're you tonight?"

"Hi, Sally." Margaret's smile was a thing of beauty, and Ben forgot all about the food in his mouth as she walked toward the booth across from his.

"You want your usual?" The woman didn't wait for an answer, but instead moved to grab a cup of coffee and brought it over to her. "I was just telling Ben over here that the mushroom and sausage was the best omelet in the house."

He managed to swallow the lump in his mouth as Margaret looked in his direction. Amazing, he couldn't breathe, but he still got the food down without dying on the spot.

"So how is it?" Margaret Preston was speaking to him. He had absolutely no idea how to respond without sounding like a complete idiot.

Words! Come on, words! You can speak, I know you can! "Umm . . . I think Sally's right, actually."

Margaret nodded and gratefully took the cup of coffee Sally offered her. "She normally is." Margaret looked away and he felt his ability to think come back as her eyes left his. "I'll have what he's having."

Sally chuckled. "So, the usual then." The waitress walked toward the counter that separated them from the kitchen and called out for an encore of the last order. Someone behind the wall made a comment that had her laughing as she moved to another table that she had claimed as her own.

Ben looked back in Margaret's direction and saw that she was looking at him again. He wanted to crawl under the table and hide, but felt that might be socially awkward.

"You're in my Lit class, aren't you?"

She was talking to him again. It was really not a comfortable thing for him to deal with. Like as not, she'd expect him to answer.

"Um. Yes. Same class." Nope, not his best witty response.

"Did you get the notes from last Friday? I can't remember what we were supposed to read."

Shit. Now she was asking questions that required thought processes that were functioning. "Lord Byron. There're four examples of his work in there. We're supposed to take notes on the symbolism."

"I love his stuff. God, the man knew how to write." Her voice was wistful and her eyes had a faraway look that seemed one part wishful thinking and one part exhaustion.

Ben nodded hard, remembering her expression when she found the poem he'd written down for her. He knew she loved Byron's work. He also knew that "She Walks in Beauty" must have been written about a girl who looked exactly like the one he was trying hard not to stare at.

"So what are you doing out this late at night, Ben? I thought I was the only one crazy enough to live without sleep."

He grinned, thinking about what the faceless cop he'd decided to target would be doing in a few hours. "Hunting."

"What are you hunting?" He loved to watch her face. She had a thousand expressions that he had never seen, because she wore so few of them at school. She was intrigued by his one word answer, and maybe amused, too. It was hard to tell, because, of course, he didn't really know her. He just loved her. The two did not always go hand in hand in the world of Ben Kirby.

Okay, he was a little more socially awake now, and maybe even a little less intimidated by her presence, so he thought before he answered. "I am hunting revenge and a way to make a friend of mine smile again. She has a nice smile. I like to see it."

Margaret Preston rose from her booth across from his and slid into the seat on the opposite side of his table. He managed not to dance where he was sitting, or even to let out a scream of pure delighted terror, but only because having her sitting this close was enough to stun him for a moment.

"See? You get bonus points for a neat answer." How did she do that? How did she make him feel so comfortable when he knew good and damned well that being anywhere near her could only devastate him later? He wasn't stupid; he knew it was dangerous to get close to anyone.

"What? You want all the juicy details?" There, his mouth was still working, even if his brain was rebelling.

"Only if you want to share them." She stretched and then smiled as Sally brought her food over to her. He tried not to stare and failed.

The waitress shot a look at each of them and smiled, then headed back to her island of sanity in the corner. It wouldn't be all that long before the breakfast rush started pouring in, and he suspected she wanted to rest up for it as much as possible.

"Well, that depends." Ben leaned back in his seat and decided he'd trust her. How else could he keep the conversation going? "Can you keep a secret, Margaret?"

"Yes I can. And you can call me Maggie."

"Okay, here's the deal. I'm about to make a phone call, and when I'm done with that, I'll tell you what the call was all about."

She sliced a neat little wedge of omelet away from the mass spilling over the edges of her plate and nodded, a smile playing at her lips and mischief in her eyes.

Ben very carefully pulled the cell phone from his pocket and pulled it from its bag. He dialed the first number from his list of several and waited until he heard an irritated, sleep-muted voice answer.

And Maggie watched him, her face alight with naughty amusement.

III

The Lister house was silent. Kelli woke up only because she thought she heard a sound from Teddy's room. She wasn't technically working right now; his folks had eventually managed to come home, and when they were in the house, she was not in charge of Teddy's welfare. That didn't stop her from listening for any sounds he might make anyway.

A few seconds later, she heard another sound from the direction of his room and moved out of bed, shivering a little when the covers slid away from her body. The hardwood floors felt like someone had left them in the freezer overnight and she stepped as lightly as she could to avoid the chill.

Teddy's room was across the hallway and to the right. She slipped over to his door and carefully opened it, mindful of any noises she might make.

He was asleep in his bed, but his rest was not an easy one. Teddy's face was drawn down in a fearful expression and his skin was covered with light sweat. Kelli moved into the room and touched his forehead, feeling for any sign of a fever.

Teddy's eyes opened, stared dazedly at her for a second and then closed again. He didn't wake up. The good news was that, while he might be having a bad dream, he didn't have a temperature.

She saw motion outside of the bedroom window and tried to catch it again. All she saw were shadows on shadows, fleeing from the streetlights. It would be impossible to see much of anything out there.

"Noooo . . . unnh . . . sabadeeng." Teddy's voice sent shivers running from her neck to her lower back and she looked back at him, the motions from outside the window completely forgotten.

"Teddy? Wake up, hon." She shook his shoulder lightly and Teddy woke in an instant, his eyes wide in the darkness, his voice a faint gasp as he sat up.

He reached out for her, for comfort, and she pulled him into a hug. At ten he was still a sweet kid. He hugged her back for a few seconds, breathing hard.

"You're okay, Teddy. It was just a dream." He clutched at her and held on with desperation and she let him for a few moments before breaking his grip and urging him back into the bed.

"It wasn't a dream, Kelli." His voice was still shaken, but, happily, it was also drowsy.

"I was here, hon. I saw you having a nightmare."

He closed his eyes, already halfway back to slumber. "Will you stay with me? Please?"

She stifled a sigh. Her bed was calling and she wanted to answer it, but Teddy was scared and she knew she'd cave in. Her own fault, really, for letting him watch those stupid horror movies. Well, and for suggesting them in the first place.

"I'll stay." She rubbed his arm lightly and was rewarded by a half smile that faded into sleep. "You sleep, Teddy. I'll be right here."

She kept her word, but it had cost her a stiff neck a few hours later when she woke up on the floor at the foot of his bed.

Teddy managed the first three hours of school before he had to come home. He was exhausted, and looked about as pale as a bar of Ivory soap. Kelli had just gotten to her class when the school nurse called on her cell phone to let her know that he was ill. Both of the Listers had work, and someone had to take care of their child. That was what they paid Kelli for.

IV

"This better be good." Brian's voice was scratchy from the lack of any moisture and his teeth were already clenched. Some asshole was calling his house and it wasn't even five in the morning. Either someone he knew was in the hospital already, or they would be before he was done with them.

"It's very good, Officer Freemont." Oh, perfect! The prick was whispering into the phone, trying to disguise his voice.

Brian stood up and moved away from the bed, where Angie was mumbling sleepily. Ever since the baby started to show, she was tired all the time. He looked back at her; she was starting to look like a bloated cow. He didn't need to hear her bitching because someone woke her from her much-needed beauty sleep.

"Talk to me and give me a reason not to find you."

"Good luck with that. I'm not planning on having you find me. You have something I want. Watch what the day brings you. You're not going to have fun. But I can make it better if you work with me. I'll call you later today and we can discuss how fast you want to give it to me."

"Listen, you little shit." He didn't get any further before the prick hung up on him. He tried calling the number back with the option he was paying extra money for, and of course it didn't work.

"Fucker." He resisted the urge to throw the phone down.

One look at his watch and he knew he wasn't going to get any more sleep. Hell, he had to be up in an hour anyway.

Brian Freemont put the phone back in its cradle, scowling the entire time. He was not a happy man.

He was about to be a lot less happy.

V

The sun was coming soon. It wouldn't be long before the light of the new day covered the town and the people of Black Stone Bay rose from their sleepy little beds to start a new day among the conscious.

Out on the bay itself, the waters were almost calm. The waves that ran to the jagged shoreline merely tapped the stones instead of shattering against them.

Jason Soulis looked out at the waters and listened to the sighs of the wind and the water.

He was going to like this town. He did already. It was perfect for him.

The waters below him stretched as far as he could see, and the sky at their horizon was changing quickly, growing brighter. He smiled to himself and turned back to the great black mansion behind him. Albert Miles had promised he would like the place, and his old friend had been absolutely right. He had also promised that Maggie would be everything Jason was looking for, and so far she was showing a great deal of promise. Two of them in one day; he let himself chuckle at the thought. The lady in question certainly had initiative.

Yes, he supposed he would keep her.

Assuming she would be willing to be kept, which he doubted.

Jason Soulis walked to his new home, casting his eyes briefly through the window of the boy he had visited during the night. He could sense the woman that slept next to him, fitfully turning in her sleep: he suspected she was a lovely young lady, friendly and shy, and innocent. He would watch her over the next few weeks. She would probably surprise him if he let her.

The wind was still a soft murmur at his back, playing idly with his hair as he closed his eyes for a moment and listened. To the west, not too far distant, he heard a scream that brought a thin smile to his lips.

Someone had found his first victim. He'd been wondering how long it would take.

CHAPTER 4

I

The car was a complete wreck. The front end had wrapped itself very neatly around a telephone pole, and the engine was halfway out of the hood. What was left of the windshield lay across the entire mess, covered with strands of hair and lightly drizzled in blood. The steering wheel looked more like a pretzel than a proper circle, and the seatbelt had been completely torn free of its moorings.

Brian Freemont looked at Alan Coswell and shook his head. "You mean to tell me someone got out of this and walked away?"

"Screw that." Coswell lit a cigarette, careful to step away from the wreckage, just in case there might be some gasoline left in the area. It wasn't very likely. The car had been there for at least a day and the spillage from the ruined tank had long since evaporated. "What I want to know is how anyone driving down this road could miss the fucking car sitting here."

Brian kept his voice as calm as he could; he was doing a damned fine impersonation of a sane man as far as he was concerned. "No street lights. Not a lot of traffic out here, except on the weekends. Hell, the only thing down this way is a make-out spot." He knew it well. He'd used it a few times back in high school and a lot more often since he'd joined the force. This was one of his favorite roads for finding a little action on the side.

He thought about a few of his recent conquests. The girls he'd had along the side of the road were pleasant distractions. It was easier than focusing on the shit his life had become in less than twenty-four hours.

Coswell snorted and coughed, a chest cold doing its best to work itself deep into his lungs. That was what he got for being a smoker as far as Brian was concerned. The fact that Coswell felt like shit also helped Brian stay outwardly calm in the face of personal disaster.

His life had become absolute hell since the phone call the day before. Piece by little piece his entire life had slipped down into a cesspool, and it didn't look like he could do a damned thing about it until the next time the badly disguised voice on the phone called him.

"Jesus Christ, Freemont! Are you even listening to me?" He turned to see Coswell glaring at him. The man's fat face and walrus mustache always annoyed him, but he was a sergeant, so Brian faked giving a damn.

"Sorry. I was trying to figure out what happened to the body." It was a lie, of course. He couldn't have cared less. Nothing much mattered right now except getting his world back in order, before everything else could crumble away.

"Come look at this shit." He moved his flashlight over a section of the car's front. Brian nodded as he walked around the rear of the vehicle. They hadn't looked over there yet.

It was hard not to see the marks once they were in view; there was nothing subtle about them. There were two handprints imbedded deep into the metal on the front passenger's side. The metal had crumpled around the indentations, and the paint had been lifted completely away, as if it had adhered to the hands that struck the side of the car.

"What the fuck?" He moved closer, crouching next to the door to study the deep dents. "I mean, damn. Should we get the fingerprint kit out?"

Coswell snorted his laughter. "Yeah, kid. Lemme just yank that outta my ass for ya." He rolled his eyes and started back toward the cruiser. "I'm gonna see what's taking the damned detectives so long."

Freemont glared at the other officer's back, and looked again at the car in front of him. The sheer force of the blow that would have left a mark like what he was staring at now would have been enough to shatter the bones in any person's arms like they were cheap glass. It might explain why the car had been abandoned. No one would want to stay around to face the police if they'd smeared someone all over the side of the road. The police seldom understood about that sort of thing. They tended to suggest a few years in jail as a good method of getting over the guilt.

The longer he looked, the more puzzled he grew. He looked at the trajectory of the car and studied the ground leading to the crash site. The skid marks were obvious for only around four feet and then they left the road a good fifty feet or more from where the vehicle now rested. It was either going at an incredible speed on the back road or . . .

"No fucking way." He scowled and walked up to the road and the deep black rubber trails that were obviously new enough to associate with the crash.

Brian Freemont was not stupid. He might not have been a rocket scientist, but he'd studied hard to get through the academy and he'd also studied on the side as well, learning all he could about accident scenes and forensic pathology along the way. One day he planned to get back to school and learn enough to get himself set up as a coroner. It was an elected position and technically you didn't even need to have a medical degree, but he wanted to do it right. He had dreams, and they didn't end with a little college-grade pussy on the side of the road now and again. His conquests with the girls were strictly a bonus, not a life-long ambition. The point being that, even though he was hardly the most honorable man, he knew what he was looking at with better than average knowledge.

The skid marks never even turned away from the course of the road. The vehicle had never swerved. It had been driving along nice and easy—probably at around 30 miles per hour too fast for the road conditions—and then it met something that hit it hard enough to push it off the asphalt and through the air, at least fifty feet.

And that something had hands.

Brian looked the evidence over again, ignoring Coswell as the man came back from the patrol car and stared hard at him.

"You look like you ate a bug. What's wrong?"

Brian looked over at the sergeant and thought about giving him a straight answer. "I just can't get this. It doesn't add up."

"Yeah? That's why you're not a detective. Leave it to the professionals, Brian." The slob seemed to think the whole thing was a joke, but as much as he wanted to respond that it was a serious situation, he bit his tongue instead. He had enough shit going down in his day without adding anything else to his list of bad events. Coswell was exactly the sort of sorry asshole that would take any comments he made and turn them around on him later. He was a prick.

His cell phone vibrated in his pants pocket and Brian answered it without even considering that he wasn't supposed to carry the damned thing on duty. Screw Coswell on that one, at least. He knew the man was carrying a phone of his own.

"Hello?"

The voice from the previous morning spoke into his ear. "How has your day been, Officer Freemont?"

He looked at Coswell. The man was busily scratching his nuts as he looked at the marks on the car again.

Brian walked away from the site, wanting to make sure his sergeant didn't hear any of the conversation.

"What did you do, you son of a bitch?"

"Nothing that I can't fix."

"Then you better get to fixing it!" He forced himself to calm down. It wasn't easy. As of nine A.M., Brian Freemont had discovered that he had no checking accounts, no savings accounts, and was two months behind on his house payments. His finances were in ruins. He had to come to work and act like nothing was wrong in his life, but everything was wrong. Every single damned thing was very, very wrong.

"Listen to me carefully. Listen to the numbers I'm going to read to you, and pay very close attention, Officer Freemont." Brian held his breath. "Are you listening? Are you there?"

"I'm here."

"Good, because I want this over with as much as you do." The man started talking, firing off a litany of numbers that Brian knew very well. They were the numbers for his car note, his mortgage, his different bank accounts. His blood seemed to slow down in his veins as he listened and he had trouble catching his breath. The voice read off his Social Security number, the policies for his life insurance, for his vehicle insurance, for his retirement accounts. By the time he was done, Brian Freemont was sweating bullets.

"Okay. Okay. What do you want?" He could barely recognize his own voice.

"You have files at your home, or hidden away somewhere else. I'm guessing you have a lot of files; police files that could cause a lot of trouble for a few friends of mine."

"I don't know what you're talking about."

The voice on the other end did not suddenly break into laughter, but he heard humor when it spoke again. "Yes, you do. You know exactly what I'm talking about. We're not mentioning names yet, Officer Freemont. I could. I could give you several. But we haven't reached that level of unpleasantness."

"What do you want?" His chest was burning, and Brian had to wonder if he was having a coronary.

"I have five things to say, so listen carefully. One: I haven't even hurt you yet. The worst thing you have going so far is a bounced check fee or two. Do you understand me?"

"Yes."

"Good. Number two: I can hurt you. I have everything that makes you a person in this country. I can have you audited by the IRS. I can have your back taxes examined with a microscope and make sure you pay interest on every penny that you ever earned. I can make sure that all proof you ever paid any taxes goes away as easily as your bank accounts did. I can ruin you so badly that Humpty Dumpty will look good next to you. Do you understand?"

"Yeah. Yes, I do." Had he ever wanted to cry so badly? His hands were shaking and the world had bleached to a dark pulsing gray in his eyes.

"Three: one of the girls you did wrong is pregnant. She wasn't with anyone but you. That means she's carrying your baby, and that means you are going to lose your wife if you aren't very, very careful about how you handle this. She doesn't want your child, but she'll carry to term if I ask her to because she knows she can ruin you like you did her. Do you understand?"

"Oh. Oh God." His voice was cracking and he couldn't feel his legs. "Oh, please, don't do this to me."

"Be quiet. We aren't done yet." The voice spoke without malice and that made it worse. "Number four: You get off work at seven P.M. tonight. By eight P.M., I want you to gather all of the evidence from all of the girls you did wrong and I want you to bring it to the edge of the Cliff Walk, right next to the spot where you're parked now. I want you to set that evidence down and I want you to go back to your home and wait for a call from me. Do you understand me, Officer Freemont?"

He nodded, forgetting that he was on the phone for a moment.

"I have spoken to several girls about you. You will bring all of the evidence packets, because if you miss one of the girls I spoke to, I will carry out every threat I just made. Do you understand me?"

"Yes. Yes, I do understand." His mouth felt so dry, so painfully wretchedly dry, that he could barely make the words form properly.

"Number five: If you do everything I just told you to do and you follow my instructions exactly, I will give you back your life. This is your one warning, Officer Freemont. If you deviate from what I've told you in any way, I will ruin you."

The phone went dead in Brian's hand. He barely noticed. His body shook and his face glistened with sweat, but he was unaware. His mind went numb for several minutes. When he could think clearly again, Coswell was talking to the detectives and they were looking over the crash site carefully.

Brian Freemont had planned to discuss the tire tracks with the detectives, but the idea had slipped his mind.

He only had one thought that didn't escape him. He had to get those damned files down here by eight o'clock or he was royally fucked.

At least as fucked as every girl he'd set up for a little fun.

The irony was not missed by him, but it was most assuredly unappreciated.

II

Ben had experienced two of his favorite things the night before and well into the morning. He'd had a wonderful conversation that covered the whole spectrum of discussions, and he'd spent time with Margaret, no, with Maggie Preston. The worst of the morning breakfast crowd had overrun the diner and then left for other places by the time they left the diner, and he'd felt so bad about it he'd left Sally an embarrassingly large tip. Funny, she didn't seem at all embarrassed. She just smiled and told him to come back any time.

After that he walked Maggie home, the conversation slowing down only because both of them were tired and even all the extra cups of coffee only went so far to keep them conscious.

"I had fun." She stretched and smiled as she spoke and Ben found himself smiling right back.

"Me too. It's nice to meet an insomniac with a personality now and then."

Maggie laughed and her hand moved over to squeeze his fingers for a second. Then she leaned in and kissed his cheek. A moment later she was pulling out her apartment key and slipping through the door. "See you in class, Ben."

He'd walked numbly into his own apartment, and sat down on the couch. The smile lingered long after he sat down and he was almost certain he'd never wash his cheek again. Well, not for a while at least.

And now, one day later, he was still amazed by the kiss on

his cheek. Maggie had gone to school and he had seen her there, but once again she was strictly there to study. She smiled and waved, but beyond that there was no contact. Not that he had expected any.

The policeman on the other end of the line was not at all happy to receive the call. He sounded stunned when he heard that Ben knew where he was. The chances were decent that he'd even looked around the area in a panic, trying to figure out where Ben was hiding. It wouldn't do him any good, because he'd never even seen Brian Freemont and he certainly hadn't gone out into the woods to watch for him. All it took was listening to the police radio broadcasts to know where the man was.

Ben smiled when he thought about the desperation in the sick bastard's voice. He forced the smile to go away. He couldn't take this as a game. It was serious business.

He turned off the cell phone and started wiping it clean. That was the second phone he'd used, and it was going into the trash.

Somewhere across the way, Maggie was probably sound asleep. He was thinking about getting some rest himself, as he had a test to study for later and his eyes were dangerously close to crossing. He wasn't going to do himself any good if he didn't catch up with the Sandman at some point.

And then Maggie walked out of her apartment and he was wide awake again. She was dressed in a simple gray skirt and silk blouse, with a matching jacket, and her hair was pulled back in a ponytail. He watched her as she left, amazed by her as always. It wasn't something he could define; it went beyond her obvious looks, but whenever he saw her, his day was made more complete.

"Romantic pabulum." He sighed and turned on the CD player near his laptop. He had a paper to finish and it wasn't going to write itself. Norah Jones started singing songs directly into his soul and he let her.

He wrote, just as he was supposed to, but in the back of his mind he was looking forward to being out near the accident site where he'd called Freemont. There would be packages waiting for him and he intended to go through them meticulously.

Danni Hopkins was a sweet girl, and he intended to make sure she got her life back. He also intended to make a few phone calls to the other victims of Freemont's game and let them know that they were free and clear.

Then, and only then, he'd consider giving the crooked cop back his life.

III

Kelli walked into the nurse's station at the elementary school with a frown on her face. Teddy was lying back on the small cot they had in the corner, his hand over his eyes. He was asleep, but it was a fitful slumber at best.

"Teddy? Sweetie?" She moved over to him and sat on the edge of the cot, careful not to knock them both through the air. It was hardly designed to have a grown-up sitting on its edge.

He looked as pale as death and for a second, even knowing that he was breathing, she thought he was dead.

Then Teddy opened his eyes and smiled apologetically at her. "Hi, Kelli. I'm sorry." His voice was weaker than she'd heard come from him in the past and it bothered her a bit.

"What for, honey?"

"You have school today."

"It doesn't matter. You're way more important." She ran her fingers through his hair and smiled at him. He closed his eyes and his face relaxed a bit. "Why don't we see about taking you home, okay?"

He nodded his head, and closed his eyes as he waited for her to speak with the nurse.

A few moments later, the portly woman who worked as the school's medical expert sat down with Kelli and they had a brief discussion. Ellen Cranst was in her late thirties, if Kelli had to guess, and while her face was heavy and her hair was pulled back in a harsh bun, she had a pleasant demeanor that took away from her otherwise harsh appearance.

"He seemed to be doing just fine this morning, but as soon as the kids went out for recess he just dropped like a stone. I was afraid he'd been stung at first, but I didn't see any evidence of it."

"I don't think he's allergic anyway." She tried to think back to any allergies at all, but Teddy was a strong little kid, and there was nothing to remember.

"Well, he seems to be doing better now, but it might be best if he took the rest of the day to rest. If he's bad in the morning, it might be time to see a doctor. You never can trust the flu season to wait."

She thanked the woman for her time and bit her tongue on the patronizing tones the nurse employed, and then took Teddy with her toward the parking lot outside.

They hadn't made seven steps out the door before Teddy grew pastier than ever and swooned. Kelli was strong enough to carry him the rest of the way to her car. She tucked him into the passenger's seat and drove as calmly as she could.

He was sweating rivers of perspiration and she almost took him directly to the hospital, but decided to check with his parents first.

The new neighbor was outside, gardening of all things, when she pulled into the long driveway of the Lister house. Jason Soulis looked her way as she tried to lift Teddy's dead weight from the car, and then moved in her direction.

He moved across the street without bothering to look in either direction, and was by her side long before she could finally pull Teddy from the side door. Without bothering to ask her, he gently urged her aside and swept the boy into his arms.

Soulis moved with her, asking her to open the door of the house and she did, gesturing for him to go ahead inside. He carried Teddy into the living room and placed him on the couch.

"Have you called a physician yet?" His tone was calm, but almost completely professional.

"No, it just happened."

"Perhaps you should do so now."

He opened Teddy's shirt and began rubbing his palms over her charge's chest. Then lowered his head and placed his ear against the pale adolescent skin, listening.

"His pulse is strong, but erratic. It's possible he was bitten by something or ate the wrong foods. I would guess he's having an allergic reaction."

She dialed William Lister's office number and got him on the first ring.

"This is Bill Lister, what can I do for you?"

"Bill? This is Kelli. Teddy got sick at school and he's not doing well. I didn't want to take him to the doctor without checking in with you first."

Soulis had removed Teddy's shirt and was now working on his shoes and his pants. He showed little emotion, save for a small expression of concern. She was tempted to question his motives, but his approach was clinical.

"Is he all right now?"

"Well he's really weak and the new neighbor, Mr. Soulis, helped me get him inside. He thinks it might be an allergic reaction to something."

"Oh, Kelli. We trust you. If you think he needs to be at the doctor's, go." He paused for a moment. "But please, call me as soon as you know anything. I'd be on my way to there right now, but I'm due in court in less than fifteen minutes."

"All right, Bill. Should I call Michelle?"

"I'll take care of it, Kelli. You just get Teddy squared away, okay?"

She looked over at Teddy, where Soulis was rubbing his extremities as if to warm them. "Okay, I'll let you know when we get there."

She hung up the phone and Soulis looked at her. "I think an ambulance might be a better way to go, Miss." He pointed to an angry red mark on Teddy's leg. "It would seem your friend has been bitten by something."

Teddy's head rolled to the side, and a small moan crept past his pasty lips. Kelli dialed 911.

IV

Tom Pardue woke up just after noon and glared at the sunlight pouring through his opened curtains. He could have sworn he'd closed them the night before. Then again, there'd been a girl in his bed the night before, too.

He sat up and looked around his bedroom. Clothes were scattered around the floor, his cast-offs from last night, but no one else's things were there.

"Stupid bitch." He'd been thinking of going at Liz a second time. She was good in the sack. Also, she made the sweetest sounds when she was crying. He liked a girl that could cry for him.

Just thinking about it got him in the mood, and he climbed from his bed, annoyed all over again that she wasn't there.

He walked from the bedroom into the hallway, and stopped for a moment to listen. A small noise from the kitchen caught his attention and Tom nodded as a smile slipped across his lips.

He walked the rest of the way on his toes, and as quietly as he could manage. He had a feeling that Liz was about to make his whole day better.

The kitchen was big; it was one of the things he liked about the house. There was an island in the center, complete with a chopping block, and several stainless steel countertops ran along the entire wall of the room. Most of Tom's food was delivery, but he liked the appearance of a professional kitchen for those rare occasions when he had something catered. It didn't happen often, but now and then he had get-togethers for his more prestigious clientele.

Mostly it was for show, but it was also a great place to sit and relax. It was also one of the first places a lot of the girls looked if they were trying to find out where he hid his dope.

Liz might be making him breakfast, or she might be trying to steal his stash. The former would get her a few brownie points. The latter would take care of his desire to hear her cry again.

Liz Montclair was a good-looking girl; she was cheerleader material, with lustrous sandy hair and wide hazel eyes.

She also had a mouth that was beyond generous. Like most of his hookers, she was a college student. He liked to get the girls young, before the shit they went through on the streets could make them look older than their years. Liz was already starting to show the signs of her bad habits. She was starting to get a little too hooked on the heavier shit. Her weight was going down and she was going to lose her looks if he didn't make her curb her taste for partying.

That, or he could just find a few more whores.

He watched her as she carefully moved from cupboard to cupboard; searching the various containers for where he might have hidden what she was looking for.

He waited patiently, knowing full well that she was getting closer to being in deep trouble. It only took her four more minutes to find the stash, and by then she was so desperate that she wasn't even paying attention.

He waited until her hand was deep inside the container of rice before he stepped all the way into the room. She was on her hands and knees, her face focused solely on the contents of the container.

He waited for the look of triumph when she found the baggie inside and then cleared his throat. Liz started, shocked by the sudden sound, and dropped the canister of rice. It rolled twice, spilling easily a pound of grain across the hardwood floor.

"You having fun there, Lizzie?" He walked closer, looking at the mess she'd made, his eyes taking their time in reaching the shocked and frightened features on her face. She was a pretty girl, with the sort of face that every guy would love to take home to meet the folks. She also looked so damned sexy when she was afraid.

"Tom!" Her voice broke and she stuttered. "I was just going to make you breakfast in bed!"

"I'm sure you were." He walked closer until he was looming above her. Liz looked up, her bottom lip trembling and her eyes already starting to tear. "Lizzie? Honey? We seem to have a problem here."

"I was just . . . I was gonna pay you, but I need a fix."

"Of course you do." He reached out with his hands and pulled the baggie from her fingers. He tore the package open and threw the contents in her face, watching her as she coughed uncontrollably, her face going red from the violence of her fit. "Help yourself, honey. It's nice and pure."

And it was, too; Tom doubted there was a better source anywhere for powdered sugar. Liz's lungs tried to compensate for the inhaled confection; it wasn't working out. She kept coughing for almost a minute, and when she was finished, she stared at the floor, her lips licking at the white powder on her face.

"What is that?" She wiped at her face, smearing white paste across her features and wiping a few spots of moisture away.

"Do you really think I'd be stupid enough to leave anything like that lying around my house?" Tom reached out and grabbed a thick handful of her sandy blond hair. "Time for you to learn a few lessons, Lizzie."

She started crying, her eyes grew wide and her hands reached up to stop him from pulling as hard as he was. He repressed a shiver of lust. First the discipline, then the sex. He had to make sure she understood who was boss, and then he'd demonstrate his affections.

Tom hauled back on her hair as hard as he could, and Lizzie wailed out in pain as her hair separated from her scalp. He knew she was going to be feeling that for a few days, oh yes, and he knew she'd be feeling a lot worse before it was done.

His knee slammed into her taut belly and doubled her over. To make sure she was really, really getting his point, he struck her there again as she coughed and dry heaved.

By the time she was done retching, he was sporting an erection. "Never try to steal from me, Lizzie. And never try to just borrow something of mine without asking. I let you off with a warning last night. I told you if you stole from me, we would have to work things out."

Liz nodded her pretty head, the tears still flowing from her eyes, though she no longer had the strength to actually cry. He walked into the living room for a moment and reached into his very small stash, the one he'd taped to the inside of the closet, far from where people would be able to see it with a casual glance.

When he returned to the kitchen, Liz was back on her hands and knees, and trying to sweep up the crap all over the floor with her hands. She was hyperventilating, her chest hitching at high speed, sucking in air without really getting much relief for her lack of breath. It did lovely things to her perky little tits.

He dropped the nickel bag on top of the rice and watched her pick it up. Liz looked at him with wide, desperate eyes, asking for his permission. He nodded and she attacked. When she was done, she had white along her nostrils that was a slightly different color than the trail left by the confectioner's sugar.

He could see when the coke hit her system. Her body relaxed and she almost managed a smile.

He was pretty sure she was about to say thanks to him when he tackled her and started tearing the clothes from her body.

She wasn't even considering the idea of thanking him before he was done. Now and then a girl got uppity and he was forced to put her back in her place. Liz had broken the rules twice in one day. For that reason, he got inventive.

When he was finished and she was pinned under him, he leaned in close and licked her earlobe. Liz twitched, but couldn't possibly get away from him. Then he withdrew from her, his erection fading as he rolled off of her sweet little body.

Tom leaned over and winked at her crying face. "Bet you didn't even know you were still a virgin anywhere, did you, Lizzie?"

She shook her head and started crying again.

Tom ran his hand over the side of her face, leaving streaks in her white sugar makeup. "You remember something, Liz. I choose your clients. I've been nice with you and kept you away from the rough ones." She tried to nod her head, but didn't seem to have the energy. "You mess with me again and I'll leave you for a couple of really sick fucks. Those boys like to use knives to make their own fuck holes."

She broke down again and Tom let himself smile. Sometimes life was good.

V

Maggie waited until the other two priests had left before she approached Father Wilson. He was a lean man, with less hair than he'd had the year before and a warm smile for all of his parishioners. He was also a man who was accustomed, if she was reading him the right way, to the finer things in life.

He'd had a sermon once about the wild things he'd done when he was younger, and how he'd almost lost himself in the decadent ways of his youth before God called him home.

That made him a little bit different as challenges went. He'd had sex before and probably on several occasions. His face still held on to some of the looks that had probably made him very popular with the girls in his neighborhood when he was younger. Mostly, he looked at the women in the audience when he gave his sermons, and she had little doubt that part of him still longed for the good old days.

She was wearing her Sunday best today. She wanted to make sure he noticed her. Father Flannery had been easy; he was lonely and he liked younger women. Father Harris had been more challenging, but she'd figured the best way to handle him was to basically assault him in his bedroom. She was fairly confident that she could manage with Father Wilson as well, but he was an intriguing challenge.

He seemed so set in his ways, and even if he looked at the women in the church more than he looked at the men, that was almost to be expected. Also, he didn't try to look down her blouse nearly as often as the other two did. They were subtle, but she knew how to read them. Father Wilson wasn't quite as easy to peg.

She couldn't find him at first and wondered if she had made a mistake. It was possible that he'd left before she got there, or that he was off doing any number of things that she had no desire to learn about. The business of running a church was hardly what she thought of as exciting news.

She found him in the vestibule behind the altar. Donald Wilson had been waiting for a moment alone. He had his eyes closed and was masturbating as quietly as he could, his mouth making motions as if he were speaking, but no sounds came from him.

Maggie watched him for several seconds, taken aback by his actions. Then she cleared her throat and got his attention.

He might have been more horrified if she'd been the Pope, but probably not. Wilson tried to stand and pull his dark slacks up at the same time, his face beet red and his hands trembling. He was close to the point of no return in his ministrations, and she looked where he had been attending to himself with a certain level of amusement, but she also tried to hide it.

"I—"

She didn't let him get any further than the one word. His blue eyes were wide and his entire body was prepared for flight before she reached out to give him a little assistance.

A few moments later he was leaning against her, his face buried in her hair, and begging her not to tell anyone. Maggie turned her head and kissed his forehead softly, and then lowered to her knees in front of him and did things with her mouth that kept him speechless for quite some time.

A short while later she stared at the statue of the Virgin Mary that stood near the front door of the church as she leaned over the altar and he entered her from behind.

He was more imaginative than the other two priests had been. He was also less vocal. When they were done, she walked him back over to the alcove where she had caught him in the act and gave him one kiss on the lips before she left. His secret would be safe with her.

Maggie felt invigorated as she started back for home, and she felt as relaxed as she ever had. Several people who saw her thought to themselves that she was a woman in love as she walked; the soft, sweet smile on her face was a wonderful sight to behold.

It wasn't love, but it was as close as she ever let herself get. The three men she had been with in the last couple of days had all managed to bring her more pleasure than she'd experienced sexually in her life. Maybe it was something about priests, or maybe it was the fact that they all so desperately wanted her again. Whatever the reason for her pleasure, she wasn't even trying to hide it.

She made a short visit to the library, where she checked out three books she knew would be useful for her term paper. It was still a few weeks before she'd really have to worry, but it was best to get the work done early and she had the time.

Ben, from across the hallway, was just getting ready to leave when she came home. He smiled sweetly and made a quick wave before he closed and locked his door.

"Hi, Ben." She smiled back, pleased to see him. He was funny and he was cute and she liked him. "You heading out somewhere?"

"Yep. I have to pick up a few packages. From my friend. The one I called."

She stared blankly for a second and then remembered what he said he was doing to a crooked cop. "Really?"

"Yep. He's supposed to leave them out for me and I'm going to check on them." He looked at his watch. "He should just about be done setting everything in place."

"Want company?" The last thing she'd expected to come out of her mouth was a request to come along on what could be a dangerous little trip. She didn't need to get into any trouble with the law, that was all there was to it. But she was curious about Ben and she was doubly curious about what he had planned. And she was restless. Very, very restless.

Ben looked at her for a few seconds and she could almost see him working out all of the details in his brain.

"If you don't, it's okay." She laughed to show him the truth of her words. "I won't be offended or anything."

He blushed, even in the growing darkness, she could see it. "Well, it's not exactly legal. I just don't want you getting into any trouble if he's outsmarted me."

"I could be your alibi." She smiled and brightened, then

winked conspiratorially. "You could say we were just making out if anyone gives you trouble."

Ben looked away for a second and she saw a smile start on his face. He was blushing worse than ever.

"Okay. If you want to." He put his hands into his jacket pockets. "You need to change first, or anything?"

"Yeah, gimme just a sec." She slid into her apartment and shimmied out of her skirt as she walked toward her bedroom. There was a nice dark pair of jeans and a sweater that would be perfect for sneaking around in the woods. By the time she'd changed her clothes, she was actually looking forward to the trip more than she had expected.

It was the risk. That was the conclusion she came to. It was the risk that made it so damned exciting with the priests, and it was the thrill of being mischievous that had her heading into the woods with a man she barely knew, all so she could watch him commit a crime.

Too many years of playing it safe and working hard had made her a thrill junkie. She hoped it was temporary insanity, because she didn't need the complications in her life.

But that was okay, too. Now and then everyone needed to have a little fun.

Later, she'd have reason to doubt the wisdom of those words.

CHAPTER 5

I

Kelli Entwhistle slumped on the front porch and rubbed at her temples. The night had gone on and on, but at least the crisis seemed to be over.

Of course, the eight hours at the hospital and the numerous tests hadn't told them a damned thing. They would probably have kept Teddy, too, but Bill was having none of it and Michelle was furious that they'd failed to uncover anything.

The Listers were inside now, tucking in their son. His color was better at least, but he still seemed listless. The plan was for Kelli to take him to a specialist the next day, one of the family doctors who had known Teddy since he was born and could, presumably, find out answers with more ease.

Kelli was scared for him. Thinking about his situation made her stomach want to knot up, and made her want to puke her guts out. He was such a sweet kid. Her cousin Amy had been a sweet kid, too, and had always been so energetic. Right up until the time she suddenly couldn't keep any food down.

By the time the doctors discovered the stomach cancer, it was too late. Kelli had watched the girl who was almost like a sister to her waste away in a matter of months. The idea of that happening to Teddy was enough to wrench her heart out of place.

"Kids shouldn't get sick. It ought to be a law." She was talking to herself, of course.

So she almost had a coronary on the spot when she got a response. "I agree. I was just coming over to see how your little friend was doing."

Jason Soulis stood in front of her, dressed in a dark gray suit and a heavy black overcoat. He was either just going out for an evening or just coming back, she had no idea which.

"Oh, shit." She clutched at her chest and felt her heart beating. That was good, because he'd scared the life out of her. "I didn't see you come up." She laughed lightly.

He lowered his head and raised it again, a slight bow of apology. His eyes never left hers. "I certainly meant no harm. Forgive me."

"Oh, no, please. That's just me freaking out a bit."

"You've had a long day; I did not mean to make it longer." He took a step back and did a more formal bow. She got the impression the man could have managed to look just as polite and proper if he were carrying a bucket of pig slop in each hand. He was just that smooth. "I hope all is well with your friend."

As he started down the stairs she realized she didn't want him to leave. He was interesting, and obviously a nice man. "We don't know yet."

Soulis stopped and looked back at her. His face was half submerged in shadows, making him look slightly gaunt as the darkness caressed his features. "They have no diagnosis as yet?"

"No. They took all sorts of tests, but they couldn't figure out what was wrong. His blood pressure is doing strange things and he is too tired, but they didn't find anything that should have made him sick."

"You must be patient. Sometimes the mysteries of the body hide themselves. The doctors will undoubtedly find the problem given a little more time."

Yes, he talked with an accent, but it was faint, and she could have listened to him speak for hours. She shook the thought away and smiled for his benefit. Amy's death had long since crushed her faith in doctors and modern medicine.

"Have a good night. I will keep your friend in my thoughts." Jason turned and walked away, his steps as graceful as a dancer's. He was gone before she remembered to say good night herself.

A few minutes later, Bill came out to the porch and snuck one of his rare cigarettes. He only smoked when he'd had a particularly bad day. This one qualified.

He sat down near her on the wooden bench, and sighed. "Did I mention you're a lifesaver, Kelli?"

She smiled and nodded. "About ten times, but don't stop on my account."

"Teddy's a good kid. And he's lucky—he has a good home and a super nanny to watch over him." His voice sounded a little lost. She could hear guilt riding along with the compliments.

"Don't be too hard on yourself, Bill. You work yourself half to death and I know you do it to make sure Teddy has a good future." She knew no such thing, but it seemed like the right thing to say.

Bill inhaled deeply and held the smoke in his lungs, savoring it before he exhaled. "Teddy's future is all taken care of, Kelli. He'll never want for anything, at least not financially."

"So why do you work so hard, then?"

He looked her way and she couldn't help but notice that his eyes lingered for a few seconds in places where married men should not let their attention stray. "I like to stay busy, and I like to take on new challenges."

She opted not to take any possible innuendoes to heart. Her fantasies were just that, and not something she ever intended to act on.

"Well, I guess I better go hit the books." Kelli stood up and rolled her head a few times, getting the blood flow back into her tense muscles.

"Have a good night, Kelli. Thanks again." Bill stood up and put a companionable arm around her shoulders, giving her a half hug. He kissed the top of her head and then let her pass.

"Nothing to thank me for, Bill. Sweet dreams."

She left him out in the deepening cold of the night, and went up to her bedroom, across from Teddy's. Michelle Lister was still in the room looking down on her sleeping son. She had a few lines from crying on her face, but Kelli didn't look for long or offer any sort of comfort. Michelle was a very private woman, and she knew the lady would prefer to be by herself with her sleeping child.

There was surprisingly little traffic on Cliff Walk. Normally, even in the dead of winter, she could expect to see a few cars traveling up and down the long stretch of road. Kelli stared at the road and the house across the street for several minutes, her mind wandering from her employer on the porch to the man who had just recently come to town.

She closed her eyes and drifted to sleep still fully clothed and far too tired to care about the discomfort of wearing her jeans to slumber land.

Across the street, Jason watched her from the shadows of an oak tree. He barely moved until the moon had risen into the sky.

II

Brian Freemont drove like a madman, desperate to get back to his house and the phone call he knew he had to expect. He'd had more than enough of his mystery caller and the threats the man had delivered. He wanted the situation resolved.

"I just want my life back. That's all. Please, God, let me have my life back."

His stomach seethed with tension. Angie was at home and he dreaded the idea that she would answer that particular phone call. If she did, she could make his life a living hell. He didn't like the idea of a divorce, and he liked the idea of child support even less.

Sometimes, when he was halfway to sleep, he looked back and wondered if he had ever loved Angie. He thought so. These days she was too high maintenance and her moods were pissing him off to the point that he didn't fucking care what happened to her.

That was a lie. He did care, he just didn't know if he cared as much as he should. She was a good woman, one of the best he'd ever known, but her mood swings and weight gain were taxing his patience.

Mostly, these days, he was worried about what was going to happen if he didn't get this all worked out. Everything he had was gone; all of the money in his accounts, except for his last paycheck. He knew, because he'd looked all of the accounts over online earlier in the day. It wasn't that the money had been taken. Instead it was as if the money had never existed. Even his transaction records were screwed up beyond all repair. If this wasn't fixed to the bastard on the phone's satisfaction, his whole world was going to fall apart.

He wanted that fucker dead.

He wanted to make the son of a bitch scream and die and bleed.

But mostly he wanted his life back.

The clock on the dashboard told him he still had five minutes to get home. He parked as calmly as he could and climbed from the car. His hands were doing their best to clench into fists and he made himself calm down a bit. Angie didn't need to see him like this.

He opened the door to his house and smiled as he walked in, ready to put on a cheery face for his wife. He needn't have bothered. She was already in a bad mood.

Angie Freemont sat on the couch, the TV playing the last of the nightly news, and stared daggers at Brian.

"Angie? What's wrong?"

Her voice was hoarse and tense. "You want to tell me why the bank called four times today, Brian?"

"What did they call about, honey?"

"About the fact that we have no money, and seven checks have bounced since this morning. How's that for a starter?"

Brian felt his stomach fall a few stories and took a deep breath. "I can explain that."

"Good! Because I'm sick to death of this shit, Brian!"

"It was a mistake, I already talked to the bank and everything should be fine in the morning. Something about a hacker trying to steal from a bunch of accounts." This was closer to the truth than he liked to think about, but it made the lie easier.

She opened her mouth to speak and the phone rang. The idea of his wife grabbing the phone to speak to the man blackmailing him for screwing college trim on the side sent Brian Freemont leaping across the room. The end table with the phone was next to Angie's right hand. He knocked her arm out of the way as he grabbed the receiver.

"Hello?" Angie shot him a murderous glance and he in turn looked as apologetic as he could.

"Officer Freemont?"

"Yes, this is me."

"One second." He could hear the man moving through the underbrush. "How many boxes did you put out here?"

"Four. They should all be together." This was the moment he needed to worry about the most. He chewed on his lip and did his best not to sound too stressed.

Everything depended on the caller taking the boxes with him.

"I see four boxes; we're off to a good start here, Officer. Hold on for me."

"Of course." Angie was standing now, her face set into an ugly expression of hatred and disappointment. Brian felt like a slug. He was responsible for everything and he knew it, but he was also trying to make it all right again. If she would let him, and the little bastard would take the bait.

"I have the packages. If everything checks out, you will have your life back in two hours."

"I understand, thank you."

"Officer? Do I have to explain what will happen if you try to pull a fast one?"

"No, of course not."

"Have a good night."

Brian hung up the phone and looked at Angie. "That was the bank. Everything is settled."

"Seriously?" She smiled a tentative, nervous little smile. Her face was suddenly beautiful again.

"Yeah, babe. Seriously, it's all taken care of." He moved to her and she hugged him tightly, awkwardly shifting a bit to protect their unborn child. That thought suddenly filled him with wonder. He had a child coming into the world. A new life that was forming in the belly of the woman he'd married and promised to love, honor, and respect.

Something had to change. He knew that. He just didn't want it to. He liked his secret life, and he liked the power to screw with girls' minds and leave them worrying.

He didn't want to give that up.

So, of course, he had made proper provisions.

For the next hour or so, he was going to stay home. Then he would go back to the car and find his little Radio Shack tracking device, the one he'd slipped into the cardboard box that was probably being carried away right now.

And then he would make good and damned sure that someone never messed with him again.

Angie kissed his mouth and he kissed back, remembering all the reasons that he loved her. She was sore and pregnant, and she still wanted him.

Really, that was all he'd ever wanted out of life, to be needed. And if he was getting a little on the side, it was just gravy.

They made love, carefully, but they made love. This was different. Angie was special. She wasn't like the girls he spent time with. She didn't cry when it was happening, or when it was over.

III

Avery Tripp slipped out of the house as carefully as he could. The folks were still busy "talking," which made it a little easier. Talking was what they called it whenever they needed down time and decided to close the bedroom door. He had no idea what they were up to, but it left Dad in a good mood, so it couldn't be a bad thing.

The yard was dark, but the lawn was so precisely mowed it could have been done by the barber that handled his crew cut, so he wasn't worried. Besides, he knew the way to Teddy's place like the back of his hand.

Teddy left school early and he hated when that happened. His best friend was his main reason for going to school in the first place. Okay, and because his folks would boil him in oil if he didn't. But mainly it was because Teddy was there and he was cool to hang around with.

The road was well-lit and the lawns on either side of him offered exactly enough bushes—because the people here liked their privacy—to let him move toward the Lister place without any fear of being discovered.

He saw the crows looking down at him and stopped in his tracks. They were everywhere, great skulking black shadows that moved and from time to time chattered softly to each other.

Mostly they just looked at him. Avery looked back, smiling at the gathering. What was it Dad said they were called when they were all together like that? "A murder of crows," he said, savoring the title. He liked the sound of that.

The birds didn't intimidate him; they were just birds. So Avery started down the way again, listening for cars and minding his own business. Jayce Thornton was playing havoc with his thoughts lately. She was cute. He liked her. He also knew that if she spoke to him, he would explode into flames.

The last time she'd talked to him had been to see if she could borrow his notes after she had to stay home for a day. He'd had to write them up for her, because he could barely even read his own handwriting on the originals, and he'd been drawing stuff all along the edges. Nothing dirty, just things he didn't want anyone to see.

These days he always made a copy of his notes, just in case. Funny thing about that: His grades had gotten way better ever since he had decided to make copies. If there was a connection, he refused to see it.

"It's rather late to be out by yourself, don't you think?" The voice belonged to a stranger, and Avery froze in his tracks. He looked around and saw the man a moment later, but he almost had to strain to make him out.

Dark black clothes hid most of his body, and heavy shadows obscured a good part of his face. But he was smiling pleasantly enough.

"I'm not supposed to talk to strangers." It was a good line to use when he was nervous. The man made him want to run screaming.

"Yes. I think maybe you're not supposed to be out walking alone this time of night, either."

Okay. The guy had him dead to rights on that one.

The stranger held out one hand and Avery watched as two of the crows on the phone lines above his head lowered like leaves in a graceful fall, to settle on the man's opened palm and forearm. "Where are you going so late in the evening, my young friend?"

"Whoa! How did you do that?" Avery forgot himself and talked far louder than he meant to, the excitement of watching the crows taking away his fear of being busted.

"They're friendly birds when you know how to talk to them. Would you like to hold one?"

"Can I?" He walked forward and held out his hand, reaching eagerly.

"Carefully. They are easily startled. They must come to you; you must not come to them."

Avery nodded and stopped, holding his hand like he'd seen the man do before. "What makes them so nervous?"

"Look at yourself. You are as big as twenty of them. How would you feel if a giant reached out to grab you without warning?" The man's eyes looked into his, amusement emphasizing the light crow's feet around the dark pupils. Then he moved his hand closer to Avery's and the crow bobbed its head three times before walking sullenly over to stand on Avery's palm. The feet were cold and black; he felt the pinpoints of the claws where they pinched his hand.

Avery stared, amazed by the bird now in his hand. The crow craned its head around and looked at him with one glossy black eye.

"Can I keep him, mister?"

The man laughed lightly and shook his head. "He is not to be kept, my friend. He is too wild for that. He must live his own life or he will never be happy."

Avery understood the concept, but wasn't thrilled by the news. He would have loved having a crow as a pet. How cool would that be?

The stranger lifted his hand and the crow that had been perched there flew into the air, powerful wings lifting it back to the perch it had previously abandoned. The bird in Avery's hand fidgeted a bit and danced from foot to foot for a moment. Then it took off, the wings almost striking his face before it was airborne.

Avery turned to thank the man who'd shown him the crows, but when he looked, there was no sign that he had ever been there. He frowned, and was about to call out when the hands caught him around the throat and lifted him from the ground.

Avery couldn't scream, couldn't breathe, and his feet kicked at the man again and again, but seemed to have absolutely no impact.

"Shhh . . . Avery Tripp. You and the crows will be good friends, I think."

The world faded away, lost in a darkness that was filled with the rustle of black feathers.

IV

"Have you ever seen so many birds?" Ben looked around the car in wonder, a smile playing at his lips. He was a great big kid in a lot of ways.

Maggie stood nearby, holding the last of the boxes. He took it from her and set it next to the car, then reached into a box he had brought with him. Aside from the gloves both of them wore, the box also held a small meter of some kind.

"What's that?" She sounded amused, and he was glad she was having fun.

"This is an electromagnetic emanation detector." He put on a deep scholarly voice for her.

"A what?" She was smiling and looking at him with those amazing eyes.

"It checks for radio waves and other stuff."

"What? You think he bugged you?"

He looked right back at her, his smile fading a bit. "I would. If someone was screwing with me this way, I most certainly would."

"You really think so?" He couldn't tell if she was thinking about it or doubting his sanity.

"I've made threats against him. He's a cop. And he's not a very nice cop. I don't want to take any chances." He shrugged, trying to tell himself it didn't matter if she thought he was loony.

"See? That's smart. I wouldn't have thought about it."

He turned on the meter and ran it carefully over each of the boxes. The first two were clean. The third gave off a signal. He found the source and pulled a small transmitter out of the edge, frowning at it. Not a lot of range, but it would do if the man using it was careful.

"Bastard," he was laughing as he said it.

"You're not upset?"

"No. It's like chess. Only he doesn't know all the rules."

"Yeah? Like what?" She moved closer, and he showed her the small tracking device.

"Like I don't play nicely." He moved the device over to a different part of the parking area, placing it into a knothole in one of the trees.

"Should I call him now? Or make him wait?"

"Oh, no." She shook her head, actually looking indignant. "Call his ass and break his balls." He blinked and smiled. He wasn't used to her using vulgarity. Then again, he wasn't used to her. It was nice new territory to explore.

"Okay. You win."

He picked up the phone he'd been using earlier and dialed the number for the man's house again.

The phone rang seven times before Brian Freemont answered. He didn't sound at all happy about the interruption.

"Hello?"

"Hello, Officer Freemont. I found your tracking device. Now you get to wait at least one more day before I give you back your life. Don't write any checks."

He turned off the phone and put it back into his pocket.

Maggie was smiling at him, her eyes alight with amusement. "You're a very bad man, Ben. Very bad."

"Yeah, well, I have my moments."

They left the boxes behind, taking only the evidence packages that they held.

All the way back to the apartments, Maggie kept giving him the strangest looks. He didn't know why, but he rather liked it.

V

Tom Pardue was high on life. He always got that way when he knew he was going to have a good time with someone. Right now he was going to have a party all over Maggie Preston. She was a fine-looking girl, she really was, but she'd been playing games and thinking it wouldn't get back to him.

She was supposed to be handling situations with Lance Brewster, and he'd just gotten another call from a long-term client who was not at all happy with the lack of attention he was getting. That wasn't acceptable. She knew the score: He let her *think* she was something special. He made sure she got the nonviolent johns who weren't too freaky, because she earned the money. He gave her name to only the best clientele, because she was damned good at her job. She'd told him a few things back in the day about being double-jointed and a gymnast. Until she'd proved to him how much difference that could make, he could have cared less. She could also do things with her mouth to make a man cry. She could unhinge her jaw, for God's sake! On the day he decided to give her a test session, she'd swallowed him whole and then kept him at the edge of orgasm for over an hour. Maggie could tease mercilessly and have a man begging for release. That was why she was so popular. She could also get into the most incredible positions he'd ever experienced. But that didn't mean she was in charge of her own destiny or any of that other shit she liked to spew from time to time. In the long run she was just another piece of ass, and she was his to do with as he pleased. She was a hooker who had a few special talents; it didn't make her the queen of the universe, it just made her a good commodity. If she wanted to believe she was something more than that, he could correct her ideas.

Maybe it was time to stop being so nice about how he treated her. Maybe if he gave her a few sessions like he'd given Lizzie earlier, she'd remember who was in charge of her fucking destiny.

So he was waiting around for her to show her little ass at her little apartment. Then, if she got bitchy, he was going to explain everything nicely, exactly one more time. If it was twice, he'd break her in half.

That was before she came into the courtyard of her place with some little yuppie fuck, carrying a bunch of white bags and laughing like she didn't have a care in the whole world.

Seeing her and her boyfriend just made the whole of his day better. She hadn't been producing as well as she should for almost a week, and now he knew why.

Maggie was laughing, her head thrown back at something the college boy had said.

Being a good sport, Tom walked out from his hiding place and smiled.

"Hey, Maggie." He smiled and watched her jump as the bags in her hands fell all over the ground.

"Tom . . ." Her sweet, lovely, sexy-as-all-hell face grew ghostly white, prompting a bigger grin on Tom. He sauntered over as casual as he could, and rocked back on his heels for a second.

"That's me. Tom." He looked over at the college boy. He was in decent shape for a loser, but probably wouldn't last more than three punches. "Who's your friend?"

"Ben, this is Tom. Tom, this is Ben. We have a class together." She was good, keeping it calmer than he'd expected. It made sense, the kid being a study buddy, because Tom couldn't imagine his pet whore would want to get her face shattered for a limp-wristed little piece like the one she was hanging with.

The kid set down his packages as carefully as he could and held out a hand. Almost amused by the idea, he took the offering and shook hands like a real gentleman.

"Nice to meet you, Tom." The kid's face was neutral. That was good. He didn't want to have the boy feeling like they were going to be friends or anything.

"Likewise," he said with absolutely no concern whatsoever if the loser noticed it was a lie.

"What can I do for you, Tom?"

"There's a little problem with Brewster, my puppy." He looked into her eyes and saw the minor flash of gratitude that went along with the tightening of her jaw. He could have ousted her and it wouldn't have mattered all that much, but if he pissed her off over the little shit, she'd forget to be grateful when the time came.

"What's wrong with him?"

"He misses you. He just wanted me to say hi; maybe later you could give him a visit?"

Maggie looked at him through half-lidded eyes. She had a great bitch stare. It would have worked on most guys. Tom wasn't like most guys. He knew the score and sometimes he had to remind the girls. They didn't remind him.

"Maybe," she shrugged. It always did the nicest things to her tits. "Has he learned not to bite yet?"

"Disciplining puppies is so hard, Maggie." He pouted and put on his best puppy dog face. Even he knew it wasn't a pretty sight, but he did it anyway. "But he wanted me to tell you he's really sorry and it won't happen again."

Maggie looked him up and down with an almost insolent stare that was going to cost her dearly if she didn't satisfy Brewster's needs. "Yeah, okay. I'll stop by and see him."

"Thanks, sweetheart. I know you just made his whole day

better." He looked over at Ben and winked. "You think she's gonna make it tonight, Ben? Or are you keeping her busy?"

He looked surprised by the comment. "Oh, no. She was just helping me pick up some stuff for the forensics class I'm taking." He gestured at the small mountain of white bags.

"Fake evidence folders, cute."

"Professor Holmes likes his authentic touches." Ben was looking at him now, too, with a funny expression on his face. Tom decided he'd have to check later to see if he had been insulted.

"Well, you guys have fun now." He turned and headed back to his car. Brewster would be happy and he would pay top dollar. That made Tom happy. Maggie was off the hook, for now. She'd get bitchy sooner or later, and he'd put her back in her place again. He loved teaching Maggie lessons. He shot his best smile at Ben and then winked playfully at Maggie. "But not too much fun, you hear?"

Neither of them said anything as he left. That was good. He liked to get in the last word.

CHAPTER 6

I

Alan and Meghan Tripp were beside themselves when the sun rose on their son's empty bedroom. He had been in bed by nine; they knew that, because they'd tucked him in together. He was a good kid and even though he was getting older, he still tolerated their doting on him.

Now he was gone.

By the time he should have been getting ready for school, they had torn through every room in the house. By the time he should have been finishing his breakfast, they had called everyone they could think of. No one had seen Avery after they put him into bed.

Meghan was a wreck, pacing and wringing her hands. Avery had been something of an unexpected miracle child, coming as he did after an early partial hysterectomy. There was no chance that they would ever have another child, and even if they did, he would never be able to replace Avery. He was her baby, and she was devastated by his disappearance.

Alan was holding it in better, but he wanted to scream. Instead, he did the only wise thing and called the police. They were there in less than five minutes; no one in Black Stone Bay took child abduction lightly. Not after what had happened with the Whittaker girl back in '87. Carla Whittaker had been stolen from her bedroom in the middle of the night, and at first her parents thought she had run away to get attention. For the first three days, the Whittaker family simply made polite inquiries of her friends and school chums.

Then the phone calls came. An anonymous voice spoke urgently, demanding ransom and secrecy. An hour later, the caller rang them again and almost every hour after that the calls came fast and hard, some time after the fourth day of quiet, polite searching was done. The kidnappers wanted money, of course, and they would not let anyone speak to Carla.

The story did not play out well. After the money was delivered, the phone calls stopped. Pieces of Carla were found along the coast for several months. All of them were fresh when they were located. The last piece they found was her head, which the coroner determined had only been in the water for a few hours when fishermen found it. The case had never been solved.

So, yes, it was fair to say that no one in Black Stone Bay took missing children lightly.

The questions were endless, of course. Did they have a recent picture? Yes, and also video footage. Did they know what he was wearing? The clothes he had worn to school were not in the hamper, so yes, he was wearing a green flannel shirt, blue jeans, and red Reeboks. His jacket was also missing, a dark brown leather bomber jacket that he had requested for his birthday. Did he have any friends in the area? Damned near every child in the school and in the neighborhood; he was a well-liked young man. Did he have any enemies? No. Even Lucien Hawkings liked him, and the old bastard didn't like anyone. Where were they when he disappeared? They didn't know when he vanished, but they were likely in bed. When did they realize he was missing? Five minutes before they called the police. The list went on and on.

By noon there were almost four hundred people searching for Avery Tripp. By four in the afternoon, there were closer to eight hundred. By sunset, a lot of very disappointed people were ready to call it quits.

Alan Tripp was not among them. He wandered the streets until almost two in the morning before he came home and fell into a troubled sleep. In his dreams he heard Avery crying for help, and try though he did, he could not find his son.

When he awoke in the morning, Avery was still missing. He left the house with the dawn and began searching again. There were so many places his son could be; Avery loved to explore. He was never happier than when he was out finding new things.

II

Maggie had to give credit where it was due; Lance Brewster was very good at groveling. After she had finally conceded to call the man, he spent twenty minutes apologizing for the way he'd mistreated her. She spent twenty minutes listening to his attempts at an explanation without giving an inch to him.

He swore it would never happen again and confessed that he had feelings for her that went beyond what he should have. That did not get him any further with her. Maggie didn't have the time to be his personal toy and she most certainly didn't have the time to listen as he went on about how his wife didn't understand him. She knew all about the divorce he was going through; she just did not care.

Finally, after almost an hour of his begging, she allowed that she could be free that night.

The man was in tears on the phone. It was really rather embarrassing. Still, he was normally a good client. Unless he wanted to make sure that he never saw her again, he would continue to be a good client.

Besides, after the incident with Tom the night before, she needed a little reminder that some people actually cared for her, even if they cared for all the wrong reasons.

Monkey Boy had come in on a rampage, ready to cause her no end of grief, and had managed to show mercy for whatever reason. She was grateful, which was really the main factor that made her give in to his request.

Yes, grateful; because now the one person she'd met recently who was becoming a friend wasn't suddenly looking at her like she was a whore. In the grander scheme of things, it wouldn't matter all that much what Ben Kirby thought of her, but it was still nice to have a guy she could talk to who didn't seem desperate to get into her pants.

They arranged to meet at the Windbreakers, a very fine dining establishment known for their excellent food and atrocious costs. He brought her a pair of diamond earrings that was beyond excessive, and gave her a matching necklace as well. She thanked him politely, and warmed up a small amount. They had a nice meal, with excellent food, just a little wine, and some decent conversation. Of course he had to mention his wife again and the misery she was putting him through, but that came with the territory.

After dinner, she made him beg again; in the bedroom she made him beg as well. She did not stay the night with him in his hotel suite. He wanted her to, but she had school in the morning.

She left Monkey Boy's portion of the money in the drop slot of his front door. She knew the signs that Tom was getting antsy. She also knew the best way to get him to behave was to keep her end of the bargain they'd struck some time back.

She kept the diamonds. They were hers. Any apologies that had to be made were made to her, and not to the prick who thought he owned her.

She didn't feel like going home, and she was far from tired. So it was off to the diner. Sally was probably working, and Sally was normally good for a few jokes while she ate.

No one was more surprised than she was to find Ben there. It was a nice surprise, but unexpected.

He was leaning over his laptop and typing furiously. His fingers moved so fast she would have thought the keyboard would catch fire. She slipped in across from him, moving as carefully as she could, amused by how intent he was on his typing.

When he finally looked up, he actually jumped in his seat. "Hey!" He looked embarrassed. "I mean, hi."

She laughed, and reached across the table to graze his hand with her fingers. "I didn't mean to scare you. You just looked so intent I didn't want to disturb your work."

"No, it's okay. I'm just . . . gathering my thoughts."

"Did you get what you were looking for? For your friend?" She didn't have to clarify. He knew what she was talking about.

"Yes." A quick flash of a smile that degraded into a yawn. "Excuse me. I did get it. I'm going to tell her tomorrow." He rubbed at his eyes for a second and stared at her. After a second he remembered it wasn't polite to stare and looked greedily at his now empty coffee cup.

"You're sweet to go through all of that." He blushed. She had never known anyone who blushed as often as he did. She looked around and waved to Sally, who had been taking a large order from a group of businessmen. Sally smiled and nodded as Maggie made a few gestures for food, coffee, and a refill over here.

"Why are you staring at me, Ben?"

If she thought he'd blushed before, she was mistaken. He was red all the way to his ears when she asked. It was cruel, maybe, but she couldn't help teasing him just a bit. He almost begged for a good teasing.

"Sorry. Really, I am. You just took me off guard and I've never seen you dressed that way."

Maggie hadn't even really given her clothing any consideration. She was dressed for a night out, and once the wardrobe had been chosen it was the last thing she thought about. The dress she was wearing was a formal little black thing that clung to all of her curves. She liked it and saved it for special occasions.

"I had a dinner date. Is it too much?"

"No. No, not at all." He was doing a wonderful job of not stammering.

She laughed and playfully swatted his arm. "Down, boy. It's just me under all of this goop." She gestured to her face and the makeup she had carefully applied earlier. "I'll be back in regular clothes tomorrow."

"Yeah, well, don't go changing on my behalf. You look beautiful." He stared at his monitor as he said it, and then closed the screen so he could look at her properly.

"Well, thanks. It's always nice to be appreciated."

Sally set down her omelet and coffee, then topped off Ben's cup. After she'd walked away to handle the businessmen, Ben smiled and poured a few spoonfuls of sugar into his coffee.

"I didn't expect to find you here, Ben. Why the change of scenery?"

"Because if I stared at my walls for another minute, I'd go crazy."

"Is that the only reason?"

"No. I also ran out of coffee."

Maggie laughed. It was nice to know she wasn't being stalked. She'd had enough of that to last her a lifetime.

It was nice to relax. It was beyond nice to be able to just be herself around a guy. Ben was sweet and he was cute, she was going to have to watch herself around him. She couldn't afford to fall for anyone. Her plans for the future did not include being in a relationship; at least not for a while.

They went to the apartment building together, then to their separate apartments almost immediately after they reached them. She paused long enough to give Ben another kiss on the cheek. After that, she slept. It had been a very difficult day and a taxing night. She needed the rest. There were more names on Jason Soulis's list, and she had school to consider.

III

Teddy wanted to go look for Avery. Kelli could see it in every move he made and every pace he took around the house. His parents had decided he needed to recover his strength and she couldn't exactly disagree with the idea. While he seemed far stronger than he had the day before, he was still looking as pale as a ghost.

"Honey, we can't go looking for Avery." Damn, it hurt to look at his disappointment. "You're just not strong enough yet."

"But I am, Kelli!" His voice was shrill and he looked like he was going to cry. She knew the feeling. Avery was a little munchkin and he was always in trouble, but he was also a sweet kid.

"I'll tell you what. Why don't you get on a good coat and we can drive around for a while, okay? Maybe we'll spot something or even see Avery."

He didn't have the energy to jump and cheer, but he gave it the old college try. They left the house ten minutes later, both of them bundled up in heavy coats against the risk of deeply cold rain. The day was overcast and the air was promising a downpour before it was all said and done.

Kelli drove carefully, minding the speed limit more than she usually did. Teddy rested his forehead against the passenger's side window and looked out at the street and the houses that they drove past. His body barely moved, but she could see his eyes reflected in the glass and could see that he was desperately searching for any sign that Avery might be nearby.

Just past the last of the houses on the Cliff Walk drive, they came to a small patch of woods. There was a squad car parked in the small turnaround area, and a tall, dark-haired policeman was looking over four cardboard boxes with a look of quiet fury etched into his plain features. For just a moment, she imagined she could see discarded, bloody clothing in the boxes and Kelli drove a little faster. There was something about the cop that gave her a bad vibe.

"Do you think he's dead, Kelli?"

"What? Oh no, sweetie. I think maybe he just got lost." Did she think Avery was dead? She hoped he wasn't. He was a sweet kid, and she knew Teddy would be devastated.

She thought about his face when she'd busted them with the girly magazine. Avery was a vivacious boy and he wasn't afraid of very much in the world. That could be a big benefit, but it could also be a dangerous way to live. Avery Tripp might very well be dead, and she hated that she couldn't get the notion out of her mind.

The sun broke through the clouds a bit and she took that as a good sign. Cloudy days always made her feel depressed.

They drove in silence for a while, covering the entire shoreline of Black Stone Bay and then circling the road to the downtown area. It wasn't until she got to the entrances of the universities, where they faced each other, that she realized Teddy was unconscious and drooling against the window.

It was faster to drive to the hospital than to call an ambulance.

IV

The sun set on the second day of looking for Avery Tripp with little having changed, save that his parents were staggering around like boxers who'd been hit too many times. Ben knew the police were working their collective asses off, and so were the volunteers out looking for the kid.

Danni Hopkins was wringing her hands. She felt bad about the little boy whose face adorned the front page of the newspaper, but she felt a lot worse about her own life at the moment.

Ben was supposed to be here already and she was sitting in the same park as the last time she saw him, as the sun set. She wasn't comfortable waiting alone. She was a lot less happy about being by herself in the park than she'd been only a week earlier.

Brian Freemont had taken away a few delusions about the kindness of her fellow human beings. She'd spent most of the last few nights wishing she could sleep, and hoping that somehow, somewhere down the line, she could get her mind to stop focusing on having the man on top of her and doing his best to fuck her through the ground.

Remembering what she'd done to avoid jail had certainly put her life into perspective. Danni wasn't planning on ever touching another illegal substance for as long as she lived. She was also thinking a life of celibacy wouldn't be a bad thing.

Her stomach gave a faint rumble of protest; she also hadn't been eating for the last few days. Every time she cooked something and sat down to eat, she found she lacked the energy.

Physically, she was ravenous. Her emotional appetite was gone, and maybe forever.

Ben came along a minute after the campus clock struck a single note to announce the quarter hour. He moved over to her bench and settled down next to her.

"Sorry I'm late. I had to check on a few things."

Danni looked at him for a moment, half expecting him to say something vulgar. She'd been regretting telling him what happened ever since she'd opened her mouth. It would only take one word from him and her reputation around the school would be shattered.

Still, she made herself be nice. "Hi. It's not a problem." She forced a strained smile onto her face. "You said you wanted to talk to me?"

"Yeah." He nodded and then reached into his jacket pocket to pull out a paper bag. "This is for you."

She looked at him long and hard, her mind reeling a bit. "Is this . . . ?"

"Yeah. Don't open it here." He shrugged. "You hear of any others who got . . . in trouble with him, you can tell them that I burned the evidence bags. You get yours back, because I wanted you to know."

Danni started crying, right then and there. She couldn't help it. "Oh, God, Ben . . . oh, my fucking God . . ." She cried harder, the bag in her hand held tightly.

"Oh, hey." He moved his hands around, helplessly, his face puzzled by her reaction. "Listen, I didn't mean to make you cry . . ." He looked like he wanted to run away, and she couldn't help but laugh.

"No, Ben. Oh, no, I just can't tell you how happy I am." She broke down again, and Ben nodded, looking extremely relieved.

"Well, that's good then. I don't like to see you cry, Danni."

He patted her shoulder awkwardly and she hugged him hard, breathing against his neck and knowing that she was probably covering him with slobber and tears but unable to stop herself.

She pulled back after a few minutes, when the worst of the storm was over, and wiped her face. "I cried all over you."

"It's okay." He looked uncomfortable.

"How can I thank you, Ben? I can't believe you did this for me."

Ben stood up and smiled warmly, his eyes halfway between being happy and being somewhere else in his head. "You don't have to thank me, Danni. Just, don't ever get yourself caught that way again—"

"—I won't! I swear. I'm staying clean from now on!"

He nodded, "And don't ever tell anyone what I did, okay? Somewhere out there, a very angry cop is probably looking for me right now."

"Never a word, Ben. Thank you. Thanks so much."

"Have a good night, Danni. I'll see you in class, okay?"

He walked away and she watched him, still overwhelmed by what he'd done. She had a flash of guilt ripple across her mind. Part of her had expected him to demand similar treatment in return.

The worst part was she probably would have done it; just to be sure she was safe from Brian Freemont.

She crossed her arms over her chest, suddenly cold as the wind picked up, and shivered. The chill was only partly from the weather. What did it say about her if she would screw a guy by way of saying thanks? She didn't like to think about it, but the thought wouldn't leave her alone.

Danni rose from the bench with the package still clutched tightly in her hand. She looked around the park for a second, surprised to realize that the sun was gone from the sky. The only light left came from the lamps along the walkways.

She moved toward her car, planning on heading home.

The man stepped out in front of her from the shadows, seeming to simply grow from the darkness as he stepped forward.

"Oh!" She dropped the brown bag, her heart thudding hard at the sudden appearance.

He looked at her, his eyes hidden in shadows, a smile threatening to form on his mouth.

"You scared the crap out of me." And listen to her! She was

laughing! It was amazing what one small, kind act could do to renew her belief in mankind.

He nodded amiably and then moved. One second he was standing easily fifteen or twenty feet away, and the next he was in front of her, his hand grabbing at her neck, lifting her from the ground.

She looked into the dark pools where his eyes should have been and thought she saw something in there that looked back with contempt.

"Shhh, child. We have things to discuss, you and I. Things best said in a private place."

He carried her weight with ease, and pulled her away from the park and into the darkness.

And in the darkness she felt pain, and the rhythmic pounding of the surf became her lullaby.

V

The Listers paid better attention to the doctors the second time around. They also decided to leave their son in the hospital, despite their mutual dislike of medical facilities. At home he was their son. At the hospital he was patient number L-00041-30038. There was a little problem with having their only child looked upon as a number in a large field of numbers.

Doctor Alex Houston convinced them that he would personally supervise every action that took place regarding Teddy's well-being. They took him at his word. He'd been Teddy's physician since the boy was born, and if they had to trust someone, he would have to do.

Kelli was not nearly as convinced. Especially when she heard him say that the problems might only be in her young charge's head. Teddy had never been that excitable in her eyes. He also didn't look like he was suffering from a sudden wish to not go to school. Even now he was paler than she had ever seen him.

He woke up for a while and complained of being hungry.

Kelli had been prepared for that and pulled a peanut butter and grape jelly sandwich out of her purse. It was warm, but he at least tried to eat it. When it came to the hospital's culinary offerings, he simply pushed the grayish-brown lump of what was supposed to be meatloaf around on the plate and etched lines into his pasty mashed potatoes. The only thing he ate was the Jell-O, and then only because it was cherry-flavored.

While she kept him as entertained as she could, his parents argued with the hospital staff and made clear that if anything should happen to their boy, there would be Hell to pay and a few demons sent along to charge interest besides.

Visiting hours ended at nine P.M.; Kelli left for the Lister house at five after, her eyes almost crossing from exhaustion. By the time she got to her room, she was wide awake again. She couldn't get past the very idea that Teddy might be "willing himself sick." The doctor was an imbecile. Just because they couldn't find a physical cause for his ailments didn't mean there wasn't a legitimate health risk.

The Listers got home a few minutes after she did, and Michelle immediately went up to her office. She'd let her work go all day long and now she needed to catch up on a few briefs. Kelli understood. Bill was less pleased. He had attorneys in his office that could take care of his cases for the day. Apparently his wife didn't have the same resources in her own firm.

They both sat on the porch, Kelli and her employer. She looked at the gray house across the way and saw no sign that anyone lived there at all. Bill lit a cigarette. He'd smoked three times as many in the last day as he normally did in a week.

"I don't think it's psychosomatic, Bill."

"There's no way it could be, Kelli. He's a good boy and his mind is as sharp as a razor."

She nodded in the darkness. "I think something bit him and he's having an allergic reaction."

"It's possible, but the doctors already gave him a wide spectrum of antibiotics and enough Benadryl to keep him from sneezing for the next six months." He shrugged his broad shoulders and inhaled deeply. Most people would have thought he was perfectly calm, but Kelli knew all of the Listers well enough to see the worry in his actions, even if he never let it show on his face.

She sighed. "I hope he's okay, Bill. I'm so sorry this happened."

"It's nothing you did, Kelli." He looked her way and smiled for an instant. "You've been wonderful. Remind me to give you a raise."

"Oh, no. No raises. I'll be perfectly fine with having Teddy back here and safe."

"You're too good to us, Kelli. This is two days in a row where you had to miss school."

"I'll be fine, straight As and all of that." She dismissed his compliment and waved it away like a pesky gnat.

Theodore Thomas Lister was declared legally dead twelve minutes after Kelli went to sleep that night. The cause of death was undetermined.

The body disappeared sometime during the night.

CHAPTER 7

The Cliff Walk carried the scent of the ocean and scrubbed away the filth of the city beyond its edges. The breeze was invigorating, and Alan Tripp normally loved to spend his time walking along the edge and feeling the air rush past. It was enough on most occasions to make his problems dwindle away into nothingness.

Some problems are bigger than others.

Avery Tripp was still missing, and it was killing Alan. He thought for certain that he would go absolutely insane if he didn't know what had happened to his son, one way or the other.

The stranger who walked past him nodded amiably as he watched the waves crashing against the black stones of the cliff. He nodded back out of reflex, and felt a twinge of disappointment when the man stopped not far away to look out at the ocean. He wanted to be left alone.

"You've lost your son, haven't you?" The man's voice was deep and calm, with a faint accent.

Alan nodded his head.

"Don't worry. He'll come back to you." The man smiled

briefly, and Alan looked at him, really looked at him, for the first time. "I have a good feeling about your boy."

Another well-wisher: Alan knew the man meant well, but he was not thrilled with the idea of any more false hopes. "Thank you."

"I'm very serious, Mister Tripp. Your son will come home soon. I can feel it."

Alan closed his eyes and ground his teeth. If the man didn't leave him alone, he was going to have to get angry.

When he opened his eyes again, the man was gone. He looked around and saw no sign of him. There was not a place for a hundred yards where the man could have gone except over the side of the cliff.

He stood up and double-checked. No. There was no body down there.

"Perfect," he sighed. "Now I'm fucking hallucinating."

He left the Cliff Walk and slowly headed for home. Something about the man he'd met stuck with him, his earnestness, perhaps. Or maybe he was just tired of looking for his boy and not finding him.

Whatever the case, long before he reached home he was running, his legs pumping and his feet slapping the ground roughly; his heart wanted to explode and his lungs burned, his side felt fiery twitches, and his brow was covered in sweat. Alan wanted to push the thought aside, but he was certain that the man had been right: Avery would be coming home, maybe even waiting for him when he got there.

And then the dread set in, crushing the wings his legs had grown and extinguishing his hope. What sort of pathetic lunacy had captured him? A perfect stranger was telling him that his boy would be coming home soon and in his mind he'd already painted a thousand different fantasies in which Avery was there, waiting just ahead of him and around the corner of the neighbor's house.

Alan stopped himself; his hands on his knees and his head lowered; he gasped and gulped for sweet oxygen until he felt less lightheaded and more like a rational adult again. Sore and tired, his legs still protesting his sudden jaunt into energetic adolescence, Alan Tripp rounded the final corner to his house.

He found his son waiting for him at the front door and suddenly believed in miracles.

II

Avery Tripp was all over the news broadcasts that night. Every local channel in the area tried for an exclusive interview and instead got the same fifteen-second sound bite of the boy mumbling that he was glad he was home. It wasn't the best they could have hoped for, but it was newsworthy. Naturally, every station felt obliged to rip open old wounds and remind the world at large that Black Stone Bay had been lucky this time. Three of the four local stations made a point of retelling the story of Carla Whittaker in graphic detail; two of them ran specials called "Remembering Carla." Both thought they were being original. The fourth failed to give blow-by-blow descriptions of the body parts and when they were found, instead merely making mention of the tragedy.

Kelli was happy that Avery was back, but could find little to be excited about otherwise. First they said that Teddy was dead and now they said they couldn't find the body. The hospital was in a complete panic, and the Listers were in an unholy outrage. Currently the Tripps were explaining in vivid detail how completely and utterly the hospital staff had fucked up when they lost the son of two lawyers.

Until the situation was resolved, they'd asked her to stay on, just in case Teddy should be found alive.

She hadn't planned on leaving before then, anyway. He was a part of her life and had been for over two years.

She tried studying and gave up in disgust within twenty minutes. Her mind couldn't focus on anything other than Teddy's disappearance, and she refused to accept that he was dead until she saw a body.

Avery had come back, hadn't he?

Teddy could come back, too.

She had to hope. Kelli looked out the front window of the house and stared at her neighbor's place. A car had just pulled up and moved up the driveway all the way to the distant front door. She couldn't see who it was that got out, aside from the fact that it was female and shapely.

I can hope, she thought. *I have to hope. He's my little baby boy.*

III

Maggie pulled up outside of Jason Soulis's house and stared in awe again. The place was incredible.

As soon as she opened the door, the man was waiting at the threshold. He smiled as she approached, and she smiled back. Whether or not he'd meant to, Soulis had given her an opportunity that had proved to be very rewarding.

"Hello, Mr. Soulis." She moved toward him and smiled. He watched her the entire time she came in his direction, and returned the smile. He stepped back from her as she entered the house, and gestured for her to move toward the dining room.

Another feast had been laid out.

"Please, my dear, call me Jason." He pulled out the chair for her and waited for her to be properly seated. "You are well, Maggie?"

"I am, thanks for asking."

She was dressed in casual clothes again and so was he. Well, what passed for casual with him at any rate. He was wearing a pair of navy Dockers and a burgundy turtleneck sweater that she suspected was extremely overpriced. He carried it off well.

"You look lovely." His dark eyes drank her in with the patience and reverence of a wine connoisseur. She smiled back and gave a small nod of her head in acknowledgment of the compliment.

This time when she sat down to eat, he joined her. He ate only a little, but as with everything else, he seemed to savor the meal. Only when they were done and having brandy in the study did he discuss business.

"You have concluded your business with the Catholic Church?"

"Yes, and with the Lutheran pastor and the Baptist minister." She wasn't lying. The latter two had been arranged earlier in the day. Pastor Henderson had been a hard sell, but the Baptist minister had been only too eager to accommodate.

"Wonderful." Once again he looked her over, his face almost expressionless and his eyes alight with pleasure. "You are a very resourceful woman, Maggie. I had feared you wouldn't be able to accomplish the task I set for you."

The conversation was a little surreal, but she did her best to take it in stride. "Well, there are still more names on your list, Jason."

"True, but I think you've already proven to be up to the challenge. I had serious doubts about you managing to seduce the Lutheran minister."

"Really?" She smiled a little, remembering how reluctant he had been. "Why is that?"

"Well, I have it on good authority that the man is homosexual."

Maggie chuckled. "Well, that explains a lot, actually."

"So, you wish to continue with our arrangement?"

"As long as you want me to," she kept her cool. It wouldn't do to sound too excited about the prospect.

Jason nodded and walked over to his desk at the far end of the room. He counted out a preposterous amount of money in hundred-dollar bills, and set them down on the small table where her empty brandy snifter now rested.

"That's double what we had agreed to." Not that she would complain, but better to be honest than lose out on the rest of the take.

"No, Maggie. That is the agreed-upon amount, with a bonus if you spend the night here, with me."

"I was hired for the night anyway, Jason."

"No. I hired your services from Tom, and that money has already been delivered. This is a different matter entirely."

"I'm not one to turn down a generous offer, but aren't you paying twice for the same services?"

"No, Maggie." He looked her in the eyes, his stare intense enough to damn near hypnotize her. "No. I do not see the two as inseparable. Yes, I paid to have you here for the night. I did not pay Tom to have your sexual favors. That is a separate transaction, between you and me."

"Not in his eyes."

"His eyes are insignificant. It is your eyes that interest me. If you wish, you may stay with me and have a separate room for the night. That concludes any business I have with Tom Pardue." He shrugged. "If you wish, you may also take the bonus I have offered you to be with me for the rest of the night. The decision is yours."

The damnedest thing about it was that she knew he was completely serious. If she said she wanted to sleep in a separate room, he'd let her. "I want to stay with you, Jason."

He smiled and held out one hand. She took it, marveling at the cool, soft feel of his fingers.

IV

They poked and prodded Avery for over two hours before Alan told them enough was enough. He sent the doctors packing with their blood samples and their heart rate monitors. His boy was home and tired. That was all that mattered. He wanted to rest in his own bed, and Alan intended to give his son everything he could possibly want.

And even if he hadn't wanted it that way, Meghan would have settled the situation. Had he waited much longer his wife would have gone down to his workshop and come up with his chainsaw, gunning the engine for all it was worth.

Avery was weak, but seemed unharmed otherwise. He was happy to be home and had almost become fused to his mother's side. Alan couldn't blame him. The poor kid had been gone for two days.

When the doctors were finally done and he'd shooed away

the news people and even the police, Alan went up to tuck his wife and son into Avery's bed. Meghan had made very clear that she would not be leaving her son alone for a few nights and that was just fine. He needed to get a little rest himself.

Meghan was still awake when he entered the room. Avery was sound asleep, his eyes closed and his breathing regular.

"You okay, hon?" He spoke in a whisper, just in case Avery had suddenly become a light sleeper.

"Yeah," she nodded and started to tear up again. He leaned over and kissed her on the lips and then held her against his shoulder as she cried for a few minutes. He cried, too. The thought that he'd almost lost his son was enough to make him want to wither up and die.

"Yeah, baby. I'm good. I couldn't be better."

"I love you, Meghan. Get yourself some sleep."

"You too, okay?"

"Oh, yeah," he nodded his emphasis and wiped at his eyes. "Yeah, baby, I plan to. I'm just going to lock everything up."

He left the two most important people in his world in each other's arms, and turned off the light. Then he moved back down the stairs and systematically switched every light off that illuminated the lower level. He also checked every door and window, even going so far as to search the basement, because the one thing that Avery couldn't answer so far was where he had been. The only thing he could tell them was that it had been very dark and there were other people down there as well.

So he wasn't taking any chances. He checked everywhere twice before he went upstairs and into the empty master bedroom.

He was asleep before he even hit the bed. The last seventy-two hours had been hellish at best.

He was unconscious before the reporter from the local rag came snooping around outside of the house. He remained unaware of the attempt to open the locked doors.

Leo Marconelli was a busy man and he wanted to get a scoop that would rock the area. He didn't have time to get into investigative reporting, but he was pretty sure he could make up a good tale. The panties had cost him a small fortune, but his source promised they belonged to Carla Whittaker. Once they were planted in the workshop he'd spotted when he was sneaking around the house earlier, he could point a finger at Alan Tripp and make sure that everyone knew it was his investigative reporting that caught her killer. After that, no one would give a good goddamn about a little kid that managed to get un-lost, or a corpse that disappeared from the hospital. Oh sure, later there would be all sorts of questions about how the panties had gotten there, and about how Leo had known. But that would be later after the celebrity had stuck to him, and he would deal with those situations as they arose.

"Excuse me, mister?"

Marconelli didn't actually let out a shriek. It was more of a squeak.

He turned to see who was behind him and almost wet himself when he saw the kid. Not the one from this house, but the one who was supposed to be dead.

"Holy shit, kid! What are you doing, trying to give me a heart attack?"

"I'm lost. Will you help me?"

"Yeah, of course I will." He tried to smile in a friendly manner. "You bet I will. What's your name?" He knew, of course, but he needed to confirm.

"Teddy Lister."

"Well, Teddy, why don't we get you home. I'll drive you."

The Lister kid backed up a bit, looking nervous. "I don't need to go home. That isn't what I lost."

"Yeah? What did you lose?" He was afraid of going home. Suddenly Marconelli was glad he hadn't managed to slip the panties into the Tripp house. The Lister kid's family was already sounding like a juicier target. If the kid didn't want to go home, there had to be a good reason.

Teddy Lister smiled for his new friend, his eyes blazing in the darkness. "I lost my soul. Can I have yours?"

Marconelli never even had a chance to scream before the kid was all over him. Small, powerful hands grabbed his mouth and clamped it shut with enough pressure to burst the reporter's lips. When he tried to pull back, the boy added more pressure until he felt his cheekbone crack and fracture from the force.

He punched the kid in his sweetly smiling face and almost broke his own hand. The kid didn't even blink. He just squeezed even harder, until his fingers suddenly pressed together in the shattered ruin of the reporter's lower jaw and sinus passages.

Marconelli was lucky. He wasn't awake for the rest of what was done to him.

V

Ben waited until the sun rose before he went to sleep. Maggie didn't make it home.

He tried not to think about that too much as he slipped into his own bed. He had no claim on her. There was nothing that had happened between them that gave him the remotest right to be upset when she didn't come home.

But he was upset, just the same.

VI

He'd left the lights on to savor every moment. He told her as much as he disrobed her. At first it was just the same as always, there was no connection, no difference between Jason and a hundred others she'd been with before. That suited her just fine. She didn't want to experience anything different.

That changed when he went down on her, starting at the back of her neck and working his way slowly down her spine to her buttocks and then her sex. He did things with his tongue that left her shuddering, every muscle in her body drawn taught and her skin almost feverish with arousal.

She lost track of all time after a while and gave herself over to the sensations. It wasn't love or even a parody of love; it was pure carnal knowledge and she reveled in it.

She was normally in control of what happened, but he never gave her a chance to take command. He assaulted her again and again with sensations that seemed to almost go beyond physical. It wasn't like with the priests. That was different from this. That was natural. Whatever it was that Jason did, it seemed to defy reason and mock what she knew of the realms of possibility.

Eventually, he tired of foreplay and the actual sexual encounters began. Jason screamed several times and Maggie joined him. She didn't drift into sated sleep; she was knocked into unconsciousness by the experience.

When she woke in the morning, Jason was making coffee. She knew she should have been tender at the very least, but she felt wonderful. It was nice to relax for a while before he came into the room and served her breakfast in bed.

She drank the coffee eagerly, almost scalding her tongue but not minding in the least. Her mouth tasted funny; a taste that she thought she knew but couldn't place.

CHAPTER 8

I

Richard Boyd was not a happy man. He was, in fact, a very annoyed police detective. His life would have been easier if people would have just stopped putting files into his IN box.

Instead, they kept giving him new cases. *Not a bad job*, he mused, *except that people around these parts are disappearing in a damned big hurry.* That was the problem; he wasn't a homicide detective, he was just a schmuck in charge of missing persons.

He leaned up against the railing along the Cliff Walk, lighting his cigar with a lighter that resembled a blowtorch and had a flame strong enough to resist the winds.

All along the side of the cliffs there were lawns that seemed impossibly green for autumn, and trees that were exploding into spectacular arrays of colors. This was the time of year he liked best. Screw the summers when there were too many tourists. He didn't need extra people in town any more than he needed increased prices at the gas pump. Then there were the winters to consider, when scraping ice off his car and shoveling snow off his sidewalks seemed to take most of his free time.

"You must think you make a pretty picture there, Richie." The smart-ass was his partner, Danforth Edward Holdstedter the Third; better known to Boyd as either Danny or dickhead, depending on his state of mind. Right now he was Danny, but he was pushing it. Danny looked just as preppy as his name implied, with perfect blond hair, blue eyes, and a dimple on his chin. He was also so damned cheerful it hurt to be around him for too long. Unfortunately, he was very good at finding missing people.

"I think I'm gonna put this cigar out in your eye if you don't shut your face and let me think." Most people would have thought the threat was serious. Danny knew better. Boyd was happiest when he was threatening physical injury. Besides, Danny had him by a good sixty pounds.

"So why are we out here, exactly?" Danny moved closer and leaned over the side of the railing, staring down at the waves where they were lapping against the rocks. Danny did that every time, convinced that at least half of the people who disappeared in the area were actually so much jelly after falling into the waters of the bay. It would certainly explain the recent track record.

"Well, Danny, my boy. We have eight cases in this area that have something in common; can you guess what that is?"

"They all fell off the side here and became jelly?" The kid always sounded so hopeful when he said that.

"No, not quite." He thought about it for a second and shrugged. "Well, maybe, but we don't know it for sure."

"Then tell me."

"They all live in this area."

Danny stopped kidding around when he heard that little tidbit. There was nothing remotely funny about the idea that eight people from the Cliff Walk had mysteriously vanished.

Sure as hell, it would be a bad thing if someone else made the same conclusions.

II

Maggie went to school just like she was supposed to, but she felt sick. Her stomach churned and her heartbeat seemed to triple throughout the day. The nausea started strong and faded after a while. By the time school was finished she was feeling better and gave it no more thought.

She saw Ben in class and smiled for him. He smiled back, but neither of them spoke. They almost never did in school. It was just when they ran across each other on the street that they were friends. Here they may as well have been complete strangers. Still, she hoped he'd show up at the diner again. It was fun having someone to talk to and not having to worry about him trying to get into her pants.

Maggie found herself wondering for a few moments if Ben was homosexual and then dismissed the notion. He still looked, and he was still shy around her. It seemed that somehow she had run across a man who was actually a gentleman, and chivalrous to boot. She made a mental note to keep a fair distance from him, unless he ran across her first. It would have been too easy to let him into her world and that would be disastrous.

She didn't want or need a man in her life. She didn't want or need a relationship. Emotions were not a part of her plan, and she fully intended to keep any affection in check until after she graduated.

Just a shame he was cute. It would have been easier to ignore him if he at least had a big mole on his forehead or something.

After school she cased the synagogue until she saw Rabbi Lefkowitcz. He was a good-looking man in his forties; while he was harder to seduce than she'd expected, he eventually fell for her charms. They went to his office and she kept him occupied until the sun was almost down. He managed to look grateful for the experience and miserable for cheating on his wife at the same time. He even called her by the woman's name: Elizabeth. Her picture was on his desk: she looked nothing at all like Maggie. She didn't correct him.

Afterward, she went to the movies. John Cusack had a new comedy playing and she absolutely loved him. He was funny and sweet and managed to look sexy as hell when he was confused or pouty; kind of like Ben, despite the fact that they looked nothing alike.

She left the movie understanding the rabbi's mentality a little better.

The plan was to be home by ten; she was on schedule and thinking about calling for a pizza. She hadn't counted on Tom being there and waiting on her again.

But there he was, in all of his hip-hop glory. He was trying to look like a college kid again and failing. His long, oversized shorts and muscle shirt just looked stupid when she considered how cold it was getting, and no one, she didn't care who they were or how hot they might look, ever looked good in a baseball cap turned sideways. It worked when a kid was six, not when a man was almost thirty.

"Where have you been?" His voice was harsh and demanding of answers.

"The movies," she explained as she shook her head. One look in his eyes and she could tell he'd been sampling his own drugs again. He was normally smart enough not to, but this seemed to be one of his stupid days.

"Yeah? So why were you at a synagogue for three hours? When did you become a kike?" That was the thing about Monkey Boy: she could always count on him to be an insensitive prick, but now and then he was a smart insensitive prick.

Fortunately, she was smarter and had already come up with a proper answer in case he saw her handling her tasks for Soulis. "Hello? Student, here. I'm studying comparative religions in my sociology class."

He rocked back on his heels for a moment, nodding too fast; a sure sign he was hopped on speed. "Really? Why don't we ask Ben about that? I bet Ben's just the kind of guy who will tell me the truth about what you were doing all day."

Without any warning, Tom stepped over and pounded his fist into Ben's front door hard enough to rattle the window off to the side.

Maggie saw movement through the darkened window and a moment later a very tired-looking Ben was opening the door, his face set in a polite expression of curiosity.

"Hi, Ben!" Tom's voice boomed between the two apartments.

Ben winced. "Hi, Tom." He looked over her way and nodded his head once. "Hi, Maggie. What's up?"

"You in the same classes as Maggie, Ben?"

"A couple of them, why?"

"Oh, we were just having a discussion and I was teasing her because I saw her go into a synagogue today. I asked her when she switched from Catholicism to Judaism, and she said she was studying for a religion class."

Ben nodded his head, never taking his eyes off Pardue. "Comparative religions, a big part of our sociology class. In fact, I have to take about half of the churches around here and she has the other half. We're sort of lab partners." He never even blinked while he was spewing a line of shit right in Tom's ugly face.

"Really? Why did she get the Jews?"

"Because I have to take the Muslims. It's easier for me, because everyone knows the Muslim faith isn't exactly girl-friendly."

"Who's doing the Catholics?"

"Me. We're supposed to look at the faiths from an outsider's perspective and I'm a Methodist." Ben never once took his eyes off Tom as he spoke.

"Cool. Thanks, Ben."

"No problem. Anything else, guys?"

Maggie flashed him a quick smile and shook her head. Tom spoke before she could. "Yeah, Ben. Is that why you two keep meeting at the Silver Dollar Diner?"

Ben looked at Pardue carefully and shook his head. "No. That's just been because neither of us ever sleeps and they make good omelets there."

"That's cool." Tom smiled and moved closer to Maggie, putting his apish arm around her shoulders and hugging her to his side. "Just wanted to make sure you weren't making moves on my girl, Ben." He was smiling as he spoke, but it wasn't a smile that had anything to say about humor.

Ben shrugged and kept staring at Pardue. "Always best to know when you're out of your league, Tom."

Monkey Boy laughed and Maggie expelled a soft breath of relief.

Ben nodded and went back into his apartment.

When he was gone, Tom looked back over at her and nodded too, satisfied with the explanation. "Just making sure we still understand each other, Maggie."

"Never do that again." She slipped away from his thuggish arm around her shoulder and added a few layers of permafrost to her voice.

"Do what?" He put on his best look of wide-eyed innocence. It wasn't a pretty thing to see.

"Never check up on me again and never bother one of my friends again with this sort of shit, or we're done doing business together."

"You're wrong about that, Maggie." He was still smiling, and he was still sounding just as amiable as ever, but Maggie knew the danger signs well enough.

She just didn't care much right then. "Excuse me?"

"You're wrong." He shrugged his shoulders and leaned in close enough that she could see something green, like spinach, wedged between two of his teeth. "I own you. I was just testing the waters today, baby. I find out you've been doing business on the side or giving away pussy for free, and I'll make sure you know it, too."

Shit, he was getting all possessive again and she hated when he started that.

"Go get sober, Tom. Before you say something you'll regret later."

"Maybe you should come home and get me sober."

"I have a paper to work on."

"Shit's only gonna hold water for a few more months, Maggie. Then maybe I'll have to see about you moving in with me."

"That's not gonna happen and you know it."

"We'll see."

Tom went on his way and Maggie watched him go, suddenly cold inside and goose-fleshed. Tom wanted her to move in? She hoped that was just the coke talking, because that wasn't going to happen. She'd find a way to work her own deals before that would ever happen.

Thinking about the money she'd gotten from Jason helped. It wasn't exactly retirement money, but it put her a lot closer to her goals than she'd expected to be.

Ben's front door opened. He looked at her with a tentative smile.

"You okay, Maggie?"

"Yeah, Ben. Thanks. You saved my ass."

"Anytime." He stepped back into his apartment and waved. "Have a good night, Maggie."

"You too, Ben." She smiled for him and resisted the urge to ask him out to the diner. She could have used a friend just then. But as Monkey Boy had just reminded her, friends were a luxury she could hardly afford.

III

Brian sat in his patrol car and waited. He'd been waiting for a long while now, hoping to hear back from the bastard that had ruined his life.

He wanted to have a long, long talk with the motherfucker.

His accounts were still screwed up. He still had no money, no credit history, and a very serious problem if he wanted to keep his house and everything else in his life.

Angie was making his life a living hell. She'd called him seven times during the day, wanting to know why the bank was still calling, wanting to know who he'd really talked to on the phone, wanting to know a dozen different things that he couldn't answer if he didn't want a divorce. And he did not want to lose her. Just because he needed a little action on the side didn't mean he wanted to lose his wife.

She was important to him.

So he was fucked, unless he could figure out what to do

about the man who'd taken everything from him. He just had no idea where to start looking.

The little Mazda Miata ripped past him in the darkness, swerving erratically around the bend in the road. He caught a glimpse of long brown hair and turned on his flashers. This could be fun.

The car pulled off the road, narrowly missing a tree near the edge. A quick license plate check told him what he already knew: the owner was a college student and had a record. The night was looking better already.

He pulled over behind the sporty two-seater and moved to the driver's side window. The girl inside was already terrified. She had long brown hair, dark brown eyes and a mouth made for pleasing men.

"Did I do something wrong, officer?"

"I need to see your license and registration, please."

"What was I doing wrong?" She had the audacity to sound offended.

"You were weaving all over the road, for one." He sighed and shook his head. "I need to see your license and registration, please. Now."

She sighed and pulled out her purse, digging through layers of debris while he waited. "I'm not drunk, you know." Her voice had taken on an edge that he found annoying. Now and then he ran across one that got bitchy and that took all the fun out of his evenings. Unfortunately, it was looking like he'd found one with attitude.

"That's one of the things we're here to find out, miss."

Her ID said her name was Veronica Miller. She was nineteen, officially too young to have alcohol on her breath, but he smelled it. "Have you been drinking, Ms. Miller?"

"No. I haven't been drinking. I don't drink." Now she was rolling her eyes, so obviously put out by his daring to question her. Brian clenched his jaw, ready to just lock her in cuffs and get it over with.

"Why don't you step out of the car?"

"Look, I told you I haven't been drinking, okay?" There.

She was starting to break a bit, putting on the wide eyes as soon as she realized he was serious.

"Just step out of the car, please."

She climbed out, but very reluctantly. Her big brown eyes were doing the fast blinks that normally meant the water works would be coming soon. She swayed a bit as she stood in front of him; just shy of five and a half feet in height, she was slender and pretty and drunk enough that he would be justified in taking her to the jail for a sobering night. Brian pulled out the Breathalyzer test kit and watched in satisfaction as she got closer to tears.

"Please don't do this, mister."

"Just doing my job, Ms. Miller."

"I mean it. I can't get another ticket."

"You were driving while intoxicated. You're too young to be drinking at all."

"Are you going to give me a ticket?"

"What other choice do I have?" He let his eyes roam over her body for a moment, knowing he shouldn't be looking so blatantly. It had to be her idea.

"My dad's gonna freak out."

"I can't help with that. I can't just let you go. You were weaving all over the road. You might have killed someone."

"Come on, have a heart, I'm just at the limit."

"I don't make the rules, I just enforce them."

Three minutes later, just when he was thinking he might have to actually book her, she decided to try offering her body instead of getting locked up. Naturally he agreed and they moved into the woods. She was trembling and that made it all the sweeter when he started taking off her clothes, peeling away layers to reveal the beautiful body underneath. She was trembling and whimpering by the time he had her fully disrobed. He wanted her so badly he would have actually paid her for the pleasure, but knowing she was scared of him and what he could do to her made it all that much sweeter.

They kissed for several minutes while he explored her with his hands. She was hesitant to return the favor, but eventually started making life interesting again. Finally he moved into position, savoring the way she looked on all fours. Just as he was preparing to penetrate her, she ran. One second he was moving behind her tight, little ass and ready to get a home run—she shaved, which was a new one for him—and the next, she was up and running, leaving him humping air.

Brian cursed and gave chase, pulling up his pants as he started after the damned fool girl. Now he knew fear, too, because she could ruin him with a word. The accusation was all it took for a girl to cause him troubles, which was why he normally made sure they had at least a few drugs on them.

She was fast, moving with surprising speed and grace for a naked coed. He watched her as she ran, his eyes still taking in the sight of her body as she managed to avoid obstacles that should have had her down in the dirt. In the long run, he was faster. He had more on the line than she did and desperation fueled his pace; all she was risking was being sore in the morning. If he got busted by some little cunt telling people what he'd done, he'd lose what little remained in his life worth having.

The area was already dark, and she was drunk. That didn't stop her from giving him one hell of a run and didn't stop him from getting angrier and angrier as they ran through the woods. But as he knew would happen eventually, she slipped and fell, hitting the ground hard and whimpering as he came up on her.

He took her in the mulch and dirt, forcing himself on her and listening to her screams; they were sounds of beauty. Her sweet young face was a beautiful thing to see; dirtied and tear streaked, her eyes looking everywhere but at him until he grabbed her long hair and made her see his face. When he was done, he pulled himself from her and savored her tears.

She was still crying when he got dressed. She was still lying in the carpet of the woods when he pulled out his night stick and cracked her skull open. Just to make sure that he could hide the evidence properly, he used a rock to hide the marks left by his bludgeon.

Looking down at the ruins of a girl he'd stopped for driving badly, Brian Freemont felt at peace for the first time in several days.

IV

A house is not always a home.

Angie Freemont was learning that and learning to live with it. Brian used to be a sweet man, attentive and loving. Something about working on the police force had changed him, and not for the better.

She was in the kitchen and cooking for him, preparing his early morning dinner. It was something she always insisted on doing, having his meals ready for him. She felt she had to, not because it was her wifely duty, but because he was the one providing for her and he was the one working his ass off.

She chopped the onions with the skill of a chef, which was appropriate enough. She'd worked as a line cook all the way through high school and had done it through her three years of college, too. In her mother's words, she came from a long line of have-nots and in order to get what she wanted she had to work for a living.

Not working was driving her crazy, but the baby's health had to be considered and even now her unborn child was considered at risk. The pregnancy had not been an easy one, and it wasn't getting any less difficult. Something about the blood types for her and Brian put their child at risk. There were medicines to take, and endless warnings that she couldn't get too active.

That hadn't made Brian a very happy man. He was constantly horny. She was too, but now with the baby on the way, she normally felt too crappy to do anything about it. Besides, it was hard to get down and get funky all over her husband when there was a basketball stuck inside her stomach and her back felt like she'd been wearing a damned saddle all day.

She sautéed the onions in butter and tossed in the meat she'd been marinating. He liked cheese steaks. It was Friday night and he was stuck working the worst shift the department could throw at him. He told her he'd asked for a switch to dayshift half a dozen times, but so far he was still stuck with the shit detail.

The peppers went in next, and their aroma permeated the air. The spatula cut through the already sliced meat and blended in the vegetables as the steak cooked. Next came a little olive oil, and then the white American cheese. The crusty bread was done already, and merely waited for her husband's return to the house. Finally she tossed in the finely sliced mushrooms and stirred again before deftly flipping the meat into the hard rolls.

He would be home soon, and dinner was done. She slipped on her jacket after everything was set up and then stepped outside to catch a breath of clean air and to cool off. The house was nice, but she always felt like she was going to melt if she spent too much time in the kitchen.

They came for her in the darkness; a little boy of maybe nine or ten and a young girl who was only a few years older.

She never even had a chance to scream before they attacked, inhumanly strong hands clutching at her arms and pinning her to the hard wood of the porch, pressing her belly into the wood as they tore at her coat.

Angie fought hard; straining her wrists to break free of the demons and grunting as the girl finally ripped the fabric of her jacket away and bared her skin.

She should have been able to take them, should have been able to at least slap the little boy away from her and fight the girl. She had never been a weak woman, physically, and she could still put a hurting on a man a hundred pounds bigger than she was, as Brian had learned the one time he decided to slap her.

But the kids were too strong and seemed to feel nothing when she managed to land a kick. The girl looked at her with dead eyes. Dead, as in glazed over and dry enough that it looked painful to stare into them.

Angie finally found enough breath to scream, wrenching her hands free of the monster's grasp. She landed a beautiful punch in the girl's face and felt the delicate, teenaged nose break under her knuckles.

The little boy only seemed intent on getting her clothes off of her, and his fingers found purchase enough to rip her blouse open in an explosion of buttons and thread.

The girl she'd hit kept moving in, her hands bruising Angie's flesh, and Angie screamed again as she was pinned for the second time. Her breasts were tender, made sensitive by the changes brought on from her pregnancy. She screamed a third time when she felt the boy's teeth break the skin around her nipple.

And then the teenaged girl with the blond hair and mashed nose hit her hard enough to knock her unconscious.

She felt herself moved, heard the girl tell the boy to stop being a pig and heard the boy make a rude comment that had both of them laughing. The world faded in and out for her, an endless blur of motion that ceased only when the ringing in her head got too extreme.

The wind around her became a roaring voice. No, not the wind: the sound of crashing waves.

Angie woke up just in time to feel the water closing in around her head. She tried to catch her breath but failed, and instead sucked in water. She thrashed, drowning and terrified, but it did no good. They held her under the water with their thin hands and incredible strength. She tried to escape again and again, but soon the burning in her lungs was too much and the blackness came back to swallow her again.

And finally she awoke, soaked and naked and shivering in a different sort of darkness. There was no light of any kind, but she could hear just fine, hear the sounds of the things that moved around her, and feel their hands as they touched her in the lightless, echoing void.

"Who's there?" Her voice, weakened though it was, echoed around her.

A voice giggled off to the right. "Mommy? Is that you, Mommy?"

"Shhhh. Be nice. She is with child."

"Mmmmm. Babies."

"Leave me alone!" her voice boomed in the darkness and ricocheted off distant walls.

"No, Mommy. I'm hungry now. Feed me."

The teeth clamped down on her breast again and then there were more mouths, all of them biting at her skin, all of them penetrating flesh and meat and sometimes even bone.

Angie Freemont screamed for what seemed an eternity,

pushing and fighting and trying desperately to escape from the agonies they delivered onto her. She tried to stand and they knocked her back down. She tried to claw at their flesh and they ignored her best attacks. Finally she stopped struggling, feeling every last bite.

She took a long time to die.

CHAPTER 9

I

He wanted to be truthful with the detectives, but he couldn't, not even if it meant Angie's life.

He knew that, and hated himself for it.

Brian Freemont came home to an empty house and at first thought Angie had finally decided to leave him. It didn't take him long to realize that her clothes were still there, along with her suitcases and everything else she owned. Her purse was still exactly where she'd left it, on the edge of the couch. After that, it took about ten minutes of looking around to see the shreds of her clothes on the darkened porch.

He dialed 911 and sat down on the edge of the stairs leading up to his house. He wasn't about to touch anything else until the detectives got there. His heart was beating too fast and he was sweating despite the late October chill.

When the phone rang on his hip, he jumped. His fingers scrabbled madly to answer the damned device, and he hoped beyond all of his wildly growing doubts that Angie was calling him.

"Angie?" His voice was trembling as much as his hands.

"No, Officer Freemont," he knew the voice as soon as the

man spoke, and he felt rage blossom in his chest. "It's not your wife. I'm just calling to let you know that your accounts are back where they should be."

"What did you do with Angie, you sick fuck!"

"Your wife?" The voice sounded surprised enough that Brian guessed the man either knew nothing about her disappearance or he was an actor with supreme skills. "I don't know anything about your wife, Freemont. Maybe she found out about your extra job benefits."

The man hung up before he could respond, and much as he wanted to hunt the bastard down, he was forced to put his cell phone away when the detectives showed up.

Boyd and Holdstedter got out of their car and moved toward his house, their faces lacking any of the usual expressions he saw on the department's local clowns. The odds were good neither of the men had slept more than a couple of hours before he called for assistance. There were a total of four detectives in Black Stone Bay's police department. The other two dealt with murders. These two dealt with everything else.

Holdstedter looked like the sort of guy who got women without even trying. Boyd, at five feet, eight inches tall, was thin and balding and usually looked constipated, even when he was having a good time. Currently both of them looked like sleep was the only thing on their minds.

Boyd nodded to him and asked, "Have you heard anything at all since you called it in, Brian?" Despite his gruff exterior, Boyd's voice and demeanor were considerate to the point of being unsettling.

He shook his head. "I wish I had, Rich." His stomach felt like it wanted to tear free of its moorings and make a run for it.

"You know I have to ask these questions, Brian."

"You ask whatever you need to."

"Have you been seeing anyone on the side?"

"No. No one." The lie came out easier than he'd expected.

"Has Angie been seeing anyone?"

"No. Come on, Rich, she's six months pregnant."

Boyd shook his head and shrugged. "You'd be surprised

how many people find that a turn-on, sport." He looked around the porch and then looked at Holdstedter. "Danny? Why don't you give the place a look-over?"

The Nordic cop nodded and moved up the stairs, his eyes suddenly cold and calculating.

"Okay, Brian. Can you think of anyone who would have a reason to harm Angie?"

The damnedest thing was that he couldn't. She could be a complete bitch with him when her back was hurting or the bloating she'd been experiencing made her feel like shit, but other than that, Angie was one of the sweetest women he'd ever known.

"No. She has fewer enemies than Santa Claus."

"How about you, Brian? Have you pissed anyone off lately? I mean bad enough for them to want to get back at you through your wife?"

And there it was: the other big lie. Had he pissed anyone off? Well, there was the guy already doing everything he could to fuck up Brian's whole universe and about thirty or so women he'd blackmailed into sex that ranged from uncomfortable to borderline rape. Oh, and then there was that little rape and murder a few hours earlier. He couldn't well forget about that, now could he?

He wanted to tell the truth, he wanted to do anything he could that would help bring his Angie home safely. What he wanted to say and what he finally said had nothing in common; Brian lied through his teeth. "The meanest thing I've done to a perp lately was write a ticket for jaywalking, Rich."

"Why don't you sit down for a few more minutes, Brian, and we'll look everything over?"

Brian nodded his thanks and watched the man as he went onto the porch to talk to his partner. They were supposed to be very good detectives. He'd never worked with them, only run across them at the station. He didn't often run across cases where people were missing. Well, he didn't normally get assigned to them, being as he was a traffic cop and not a detective.

The two detectives very carefully looked over the area

where he'd found Angie's clothes, not touching anything for several minutes, until finally going back to their car to get cameras and other supplies for their investigation.

The sun finally rose around the time they were bagging her clothes and putting them into an evidence box. The detectives were good guys when he was around them and they were all kidding each other at the office. Hell, half of the practical jokes that were pulled around the department could be traced back to Boyd and Holdstedter.

They weren't clowning around now, and he doubted they would be comfortable pulling any jokes in the near future.

And that scared him a bit. The detectives were looking into the disappearance of his wife. Everyone knew that in a case like his, he would be one of the prime suspects. And if they started looking too closely at the details of Brian Freemont's daily activities, he had little doubt that they could come up with a few unusual discrepancies.

The only thing he had going for him was that he'd been on duty for ten hours. Unfortunately, that wasn't much of an alibi these days.

II

Kelli spent a lot of time going to her classes with a renewed passion for education. Well, perhaps that wasn't completely accurate: what she had a passion for was not sitting around an empty house.

There was always something she could work on, and she found new and interesting diversions. There were several reports and essays she could lose herself in, and she did, earning extra credits toward a better final grade. Her GPA was always good, but seldom excellent. She intended to rectify that.

Because, really, as long as she was busy, she didn't focus on the dreams. For the last two nights she'd dreamt of Teddy standing outside her window in the Lister house and asking her to come keep him warm. He was barely even a shape in the darkness, a shadow against the night. But he sounded so cold and so miserable that she almost got out of bed and went to him. There was something frightening about him in the dreams. He wasn't the little boy she'd helped raise for the last few years, but only something that seemed to look like him.

The first night the dream had been unsettling. The second night it had made her sleepwalk. She didn't want to know what the third night would bring if she weren't careful.

So, college work. She was going to study herself into exhaustion and hope that would be enough to keep her from dreaming anything else that disturbing.

Poor Teddy was missing and maybe dead. She knew that. She didn't need dreams to remind her of the fact. The Listers had become strangers in a lot of ways. Since Teddy's body had disappeared from the hospital, they'd given up all pretense of civility and gone on the warpath.

Kelli was in mourning. The Listers were on a revenge kick and the target of their collective wrath was the hospital. She could understand their anger, but wanted nothing to do with the couple when they were going into a self-destructive rampage.

Kelli wandered the stacks of the library, her eyes roaming from bookshelf to bookshelf in an effort to find anything that would keep her properly distracted. It was getting harder to focus, but she kept trying.

She found Ben Kirby sitting at the end of Sociology, his head in his hands. Ben was a good guy, even if he was so shy he made her look like a socialite. At the moment, he looked like he was ready to have a heart attack: his face was pale, his eyes were wide and he was staring off into outer space.

"Ben? You okay?"

He jumped when she spoke and looked around for a second before he focused on her. "Hi, Kelli." He stared at her for several seconds without answering, and finally he shook his head. "No. I don't think I am. I think I'm in big trouble."

"Anything I can do to help?" Ben was never going to be the sort of guy she found attractive: he wasn't nearly muscular enough for her tastes. He was, however, the sort of guy that made her want to mother him. If ever there had been a damaged person who was more likeable than Ben, she'd failed to run across him.

"No," he frowned and stood up. "No, but thanks a lot for asking." He moved past her before she could answer him and headed toward the library's exit. Much as she wanted to see if he really did need her help, she couldn't bring herself to follow him. His eyes were too haunted, and she'd seen enough of that sort of expression in the last few days; she saw it on the Listers and when she caught her face in the occasional reflection.

III

Avery Tripp was staying home for a few more days. His mother had already decided that. She was around constantly, and he didn't mind at all.

Alan Tripp went back to work, dodging as many questions as he could and focusing instead on getting his job done. It was the sort of work he could do in his sleep, but he needed to get the hell out of the house before he lost his temper.

Avery was home, and that was a blessing, but his son was acting a little too strangely for his comfort. Something had happened to him while he was gone, but for the life of him, Alan couldn't guess what it might have been. He'd been afraid of sexual molestation or the like, but there were no signs that he'd been misused that wretchedly.

But he wasn't himself. And Meghan was exhausted from hanging around with him constantly. His wife was acting as strangely as her son, as if the idea of being separated from her only child for even a minute should be considered a sin. It wasn't healthy and he didn't like it. He needed her to calm down and he needed Avery to grow up. The problem was that he couldn't articulate those facts without coming across like a monster without any feelings, and for that reason he was doing his best to avoid being home with them.

If that made him an insensitive bastard, he'd have to deal

with it, because the notion of being around the two most important people in his life was making his skin crawl.

"I need to see a fucking shrink." He stepped outside of the offices and moved to the smoke hole at the back of the building. There were times when his boss rode his ass hard for taking too many smoke breaks. At least for the present time, he was being allowed to come and go as he pleased.

Martin Sullivan was already outside when he got there. Martin was in the shipping and receiving department. He was a nice guy who was ten years younger than Alan and loved to go on and on about his sexual exploits. Alan would have taken offense, but Martin was just weird enough to make up stories that were humorous instead of just vulgar. Alan still got a chuckle whenever Martin went off about the female clown he'd scored with at the circus. Something about getting stuck in a clown car in a compromising position with a woman who wore more makeup than Tammy Faye Bakker. It was funny, but after the first few stories from Martin, everything sort of blurred together.

Today the man wasn't smiling. His expression was anything but happy.

"How's things, Martin?"

"Hi, Alan. Not so good."

"What's up?"

Martin looked at him and shook his head. "I think there's something wrong with me."

"Wrong how?"

"I'm having trouble keeping food down." He looked more closely at Martin and wondered if the man might have caught a bad bug. He couldn't have managed to look less energetic without being in a coffin.

"Maybe you need to take the rest of the day off."

Martin nodded and, without another word, started walking toward the parking lot. It wasn't Alan's place to stop him, but he figured he could make the guy's life a little easier and let his manager know he'd gone home.

Four more people went home early that day. In an office of only twenty workers, it was a noticeable difference.

Alan stayed until it was almost dark out before finally deciding that he, too, should get home at some point.

The house roads were relatively calm—they were almost always calm, except in the summer and on weekends when they had tall ship events in the bay—and he made good time.

But the house was dark when he got home, and for a moment he was filled with a deep, abiding dread. There should have been some lights on, somewhere in the place. Even if all the lamps were shut off, the TV screen should have been putting off a glow.

"Quit being an asshole," he told himself as he climbed out of his Subaru. "So the lights are off. Maybe they're taking a nap, or they went to see someone."

He stood outside the door for almost five minutes, his fingers cold and thick, before he finally opened the front door. There was nothing but darkness to see until he finally fumbled for the light switch in the hallway and flipped it to the on position. The room came into view and he sighed with relief. There was a part of him that had expected the bulb to have been removed or shattered.

What the hell had him so paranoid? He couldn't begin to imagine. All he knew was that the last time he'd felt this nervous without a reason was when he'd been standing at the altar and waiting for Meghan to walk down the aisle.

"Anybody home?" His voice seemed to echo through the hallway.

There was no answer at first, and the fine hairs on his neck rose. Then there was a noise from upstairs and he cocked his head to listen more carefully.

There it was again: a moan, soft and feathery faint.

He moved across the hardwood floors and up the long run of stairs as quickly and quietly as he could, barely even allowing himself the luxury of a breath as his mind was filled with images of what might have gone wrong. He saw phantasmal pictures of Meghan dead or held at the mercy of a rapist while Avery was forced to watch. He imagined Avery, dead and bled out across the floor of his bedroom, with Meghan's cold body over his, her body used to shield her dead boy. As he moved up the stairs quietly, his mind painted a thousand scenarios in which he found his family murdered or simply missing amid signs of a struggle. He had no strength at all and was so afraid of what he might find; his legs felt like someone had carefully removed the bones and replaced them with fiberfill.

Avery met him in the darkened hallway, his body seeming little more than a stain against the shadows.

"Avery? Where's your mom, son?"

Avery moved a little closer and looked up at him, his eyes glittering in the near darkness. "Hi, Daddy." He pointed to the master bedroom. "Mommy's asleep. She's tired."

Alan frowned. "Tired? What did she do all day?"

"I don't think she feels so good. She looks a little green."

Meghan was normally the last person to get a cold or even a case of the sniffles. She had a constitution like iron. "Well, I guess I better see how she's doing, sport."

"She's tired." He sounded like he was talking to a little kid.

"I got that, Avery. I just want to check on her myself."

He moved past his son, unconsciously skirting any contact with his own flesh and blood. Something wasn't right here and it was driving him crazy.

He entered the master bedroom and flicked on the light, his eyes aching in the sudden illumination. Meghan was on the bed, dressed in the same nightgown she'd worn to sleep the previous night. She didn't look like she'd moved much at all since he'd left for work almost ten hours earlier.

"Meghan?" He moved closer, feeling that cold spot in the pit of his stomach grow a few degrees colder still as he looked down on his wife's prone body.

She opened her eyes and took a few seconds to focus on him. "Hey." Her voice was raspy and dry.

"Hi, angel." He leaned down and ran a hand over her forehead. Her skin was cool to the touch, but felt a little sweaty. "Are you feeling all right? Avery said you looked a little green, and I have to agree, honey."

"Jus' tired." She smiled, her eyes focusing on him with the same clarity that she always seemed to have, and he felt relief thaw the ice in his stomach. "Feel like I haven't slept all week."

Alan leaned over and kissed her forehead, the taste of her running over his lips. "That's because you *haven't* slept all week." He leaned back away and pushed a few errant hairs from her brow. "You've been worrying too much about Avery and other things."

She nodded and closed her eyes. "I'm gonna sleep now, baby, okay?"

"Of course it is. Don't worry. I'll get something set up for dinner. Do you want anything?"

"No. Just sleep." Seconds after the words were out of her mouth she closed her eyes and drifted into slumber. He sat with her for a while and watched her, amazed by her as he always was.

Downstairs, in the darkness, his son was waiting for him. Alan stood and stretched and then got into more comfortable clothes. His little boy would want company, and he'd already promised Meghan that Avery wouldn't be left alone.

IV

There was a tension in the air that none of them would willingly acknowledge. There had been for several days and it wasn't likely that the tension was going away anytime soon.

They were all independent men, the priests of the Sacred Hearts congregation. As a rule they worked together and then went their separate ways. But every Saturday night they got together and had a proper dinner. It was tradition and they never even discussed the matter anymore. It was simply a part of their regular routine and there was no reason for it to suddenly change.

Patrick was doing the cooking that particular Saturday and, as was often the case, he decided on pasta. The man should have been Italian with the way he went for pasta. Tonight it was lasagna and it very likely tasted as wonderful as it smelled. But all three men sat in silence as they ate, lost in their own thoughts.

And each and every one of them was remembering the girl

they had seen in the church every Sunday for over a decade now, the girl who would be in the pews tomorrow and likely praying as fervently as she always did.

Each of them dreaded seeing Margaret Preston, the sweet-faced youth who had come to them and brought them pleasures of the flesh the likes of which they had never experienced before. She did so, as far as they knew, without provocation. She had surely never given any indication in the past that she found them attractive, and most assuredly she had never made advances before the week that had just come around. That she had been knowledgeable was a given. Maggie was talented and eager to teach things they had never willingly admitted to dreaming about, let alone ever expected to experience in their lives.

She had brought each of the men pleasure, deep abiding pleasure, and memories that would linger and haunt them for a long time to come. She had also brought each of them doubt. They doubted their own strengths and the strength of their faith in the Lord, if they were weak enough to give themselves over to a beautiful woman.

Each of the priests had thought of little else in their free time. The guilt was powerful and burned at them, as surely as her kisses had seared their flesh, as surely as their bodies burned for her, to be with her again, to experience the sensual gratification she had given to them once before.

They would see her at Mass and each of the men would remember what had happened. They would feel the guilt they shared more profoundly than ever and the desires as well. Each of the priests knew that this would happen but only knew it would happen for one individual. The men had often shared tales of their pasts during their Saturday night meals, and Donald Wilson had heard the confessions of his subordinates on many occasions.

There had been no confessions of their secret shared sins. Not a one of them ever seriously considered confessing. It was a secret, and it was a sin, but in each case, it was a sin that was still being savored.

And each of them had one more secret that they did not

desire to share: despite the guilt involved, each and every one of them wanted to be with her again.

It was a silent meal that Saturday night. It was the last meal that all three men would share together. One of them would be dead before the week was over.

They ate in silence, lost in their sins and their urges. None of them even noticed. They were far too distracted to pay any attention to the men they were with.

And that, of course, was exactly what Jason Soulis had been counting on when he hired Maggie: a secret shared is no longer a secret, and a sin held close to the heart is more often treasured than reviled.

Can you say Amen?

V

The night was starting to get long in the tooth and Boyd was beginning to feel married to Holstedter, which wouldn't have been that bad if the man looked as good as his sister did. Sadly, his partner was the wrong gender for him to even consider looking to get lucky.

"Are you thinking about my sister again?" Danny looked at him as he raised his mug of Sam Adams and smiled.

"Why would I be thinking about your sister?"

"You've got that look on your face that says you're thinking about getting into the sack with a well-built blonde."

"Only in your dreams, you loser." That was another thing that annoyed him about his partner: the bastard could read him like a book and he didn't like to be read.

"I can give you her number. She'll probably chew you up and spit out the bones, but you'd have a good time."

"Do you have any idea how wrong it is to hear you talk about your own sister that way?"

"Do you have any idea how wrong it is to know your partner is checking you out while you're trying to drink yourself into a stupor?"

"You're a sick man, Danny."

"Yes, yes I am. Remind me never to change."

"So how many are we up to for the day?"

"Seven. Seven more people who didn't show up where they were supposed to or anywhere else. That's seventeen to date, but who's counting?"

"That prick we have to call sir."

"O'Neill can eat my shorts."

"He probably would. I hear he swings both ways."

"That's more than I need to know, Boyd."

"Serves you right, talking about your sister that way."

"You saying you don't want to bang my sister?"

"What? You crazy? I'd fuck her through a wall. But that isn't why we're here."

"No," Holdstedter agreed. "We're here to get drunk and bitch about the disappearing populace."

"You think Freemont did in his wife?"

Holdstedter looked around to make sure none of the people in the bar was paying them any attention. No one was, except there was a brunette looking him over like he was a fine cut of meat. "I think he either did something to his wife, or he did something to someone else. He looked like he was ready to shit his pants when we pulled up."

"Maybe. I don't think he has the balls."

"Listen here, Boyd, and listen well. Brian Freemont is a dangerous man. He gets into power."

"Why do you say that?"

"He thinks too much like me, and I get into power."

"Yeah? What do you do about it?"

"I have a beer and then hope I can get lucky. Nice game of hide-the-salami and I feel plenty powerful again."

"You're gonna have a kid that way, you know. You should wait until you're married."

"Yeah, that's not happening."

"So we put him down as a suspect?"

"Yeah, we do. I looked over dispatch's records. There's a while last night when he didn't call in to report his location and he didn't write a single ticket. He had time to get home and do something to her if he really wanted to."

"You think it was that bad between them?"

Holdstedter shrugged his broad shoulders and got a sour look on his pretty-boy face. "I think anyone married to him would be miserable. I also think he looks at other women too much to be a good husband."

"Nothing wrong with looking, Danny."

"There's looking and then there's looking. If that boy had x-ray vision, every woman in this town would have reason to slap his face off."

"Okay. We keep him as a suspect." Boyd picked at the fries surrounding his burger and then decided to have a sip of beer instead. "So what the hell is going on in this town, Danny? How come we have so many missing people and not a body anywhere?"

"Maybe they're all leaving town."

"Some of them, sure. I can see that with the college girl and all, but ten-year-old corpses don't walk away. And whatever the hell happened with the Falcones, I can bet they didn't climb out of that car and skip their asses out of town for a little fun."

"Yeah," he grinned and took another sip of beer. "So a few maybe stayed here, but other than the corpses and car-crash victims, maybe they just left town."

"That's what I like about you, Danny. You're an optimist."

VI

Maggie was feeling a little tender when she got back to her apartment. The Baptist minister apparently liked his women submissive and he liked to fuck like a bunny on Spanish fly. Maggie visited him right after the Presbyterian. She was almost done with the list. Part of her was happy about that, because it was a lot of work with men who apparently weren't getting any regularly. She was also a little saddened because she was having a good time with the whole lot of them.

Ben was outside, sitting on the ground near his front door. His head was hanging low and his knees were up so high they almost reached his shoulders.

"Ben? What are you doing out here?"

He looked up slowly, and she saw that he'd been drinking. He was ripped.

Ben shrugged his shoulders and waved his hands around aimlessly. "Thinking I maybe fucked up."

He didn't normally curse, and he wasn't exactly a legend around school for his drinking habits. She walked over to where he was sitting and looked down at him. "What's wrong?"

"That damned cop."

"Oh, shit, Ben. He didn't find out it was you, did he?"

"No. His wife is missing." He looked miserable.

She shook her head. "What's that got to do with you?"

"He said it was my fault. Accused me of doing something to her." He shook his head with the slow, deliberate actions of a drunk who didn't want to lose everything in his stomach.

"Did you do anything to his wife?"

"What?" He looked up sharply and immediately regretted it. Ben leaned back against the wall, his eyes moving fast behind closed lids and his face an unpleasant shade of green in the darkness. "No, Maggie. I don't even know what she looks like."

Maggie squatted down on her haunches next to Ben and tried to look into his eyes. His face was tear-streaked and he was sweating alcohol in the cool night air. She reached out her hand and touched his cheek, making him look at her.

"Then you didn't do anything and he's just a dick, Ben."

"But maybe she left him because of me."

"What? Because you hid his money and put it back?"

He nodded his head and simultaneously leaned his face against her palm. "Yeah. 'Cause I'm a bastard and hid his money."

"Ben, he was blackmailing girls and raping them; they didn't want it, but he made them do it. The only bastard here is him. If she left him because of anything, it's because she finally saw what you saw."

He shook his head and blinked his eyes several times. His bottom lip jutted out and pulled toward his chin. He was on the verge of tears over something he had no control over, because he'd been doing something genuinely nice for a girl he barely even knew.

"Still my fault. Maybe he deserved what I did, but what did she ever do?"

"Honey, for all you know she'd been hearing about everything he did and never reported him. Some people are like that."

Ben shook his head again and rolled his eyes around until he could look in her face. "Why are you so nice to me?"

"Because you're a nice guy, Ben."

"No I'm not."

"You just stop being a nutcase, okay?" She sighed. He really was a nice guy, but he was also a very drunk nice guy who was depressed as all hell.

"Tom is lucky. He knows that, right?"

"Let's not talk about him, okay?" The last thing she wanted to think about was Monkey Boy. "Let's get you back inside your place."

Ben nodded and managed to stand on the first try. She'd expected him to fall on his ass. It still took almost five minutes to navigate into his apartment and move him toward his bedroom.

She helped him get his shoes and socks off. After that he was on his own. He didn't try to get undressed.

As she was leaving he called out to her. "Maggie?"

"Yeah, Ben?"

"Thanks. Sorry to be a pain."

"You're not. Get some sleep. Feel better tomorrow, okay?"

"Okay. Good night."

She let herself out and crossed the courtyard to her own place.

After she'd cleaned up and gotten comfortable, she lay back on her own bed and thought about Ben for a moment. He had a few homemade posters on his walls, and one of them looked very familiar. It was a poem by Byron; the same poem that she had pinned to the wall above her desk.

She drifted to sleep thinking about the poem and about the boy next door.

VII

The view from his new home was spectacular, but not good enough for what he needed to see, so Jason Soulis lifted into the air and rose until he could properly view the entire town of Black Stone Bay.

Their faith was like a beacon to him, a light that shone brightly even in the darkest hours of the morning. Through the centuries, he had seen many of the powerful auras on thousands of people.

These days it happened less and less. That suited him very well.

Inevitably, there were the ones who served their god with undying devotion and they were always a burden to him. Most times the truly devout served in a church, either in an official capacity or as a volunteer. They were the ones who could make his life uncomfortable. Through their piety, they served to protect the holy places from his influence and to protect their unwitting associates from his needs.

His eyes scanned the town, looking for the places of worship that had nearly blinded him when he first came into Black Stone Bay. There had been several places that were painful to see when he arrived. Most were barely noticeable anymore.

He smiled, looking to the buildings that had grown dark, pleased that his suspicions had been correct. It was not the building so much as those who attended to the structures that provided them shelter. Faith was a fleeting thing when laced with sin and guilt.

Every place that Maggie had visited had been tainted, not by the acts committed there but by the crisis of faith the acts had brought about.

Throughout Black Stone Bay people slept and, in some cases, worked. The proud were here in abundance, as were the wealthy and the vain. That was true in most towns. The difference was simply that the faithful were becoming an endangered species.

In the far distance a siren called out, an ambulance racing to save some fool driver who'd hit another vehicle and was now pinned in the metal that folded around his body on impact.

Slowly, very slowly, he descended back to the earth below and finally settled on the lawn of his home. He moved to the Cliff Walk, staring out at the ocean and the increasingly violent waves.

Somewhere below, deep beneath the waves, he could feel them as they moved about, growing stronger and more desperate. They were his now, to use as he saw fit, or to discard as they became redundant.

Soon they would be freed, but for now they suffered, lost in darkness and growing tired of their prison.

"Soon," he promised them. "Soon, but not just yet. The way has not been cleared."

CHAPTER 10

I

There were two abiding pains in Ben Kirby's world when he woke up. The first was the throbbing, shrieking thing that had been his brain trying to crawl out of his head and find a place to die in peace. The second was the raw humiliation of having the girl he loved find him outside his apartment and help him inside.

The head he could do something about with a few hundred aspirin and a gallon or two of water; the heart was just something he had to endure. The only good news for him was that it was Sunday and he could sleep in for a while. Being a proper masochist, he made himself climb out of bed as soon as the sun's rays tried to fry his eyeballs.

He made it out to the living room and sat down on the couch just in time to see Maggie leaving her apartment dressed in her Sunday best. One look at her and his headache faded to a whisper. Her hair was free to run around for a change of pace, instead of pulled back into her traditional ponytail; the thick, dark cascade of curls held his attention as surely as her smile always did.

She cast her eyes in the direction of his door for a second, warring with whether or not to check on him. Her teeth worried at her lower lip and he decided to make it easy for her.

Ben opened his door and looked out at her, smiling against the glare of the sun. "Good morning."

"I was just thinking about you. You all right?"

"I think my head exploded, but otherwise, yeah, I'm good."

She had a wonderful laugh. "It looks like it's still attached to me."

"I meant what I said last night, Maggie. Thanks for being a friend."

"You saved my ass the other day, Ben." She shrugged and looked away. Then she got a playful grin on her face. "Besides, I couldn't leave you to puke in the courtyard. Somebody would have to clean it up." She smiled, fired a wink over her shoulder, and headed toward the parking lot. "See you around."

He watched her walk away, savoring the chance to look at her without being noticed. When she was gone, it was back inside to medicate his aching brain.

II

Maggie sat in the center of the third row of pews and found herself staring at Father Wilson as he stood behind the altar and started speaking of sin and the wages it most certainly brought about. He looked a little twitchy up there, which was rare for him. He certainly wasn't quite as calm as he had been in the past, and while he looked at her several times, he didn't wear the same expression of fatherly kindness she'd gotten so used to seeing.

His desire was torn between giving his all to the parishioners and simply bending her over the altar a second time: she could see it in his face and his troubled eyes. She couldn't keep a small smile from playing around her lips, and the more she thought about what they had done right where he was standing in front of his congregation, the more aroused she became. It wasn't just the act of sex; it was everything else as well. The man was trying his best to behave, but she knew what he was thinking. He wanted her; he wanted to run away from her. He wanted to speak with her and tell her what a mistake it had been, and he wanted to make sure she would keep her word about never telling another soul.

Wilson's voice faltered for a second and she looked into his eyes. Maggie smiled for him, a fast sultry expression, and her eyes traveled the length of his body. She placed one finger against her lips, just for a moment, and licked her fingernail for his benefit. Nothing overt about the gesture; it would mean nothing at all to anyone but him, but for Father Wilson that gesture had powerful meaning.

He cleared his throat and looked away as if burned. Part of her was appalled by her own actions; part of her was amused by his reactions. Part of her wanted to bare her breast to him and see how long it took him to hurtle the rows of faithful churchgoers between them in order to take her again.

He turned his back to the parish and gathered his thoughts. Maggie looked off to the right and saw Patrick Flannery staring at her, his eyes slightly wider than usual and his lips parted as he watched her. She looked back in his direction and smiled again, a secretive, appreciative expression that told him exactly how much she had enjoyed her last confession. His hands were placed strategically in front of his crotch. She could still see his arousal.

When the sermon was done and everyone rose to pray, she felt the eyes of several men in the church seek her out. She stood before them all, hidden behind her proper clothing, and gave lip service to the words that were supposed to be spoken. They watched her as she left the church, and she in turn watched them as surreptitiously as she could.

Maggie knew good and damned well that she would be on the minds of the priests who attended to Sacred Hearts, and she reveled in that knowledge.

It was good to be wanted; sometimes it was better to be desired. Anyone that didn't know the difference between the two hadn't been paying attention.

III

Brian sat in the congregation, the space next to him left empty, held for Angie. There had even been a prayer said at the very beginning for her safe return to him. He watched the girl with the dark lustrous curls and just possibly the finest ass he'd ever seen, and thought about how much he would love to give her a ticket. It was a brief thought, a respite from the fear that was growing inside of him and mingling with the rage that was already dominating his thoughts. *I bet she'd be a screamer. I bet she'd fight and scream and bite and beg. I'd love to hear her begging me to stop. I'd love to make her crawl and—*

He cut the thoughts off; he was in a church after all, it wasn't appropriate.

Angie should have been next to him. He'd never even bothered with the church before they'd met. She'd changed him in a lot of ways and even he had to admit that most of the changes were for the better. Only now that she wasn't here, he actually came to the church seeking solace. It wasn't working very well though. All he could think about was how much he missed his wife and how badly he wanted to nail the piece of ass a few seats over and in front of him. *She's a college girl, I bet. Probably goes speeding around corners more than she should. Maybe I'd be doing her a favor if I tailed her for a few days. Gotta remember to check what kind of car she drives.* He shook his head, trying to get his mind off the girl a few seats away. He had to focus on Angie and their baby. That was what was important. But remembering the little bitch he'd raped in the woods was becoming a little bit of an obsession, and he wanted to get relief from the hard-on that was making his balls ache.

Still, not here and not with a member of the congregation. Too close to home. Even if she didn't protest enough to warrant getting her pretty little head bashed in, she might decide to confess it to one of the priests, and then if Angie did come home—*no, not if, when*—he'd have one hell of a lot of explaining to do.

After what seemed like hours of genuflecting, the Mass was finally said and done. He rose and headed for the doors, accepting best wishes from several people he knew and a lot he didn't. There was one girl back in the corner that he'd been with a few months back. She barely looked at him. She was still afraid of him and what he could do to her. That was a lovely thing.

The brunette with the pin-up body got outside before he did. That was all right. He wanted to see where she went, not follow her right now. All he had to do was get a tag number and the odds were beyond good that he could follow her anywhere: it was one of the advantages of being a cop.

There was a traffic jam at the threshold. Several people were standing in the doorway and looking out at the lawn of the church, not scared by whatever they saw, but certainly taken aback. Brian moved through them as carefully as he could until he saw what had them all so overwhelmed.

The girl was out there, and a few others were as well. And so were the crows. The birds were on every car, every open space around the entire church, on the telephone poles and trees, and even, he guessed, on the cross that adorned the top of the building.

They were just there, barely moving, not at all perturbed by the world around them. It had to be close to a thousand of the black carrion eaters. No, maybe closer to two thousand. But that wasn't possible, was it? Could there be that many crows in the entire state?

The sexpot walked toward her car and Brian's eyes were drawn to the movement; so, too, the eyes of the birds. Without any warning, they were airborne, black wings were flapping and generating an unsettling amount of wind. Autumn leaves blasted through the air in their wake and for a moment the air was as thick and fierce as a hurricane.

Brian backed up hastily as several of the crows suddenly veered and banked and came for the front entrance to the church. One of them came within inches of plucking his eye from his face, screaming indignantly as it came closer. His hand tried to settle on the holster he carried at work and clutched

only air. It was probably for the best that he was off-duty, because he wanted the damned thing dead. That screeching noise
reminded him too much of Angie when she was having a bitch
fit about damned near anything.

The birds rose in a spiral, a storm of feathers and beaks and
cackling cries of derision, circling the church and its parking
lot several times before they dispersed.

By the time the crows had finished their aerial dance, the
girl he'd been looking at was gone. If she walked or took a car,
he had no way of knowing.

Sullen and bitter, Brian Freemont headed for his empty
home. It was his day off, and he had nothing planned. He
thought he might go for a drive, however, and see if he could
find a few places with pleasant memories attached.

IV

Danny was being a big baby. He wanted to be in church but
there was too much work to do. He didn't want to go to church
because of his devout faith, mind you. No, he wanted to go because there were about five women there that he said dressed
up so nicely he could go without seeing a girly magazine for a
whole day after ogling them. "They're good for my soul, I tell
ya," was his favorite line on any Sunday when he had to work.

Boyd didn't care about church one way or the other, and as
for ogling women, he could do that when they were dressed
like angels, hookers, or even if they were naked. He was, in
his own words, an equal opportunity leerer.

So it was IHOP instead of Sacred Hearts. That was okay.
The food was better at the pancake place.

"Any leads on the Falcones' car?" Danny was also nursing
a mild hangover, so his normal cheer was down to a dull roar
and that was good, because Boyd was nursing a slight hangover too. He blamed his partner; it was just too embarrassing
to watch the bastard get drunk on his own.

"Yeah. According to Maria Falcone, it was her husband
driving. She has no idea who would have been in the car with

him. Says he was always picking up street trash to play hide-the-pepperoni with."

The lady at the next booth over was listening to their conversation and her eyes went wide when he talked about hiding sausages. She got an indignant expression on her face—she was either on her way to church or on her way back, he could tell by the fancy clothes—and he skewered her with a glare that had her suddenly looking elsewhere.

"What is it about Italian men having to find it elsewhere, Boyd? I swear, fidelity and Italian do not mix."

"It's the culture. And don't be an asshole. Not every Italian man is that way."

"Name one who isn't."

"I'll get back to you on that. It could take a while."

"Yeah, call me next decade, Boyd."

"Anyway, the lady says she wasn't in the car and she doesn't have any family with blond hair. So maybe we need to start checking with the hookers."

"We have hookers in Black Stone Bay?" Danny was waking up, his smart-ass was showing.

"What about the college girls?"

"We got Veronica Miller, and we got Danielle Hopkins . . ."

"Yeah, those two. Any news?"

"Witnesses say one of them was talking to a kid in the park, named Ben, but no last name."

"Physical description?"

"He's allegedly 'really cute.'"

"Can we just once not interview only the cute college students?" Boyd rolled his eyes.

"Umm. That was a guy, smart-ass."

"Of course." The woman at the next booth was making fish faces. She could go screw herself; which, he decided, was about as close as she ever got to lucky.

"Are we seeing a pattern yet?"

"Aside from what I said yesterday, no."

"And then we have Freemont's wife."

"I'm telling you, he's up to something." Boyd scratched at

his chin and continued to glare at the fish woman. "You know what? I want you to go over the car in the Veronica Miller case."

"We already did that."

"You said her purse was in there?"

"Yeah, so?"

"So, I want you to personally supervise taking fingerprints off her wallet and her photo ID. What the hell, let's go for broke here. I want you to go over her insurance card and her registration, too."

"Why, you think a cop did something?"

"I got twenty dollars that says Freemont was the cop on duty when her car was pulled over."

"You seriously think he did something to her?"

"You said it yourself yesterday." He started ticking off points on his fingers. "He had an hour of radio silence. He had a chance to do it and he was in the area. And I don't trust that slimy little prick."

"Will you please watch your language?" The church lady was making even more fishy faces as she stood up.

"You know what? Why don't you sit your ass down and mind your own business, lady, before I book you for interfering with official police business."

He took great satisfaction in watching her do exactly that.

V

It was almost sundown, and the day had dragged on for what seemed like a dozen or so eternities. Kelli sat back in her favorite seat on the porch, nestled in a coat and staring at the leaves on the trees.

The Listers were not having a good day and, as a result, neither was she. Despite her best efforts to remain strong and to be supportive for Teddy's parents, she was ready to scream.

How is it that two people can live their lives together, have a child together, and not love each other at all? That makes as much sense as peanut butter and tuna fish salad egg rolls.

They were breaking, or they had already broken. Kelli wasn't sure which, only that she was just now noticing the situation. Every time she'd seen them they seemed like the perfect couple. It was only now, with Teddy out of the picture, that she saw how little they had to say to each other. The only common denominator in their lives was their son. With Teddy gone, they were barely civil to each other, and most of what they had to say revolved around their mutual desire to make the hospital suffer as much as they were suffering.

They were inside the house, which was why she was outside. What had started as a nice, simple discussion about whether or not they were going to hire a private investigator to check on the possible incompetence of the hospital staff had exploded around the same time that Bill suggested using an agency he had hired previously from Boston. It seemed that Michelle's firm had used the detectives before and found them wanting.

Right after that, the screaming match began. She hadn't heard any of the conversation beforehand; it wasn't in her nature to eavesdrop under most circumstances. But when the argument started growing, she really didn't have a choice. The neighbors were probably hearing the damned fight a half a block away.

Bill started the actual yelling: "What the hell does it matter, Michelle? So your fucking boss had a bad experience with the Harkers! I don't care! They've done damned good work for me for over ten years!"

"Yeah, I've seen the little bitch you keep hiring, too! Who do you think you're kidding, Bill? How long have you been fucking her on the side?"

"You've got to be kidding me! I've never done anything with Denise and you know it, Michelle. She's a fucking detective who does work for me. I can't believe you'd even make an accusation like that."

"Really?" she asked. "Are you really having trouble with this after what happened at the goddamned New Year's Eve party back in 2000?"

"Oh, give it a rest already!" He was really cooking after that comment. That was about the time Kelli left the house.

"That was five years ago, Michelle! Five damned years, and nothing happened!"

"I don't call a pregnancy scare nothing, you bastard. You're lucky you didn't get AIDS from that skank!"

She did her best to ignore the words that the Listers threw at each other. It might have been easier to do if they weren't throwing more than just words. When she heard the fighting escalate to Michelle Factor Four—the point where breakables were normally hurled through the air—Kelli decided it was time to take a walk.

The woods were beautiful, of course. The colors of the leaves were brilliant and almost explosive. But that didn't do a damned thing to cheer her up. The more she thought about Bill and Michelle fighting, the less she wanted to return to their home.

By the time she finally did return, the silence from inside the house was almost worse than the earlier screaming match. The tensions were high enough that she wanted a chainsaw to cut through the oppressive atmosphere.

So she sat here, on the porch, and watched as the sun fell lower. The trees finally obscured her view after a few minutes. Bill Lister stepped out of the front door and lit a cigarette. He sat down on the far end of the couch, ignoring the wicker's creaking protests. Kelli smiled in his direction and he smiled back, a little shamefaced by what he suspected she'd heard.

"It's safe now, if you want to go inside. We've reached the I'm-Not-Talking-To-You stage." He tried to keep his voice light, but she could hear the strain.

"Oh, it's all good. I'm just enjoying the dusk."

"It's a beautiful night. Or it will be."

She looked away and was surprised to feel her eyes threatening tears. "Teddy should be here. He liked to sit in my lap and have me read to him when he was younger, and lately he'd just sit right where you are and read his own stuff."

Bill looked away, and she could tell by the way he was swallowing in rapid gulps that he was trying not to lose it.

After almost a full minute he nodded his head. "Yeah, he should be here." He looked at Kelli and she could see the ghost of Teddy's future looking back. In that light, with that expression, Bill looked exactly like she thought Teddy would look when he was done growing up. "Do you think he's alive, Kelli?"

She drank in the sight of him, not only because he was a handsome man and a crush she knew she would never act on, but because he was Teddy's father and the closest link she had to a kid she cared for more than she expected to. *Handsome. Teddy would have been a very handsome man someday. He would have gone on dates and the girls would have swarmed around him. He would have probably kept playing sports, maybe even football, and he would have been good at it. But he's dead. I know he is. I can feel it. Death feels like autumn; cold and sad and so very lonely, even in a crowd.*

"All we can do now is hope, Bill."

She got up and went inside, because if she didn't she could feel that things were going to go where they shouldn't between her and Teddy's father. She didn't want to be the straw that broke the Listers' marital back, and she sure as hell didn't want to be the one Michelle referred to as a skank.

VI

And what the hell was he thinking? He watched Kelli stand up and had to make himself stand still. He wanted to reach out and pull her to him, look into her dark blue eyes and run his fingers through her long chestnut hair. He wanted to hold her and comfort her the way he was supposed to take care of his wife and he was ashamed of himself for these feelings.

Kelli was half his age: it would have been close, but he was old enough to be her father. But she had exactly the sort of body he'd always loved—lean with small, shapely breasts and wide hips—and she was always so sweet. In the back of his mind, he played over another fantasy where she had her long legs wrapped around his body and her fingers locked in his hair and her mouth was bruising his lips.

He crushed out his cigarette and stood up, heading away

from the house. The sun was down now and the air was getting colder, but he didn't go back in for his jacket; he was pretty damned sure that if he saw Kelli in the next few minutes he would do something incredibly stupid.

Like kiss her and ask her to run away from all of this with me, and just for one time in my fucking life it would be so nice to forget everything but the freedom to do whatever I wanted. When the hell did I grow old and bitter? He chuckled to himself as he lit another cigarette. *Around the same time I married Michelle, I guess. The same time I couldn't just be free to go where I wanted and do all the things I kept meaning to do.*

There had been college and then law school and then interning for a group of self-righteous bastards who knew their business and knew a good thing when they saw it. And damn, they'd paid him handsomely as soon as he graduated. But he sometimes wondered how different everything would have been if he'd decided to learn something other than corporate law when he was studying for the rest of his miserable life. Because there were days, and they were coming around more and more often, when he hated his job and he could barely stand to look at his wife.

Teddy had made it all worthwhile. The days when he and Michelle could barely stand each other, all his son had to do was walk into the room and they both remembered why they loved each other and why they'd been struggling to stay together for so long. All of the old clichés seemed to be true: he loved his wife, but was not sure if he was in love with her; she was his wife and his mate, but she wasn't really his friend. She didn't understand him, and he loathed himself for having those oversimplified, miserable excuses filling his head constantly. They were all easier to ignore when Teddy was there and filling not just the room but the whole fucking *house* with his sweet, silly smile and his endless childhood energy.

And now he was missing from the equation and it was painful to be in the same room with his wife, because they were both hurting, both desperate to lash out and not really much in the mood to be forgiving.

Teddy peered around a tree and looked at Bill, his eyes flashing with merriment and an impish smile on his face. He wore clothes that were unfamiliar to Bill, and his hair was a little wild, but oh, dear God, how sweet he looked; an angel made flesh, alive despite everything Bill had allowed himself to think.

"Teddy?" It felt like his heart had stopped when he saw his son.

Teddy didn't answer. Instead his boy ran into the woods, laughing, moving with the sort of wild abandon that Bill had almost forgotten existed. Almost forgotten because, right then, seeing his sweet boy's face after three days without him in the world, Bill was like a child again. He was angry, to be sure, but he was so very happy too, and he felt like he could run a thousand miles and easily, if he could just catch up with his son.

"Teddy!" In that one word he cried his joy to the universe and released himself from the bonds that kept him anchored to the world. With each step he took, he felt younger and stronger, and he gave chase, pushing himself hard to catch up to the most important person in his entire existence.

He ran, and Teddy ran before him, almost dancing with each movement as he looked over his shoulder and smiled back at Bill. The leaves on the ground exploded away from them, leaving wakes in the mulch as surely as a clipper cuts through waves on a mild sea.

Bill felt like he'd grown wings; his feet knew just where to touch and exactly how to push off from every obstacle that should have tripped him. His hands stretched out in front of him, closing in on his sweet boy and coming closer to catching him, holding him, loving him fiercely.

He caught his son in his hands and Teddy giggled. And then he had Teddy in his arms, and was holding him tightly enough to practically crush his wonderful, crazy, beautiful boy. He pulled his son closer still and smelled the charnel scent on his ten-year-old hair and thought it surely the sweetest perfume.

And then Teddy was hugging him back and his son was so

unbelievably strong. His precious, lovely boy was smiling in his face; Teddy's skin and eyes seemed the wrong color and his hair was rippling in a wind that Bill had not expected.

And then his son was killing him.

Despite the pain, Bill Lister died happy, reunited with his boy in the end.

VII

Tom Pardue waited patiently. He was good at being patient. It was one of the things that set him aside from the others of his ilk. He didn't need to beat information from his girls, he just had to watch and wait.

He was watching Maggie when she went into the Methodist Church. It took some doing, but he was watching when she went into the minister's office, too. He spent a little over an hour watching her fuck the middle-aged pastor four ways to Sunday, leaving him gasping and red-faced when she was done with him. His only real regret was that he didn't have a camera to film the entire fuckfest, because she could have been teaching the rest of his whores a trick or two and he could have sold the resulting video for fifty bucks a pop to every college boy in town that wanted a piece of her sweet, little ass.

Which reminded him; this time when he taught her a lesson he was going to have to make her squeal like a pig and nail her there, too. Hadn't done that one on her yet, but he'd thought about it a few hundred times.

He thought about confronting her when she left the church, and changed his mind when the phone call from Nichole came in: her john was being stupid and refusing to pay. That was not acceptable.

So he let Maggie go about her business. He could be patient. He'd be teaching her a lesson soon enough and this way he could let the anger burn for a while. He liked to let things simmer and boil; it made the final payoff ever so much sweeter.

"You fucking your buddy Ben, too, Maggie?" He spoke only

to himself and didn't expect an answer. But yes, he suspected she was. And even if she wasn't, she liked the boy. That was good enough reason to put a hurt on the skinny little prick.

Maybe he'd make her watch. Maybe they'd play a game or two, where she got to beg him long and hard to see how many fingers he left on little Benny's hands.

Hell, maybe he'd make *Ben* squeal like a pig first. He wasn't into guys, but it might be worth changing his ways just to see if raping her boyfriend hurt Maggie as much as when he did it to her.

He wasn't sure yet, but either way, he had time to decide.

For now, he had to go ahead and work over one of the assholes who owed him money. No one got to owe him and walk away without a few broken bones at the very least.

Tom loved his job. It paid well, and the fringe benefits were positively the sweetest things he could think of: sex and violence in equally large doses.

CHAPTER 11

I

Boyd looked down at the body and then he looked back at his partner and the two homicide detectives, Nancy Whalen and Bob Longwood.

"I want this between us for now, okay? I don't want anyone talking about this case to anyone on the force."

"You know we could take this case from you, right?" Bob looked over his way, the cigar Boyd had given him sticking from the side of his mouth. Bob Longwood was not a good-looking man, but he was definitely an intimidating one. He was too heavy and too damned tall not to be intimidating.

Nancy shook her head. "Shut the fuck up, Bob." Nancy was a short woman with big hair. He'd seen her wear it down once and it ran almost to her knees. When she was off duty, there was probably no one he'd ever met who was sweeter, but when she was working, she could out-swear a sailor and out-glare the sun. One hundred percent lean, mean law machine. There had been a few occasions when they'd almost gone at it like bunnies, and both of them still wanted to, but they had enough common sense not to mix work and pleasure that way.

Besides, her husband liked to bench-press Mack trucks to stay in shape and Boyd wasn't really sure he was willing to get himself torn into itsy bitsy pieces and buried alive just yet.

"What? I didn't say we would take the case from them, I'm just saying we could." Boyd didn't take any offense and neither did Danny. Bob was teasing and they all knew it. It wasn't like he didn't have enough cases on his plate, and a couple of years back, Boyd had been partnered with him. That was back when the department had tried to actually have separate detectives for Vice. They gave up on that in a hurry. The department was well-off, but not filthy stinking rich. They were cops, after all, and it was much more important to have the extra money they could have used for detectives doing something important, like planting flowers on all the curbs in the springtime. Not that Boyd was bitter about it or anything. Much.

Boyd lit his own cigar, standing a long way off from the body when he did it. No one had touched the body since it had been found the night before by a couple of high school kids who wanted to get frisky. They were good kids; they were smart enough not to touch anything. He could see the spot where they'd had their blanket laid out a good thirty yards away from the actual crime scene.

Veronica Miller was not looking her prettiest. A couple of days in the woods will do that to a corpse. The crows had been picking at her face and chest; they'd removed her eyes and most of her nose. Not even Danny could look at what remained and think anything sexual. That was saying something, as Danny could probably look at his own grandmother and wonder if she was a good lay. No, that wasn't really fair. Someone else's grandmother, maybe, but he wasn't a complete pig.

"Hey, Danny Boy!"

"Yeah, Richie?"

"You ever wonder if your grandmother was good in the sack?"

"Of course. I asked my grandfather about it."

"Yeah? What did he say?"

"He said your grandmother was better."

"Fuck you."

"Are you two ever serious?" Nancy was being all professional again. Well, mostly, she had a little laugh when she asked.

He looked her way and smiled past the plume of smoke from his stogie. Damn, she was a good-looking woman.

"Of course, hon. I'm serious about this case. Veronica Miller needs to be our little secret."

"Why, Rich?"

" 'Cause we think maybe a cop did this."

"No shit?" Bob looked over at the corpse again and got a little pastier. Boyd wondered exactly which bright boy at the top had chosen to make him a homicide detective. It wasn't that he couldn't do the job, because he could. It was that he hated the sight of blood. Okay, so most of the blood here was dried up and flaking, but still.

"Want to tell us which one?"

"Well, neither of you."

Nancy nodded her head. "So let's get the equipment and get this done."

"We owe you, guys. Dinner's on us tonight."

Nancy looked at him long and hard, and he knew she was thinking the same thing that he was: no drinking tonight or things could get dangerous and her husband could find reasons to twist Boyd into a pretzel.

"By the book, guys. I want to make sure we find everything, okay? If we have a crooked cop, I want him going down hard."

"You looking for a good fuck, Rich?" That was Nancy, and hearing her talk like that made him swear off drinking a second time.

"Only every day of his life, Nancy."

"Shut the fuck up, Danny."

They got to work. They were very meticulous and found the condom Brian Freemont had dropped when he was murdering Veronica Miller.

II

Brian woke up in a decent mood. He had the day off again, and planned on using it to just relax. That was the problem here. He needed to relax in a big way.

If he didn't calm his ass down and soon, he was going to screw up.

His mood darkened when he realized Angie wasn't there. For a minute he'd let himself forget that she was gone.

He missed her, even missed her being a bloated, irritable, screaming bitch.

Mostly though, he missed seeing her face in the morning.

Damnedest thing about it was he was a little surprised by how much he missed her.

"Get over it. She's gone. Move on with your life."

The problem was that as much as he loved her, he knew that he couldn't stop chasing the college girls. It was heady stuff when they were begging him and thinking of ways to get out of their troubles. Even thinking about it was getting him in the mood to go out and do it again.

But he couldn't do it. He wasn't working. That was a problem.

On the other hand, there was always the campus.

What the hell are you, crazy? You can't just go to the campus and grab some piece off the sidewalk. He stopped and thought about that for a minute. Maybe he could. He'd never really considered using the files he had—or that the students there thought he had on them—for a second tumble before, but the more he thought about it, the better he liked the idea.

He just had to be smart about it and look for the ones who were looking properly scared when they saw him again. And he had to mark any of them that looked smug when they saw him, because, really, he wanted to find the bastard that had screwed up his good thing. He wanted to find him in a bad way.

Maybe he'd get lucky. Maybe he could find one of the smug little bitches and make her forget about being cocky, and in the process maybe he could get a name to go with the voice he'd had in his nightmares for the last week.

Brian showered and got dressed. He took his gloves with him. You never knew what the day would bring.

He didn't know the half of it.

III

Michelle was on a rampage. She was quiet about it, but she was pretty close to the homicidal stage. Kelli had the good sense to stay out of her way.

Bill hadn't come home last night.

Michelle was thinking the worst, and so was Kelli, though they had drawn different conclusions. His wife was muttering now and then, mentioning half a dozen different names belonging to different women. She could figure out the context from the previous night.

Kelli was worried for different reasons. It wasn't like Bill not to come home. She knew that. She knew he wouldn't really sleep around on his wife, either. It wasn't the way he was designed.

So now two of the guys she cared for were missing. She didn't have time to think about it. She had to get to school. Mercenary? Yes, but if she stayed here and thought about it, she was going to get herself doubled over and turn into an ulcerating knot.

Kelli grabbed her things and started out the front door. She only made it a third of the way to her car before she saw Bill's shoe. It was sticking up like a finger aiming at the sky and she walked over toward it, frowning in concentration.

It was the same loafer that had adorned his left foot last night. There looked to be a spill of drying stain across the top and she looked again, carefully, and saw that it was blood.

Kelli walked as calmly as she could back to the house and dialed for the police.

The detectives showed up twenty minutes later, looking exhausted and fed up. Not fed up with her, but with the way their day was going.

By the time they arrived, she'd calmed Michelle down to a

dull simmer. Now that there was a chance her husband wasn't fooling around, she was back to her normal self, only stressed out.

"I'm Detective Boyd. This is Detective Holdstedter." The short one spoke, his face placed as carefully to neutral as he could manage. The tall one, the Ken doll in the expensive suit, looked at each of the women with a fast eye. She looked back. He was cute.

"Hi, thanks for coming." She was trying to sound professional, because Michelle wasn't in any frame of mind for that. "Do you want me to show you where I found the shoe?"

"Yeah, if you could, ma'am." Boyd followed her, his eyes looking at the ground. He pointed to something and shot a look at his partner. Ken stopped moving and looked where he'd gestured. She resisted the temptation to look over where Ken went and walked on to where she saw the shoe.

Boyd stood next to her and stared for a moment, then he cast his eyes all over the place, like a man watching a tennis match played by octopi. His facial expression was nearly blank of emotion, unchanging, but she stared at him anyway as he looked over the trees, the grass, and the bushes, focused intently on seeing everything there was to be seen.

"Get the kit, Danny. We have a few things to pick up."

"I'm on it," and as he said the words, Holdstedter stood from where he had been crouching, a glove now on his hand and something small pressed between two fingers.

"What did he find?" She hadn't meant to speak, but the words fired out anyway.

"Looked like a button," the detective shrugged and took enough time to look into her face. She had no doubt at all that he was reading every little sin she'd ever thought of committing. He had eyes like that. "Might be nothing, might be a clue." He smiled and she felt more at ease.

"Do you think he was abducted?"

"Honestly? Yes, I do. I think Mr. Lister was taken by force. But I don't know that yet, so don't go panicking."

"Do you want me to stay here for a while?"

"Do you have somewhere else to be?"

"I have school."

He looked at her again and nodded. "So why don't you head off to school then, miss. I'll give you my card and you can call me when you have a little free time."

"Are you sure that's okay?"

"Oh, yeah. You go do what you have to do. I'll be here for a couple of hours at least."

She nodded and took the card he offered. She nodded to the Ken doll, too. He smiled for her and suddenly had a lot more personality than she had been giving him credit for. He graduated up from cute to handsome.

It was time for class and definitely not time to think about good-looking cops, so she went on her way. She went reluctantly; she'd wanted to stay and learn more about what might have happened to Bill.

IV

Ben wasn't really expecting any policemen at his door. The detectives introduced themselves and looked at him with expressionless faces; they asked if he could answer a few questions. He nodded and stepped out of his apartment.

"What can I do for you, Detective Boyd?"

"It's just a few routine questions, sir. We have a missing person's report filed on a fellow student at your school . . . Danielle Hopkins."

"Danni's missing?" He hadn't really given much thought to her not being in class. Danni wasn't exactly known for her perfect attendance. "I saw her just the other night. When was that . . . I think it was Thursday."

"You look worried. Was she having troubles with someone?"

Looked worried? He was terrified. How was he supposed to help her without getting himself into deep trouble?

"She . . . was having troubles with a man. I helped her get them resolved, I thought." *Shit. Damn, damn, damn.* This wasn't at all what he wanted to talk about.

"Anyone you care to tell us about?" Detective Boyd was looking at him and looking hard. The big guy next to him was looking, too. Neither of them was making it easy to read what they might be thinking, and he decided that if he ever took up poker, it wouldn't be a game he played with either of the policemen.

"Okay, here's the thing. If I talk to you, you're gonna get really, really pissed off with me, and then you're going to take me to jail or worse. I'm in a dilemma here, gentlemen. I do not want to go to jail."

"Did you commit a crime?" That was the tall one, Holdstedter. That was good, because for a minute he was beginning to think the poor guy couldn't talk.

"Sort of. Yes, but it's something I already fixed, so, I'm not sure."

"Okay. Was anyone hurt during the commitment of this crime?"

"More temporarily inconvenienced and probably really, really pissed at me."

"So it was a joke?"

"Absolutely not."

The two detectives looked at each other and had a completely silent conversation that involved nothing but facial expressions. "Okay, Mr. Kirby. Let's try this again. I'm going to ask you questions and I will want answers." Boyd held up a hand before he could protest. "If in the course of this discussion you should happen to mention a non-violent crime that does not involve dealing drugs to children or peddling little girls on the sex market, I am willing to overlook it for the present time."

"Are you completely serious?"

"Deadly serious. I want to find Danielle Hopkins. Anything else you talk about is going to slide as long as it helps me in that process."

He thought about that for a minute and finally nodded.

"Okay. So what if I tell you the guy I was . . . helping Danielle deal with was a cop?"

"That would depend on what the cop did, and what you did."

"Well, okay. So here's the thing: I was blackmailing the cop to leave Danni alone."

"What was he doing to Danni?"

"Forced sexual encounters to avoid possible jail time."

"Talk to me. Tell me everything." The two detectives didn't look neutral anymore, they looked like they wanted to find a blackmailing cop and have a sit-down chat with him.

"You don't push on me or Danni?"

"Same conditions as before: no drugs, kids, or murder, and we have a deal."

"None of that stuff. I was blackmailing a police officer named Brian Freemont."

What he expected was either a nice, calm questioning session or to find himself in jail in around five minutes. What he got was two very menacing detectives who were suddenly smiling and looking at him as if he were a long-lost cousin they'd been dying to meet.

"Brian Freemont? Really?"

"Ummm . . . I'm a little scared to answer this, but yes."

"Come on, boy, let's take you out to lunch." The detective looked at his watch. "This could take a while."

Ben had a feeling his day was about to get very interesting.

He wasn't wrong.

Ben was just starting to realize he wasn't likely to go to jail when he saw Tom Pardue coming around the corner; Tom took one look at him and the men with him and his normal shit-eating grin dropped like a soufflé at a rap concert.

V

Well, the day had started crappy, but it was getting better and better by the second. Who should walk right into the very place he was leaving than good old Tommy Pardue? Boyd felt a smile grow across his face when the punk saw him. First the treasure-trove kid who was about to make his life easier, and now a chew toy as a bonus.

Pardue did an about-face and got half a step before Boyd

was bellowing loud enough to have the kid next to him let out a little gasp. "FREEEEEZE!"

The baboon stopped where he was. He was well trained like that.

"I didn't do anything."

"Bullshit. You're always doing something." He walked over and moved around until he was in front of the slimebag. Tom Pardue had a nice, long record, but he was normally smart enough to avoid getting busted. Boyd made it a point to stop him every single time he saw him, because he kept hoping he'd get lucky.

Pardue was looking scared enough to rabbit, smart enough to stay exactly where he was, and angry enough to throw a tantrum.

"I'm just here to see a friend." His voice was shaking; either he was up to something, or he was carrying something.

"Yeah? Who you coming to see?" Boyd did his best to sound bored. He was very good at sounding that way. It was a gift.

"A girl I know."

"One of your hookers?"

Pardue started looking nervous. "Um. No, just a girl I date."

Boyd saw it from the corner of his eye, the way Ben Kirby jumped as if slapped. He checked the reaction again when he continued. "You don't date girls, Tommy. You just do quality checks on your own stable; who do you think you're kidding?"

Yep. Ben got a look of absolute shock on his face. He didn't even try to hide it.

"Get up against the wall, boyo, now." He complied, but to make sure he got it right the first time, Boyd had Danny help him. Danny was only as gentle as he was obligated to be by law.

When he was done, Danny got that little sad look he always got when a beautiful girl was married, or when he didn't get to have fun with a perp. "He's clean."

Boyd snorted. "He ain't clean, just smarter than he looks."

"Hey, I'm right here."

"Don't I know it. Now don't you think you should be

somewhere else? Before I forget you're a nice, upstanding citizen and find something to arrest your sorry ass for?"

"Yeah. Whatever."

"And Tommy? If I find you around here again, I'll think of something inventive." He looked at Pardue as hard as he could. He hated the little shit. He'd hated Pardue back when he was on vice and knew he was beating the crap out of the college girls working for him. Boyd just never could find a way to get any of them to talk. The notion that the little fucker was slippery enough to escape him still stuck in the back of his throat.

"That sounds like harassment." See? That was what he was talking about. There he was getting all smug again, because there was no evidence.

"No, Tommy. That isn't harassment. That's a promise." He moved in closer until their faces were two inches apart, his eyes felt like they would pop out of his head he was staring so hard. "Harassment doesn't happen to little fucks like you. I happen. Try me."

Pardue nodded his head, all semblance of uppity asshole removed for the moment. Then he wised up and got the hell out of the way.

But as he was standing to the side, he looked back at Ben with a murderous glare.

"You got a problem with my suspect, loser?" Whatever the problem was between Pardue and Kirby, he figured the least he could do was make it a little easier on the kid. Christ, the kid was definitely returning the favor over lunch.

"What?" Pardue looked at him suddenly all innocent again.

"I said do you have a problem with my suspect?"

"No. I don't even know him."

"Good. Now get the hell out of here." This time he waited until the walking ape ass was gone before he moved on with Ben and Danny.

"Friend of yours?"

Ben looked distracted. Boyd was pretty sure he could guess why.

"No. I've only met him twice."

"Knows somebody that you know?"

"Yeah."

"Tell your friend to watch herself. Do that, okay?" If his voice was softer than usual, he didn't notice.

"I will. I definitely will." The open book of Ben Kirby's facial expressions closed down hard and fast.

As long as he was still willing to talk about Freemont, it was all right in Boyd's book. Still, if he'd screwed up something in the kid's life, he'd probably feel sorry about it later.

VI

Maggie sat in class and did her work. Ben wasn't there, and that bothered her a bit, but she tried not to let it drag her down. When her work was done and it was time to be on the way, she packed up her notes and grabbed her belongings.

Today was payday.

Big payday. Her duties for Soulis were completed, and again she felt elation and depression at the thought. Still, she had a nice sum of money coming her way and that helped salve the thoughts going through her head.

She walked out of the classroom and into the middle of a bright day that made her wish she'd brought her sunglasses. They were still in the car, where they did her absolutely no good.

She checked her cell phone for messages: there were three. Two were from clients who wanted to know when she could see them. One was from Jason. The other two would have to wait for a bit.

She called him back and he answered on the fourth ring. "This is Jason Soulis."

"Hi, Jason. This is Maggie."

"How lovely to hear from you." That accent of his still puzzled her. Somewhere in Europe was a guess, but beyond that, she had no idea. "Thank you for returning my call."

"I was going to call you, actually. I'm finished with your project."

A tall man with a military haircut stared at her as she

walked past, and she felt the fine hairs on the back of her neck
rise.

At exactly the same time as she caught the freak staring at
her, she saw the first of the crows. They came in fast and hard
and began landing on the edges of the building around her.
Weird.

"That's wonderful news, Maggie. You've made me a very
happy man."

"I'm glad I could help." What else could she say?

"Do you have plans for tonight? I was thinking about dis-
cussing having you stay for the evening."

"I think I can manage that, Jason."

"Excellent. I shall make the arrangements with our mutual
contact." The tall man was still watching her. She could feel
his eyes on her like oil on water: slick but not sticking, and
definitely a little disgusting.

"Please do." She had no desire whatsoever to speak with
Tom. He was being a prick lately and she was thinking more
and more of ending her business deals with him. Of course, he
probably wouldn't be thrilled about that. Okay, he might be
homicidal.

"I shall see you around seven then?"

She checked her watch. That gave her three hours and spare
change. "It sounds perfect, Jason. I'll see you then."

"Maggie?"

"Yes?"

"Wear something nice for me, please."

"I will, just for you."

VII

The conversation went on for what seemed like forever. Ben
felt numb inside, but he did his best to answer the questions
one last time.

Boyd pushed another cola at him as soon as the waitress
brought it over. "Okay, Ben. I want to go over this last part, and
then we'll be done. Honest."

"Hey. You bought me a burger and a lot of caffeine. It's okay."

Boyd smiled and nodded. "Okay, what happened to the files he dropped off?"

"I found the one I needed and burned the rest."

Holdstedter looked at him, his broad Nordic face puzzled. "Why did you burn them?"

"Because, I didn't want anyone to find out what those girls went through."

"You didn't even look through the files first? To see what was in them?"

"Look, I was trying to do someone a favor, okay? She was depressed and she was probably ready to have a meltdown and I wanted to see her happy again. Is that so hard to understand?"

Boyd answered for his partner. "Honestly? Yes, it is."

"Why?"

"Do you have any idea what most people would have done in your situation?"

"No," he shrugged. He hadn't really given it much thought.

"My guess is a lot of guys would have used it to their advantage."

"Jesus. I could never do that."

Boyd looked at him hard and then his expression softened just a little. "Yeah. I believe you. But you're the exception that proves the rule, Ben. I've dealt with a lot of kids your age who would have done all sorts of things with the information you had, but you're the only one I can think of who would have burned the stuff."

"Well, maybe that was my way of stopping myself from becoming a statistic."

"Then good for you. For the record, you did break a lot of laws, and some of them would land you in prison with some damned mean characters. But even if I hadn't made a promise to you, I wouldn't press charges. You're good people, Ben Kirby. Try to stay that way."

The detective stood up and his partner did the same. Boyd

handed him a business card. "You have any problems from Pardue, you give me a call."

"Why did you tell him I was a suspect?"

"Because I saw you two knew each other. This way, when I come down on him, and I will come down on him, he won't blame you."

"What . . . what exactly does he do?"

"What doesn't he do?" Boyd looked him up and down and then shrugged. "He deals dope, he works a few small protection rackets, and he pimps college girls."

Something cold grew through the lining of Ben's stomach.

Boyd watched him and got a strange expression on his face. It was strange, Ben suspected, because it seldom showed up on his features. It was pity.

Ben hated him a little for that, but he hid it. The detectives left, and Ben stayed where he was. He knew he'd have to move eventually, but he didn't like the idea. He didn't like much of anything at the moment.

Some truths hurt more than others.

This particular revelation hurt like hell.

VIII

Alan came home to absolute silence. He'd tried calling several times, but without much success. No one answered but the machine.

The sun was just setting by the time he opened the door to his house and stepped inside. He walked through the living room and then up the stairs, his emotions doing the exact same thing they had the day before. He should have been calm, but it wasn't working out that way.

The stairs creaked, but he heard no other noises.

The hallway was dark and he walked softly, ignoring the way his knees wanted to shake. What the hell was wrong with him? This was his home, his castle, the place where he should have felt safest. *So why am I so fucking scared?*

He shook the thought away angrily and moved to the master bedroom's closed door. He didn't knock, it was his room.

When the door creaked open he saw Avery and Meghan. For just one second, he thought they were both asleep, nestled together. Then he saw the blood that ran from Avery's mouth and his mother's neck.

Avery lifted away from the wound he'd made, and Alan saw the dead staring eyes of his wife as she lay where she had for what was probably a couple of hours. She was dead. He could tell that from ten feet away.

He'd known something was wrong with his son, had tried to deny it to himself, but he'd never guessed.

"Oh, fuck. Avery, what did you do?"

Avery looked at him with eyes as dead as his mother's and smiled a bloody, sweet smile only granted to ten-year-olds.

"She's okay, Dad. She will be."

The pit of his stomach disappeared into an ice storm and he tried to breathe, but nothing came to his lungs. "Unnngh."

He wanted to speak, to tell Avery to get away from Meghan and let her breathe, let her get some air, because she looked horrible. Her face was completely slack and her eyes stared at the ceiling with rapt fascination. He wanted to reach out and pull his son away from his wife, drag him out of the room and kill him. He wanted to hold Meghan and have her come back to him.

Avery wiped the blood from his lips with his left sleeve. It helped make him look more like he was supposed to look, like he was just a little boy again.

The eyes gave it away; even if he hadn't seen what Avery was doing to Meghan—and at that thought, he wanted to fall down and die on the spot because the notion of being without her was destroying him—his son's eyes, gleaming with an odd silvery light, would have destroyed the illusion beyond all repair.

"What did you do?"

"She'll get better, Dad. I did." He moved, a small boy, only ten and still waiting for his first growth spurt for the love of

God, and before Alan could fully grasp what was happening,
his only son was standing at the foot of the bed, at eye level
with him.

"What . . . did . . . you . . . do?" This thing could no more
be Avery than the pallid dead thing on the bed could be
Meghan. That was the realization that let the anger in. It
looked like Avery. It called him Dad like Avery, but there was
no way that his son could be a killer.

"I'm making her better, Daddy."

"Where's my son?" He didn't recognize his own voice.

"I'm right here." Avery flashed a smile that belonged on
Jack the Ripper far more than it belonged anywhere near the
face of his only child. The eyes glittered at him, mocked him,
challenged him.

And Alan saw the challenge, heard it in his heart, and accepted it. In two steps he was across the room, covering the
distance to the mockery of his beautiful boy. By the third foot-
fall, he had his hands around the monster's throat and was lifting the fragile weight of a ten-year-old child into the air, his
fingers crushing down in rage.

Avery backhanded him hard enough to make him see stars.
Alan dropped his hold on the thing with Avery's face and staggered, his face already swelling from the violent impact.

Avery's evil twin landed with the grace of a cat and jumped
from the bed, sailing through the air until he struck the lamp
built into the ceiling. The glass exploded with a brilliant display
of sparks and showered down over Alan where he lay. Several
pieces of the light's frosted glass cover fell to the floor; three of
them took a detour and stopped in Alan's left arm, chin, and
chest. The pain was intoxicating. Then Avery hit the ground,
crouching before he scurried away at an impossible speed.

"You don't hit me, Daddy! You don't *ever* hit me!"

The room fell into complete darkness. Alan's eyes started
to adjust and he felt his pulse double as he strained to hear any
sound at all. There was nothing to hear. Avery didn't even
seem to be breathing.

Alan lowered his head to the ground and tried spying where

there might be a shadow of the boy's legs, something to indi-
cate where he might be.

The double pinpoints of silvery light under the bed gave
the thing away just before it attacked. Alan rolled, but it was
faster than he was. Sharp, savage teeth clamped down on his
hand, driving deep into the flesh between his thumb and forefinger, and he let loose a scream.

His free hand shot out in a wide arc and doubled back,
slamming into the back of Avery's head. The only noticeable
effect was the teeth slicing deeper than before.

The monster was strong, far stronger than any ten-year-old
could ever be. But it didn't weigh any more than Avery did, and
Alan rolled over, using his own weight to pin the struggling,
frantic form under him.

It seemed like a good idea at the time. Then the small feet of
the thing biting all hell out of his hand were suddenly propped
against his stomach and he felt the powerful muscles under his
son's Levi's flex. Alan Tripp was thrown through the air and hit
the bedroom window hard enough to shatter it. His head struck
a crossbeam and drove through the wood and glass alike, even
as his body bounced against the interior of the frame.

Before he could even catch his breath, he felt small hands
pushing, shoving his body out the window to the roof outside.
He barely had time to realize just what was happening before he
was pushed from the steeply angled shingles and sent rolling to
the ground below.

Alan kissed the concrete hard, and heard the sound of glass
tinkling and fast-moving feet slipping across the roof. A second
later he saw Avery's feet, spread wide apart, slap the ground.

"We'll come back for you, Daddy."

Avery loomed over him, the bulk of Meghan's dead body
slung over his shoulder. Her legs and hands scraped the ground
around him as he turned and ran, hauling the weight of a woman
a full two feet taller than him as if she were a feather pillow.

Alan tried to stand one more time, and failed miserably. The
darkness came for him a few seconds later, and he slipped away
from consciousness into the soothing balm of dark dreams.

CHAPTER 12

The sun wasn't up yet, and Jason was sleeping beside her, nearly completely motionless. Her body ached, but in the nicest ways. The man was definitely imaginative.

Technically it was morning now, and she had things to do. She rose from the bed and looked down on his sleeping form. He was handsome. He was also very strange. She liked him. He was charming and pleasant and very attentive. He was also filthy stinking rich.

She stepped over to her strapless black number and pulled it back on, starting at her feet and working it up to her chest.

Jason turned over in the bed and looked at her. He had a smile on his face. "Time to leave already?"

She smiled back, looking into his eyes in the faint light. He had lovely eyes, dark and deep. "If you don't mind, handsome. I have classes in a few hours."

"I don't mind. Thank you for the company." He stretched and she watched the muscles play across his torso. He looked almost soft when he was clothed, but once in the nude he was sinewy and powerful.

"Can I ask you something?"

"Of course. Anything you'd like."

"Not that I'm complaining, but why all the priests and such?"

He chuckled. "For now I'll simply say that they needed to relax. Ask me again after we are together again."

"We'll be together again?"

"If you'll have me, yes."

"I'll keep you to your word on the final answer, you know that, right?"

"I would be disappointed if you did not, Maggie."

She leaned over and gave him a kiss on his lips. Once again that strange flavor was in her mouth and she tasted it in his breath. He kissed her deeply and distracted her with his tongue a few seconds later. When he broke the kiss he smiled at her. "You had best leave if you plan on getting away from me, Maggie."

He was fully aroused, but not being an ass about it. She smiled down at him and slid back out of her dress. He lay back and let her take control of the situation.

The sun was up before they were finished. She didn't mind and he was most certainly not complaining. The drive home was a quiet one. Even the early morning traffic was feeling pretty subdued. She liked it like that, too. She wanted to get home and shower and get ready for school.

She got home.

But the rest of the day failed to turn out the way she had planned for it to go.

II

The sun was going to be coming up soon. Ben had thought about drinking, but somehow he never quite got around to picking up a bottle. It was too much effort.

So he sat in the darkness and listened to the night and thought long and hard about his life. So far, it was mostly un-eventful. He was at peace with that.

So Maggie had an unusual choice for a career. So what?

He was more worried about someone trying to hurt her than her having sex.

Well, most of him. Part of him was depressed as hell about it. But that wasn't important. It wasn't his life and he had no claims to make. He just wished he did.

"Grow the fuck up, loser."

"Talking to yourself, Ben?" The last thing he'd expected to hear was Tom Pardue's voice.

He turned his head and spotted the blond ape in Maggie's doorway. Tom was smiling.

"I didn't know there was anyone else here to talk to." He shrugged.

"Well, here I am." Tom was smiling. He had a very unpleasant smile.

"I don't think Maggie's home, Tom."

"Yeah. I know. She's probably not gonna be back tonight."

Ben nodded. "Well, I think I'm going to call it a night. I have class in five hours."

Tom slid two feet in his direction and leaned against his door. "You know what? I was thinking we should have a talk, you and me."

"What about?" He was doing a damned fine job of not panicking. At least in his own estimation.

"About Maggie." Tom was smiling again.

He shrugged. "Sure, talk."

"Well, I think maybe you got a little upset earlier, when you heard what she does."

"I was a little surprised, maybe. Yeah, I guess I was surprised."

"I can get that. Here's the thing though. You don't tell anyone about her," the man shrugged as he spoke. "She's a private girl."

"I wasn't planning on telling anyone, Tom. It's not their business and it's not my business."

"Good boy."

"Are we done? I have school in a few hours."

"Almost. I just need to make sure we really understand each other, okay?"

Before Ben could respond, Tom landed a fist in his solar plexus and knocked the wind from his body. Ben had never been a fighter. He didn't have any plans on becoming one, either. He dropped to his knees and tried to suck in a breath, but it didn't happen.

Tom helped him along with a knee across his cheek. Ben was already seeing constellations when his head rebounded off the door. That was pretty much all she wrote on the subject. Ben fell flat against the ground, the ringing in his head enough to make him wonder if he'd been permanently damaged.

The ugly blond giant with the acne scars leaned down and appraised his condition. Apparently he wasn't quite satisfied with his handiwork, because he kicked Ben in the ribs, and then in the stomach, the crotch, and the upper thigh.

"I'm glad we had this chance to talk, Ben. I feel much better about the situation than I did before." He crouched over Ben and looked down at him with malignant eyes. "Remember, it's our little secret. But you know what? Just to show there are no hard feelings, I can give you a night with Maggie for half-price. Would you like that?"

The nausea rolled through his stomach and mingled with the agony in his testicles.

"You give it some thought. Trust me, she's an amazing fuck."

Ben closed his eyes, wishing he could come up with a properly obnoxious retort, and settling instead for not puking out his spleen. His eyes stayed closed until Maggie woke him up.

"Shit, Ben." She was looking down at him, her eyes worriedly checking the damage to his face and head. "What happened to you?"

"Tom came by. We talked."

"That prick. He's a fucking animal." She took his arm and helped him sit up. The axis of the universe didn't completely fall away, but it sure felt to Ben like it wanted to. He coughed several times and leaned his head back against the door, hoping he wouldn't make himself look like more of a loser and hurl. "Come on, let's get you inside." She offered her hands and he took them. Maggie pulled and he leaned into it, letting her give him the much-needed boost.

A few minutes later she was helping him to his bedroom again. "We gotta stop meeting like this." He broke a smile and looked at her face, her perfect face, now marred by her anger. "People are gonna talk."

"Shut up," she was smiling as she said it. "I'm trying to stay pissed off."

"Okay. Shutting up now." He sat down hard on the bed and felt the room spin a bit.

"You don't look good. I'm gonna call you an ambulance."

"No. Don't do that. They'll have to tell the cops."

"So?"

"You don't need the grief if I talk to the cops." He lay back on his bed and clutched at the sides of the mattress to make the spinning go away. "I just need to rest."

"Why would there be trouble for me if you talked to the police?"

She wasn't getting it. He wasn't really in the mood to discuss it with her. So he closed his eyes, and a few moments later he was asleep again.

III

Some plans don't work out the way you want them to, no matter how good they look on paper. Brian Freemont knew that going into his excursion to the campus, but he'd tried anyway and met with resounding failure.

He hadn't figured that at a potted ivy university like Winslow Harper he would have trouble finding just one of the girls he'd had celebrations with before. He was mistaken. If any of his previous conquests were there, they were doing a great job of not being seen. The closest he came to finding a familiar face was the girl from the church the morning before, and while he wanted to get to know her better, he also didn't think he could intimidate that one. Maybe if he was in uniform, but not in his street clothes. And there was something weird about her: every time he saw her, there were crows all over the place.

So after spending most of the day on the campus and looking at what he could not touch, he'd decided to call it a day and head off for a couple of beers. Half a keg or so later at the Rusty Scupper, he ran across Boyd and Holdstedter, the detectives on his wife's case, as they were coming into the restaurant with the homicide detectives, Bob Longwood—the walking mountain—and Nancy Whalen, who was still on Brian's list of most fuckable cops.

He smiled at them as he was heading for the door.

As an afterthought he looked at Boyd and said, "Heard you had another disappearance."

"Yeah, we did." Boyd pinned him to the wall with his eyes. For a short little guy, he had a lot of attitude. "But we also found the body of one of our missing college students, so it's all balancing out."

Somewhere a roller coaster was dropping the apex of its first hill at high speed: Brian's stomach felt like it was in the front seat of that roller coaster. The beer he'd been drinking through the last few hours mingled with his steak dinner and threatened a violent rebellion.

"Really? Well, that's great. Not for the girl, of course, but wonderful."

Boyd looked at him for three heartbeats without saying a word, and then he smiled. There was nothing friendly or jovial about the way Boyd's lips pulled into a curl. "Yeah, the best part is, the perp left evidence."

"Really?" Forget roller coasters; his stomach lurched hard to the left and then to the right before it decided to just quiver and churn.

"Yeah," Boyd nodded and Brian was vaguely aware of the other three detectives looking at him, and each and every one of them was smirking; little I-know-a-secret expressions on their faces. "The moron left a condom behind. Just chock-full of nice, genetic tests waiting to happen." The detective came closer, and looked up into his eyes. "I got a rush job put on it, 'cause I think I'm close to getting this one solved."

All the happy had officially been drained out of Brian's day, and his stomach decided enough was enough: he muttered an "excuse me" to the detectives and ran for the men's room at high speed. He shoved the door open, knocking the man on the other side off his feet, and before he could apologize he was on his hands and knees in the room and vomiting across the tiles and the legs of the man he'd run down.

The man was understandably upset. "Jesus Christ!" He pushed himself back across the tiles with an expression of disgust plastered across his face.

Someone chuckled from the doorway behind him, but Brian was far too busy to bother with the distraction. His stomach seemed determined to remove every last iota of food and drink he'd had since graduating high school.

"You're a mess, Freemont," Holdstedter's voice was not at all sympathetic. "Call a cab. I see you get into your car and I'll lock you in cuffs myself."

"Uhhh," the voice came from near the sink. "This freak is a cop?" Brian looked at the man standing up in front of him. He was busily pulling off his blue jeans and soaking the vomit-crusted legs in the sink. A pair of bright pink boxers adorned his hips and hid the upper portion of his hairy legs; his reflection was glaring at Brian. There wasn't a part of the exposed skin that wasn't covered with a pelt of black hair, except for his face and the top of his head, which gleamed in the bright lights.

"Yes, sir. He is. Not his proudest moment, or ours, either."

"No kidding?" Sarcasm made the vomit victim's voice even more nasal. "What's your captain's name?"

"O'Neill, sir. James O'Neill."

"Well, Captain O'Neill can expect a call. I don't know if there are charges I can file, but I'm definitely filing a complaint." The man was pissed and not at all thrilled about wringing his jeans out.

"Technically, I could book him for Drunk and Disorderly

if you wanted." Holdstedter was being very professional, very helpful. Brian wanted him dead.

From a considerable height advantage, the civilian looked down at him and a smile that was far too similar to Boyd's spread across his face. "Yeah. Do that. Bust him. Please."

Holdstedter looked down at him, too, and was reaching for his cuffs. "You go right ahead and wash up, Freemont. Then we're gonna take a ride."

As it turned out, the detective did not actually haul Brian off to the processing center. He saved that for a couple of the beat cops he called to the scene.

The four detectives were all watching him as he was taken away. None of them laughed, but all of them were still smiling at him.

Life sucked.

He was released from the drunk tank at ten A.M. He was home half an hour later. He showered and shaved and then went back to sleep.

The official reprimand was waiting for him on Captain O'Neill's desk when he got to work.

Life sucked royally.

IV

Alan Tripp woke up in a hospital room. His chest felt like it was on fire and his hand was a shrieking symphony of pain. A male nurse was looking at him with wide blue eyes, and as soon as he woke up, the man moved over to take his pulse and blood pressure. He didn't know why the man was bothering: there was already a heart monitor and cuff attached to his left arm. He could hear the constant, steady beeps that mirrored the beating of his heart.

"How are you feeling, Mr. Tripp?" Friendly and professional, just like the ones that dealt with him when Avery was born.

Avery. Thinking about his son made the room swim into

clearer focus. "I'm fine," he lied. He was far from that particular state of existence. He doubted he'd ever be anywhere near fine again.

"There are some police officers who would like to talk to you." The man looked at him with sympathy. "Do you feel up to talking to them?"

No. No, he did not feel up to talking to the fucking police. He felt like crawling under the hospital bed and dying. "Sure."

Detectives Boyd and Holdstedter came into the room a few minutes later, both of them looking freshly scrubbed and well rested. They introduced themselves and the blond one poured him a Styrofoam cup full of deliciously cold water.

"Can you tell us what happened at your house, Mr. Tripp?" The shorter of the two men asked the question, his face almost masklike.

"My son killed my wife and then ran away with her body."

Detective Boyd's voice was doubtful. "Your son Avery?" He recognized the man. It had taken a moment for him to connect the pissed-off detective he'd seen during the search for Avery with the soft-spoken man standing in front of him now.

"Yes. Avery did it. I saw him."

"Do you have any idea why?"

"I think he was feeding on her."

Both detectives stared at him in horrified silence for at least half a minute. He understood how they felt.

Finally Holdstedter spoke up. "Feeding on her? He was *eating* her *flesh*?"

"I don't know. She was dead, her blood was all over her neck and the bed and his mouth and I think he was eating Meghan." He heard the sound of his voice rising, scaling up in octaves and volume alike, but he didn't seem to have any control over the words or volume. All of the horror of the previous night crawled back into his mind and left him ready to scream, so he did. "My little boy killed her and started eating her fucking neck, detective! He had blood all over his mouth and down on his shirt *and his goddamned teeth were pink with it!*"

The whole room went dark red, shading to near black at the edges of his vision. The two detectives looked at him with doubtful expressions and his excitement grew in leaps and bounds. "He wasn't Avery, but he looked like him! He was too strong! No one is that strong, you hear me? No one in the world is that strong! I tried to choke him to death and he bitch-slapped me! That goddamned freak threw me out a window!"

Somewhere near his left side the heart monitor was beeping erratically, and his vision went darker still, redder, more like the color of his wife's life as it drained all over the bed.

He was irritated by the sound of the monitor so he reached out and slapped at the thing, doing little more than bruising his fingertips. He grunted and reached for it again, this time pushing the device and the attached IVs to the ground. The needle in his arm pulled free and he barely even noticed. It was just one more pain and it didn't matter, not anymore . . . nothing mattered except that he find his son and punish him for what he'd done to Meghan. He had to know where her body was and where Avery's body must surely be, because there was no way that Avery had done what he knew the boy had done.

The nurse reached for him to calm him down and Alan screamed at the man for his efforts. "Get away from me! I want Meghan! I want Avery! You find them goddamn you!"

He looked toward Boyd and reached for the man to shake him to make his case clear. He wanted his family back because something was wrong around these parts.

His hands touched the lapels of the detective's jacket and were knocked away hard and fast. Before he could grab a second time the other detective was on him, wrenching his hands away from the shorter one and pulling them behind his back.

It didn't matter. None of it did. Alan laughed, because he couldn't make the words come out anymore, and he flexed, pulling his arms free from the larger man's grip. He was still turning to face the blond when Holdstedter's fist slammed into his face and knocked him off his feet.

He was still screaming and laughing and crying out his frustrations when the two men pinned him to the ground and called for restraints. The blood had soaked through his bandaged hand, and the sight of the dark red oozing through the cotton was enough to send him over the edge. He kicked Holdstedter in the balls, and swung his body around, determined to get out of the room and the building so he could find his family and bring them back together.

He didn't want any of this, didn't want to piss off the cops or hurt anyone, but his mind was screaming signals at him that didn't make sense and he couldn't stop himself.

Boyd stopped him instead. Alan fought back for several seconds as the detective slipped in behind him and got him into a chokehold. He was still fighting all the way back into unconsciousness.

· V

"He's a mental case. Elementary school kids do not go around eating their mothers."

"He kicks like a mule."

"I wouldn't know. I kept my balls away from him."

"Love the sympathy, man." Danny was walking like he'd been horseback riding for the last week.

"Oh, I got sympathy for you. I'm not even gonna tell the girls who give you the eye that your nuts are broken." They stepped out of the hospital and into the parking deck. Boyd reached for a cigar.

"You're all fuckin' heart."

"Yeah, I know. I'm an old softy." He plunked the cigar into his mouth and ruminated on it for a few minutes as they walked.

"Something happened to him. He wasn't like this last week."

"You see his hand?"

"The bloody one?"

"Yeah, Danny, the bloody one. I watched when they changed the bandages."

"I was a little busy trying to find my testicle."

"You get that taken care of okay, did you?"

"Yeah, they're both there now."

"Anyway. He got the shit bit out of his hand. Either he was

killing his wife or son and they bit him, or one of them went crazy."

"He didn't kill his wife or son. I'd put money on that and kiss Whalen's husband."

"You going all sweet on Nancy's husband, Danny?"

"Not as sweet as you are on Nancy."

"Shut your mouth. That sort of shit just causes troubles."

"It's mutual. I thought she was gonna crawl under the table and give you a hummer right in the fucken restaurant."

"Nothing ever happened. Nothing ever will. Now shut up about it."

"He still didn't kill his wife."

"He never let the doctors finish checking out his boy. What does that say?"

"That he wanted his son safe and at home and resting."

"I dunno. Maybe, maybe not."

"So let's pretend that I'm a detective too, Rich."

"Oh, you're a detective." He shot Danny a look. "You're a damned good one, too. I just don't know if I agree with you."

"So we get some pictures of the hand wound, see if they took any before they started sewing it up, and see if the marks match any dental records for the kid or the mom. Maybe someone else broke into the house."

"I'm pretty sure someone did."

Danny looked at him and stopped moving. "So what makes you call him crazy?"

"He is crazy. He kicked a cop in the balls. That's crazy."

"But you don't think he attacked his own family? Why?"

"Because I looked at the window while you were checking out the bedroom. Somebody big hit that glass hard, and he had glass all in his hair. I think he got pushed or thrown out that window."

"Maybe it was his son. Maybe somebody drugged the kid with PCP or something."

"Could be, he was gone for a couple of days. Anything could have happened to him."

They walked the rest of the way to the car in silence, each lost in their own little processes for working on puzzles.

"We gonna bust Freemont today?"

"Only if the lab gets those results to us." Danny started toward the driver's side door of the car and Boyd pushed in front of him. "Uh, no. I got the driving."

"What? I always drive."

"Not when your balls are still recovering. I want you able to think and relax."

"Careful, Richie. I might think you actually care."

"Hey, I do care. You're my buddy. You're lousy in a fight, but you're still my pal." He sucked and puffed at his cigar until his head was surrounded by a halo of smoke. Then he climbed into the driver's seat and started the engine. "I want to go to the Cliff Walk."

"Yeah? Why this time?"

"They live right near there. I want to see if maybe you're right and somebody is dumping bodies there."

"Jelly. I'm telling you, Richie, they're all dead and jelly on the rocks."

"You're sick and obsessed."

"You're short and a bitch."

"Maybe, but I ain't your bitch."

"No. You're Whalen's bitch, and her husband's if he ever finds out about you two."

"There's nothing to find out."

"Yet."

"Fuck you."

"No way, my balls hurt too much."

VI

Ben woke up with Maggie in the bed next to him. She was asleep, her face highlighted with shades of gold by the afternoon sun. His jaw hurt, his ribs ached, and his entire side felt like someone had parked a car on it, and he didn't care in the least. He spent almost ten minutes looking at her, studying her, loving the way she looked while she slept.

Loving her. That was the problem here. He wasn't supposed

to love her. Even if he was, he sure as hell didn't expect her to love him back.

That part he got right at least. It was sweet of her to stay, to make sure he was all right through the night, but he wasn't about to read anything into it.

Her hair was a wild mess of curls, half of which fell across her face and hid the curves and edges of her cheek and jaw. Her lips were just slightly parted and he could see the white of her teeth as she breathed in and out softly.

There was a strong desire to lean over and kiss her awake. There was also a desperate need to drain his bladder. He let common sense override his desires and climbed carefully out of the bed.

Ten minutes later he was brewing coffee. Five minutes after that, he was whipping eggs into froth and chopping ham. He didn't have any fresh mushrooms, so the canned ones would have to suffice.

He tried for an omelet; he got scrambled eggs with cheese, ham, and canned mushrooms. After that, he set the concoction on a plate, poured a cup of coffee and added the same amount of milk and sugar he'd seen Maggie add at the restaurant; it was enough sugar to put most people into a diabetic coma.

She was sitting up in his bed when he got back to the room. Maggie smiled a good morning to him and reached for the coffee gratefully as he set it down.

"Good morning." He smiled and savored the look of her for a second before heading back into his kitchen for his plate.

"You coming back?"

"Yeah." He did, carrying a plate identical to hers, but with five times as much sugar in the coffee.

"How are you feeling?" She sipped and looked over the lip of the mug at him.

"Better," he shrugged. "My face doesn't hurt that much, at least." He sat at the foot of the bed, and set his plate down. "Thanks for staying."

"Well, it was sort of my fault."

"No. It wasn't."

"If you didn't know me, he wouldn't have done that."

"He would have. He said it was nothing personal, just business."

"Did he say why?"

"So I wouldn't tell anyone what you do."

She started as if he'd slapped her. "He told you?" Her voice had dropped an octave; what came from her mouth was a sultry whisper that was purely unintentional.

"No. I sort of found out when the police were questioning me about Brian Freemont."

Maggie looked at the wall, her lower lip trembling a bit. She was angry, he could see that, but she was also humiliated and embarrassed.

"Maggie."

She didn't respond; she was still looking through the wall.

"Maggie. Look at me."

The glare she fired at him would have withered steel. Normally he would have been backing away in terror. This was different.

"Maggie, it's okay. I'm not going to tell anyone."

"Maybe I didn't want *you* to know. Did you think of that?"

"So pretend I don't."

"It doesn't work that way, Ben, and you know it."

"It does if you want it to."

"I'm sitting here thinking I've finally got a friend, you know? Someone I can just be myself with, and he pulls this shit!" The mug went flying as her hands went to her face.

There are a thousand acts of courage committed every day that will never be catalogued as the actions of heroes. There are people who face the world as little as possible and for whom the act of going to the grocery store is a monumental feat. There are children who deal with their worst fears every single time they get onto a school bus and face another day where no one cares about them and the bullies are always waiting. For Ben Kirby, the very idea of touching Maggie was an act of courage. She was his ideal and she was the only one he'd let close to him in a long time.

He reached out and put his arms around her, leaning his chin into her hair. She resisted at first. She tried to push him away, but he wouldn't let her.

Finally she relented and let herself be hugged. A few moments later she even hugged back.

"I don't think any differently now."

She laughed bitterly into his chest. "What? You always thought I was a whore?"

"Nope. Always thought you were quiet and nice to look at."

"Liar."

"It's just a job. It gets the bills paid."

"That's what I've been saying."

"Well, you're right."

She stayed there for a few more seconds and Ben closed his eyes, savoring her presence the way he always did. Perhaps he would have eventually gotten up the courage to tell her he loved her, but really, it wasn't very likely.

Only one act of courage per day, please. We have to keep up our standards.

VII

Kelli Entwhistle awoke in a silent house for the first time since she'd moved in with the Listers. There was no sound from the Listers' master bedroom. Normally there would have been at least the noise of the alarm clock or the shower running.

She spent the rest of the day feeling unsettled by the experience. She still half expected Teddy to come bounding into her room to wake her, even though he'd stopped doing that around the age of eight.

When school was done, she went back to the house and cleaned it from top to bottom. She even entered the master bedroom, despite her fear that she would find a bloodied shirt, or some sign that something had happened to Michelle.

There was nothing.

Ten minutes after she'd finished cooking herself dinner, the phone rang. She answered it, fully expecting to hear her employer's voice. It was Lori Sinclair who spoke. Lori was a nice enough woman but had all the actual brain power of a gnat. Most of her energies were focused solely on being perky.

"Hi, Kelli! It's nice to hear from you. I was just calling to double-check on the whole Halloween Block thing. You said you could take a clutch of kids trick-or-treating and I wanted you to know I've got you set up with ten, plus your own, of course. I can't talk right now, busy, busy, busy, but I'll get hold of you in a couple of days, okay? Thanks! You're a love, bye!"

The phone clicked in her ear, a warning that Lori was now gone and on to the next phone call.

"Fuck." She'd forgotten all about Halloween. Lori either hadn't heard or had forgotten that Kelli's charge was out of the scene. And damn, didn't that start her wanting to cry again.

"Okay, so maybe I should do it anyway. The kids still need to be watched, and I could use a chance to get out of the house." She leaned back in her seat and thought about it. There were some sweet kids out in the area and she liked kids. She genuinely did, which never ceased to amaze her friends from school.

"It could be fun. I'll call the girls and we'll get it going on and maybe even dress up ourselves." She smiled. "Then there're some parties to hit. So, yeah, I'll do it." She looked around and exhaled. "Christ, I'm talking to myself again."

The room did not answer her.

VIII

Michelle Lister never made it home. She had court for most of the day and then she had a meeting with another client, and after that she needed to dig into the legal research her interns had dragged up for her; the proper destruction of a hospital took effort.

Make no mistake about it: the entire situation was extremely personal. Her only child, a boy she loved as much as she had ever loved anything in her life, was dead. She knew that. She felt it in her heart. She let Kelli stay, of course, because the girl was practically family after the last few years, and it would have been wrong to turn her out.

And it would have been lonely. The damned house was always too big and now, well, now it was just plain monstrous. If Bill was indeed dead—a thought she tried not to let creep into her mind because, like the house, it was too big—then she would sell the house and move somewhere else, somewhere smaller without any of the emotional luggage.

For now, however, she was busy, and that meant she would have to wait a while to discuss everything with Kelli. Dinner was a double cheeseburger and fries; she ate while she drove and called to her assistants to get the paperwork ready. They were jumping hard and fast to keep Michelle happy right now, not only because of her losses, but also because her temper was legendary at the offices.

She spent three hours going over the papers and making her own notes. Tomorrow she would have them typed up and properly filed. For now it was enough to get everything ready.

After that, when she realized she had spent the day in a frenzy and might actually be able to sleep, she started for home. The air was thick outside: sometime after she'd gone to the offices, the weather had changed. Heavy ground fog slipped along the edges of the buildings and across the road like phantom waves, shifted by the wind. The air was colder too, and she felt a shiver run up her spine as the misty weather crept through her clothes.

"I hate this damn town." She moved over to the car and double-checked to make sure that no one was lurking around the building. College towns could get weird at night and lately this one was worse than usual. Too many disappearances, too many strangers, too many people who could be a threat.

Not enough family left.

She let herself think for a second and that was a mistake. Just like that, everything washed over her again, Teddy and Bill and everything. If Bill really was gone and the last thing she'd said to him was to accuse him of sleeping around—which he hadn't done, but it always pissed him off—she would never forgive herself.

The tears started a few seconds later and despite her best efforts they wouldn't leave her alone. Her eyes were dripping like a bad sink and she hated it.

"Screw this!" She wiped the wet works away with her palms and opened the car door. If she was going to turn into a bawling baby she was going to do it in the comfort of her own home, no matter how little comfort it provided.

The radio went up to a little lower than deafening and she popped in her Police CD. Sting always helped make her feel a little better.

Then she was on the road and heading for home. Sting was talking about a Scottish Loch and she was letting herself start to unwind, to get a little tension undone, when she saw the flash of movement up ahead in the fog.

She tapped the brakes because, for just a second that looked like . . .

"Teddy?"

Her heart stuttered, it shivered inside of her chest. She came to a complete stop and climbed out of the car. "Teddy? Are you out there?"

"Mommy?" *His voice! Oh, Jesus, his VOICE!* She didn't stop to think, she merely ran. Behind her the idling car moved forward, slowly gathering speed as it moved away. She was aware of the problem, but couldn't let herself think about a car: her son was up ahead, out in the darkness of the woods.

"Mommy? I'm scared!"

"Baby! Momma's coming!" Her heel broke and she kicked the shoe off irritably as she moved off the road and into the woods. "Momma's coming honey, where are you?"

"Mommy!"

She turned and saw him as he dropped from the air like an angel on wings. His hair streamed around his sweet face, a red-blond halo illuminated by the dwindling taillights of the car.

How did he learn to fly?

The car left the road, thudding and bumping its way across the ground and coming to rest against a thick oak tree with an audible crunch.

Teddy dropped into his mother's arms and she cried out in

an ecstasy of joy. His skin was so cold in the fog, so damp, that she had a brief horrifying notion that she was touching a corpse. But dead children couldn't move, couldn't smile with such beauty as you pulled them closer. He smelled the way a little angel should smell: of the sea breeze and the sand.

"Mommy!" God, just hearing him, touching him was all she ever needed to be complete. She realized that now, after she had almost lost him. She'd given up, had even thought—

"Oh my God, Teddy," her voice, usually so calm and in command, broke and she let it, the tears falling freely from her eyes as she hugged him fiercely. "Oh my baby, I thought you were dead! I thought I'd never see you again," she cried, pressing her hot face against his shoulder and neck and braying out her joy without any inhibitions.

His delicate little hands moved into her hair and he whispered sweetly into her ear, "Mommy, I missed you."

"Don't you ever leave me again, baby. Don't you dare ever run away again."

"I won't, Mommy. We'll be together forever. You and me and Daddy."

"Your father?" The cold came back, the void opened again beneath her as she struggled with the words that would make him hurt less when he heard them. Bill was dead; he had to be dead, because his shoe was left behind.

"Daddy will be with us. Here he comes now." Teddy's voice sounded wrong, teasing, like when he waited for her to open his present to her at Christmas. It was both a wonderful sound and an oddly chilling one.

"Honey, about your daddy . . ."

"What about me?" Bill's voice was in her ear, directly behind her, but she'd never heard him approach and never felt his breath touch her skin. Cold, hard hands slipped across her shoulders, massaging her flesh. She shivered at the touch and tried to turn her face to see if it really was Bill she felt. He pressed his body against her, his hands gripping harder than before, and she felt his excitement as he pushed still harder against her, pinning her in place.

"Bill? What the hell . . . where have you been?" She tried

to stay calm, but her voice was shaken, her heart trying to find a rhythm it was comfortable with.

"I had to find Teddy, didn't I?" His lips were against her ear, a soft cold whisper of flesh against flesh. Bill had always loved to nibble her ears during foreplay. The thought chilled her as much as the feel of his cold flesh pressing to her. "We have to be a family again, Michelle. We have to be together."

Teddy's hands were still in her hair and they clenched suddenly, hard powerful little grips that pulled her face up until she could look at him. See him for the first time. In the near darkness, his eyes were aglow, lit by fires the color of winter moonlight. His skin was sallow, pasty white. His teeth were bared in a smile that had nothing to do with joy or love or compassion. And then he leaned down as fast as a striking cobra and his teeth were biting, tearing into her flesh.

Michelle screamed, with the sudden and unbearable pain that was second only to the understanding that this was not her son. Teddy bit deeper, his cold face pressed to her neck and his tongue digging at the incisions he made, penetrating and tasting her life.

Bill bit her too, his mouth on the other side of her throat. The pain was worse by far, as his teeth punctured her skin, her muscles. His hands slid down and cupped her breasts in a sick mockery of the love they'd known, no matter how cold and distant it had become.

Michelle struggled. She fought and she pushed and she screamed loudly enough to hear her voice echo off the nearby trees. The darkness was almost complete, and even her car was too distant to bring a hope that someone would come and stop the insanity. Michelle cried and begged her family to leave her in peace.

That was not an option for her husband and child. They wanted what they always wanted: to be a family again.

One big, happy family.

CHAPTER 13

I

Some days it didn't pay to get out of bed. Truer words had never been spoken. It was just after midnight when Brian Freemont found the silver Mercedes parked against a tree. The engine was dead, but the hood was still warm. He called it in immediately.

The car belonged to Michelle Aarons Lister. There was no sign of her, but he could see the car keys were still in the ignition. He thought about going to look for her, to see if she had crawled away or been dragged, but after the verbal ass-fucking Captain O'Neill had given him earlier, he decided to follow procedure and wait.

O'Neill was not a happy man. It turned out that Brian hadn't tossed his cookies on just anyone. Oh, no, that would have been an easy enough thing to escape from. No, he'd managed to blow chunks all over the legs and pants of the police commissioner's son-in-law.

O'Neill was normally a good man to deal with; he'd always had an open-door policy and he'd been enthusiastic about his reviews for Brian since he'd joined the force. He was even sympathetic to Brian's current dilemmas; he knew all about Angie's disappearance and the fact that she was six months pregnant with their first child.

His example of mercy was to let Brian keep his job and stay on patrol. But O'Neill was not happy. He was never happy, he went on to explain, when the Commissioner himself called his house at three in the morning to rip him a new asshole. It was going to take a lot of ass-kissing to get anywhere near a promotion or raise, which sucked, because the captain had also made clear he'd been very close to stepping to the next level before the reprimand.

So now, it was by the book. End of discussion.

For ten minutes he was alone in the woods. The accident was off the road, and even with his flashers strobing through the night, it was foggy and murky; dark enough that he had to wonder if he was seeing things. There was movement around the edges of a few trees, flickering little traces that were there and then gone an instant later. He ignored them at first, but they were becoming more active, more distracting.

Brian eased his hand down to the holster on his hip. To date he'd never drawn the weapon in the line of duty, never had a reason to. He wanted to keep it that way. Still, he wasn't willing to take any chances.

"Mrs. Lister?" No one answered his call.

But there were sounds now, to go with the movements. Scratching noises and occasionally a few pieces of bark could be seen falling in the off and on lights. They made a sound like hail falling across sandpaper as they struck the ground.

And the sounds were coming from several places at once.

The hairs on Brian's neck rose and his hand unclasped the snap that held his pistol in place. "Whoever's out there better knock it off!"

The sounds continued, undaunted.

"This is police business, and I am not in the mood to play with you!" He was starting to sweat and he could hear a ringing sound in his ears that he knew had nothing at all to do with the world outside of his skull.

A pinecone bounced off the back of his head hard and sharp. He let out a little yelp as he turned to see where it had come from.

There was nothing to see, but he could swear he heard a woman giggling.

His vision went red. Some little bitch was playing games with him and that was enough to make him want to shoot first and ask questions later.

"You come on out where I can see you, right now!"

"We're right here, Freemont." The voice came from almost directly behind him and he turned fast, drawing his weapon.

He realized an instant later that he had made a horrible mistake. Detectives Richard Boyd and Daniel Holdstedter had their revolvers drawn and aimed at his face before he could finish sighting.

"PUT THE FUCKEN GUN DOWN!" Boyd didn't need a bullhorn, his voice echoed off the trees. Even in the darkness he could feel the eyes of the man burning at him.

He dropped the pistol and held his hands up. Danny Holdstedter had him on the ground and eating leaves five seconds after that.

"You outta your fuckin' mind, Freemont?"

"Danny, someone was fucking with me out here!"

The detective frisked him hard and fast, flipping him over like a fish and checking his front as well. He pulled a six-pack of condoms from Freemont's front shirt pocket, along with a pen and a shopping list.

"Nice, Freemont. Figured on getting lucky in the woods?" Holdstedter waved the package in the air for Boyd to see.

"That's sweet. Good to see a man who has faith that his wife will return to his loving arms, isn't it, Danny-Boy?"

"Oh, yeah. Makes me feel all warm and fuzzy."

"Strap his legs, too. Then we're gonna have a look around."

"What? Hey, come on, guys! It was an honest mistake."

Boyd walked closer and looked down at him. "No, Freemont, it was a stupid fucken rookie thing to do." The detective's eyes crawled over him like he was being forced to carefully examine a large pile of dog shit. "Then again, let's look at the source."

Holdstedter pulled a long white zip tie and locked his ankles together while Boyd watched. "Stay put, dipshit. We ain't done talking about this." Boyd took the time to pick up Brian's revolver and remove the shells before putting the weapon in his jacket pocket. The two detectives went over to the wrecked car and began talking.

Brian watched them as they moved around the car and examined the ground carefully. A few minutes later they were gone and Brian was left alone. He sat very still, afraid to move.

The sounds started up again when the other cops were out of hearing range. He tried to ignore them as they came closer . . . slowly, steadily.

II

Business and pleasure do not always mix. Maggie knew that very well. She was reminded when she spent the night with Leonard Morton. Leonard was a large man, half-bald and sweaty on the best days. He was pleasant enough, actually rather charming in old-fashioned ways, but he was also, simply put, a bit of a pig. He even had the nose for the assignment.

Still, she did what she had to and stayed the night as she had been paid to do. And if she felt worse about it than she normally did, well, that was to be expected when you got right down to it. She suspected Ben would know what she was doing and that bothered her more than she wanted it to.

Tom was going to pay for that. She didn't know how, but he was going to regret fucking with her. Thinking about his sorry excuse for a face made her grind her teeth together. She could feel a headache coming on and he would pay for that, too.

She just had to work out the details.

She got home a little before the sun rose. The apartments were all dark, which was about what she'd expected.

There was a note against her front door. It was written on the same antiqued stock as the poem she'd gotten a week earlier and the few pieces of artwork and poetry she'd seen in Ben's bedroom.

She opened the single piece of paper and read the words carefully.

It read:

> Alone
>
> From childhood's hour I have not been
> As others were; I have not seen
> As others saw; I could not bring
> My passions from a common spring.
> From the same source I have not taken
> My sorrow; I could not awaken
> My heart to joy at the same tone;
> And all I loved, I loved alone.
> Then—in my childhood, in the dawn
> Of a most stormy life—was drawn
> From every depth of good and ill
> The mystery which binds me still:
> From the torrent, or the fountain,
> From the red cliff of the mountain,
> From the sun that round me rolled
> In its autumn tint of gold,
> From the lightning in the sky
> As it passed me flying by,
> From the thunder and the storm,
> And the cloud that took the form
> (When the rest of Heaven was blue)
> Of a demon in my view.
>
> —Edgar Allan Poe

Thanks for keeping me not alone,

Ben

She folded the paper and looked over her shoulder to the window of his place. Silly, really, that a poem could make her feel better. But it did.

She took the paper inside her apartment and carefully set it out on the kitchen table. A few hours under a frying pan would take the worst of the wrinkles out, and after that she planned on pinning it to the wall.

She was just getting ready for a few hours of sleep when the phone rang.

"Hello?"

"Well, I kind of expected a phone call from you today." Tom's voice crawled through the receiver. He was sounding like he was ready for a fight.

"Really? Why?" He wasn't the only one who could do innocent.

There was complete silence on the other end for a few seconds. Monkey Boy had to think. It was seldom a pretty thing to watch and almost always took longer than should be necessary.

"Well, just because I haven't heard from you lately." He was puzzled. She didn't much care.

"Hey, school keeps me busy and the client list isn't getting any smaller."

"So, Jason Soulis called me. He wants to get together with you tonight."

"Okay. He can give me a ring to set up the particulars. Anything else?"

"Uhh. No, I guess that about does it."

"Well, there it is. Talk to you soon, Tom." She hung up before he could say anything else. She didn't want to hear his voice, didn't want to think about him. She wanted free of him, once and for all.

It was time to move on. She had enough money to handle it, but it would take time to work out the details: time or a gun big enough to erase Monkey Boy off the face of the earth. Maggie liked the second idea better, but wasn't stupid enough to do anything about it.

III

Ben watched Maggie go inside her apartment and breathed a sigh of relief. With all of the people who had vanished of late, he didn't exactly love the idea of her being out all night.

She cast her eyes in his direction and he studied her as he always did. Every detail of her face fascinated him. He wondered, as he did from time to time when he was feeling a bit self-conscious, whether or not he qualified as a stalker. There was something wrong with watching her as often as he did, and he knew that, but couldn't stop it.

Didn't want to stop it.

It still wasn't any of his business what she did with her life, but that didn't change how he felt. He was in love with the girl next door. The only reason she lived across the courtyard from him was because, once he decided he liked to see her, he found out where she lived and moved in. Elegant, beautiful, quiet, studious; she was all of those things and that, more than anything else, had caught his attention. She could have been a truck driver and he would have felt the same way. She was a prostitute and he knew he could deal with it. All sins were forgivable when faced with love.

Once she went inside her apartment, he sighed and let himself breathe again. Then he turned on one of the cell phones he'd purchased to deal with Brian Freemont and plugged it into the modem of his laptop. He was done with Freemont. The sick bastard would be suffering plenty in the near future.

His hand ran along his ribs and he winced. He was not done with Thomas Alexander Pardue. The long list of research notes he'd written down earlier was on his left and the computer was on his right.

"Fuck with me, Tom? Trust me; you don't know what being fucked is."

It was just possible that Pardue would figure out who was behind it when the time came, but long before then, Ben would be done with him. His fingers tapped keys with the skill

of a surgeon and he started his own symphony; a song just for
Tom, a special song of desperation and financial ruin.

He blinked away a few tears as he worked. They were not
tears of sorrow, he was beyond that and had been for a long
time. They were tears of rage. Ben had been a victim plenty of
times in his life. Pardue was hardly the first man he'd ever run
across who felt the need to kick his face in and he likely
wouldn't be the last.

He was just the first one Ben decided to play dirty with. Oh,
he'd certainly hacked a few accounts in the past, that was true
enough, but he'd always done it for what he considered a good
reason. When his uncle Dominick had run into troubles paying
his house notes, Ben had fixed the problem long enough for the
man to recover and go about his life. When the insurance com-
panies had refused to pay a few claims that were due to his father, he'd fixed that too. It was easy when you had the right
equipment and the proper tools.

Ben had both and knew how to use them. Danni had been
the latest trick he turned. He'd even promised himself he'd
stop after that, because sooner or later even the best hackers
got themselves busted and he wasn't dumb enough to think it
wouldn't happen to him if he kept it up.

But this was different. He could deal with an occasional
beating; they happened every day to people just like him. He
could even deal with the threats of more beatings, because he
never intended to announce what Maggie did; if she'd thrown
rocks at him and called him the worst names she could come
up with when she found him on the sidewalk the night before,
she still would never have had to worry about that.

So she was a prostitute. It was a job. He could deal with
that and he would pretend the knowledge didn't bother him in
the least, because he never wanted to hurt her.

But Tom? The very thought that Pardue would ever strike
her in anger, would ever touch her or know her body . . . that
was exactly enough to make him want the man to suffer.

He started with the bank accounts. After that he moved on
to land deeds and credit cards. When he was done there, he
moved into the police databases in the area and added a few

minor, niggling warrants to the list of outstanding orders; nothing that would get Tom on "America's Most Wanted"; just the sort that would cause him to be pulled over. He also cancelled Tom's car insurance and revoked his driver's license.

When he was done, Pardue had twelve thousand dollars to his name. It was enough to let a few days or even weeks pass before the man discovered he was broke.

All of Pardue's money went into a series of legitimate trust funds. They'd been established a long time ago, under several different names.

When he was finished, Ben set aside his laptop and disconnected the cell phone. He stared out the window and squinted against the glaring reflection of the sun on Maggie's side of the building.

"Fuck with me again, Tom. Fuck with me again, and you'll see how nasty I can get."

Ben closed his eyes and went to sleep on his couch. It had been a long night and he was tired. In his dreams Maggie was with him as she had been the previous afternoon: she was sleeping and he watched her while she dreamed.

IV

The International House of Pancakes was paradise: The food was plentiful and fattening and the coffee flowed in great rivers of caffeinated pleasure.

Boyd needed the caffeine and so did Holdstedter. Old Danny was looking about as white as toothpaste from lack of sleep. Real toothpaste, not that gel shit everyone thought was so cool.

"This shit ever gonna stop?"

"What? The disappearances?" There was already a backlog of cases to investigate and seven more people had vanished and been reported since midnight.

"No, Richie, the unclean love you have for Whalen. Of course the disappearances."

"Sooner or later the town's gonna run out of people to have

disappear. But don't worry, Danny. Our asses will be long fired before then." He poured more syrup over his pancakes. Sugar and caffeine, those were the secrets to keeping him happy. "And Danny?"

"Yeah?"

"You go ahead and keep it up about Whalen and me. You just do that. It gets funnier every time you say it."

Danny grinned. "Doesn't it though?"

"Not as funny as the look on Freemont's face last night."

Danny nodded and broke into a bright, sunny smile. "Does my heart good to know he shit himself."

"Boy has a bad case of the stupids going. Gonna be fun to see what O'Neill does to his sorry ass."

"Did you want to shoot him as bad as I wanted to shoot him?"

"You kidding?" He held his index finger and his thumb a quarter inch apart. "This close to popping an eye out the back of his fucken head."

The man in the booth behind Danny was looking green. Boyd savored the expression. It was never wise to eavesdrop on cops.

"See? That's the problem with you. You always gotta take the hard shots. I was gonna go for the gut. I like to see pricks like him squirm."

The excitement was getting to Danny. He had color coming back into his cheeks. "What hard shot? His eyes were bugging out." He shrugged and cut another wedge out of his remaining pancakes. "I was waiting to see if they'd just fall out on their own, but they didn't. I gotta tell you, I was disappointed."

"You think he did the Lister woman?"

"Nah. He's too sweaty right now. I bet he was figuring out whether to offer his mouth or his ass to O'Neill."

"So I guess he'll be using both today. Captain's luck just got better."

"You ever see the captain's wife?"

"Nope." Danny went to sip at his coffee.

Boyd waited to make sure his timing was just so. "Then you have no idea how true what you just said is. Gawd almighty, that woman could scare a dildo."

Danny coughed coffee out of his nose as he tried to laugh. "Oh fuck, that burns . . ."

"Schmuck. The captain isn't even married."

"Then whose picture is that on his desk?"

"The commissioner's wife. He has to pleasure her at least once a week or his life goes to hell."

"You lie like a rug."

"You don't believe me, you go ahead and ask him."

"Anyway. What have we got on Freemont?"

"We got DNA evidence that should get him in jail nice and easy."

"So where is this evidence?"

"Not with us yet."

"See? There you go getting all cocky again."

"It ain't cocky. That little shit is up to something. I don't think he did his wife, but I know he did something. And did you see his face right before he blew his dinner? He was ready to run home to momma."

"Oh, and I saw it after he tossed, too. Man, I wish I had a digital camera. He'd be all over the Internet on that one."

"So, what happened to Michelle Lister, Danny?"

"She wasn't abducted. Or if she was, she didn't get taken from the car."

"Yeah?"

"Yeah. Automatic transmission was still in drive."

"Good point. You know, with everything that woman has gone through, I gotta wonder if her family is really dead. This could be a kidnapping of some kind."

"I thought the boy was confirmed dead." Danny put a thoughtful look on his face. As far as Boyd was concerned, it didn't fit. Danny never had to think hard.

"He is. By the same people that lost him." More coffee to wash down the paste his pancakes had become. "It could be an inside job."

"I don't think so."

"Neither do I, but I had to put it out there."

"Okay, so the kid is still dead, at least as far as the hospital is concerned. We just don't take them at their word."

"Anything on the rubbers?"

Danny looked at him without any comprehension for about seven seconds and then nodded. "Oh, *those* rubbers. I was thinking galoshes."

"You would."

"Anyway, yeah, they're a match for the one found near Veronica Miller. Circumstantial, but a nice addition."

"Not so circumstantial if we work this all out. Nice catch yesterday."

"Oh, I was fishing. I wanted to find something on that fucker."

"Don't worry. He's ours. Guilty as sin, you ask me."

Danny wiped his mouth and pushed his empty plate away. "Oh, he's ours. Even if he isn't, he's mine."

"I'm sensing hostility."

"Yeah, well, creeps like him give creeps like me a bad name."

Boyd was about to answer when his cell phone went off. He answered that instead.

"Boyd."

"Where are you?" It was Nelson on the switchboard.

"Eating, and off duty."

"You wish!"

"What now, Nelson?"

"We've had a total of nineteen missing persons reported today. You need to get down to the station now."

"NINETEEN?" His bellow cut through the breakfast crowd and a few people dropped utensils or in one case, a glass full of orange juice. "You better fucken be kidding me, Nelson."

"I wish I was, Boyd. Nineteen."

Boyd pushed away his pancakes. Suddenly he had no appetite.

V

Kelli spent half the morning pacing, waiting to be questioned about Michelle's disappearance. She felt like she was going to throw up. Tension did that to her, it always had. Right now, tension was her middle name.

The entire family she had been living with for the last few years, ever since she moved up to Black Stone Bay, was missing. Not really a stretch to find that the police wanted to talk to her about it.

That didn't make her any more comfortable with the idea.

Detective Boyd said he'd be coming by to talk with her, and she was waiting. He'd also said it might take him a while to get to where she was. It seemed there were a lot of people missing in Black Stone Bay.

She walked around the house until almost noon and then she stepped outside into the overcast weather. The air was thick with fog and the sound of the waves was a resonating hiss as the ocean attacked the land on the other side of the Soulis place.

The leaves were falling in greater numbers now, and the entire area was starting to look barren. Autumn always made Kelli feel a little melancholy, but this year, it was starting to frighten her.

Jason Soulis was across the way. She saw him in the front yard of the massive place and thought about waving, but changed her mind.

He was staring at the house she lived in, his face unreadable in the gloom. A moment after that, he moved toward the far side of his own place, pausing exactly long enough to give his usual wave and nod of the head.

There was something about him she found endearing and something else that she couldn't hope to fathom; he was an enigma. He'd had a girl over several times now, but he never left with her and other than her he'd never had any visitors that she knew of. A man that good looking—even if he was miles too old for her—should have been going out and enjoying life.

Instead, Jason seemed perfectly content to just sit inside that big old mansion and do nothing.

Who are you to judge? What have you been doing with yourself except babysitting since you got to school?

She did go out; she just didn't do it often. Life kept getting in the way. First there was Teddy—brief pause for stomach lurch—and then there was school, and between the two of them she always found it was easier to get a good book and read than it was to go find a party. She didn't think she was really designed for that life, anyway. There were girls who could go party every night and find a guy and have a blast, and then there were girls like her.

Kelli was not a victim of low self-esteem. She knew she was pretty enough, she knew guys looked; she just wasn't really in it for a fast fling and a polite nod to whomever she had bagged a couple of weeks earlier.

A new car pulled up in front of Jason's place. This was a muscle machine, a Camaro with a glass-packed muffler. She knew it well enough and seeing it made her want to throw rocks.

Tom Pardue was a sleazy bastard if ever there was one. He'd actually asked her once, right after she got into town, if she wanted to hook for extra money. One look from her and he'd tried to laugh it off as a joke, but she knew better.

Her interest was piqued, so she stayed where she was and waited to see what would happen between Tom and Jason. If it was what she suspected, her estimations of Jason were about to take a plunge.

Naturally, she never got to find out. Around the same time Tom was knocking on the man's front door, Detectives Boyd and Holdstedter pulled into the long driveway.

They got out looking shell-shocked. She smiled and stood up. At least she wasn't the only one feeling that way.

"Ms. Entwhistle, how are you today?"

"Okay, I guess." She wasn't, but it was the sort of lie you were supposed to tell; and really, it was less worrisome than screaming and ripping her own hair out, which was closer to how she felt.

"I'm sorry to bug you, we just had to ask a few questions,

especially under the current circumstances. I hope you understand."

"Of course, Detective Boyd."

"Listen, just call me Boyd. It's 'detective' if you're a suspect, and you aren't."

"I'm not?" She felt a little of the storm in her stomach subside.

Boyd looked surprised by her response and Holdstedter answered for his partner. "No, not at all. We actually talked about it and decided you weren't stupid enough to kidnap your own employers. Seriously, who would you ransom them to?" He had pretty teeth in between his perfectly kissable lips. She pinched her thigh to get those sorts of notions out of her head.

"Funny, man. Very funny."

Boyd nodded. "He likes to think so. I like to keep him from crying, so I pretend he's right."

Holdstedter didn't look at all offended by the comment. "No, you were never a serious suspect."

"What we wanted to see you about is if you can think of anyone who would have reason to make the Listers disappear like this. Do you know if they had any enemies?"

She shook her head in an instant. "No. I mean I used to joke about them both being lawyers, but I don't think either of them ever really got into the sorts of cases where they would make enemies."

"Doesn't take much. Do you remember if either of them were working on big cases?"

"The only thing they talked about since . . . since Teddy disappeared was going after the hospital. They wanted to make them suffer for losing their baby." She looked away and had to fight hard to stop the tears. Damn, it was supposed to get easier, not harder.

Boyd moved closer and put a sympathetic hand on her shoulder. She was touched, because she really didn't think he was the type to do that with too many people.

"I know it's hard, but I just want to make sure we've got our bases covered."

"I know. I'm sorry."

"What for?" His voice was gruff when he asked. "For having feelings? Please. Even Danny over here has feelings and believe me, he's very superficial."

"My ass, your face. A match, Richie."

Kelli laughed. Both of the detectives smiled. Holdstedter winked at her. "I knew there was a smile in there somewhere. Now and then you have to dig for 'em."

"How about new people in their lives? New neighbors around here or new coworkers?"

Kelli looked over at Jason's place. "Only one I know of is Jason Soulis." She pointed to the great gray house across the street.

Boyd looked, and for just an instant she saw a shark's smile on his face. "Now, that ain't his car, is it?"

"Oh, please. No, that's Tom Pardue's car." He said the name at the same time that she did, and she looked back at the detective. "You know him?"

"Oh yeah. We're old friends. We've been buddies for years."

Holdstedter chuckled and shook his head. "You know, I think you should put him on your Christmas card list, Richie."

Boyd's eyes narrowed for a second and he nodded. "Or maybe we could pay him a visit sometime." Then he shook himself and looked back at her. "So, does Pardue visit this Soulis guy a lot?"

"No. I've never seen him over there before."

"Bet he ain't selling Girl Scout cookies." Holdstedter crossed his arms and looked at the car as if it were guilty of a dozen crimes, merely by being associated with Pardue.

"How long has Soulis been in town, Ms. Entwhistle?"

"If you're Boyd, I'm Kelli."

"How long, Kelli?"

"Around two weeks, I guess. Since the early part of October."

The two detectives nodded in unison. "Well, isn't that interesting." Boyd's question was rhetorical. He reached into his coat and pulled out a cigar. "You mind?"

She shook her head. "I like the smell of a good cigar."

"How do you figure?" Holdstedter was looking at Boyd, his smooth brow wrinkled in thought.

Boyd lit his cigar, filling the foggy air with plumes of the aromatic tobacco. "Two weeks. We've had a lot of things happening around here for the last two weeks."

Thinking back on that gave Kelli a case of the heebie-jeebies. A lot really had happened in the last fourteen or so days. Enough that she found herself wondering what had happened to her entire world in that amount of time.

Boyd and Holdstedter stared at the Camaro and nodded, saying nothing for several moments.

"Would you guys like some coffee or something?"

"Hmm? Oh, no. But thanks." Boyd looked at her. "Listen, not that you're a nosy neighbor or anything, but have you met that Soulis guy?"

"What the hell kind of name is Soulis, anyway?" Holdstedter scratched idly at his chiseled chin. "Sounds like a stage name for a bad magician."

Kelli laughed again. She thought it was weird herself.

"Scottish, I think. I read about a castle over there where they burned a Lord Soulis for witchcraft."

Holdstedter looked at Boyd as he answered; a smile grew on the taller detective's face. "Since when do you read?"

"Since your mother stopped putting out." Then Boyd got a horrified look on his face and looked toward Kelli. She was too busy laughing to pay much attention.

"I can't believe I said that in front of you." His eyes were wide and his face plastered with apology and shame.

"No, please," she waved aside his horrified look. "I needed that."

"Yeah, so did Danny's mom."

"You're a bad man, Boyd."

He nodded and smiled. He had a nice smile under all that gruff. "That's what Danny's mom always said."

"Okay, one more mom joke and I'm gonna open up with the Whalen comments."

"Okay, okay. You win. I'll leave your mom out of this."

"Smart move."

"Besides, your sister's better in bed anyway."

Kelli laughed again. It was good to laugh. She'd almost forgotten what it felt like.

VI

Tom walked around the side of the mansion and shook his head. He was proud of his house. He had a damned nice place. He could have fit about seven just like it inside the place he was circling.

Jason Soulis said he wanted to see him, and so here he was. Soulis was his favorite kind of client; he didn't make demands and he always paid upfront. So now and then he could make a house call for that sort of customer.

It was just a pain in the ass when they weren't where they said they would be. He went around to the back of the mansion, marveling still at the dark gray walls and the high gloss of the marble. He didn't figure he could make the sort of money that would be needed for a house this fine without pimping every single bitch on both college campuses. Not that he wouldn't be willing to, of course.

The back of the house overlooked the Cliff Walk, and he spotted Soulis over near the edge. The man was dressed in the sort of style that only worked for filthy rich people: He looked casual, but the clothes all had a fit that was too perfect. There was a chill in the air, but not much of one. Soulis was decked out in a suit and a greatcoat and gloves.

He stared out at the ocean as Tom approached. Before he was within ten feet of the man, Soulis waved to acknowledge his presence. "It's a beautiful day here."

Tom shrugged. It was a shitty day as far as he was concerned, but the customer is always right, unless, of course, he was wrong.

"I have a fondness for the ocean, Mr. Pardue. Forgive me my trifles."

"You wanted to see me, Mr. Soulis?"

Soulis reached into his coat pocket and pulled out a thick envelope. "For tonight."

Tom made the money disappear. He didn't bother counting it. He had no doubt in his mind that Soulis would take offense, and something about him was intimidating. He didn't like that feeling. He was used to being the one who intimidated just by being there. Soulis couldn't have cared less if Tom were waving a gun in his face. That was the feeling he got from the man.

"Thank you."

"Do you like Black Stone Bay, Mr. Pardue?"

"Yeah. It's home."

"Indeed. It's starting to feel that way for me as well."

"So, Maggie hasn't given you any troubles?"

Soulis finally turned to look at him, one dark eyebrow raised in a question. "Should she?"

"No, no, I just like to make sure everything is going the right way. I wouldn't want you dissatisfied."

"She has proven to be everything I expected."

"Good. That's good."

"You have excellent tastes in ladies."

"Maggie's something all right." He would never think of her as a lady, but if Soulis wanted to, that was his choice.

Soulis stared down at the waters, his eyes watching the waves shatter themselves against the rocks.

"Do you suppose there is any way to survive the waters here in the bay?"

"Yeah. Don't fall in."

Soulis smiled thinly. "No doubt."

"Was there anything else I could do for you, Mr. Soulis?"

"One more thing, actually. There is a policeman who's caught my attention: Brian Freemont."

The name meant nothing. "What about him?"

"I would like you to post his bail."

"I thought you said he was a cop."

"He is. He just isn't a very good one."

"What's he in jail for?"

"He is currently incarcerated for pulling his firearm on two other police officers."

"That's gonna be an ugly bail to post."

Soulis held out a much, much thicker envelope. "That should suffice."

Tom managed not to whistle. Soulis would have thought it rude and classless. Around Soulis, Tom wanted to look like he was in the big leagues. He wasn't, he just wanted to be.

"There anything else?"

"Yes. Let him sit a bit. I don't want him getting out until sunset."

He didn't ask questions. He knew better. Jason Soulis probably wasn't the sort of man who liked to have questions asked. The money went into his pants pocket.

"Mr. Pardue?"

"Yes sir?"

"Do I have to warn you about disappointing me?"

"Absolutely not."

"Good. Have a nice day."

Tom left, part of him offended by the casual dismissal and part of him happy to go. Soulis was a scary man and he didn't even try to be that way. It was power; the man had power and in abundance. He doubted there was much of anything Soulis could want and not get. Someday he intended to be in the same position.

VII

Maggie met with Jason Soulis and spent the night again. He was as imaginative as ever, and she was thoroughly sated.

Unfortunately, he was not. She lay back as he moved over her, his mouth starting at her feet and moving slowly, languidly up her legs, preceded by his hands.

Her skin felt feverish. Her breaths came in gasps. His tongue lapped at her flesh, his teeth nipped at her skin, his nails drew lines of sweet fire across her nerve endings. Her hands clenched the sheets, pulling at the tough silk and stretching it out of shape.

"God, Jason . . ." She whined; there was a point where pleasure bordered on pain and she had reached it. He kept going, crawling up her body, his mouth on her inner thigh and then higher, his hands sliding across her stomach, her ribs, moving to her breasts.

He was merciless and she hissed in pleasure, moaned in agony. And still he kept going. His body slowly worked over the contours of hers, his hands and mouth traveled everywhere, sliding over her front and sides and back as he explored.

He used her. She returned the favor. Enough was enough, and she decided to get inventive right back. He kissed. She bit. He scratched, she clawed. He thrust, she arched. He tasted, she drank. He bruised, she cut. Well before they were finished, both had begged for mercy and been granted none.

Finally, she solved a mystery. The taste she had in her mouth when all was said and done, so familiar but not common. It was blood. She drank his and he drank hers. It was intoxicating.

When the sun was almost up, she rose from his bed and dressed hastily. Her body still felt feverish, and she was in a daze. Jason watched her stand and move about, and smiled at her.

"Find a safe place, Maggie. Be with someone you can trust for the day."

"Why?"

"Trust me on this if nothing else. Find a safe place. Come to me tonight, when you want your questions answered."

Exhausted, elated, and nearly delirious, she nodded her head and left his house. The glow of the coming dawn seemed too bright to her eyes and she drove quickly, trying to keep her calm.

"Damn. I gotta start getting some sleep. This is crazy."

The roads were mercifully devoid of people. The trees were alive with the watchful eyes of crows. She found herself noticing the birds at nearly every corner, all of them intent on her, staring as if she were a succulent morsel of food.

Maggie pulled into the parking lot and barely avoided hitting another car parked in the space next to hers. The world was swimming and swaying by the time she got out of the car and started for her apartment. The courtyard seemed miles longer than it should have.

She was almost home, almost safe, when the ground lurched under her feet and she fell. The darkness was complete and silent and blissful.

CHAPTER 14

I

Ryan Harper wet himself when the gun pushed up against his face. It was a big gun, and he knew good and fucking well that Tom Pardue would use it on him in a heartbeat if he didn't get what he wanted.

"Tom?" His voice was subdued for obvious reasons. "Want to tell me what's wrong?"

"What's wrong is that all of my money is gone, Ryan." He'd never seen Pardue looking anywhere near this pissed off. "All of it. I got nothin' left and I'm feeling a little like killing someone. So you tell me who has my money, and I will pick that person to fucking kill instead of you."

"Tom, I don't know who has your money."

"Listen carefully, Ryan. Listen like your life depended on it." His teeth were bared and the acne scars on his face were glistening. Pardue's eyes were wide and furious. "You have five hours to find out who has my money, or I'm going to come back here and make you sorry we ever did business together."

Tom Pardue was not the smartest man in the world, but he had the good sense to know he wasn't. Ryan had helped him launder a lot of money over the years and been paid for it.

That also meant that Ryan was one of a small handful of people who knew how much Pardue was really worth and who had access to information about where he kept his life savings.

"Tom, listen to me. I didn't take your money, you know that, okay? I don't need to take your money and I'm not stupid enough to have you wanting me dead."

"That's why you're still alive, buddy boy. That's the only fucking reason." Tom's eyes were absolutely murderous. "You find out who did. That's all. You fuck this up, I fuck you up." He emphasized his words by running the business end of the pistol along Ryan's jaw line.

"I'll do what I can, Tom, but I'm only human."

"Be better than that. Be better than only human. You understand me?"

Ryan nodded.

"Good, because I've seen that little skirt you're with. She won't much care for you when I'm done. Shit. Do ya one better. You get this right, or you won't much care for her when I'm done, either. You get me?"

"Yeah, I get you, man. Just chill, okay? Just be calm. It'll work out. I'll find out who did it."

Tom put the gun into the back of his pants and stepped back two paces. Ryan let himself hope he might live through this.

Not fifteen feet away, Karley was making breakfast. The only barrier between them was a thin apartment wall. That she hadn't heard anything was something of a miracle.

"Five hours. That's all. Get to work."

Tom left the apartment and stormed off toward his car. Every stride he took, every gesture he made, was filled with anger.

Somebody was going to pay dearly for pissing him off. Ryan intended to make sure that someone wasn't himself.

II

Pissed didn't start to cover it. Pardue was wickedly, lividly enraged and wanted to take it out on someone. He just hadn't figured out who that someone would be. The list of people he wanted to hurt was monumental; his ability to do so was limited. There were the girls, Lord knew a few of them were giving him attitude, and he wanted it taken care of, but he could only go so far before they weren't marketable. Even what he'd done to Lizzie was pushing it a bit. She'd had to recover for two days before she could get enthusiastic with a client and that had cost him money.

Just right now, money was the root of all his woes. Somebody, somewhere, had raped his bank accounts and done it so well he was at a complete loss. The problem was that even with his money laundered in advance he couldn't exactly go to the cops and report the problem. He had a bit of a rep and he knew it was Boyd who would get the case. It was always that short little fuck who dealt with him.

He picked up his cell phone and dialed Lenny Simonson. Lenny was the only other person who could have touched his cash without all sorts of red flags going off. Lenny was also the more likely of the two when it came to being stupid. Ryan had enough money of his own and wasn't likely to get desperate, but it sure was fun putting the fear of God into him. Hell, that had about made his morning; would have made it, if Ryan could have pulled a half a million dollars out of his ass to make up for what was missing.

Ryan couldn't do that.

Lenny did not answer his phone. He also did not, for whatever insane reason, believe in answering machines. So he was going to have to do this the old-fashioned way and just pay the little bitch a visit.

Lenny was different than Ryan. With Ryan, a threat would be enough to make him work his ass off. Lenny would require a demonstration.

He wondered if Lenny's little girl had hit puberty yet. "Either way, bitch is gonna scream I don't get some satisfaction today."

Part of him hoped Lenny was guilty of something. He wanted to see the look on the asshole's face when he stuck it to his good buddy's little girl. Hell, knowing Lenny, he wouldn't have been surprised if he was doing the girl himself. Lenny liked them young. They had a good relationship for that reason; Tom could provide all the side dishes he wanted just as long as Lenny kept the books neat and orderly.

The books, by the way, were not looking at all good.

Neither was the chance that Lenny would be a happy man for much longer.

He drove, his eyes locked on the road and making sure he did the speed limit.

Outside, the crows were watching, waiting patiently. They had their own agendas and they were not sharing their secrets with anyone.

III

Kelli finished with her classes and tried to keep up the appearance that all was well in her world. She called on Marie, Rita, and Erika to help her with the kids. They all agreed, though she was sure it was mostly just to keep her company. They still thought she was crazy as a loon for staying in the house and helping out with the trick-or-treaters. She didn't care. The Listers were technically missing, not dead, and she intended to take care of the house as if they were still there.

It was all she had, anyway.

So she penciled in the time for taking care of the Halloween thing and went about her business.

Such as it was. Mostly she was coasting. She was doing that a lot these days.

When classes were finished, she thought about going home and instead decided to hit the library. She was curious now about Jason Soulis, so she decided to look into his background as much as she could.

Google and Yahoo! were her friends. She spent hours looking up the name Soulis and his full name. On Soulis she got a lot of stuff about a Scottish Lord who had been burned to death for witchcraft and for apparently kidnapping and torturing villagers to death. She also found references to dozens of people with the last name, articles on clubs, and people who were just living their lives but apparently did something noteworthy.

On Jason Soulis, she found nothing. Not a damned thing.

How the hell does someone afford a place like that and have no mention in even an occasional newspaper article online? That's just crazy. She didn't know enough about computers and searching to get far anyway, but she'd expected to find something.

As she was getting ready to leave, she saw the crows outside. Once again they were everywhere. The lawns were black with them, and they all seemed to be waiting for something. She just had no idea what it might be.

Apparently it was for her. The moment she stepped out of the building they exploded into activity, lifting into the air and taking off in a massive black cloud. Aside from the wind they generated, they were still eerily silent.

The crows. She hadn't really noticed them until Jason came to town.

It took her a few minutes to dig into her purse and find the business card, but she eventually found Richard Boyd's number and gave it a ring. He didn't answer so she left him a message. There was nothing solid, of course, but she wanted him to know about her search and about the crows for what little it was worth.

"Hey, Kelli!" She recognized the voice immediately. It was Todd Thatcher. He was one of the Phi Chi's, a rather notorious fraternity on the campus. They had the best parties, the best drugs, and the worst reputation for a frat house in the state as far as she could tell.

Still, she'd managed to go to a few of their parties in the past and always had a good time. Okay, so her ass got grabbed now and then, but she always had fun flirting with the jocks and the upperclassmen that made up the roster.

And they were smart enough to know it was just flirting. Mostly. Derek Benson wasn't smart enough. Todd had been there to prevent his refusal to accept "no" as answer from becoming an incident that would have landed her in the hospital,

Derek in jail, or both. When he tried forcing the issue, Todd slammed him into the wall hard enough to dent the plaster and then made him apologize to Kelli. Derek wasn't with the Phi Chi's anymore. He didn't go to the university anymore, either. He managed to screw up his grades too badly to stay.

"How are you, Todd?" She smiled in his direction and he came closer, a broad grin on his broad body. The boy was built like a door: big and blocky.

"I'm good. We're having a party tonight, thought you might like to come." He was trying to be casual, but it wasn't working all that well. He had a crush, and he was sweet when he wasn't being a typical guy.

"Oh, I don't know if I can." She doubted it, actually. There were tests to study for and she didn't like being away from the house after dark right now. There was something creepy about the nights lately. The nightmares probably had something to do with it. Sometimes she still thought Teddy was outside and asking her to let him in.

He looked a little crestfallen, but it was a survivable level. He pouted very well for such a big moose. "Oh, that's cool. Just wanted to let you know."

"I would if I could, Todd. But I'm so far behind on my schoolwork and I have to watch over the house for the Listers." She gave him her best apologetic look and he shuffled around uncomfortably for a second. "Maybe we could do something on Halloween? I have to take some kids out around five, but I should be done a little after seven, maybe seven-thirty."

He smiled and nodded. If he'd had a tail, it would have wagged. "Yeah, that'd be great. We're having a party that night too. This is just sort of a warm-up."

"Yeah, I was wondering why the party on a Wednesday night."

"Hey, why not?"

"So, you want to meet up?"

"That'd be great. Okay." He shuffled from one foot to the other, his hands moving like they had no idea what to do with themselves. Kelli's hands never had that problem; they flew around her body whenever she spoke.

"Okay, so I'll see you later, Todd."

"Yeah. I'll see you, Kelli."

She walked off, smiling again and thrilled. She hadn't had a chance at a date or even a party for over two months, and she needed the release.

Todd shuffled off, on his way to wherever he had been going. He was smiling, too.

They never got to go on the date. Todd was dead by Halloween.

IV

The Phi Chi boys wanted to have a party, and that meant they called on Tom. Tom was glad to accommodate. They wanted to spend enough to at least earn him the cash to make his next buy, which was going to be necessary if he wanted to stay in business.

He hadn't found Lenny, and he was on his way to Ryan's place when Doug Clark got hold of him. Doug was the big man on campus this year; top of the food chain as it were. That was good, because Doug had money and wasn't afraid to spend it.

"Yo, Tom, my man! Wassup?"

"Doug! How's business?"

"Rockin', that's why I need to get some party supplies."

"What are you gonna need, Doug?"

Doug gave him a list that was substantial and put Tom into a good mood for the first time all day. "I can do all of that, my man. Anything else?"

"Yeah, actually." He sounded almost embarrassed. Anything but extremely cocky was rare for the moron, but that was okay as long as there was money involved.

"Talk to me."

"Some of the guys were thinking a few girls could be fun. I heard you can supply some."

"Oh, I can get you girls. No problem there, but they aren't your standard hookers. We're talking high-end, quality ass."

"That's cool. How much?"

"How many guys?"

Doug paused for a moment before answering, "The whole frat."

"How many girls?"

"Maybe three or four." He was sounding a little nervous now. Three or four girls for one of the largest fraternities in the area probably meant a serious train job on the girls. They would not be happy when it was all done.

"Three will be four large. Four will be five large." They'd have to be placated, of course, but he needed the cash and there were a few girls who still thought they could push Tom to get what they wanted. It was time for them to learn otherwise.

"Better make it three then. Sky's the limit, but damn."

"I'm not kidding when I say they're the best."

"They do what we want?" Actually, there would probably be a lot of screaming and protesting, but when it was done, they'd be grateful to get back to the high-end boys who only wanted straight sex instead of a little gang action or to watch a girl take a donkey. He had shit to make the girls compliant, but there were limits.

"Oh, they might fuss a little, but they'll do it. That's what they get paid to do."

"Sweet stuff, my man."

"I'll have the girls rounded up by around eight o'clock. I'll have everything else sooner if you need it."

"The earlier the better with the supplies. Beer only goes so far."

Tom smiled. "You know what? Just for this occasion, I'm gonna drop you some Viagra. Make sure you can show the girls the time of their lives."

"Awesome! You're the man!"

"Oh yes. The one and only, Doug. Don't you forget it."

He hung up the phone and relaxed a bit. Playtime was over. He had just the three girls he wanted to use, and they would have no idea what was coming.

The one he was going to have the most fun with was Maggie. Bitch needed to learn her place. It was long overdue.

But first, he had to visit Ryan and find out what was going on.

And maybe he'd have to show Ryan's woman a good time. He was a little disappointed that he hadn't found Lenny and his little girl, but it was a small price to pay.

Lenny could wait until tomorrow if he had to. His daughter could wait, too, but the longer Tom had to wait, the worse he was going to make it for the girl.

Ryan didn't have any information for him.

He cried when Tom tied him up. He begged when Tom grabbed Karley and started giving her a work over.

Karley cried too. That made it more fun.

V

Maggie woke up a little after three in the afternoon. The window curtains were drawn tightly and she was in the exact same clothes she had been wearing the night before. She was also in Ben's bed.

She sat up and felt a slight twinge from her muscles. All in all she felt much better than she had the night before. She could hear the stereo playing in Ben's living room. Diana Krall sang softly but she didn't recognize the tune.

Maggie stretched, feeling the muscles slide under her skin in an oddly sensuous way. She stood up and looked around the small bedroom. She had been placed on top of the covers, and the only distortion of the bedclothes came from where her body had been resting. Ben had left her alone through the day.

Jason had said something to her the night before about finding someone she could trust, and she guessed that maybe she had.

She left his bedroom and immediately went for the toilet. It wasn't hard to find, as their apartments were mirror images.

After what seemed like a few eternities, her bladder stopped screaming at her and she flushed.

Not wanting to delay the inevitable, she walked toward the living room and found Ben asleep on the couch. His face was looking less swollen. On the coffee table in front of him, she spotted her shoes and her purse. Her keys were sitting slightly aside from everything else. Had she dropped them the night before? She wasn't sure, but she thought maybe she had. Ben must have gone looking for them after he found her.

The sunlight streaming through the window was annoyingly bright, but survivable, so she walked into the room and grabbed her purse, desperate for a cigarette. She didn't know if Ben was a smoker, but he had ashtrays so she made herself at home and lit up.

He stirred on the couch, but didn't wake up immediately. So Maggie finished her cigarette and then leaned in close and kissed him on the forehead. His eyes creaked open and he looked up to see her. His face managed a small smile as he sat up and looked at her, his eyes still bleary.

"Good morning, handsome." She looked at her watch. "Or good afternoon."

"Hi. You okay?"

"Never better." This was true. She felt rested and invigorated for the first time in forever.

"I was a little worried."

"Yeah, well, I don't normally pass out."

"Been a couple of rough days." There was no judgment in the tones, merely an acceptance of fact.

"Yeah, that's for sure." She sat down next to him, and he moved his legs away to let her.

"Guess I'm lucky you found me."

"Wasn't luck." He shrugged. "You knocked on my door."

"I did?"

"Well, fell against it."

"Well, thanks."

"Hey, you did it for me. Besides, I wasn't doing anything, anyway." He smiled and then covered his mouth as he yawned.

"It was still nice of you. So thanks."

Ben looked uncomfortable and shifted his weight a bit. She felt a flash of absolute hatred for Tom: the discomfort had never been there before. She looked at him and then leaned over. A quick kiss on the cheek and she stood back up.

"I should go."

He nodded and the smile on his face faded a bit. "Don't be a stranger."

"Not on a bet."

She slipped out the front door with another wave and crossed over to her own apartment. The sky was overcast, but the world still seemed too bright.

A moment later she was inside where everything was tolerable again. Just the act of walking across the courtyard left her feeling as weak as a baby.

She'd barely gotten into her living room before the phone rang. It was Tom. He needed to see her and he had a job for her that was going to pay well. She agreed to meet him just after six at his place.

It was a job. It was what she did.

But not for much longer. She just had to decide how to break it to Monkey Boy without him putting a few bullets through her head or doing something even worse that would leave her alive and ruined when he was done.

VI

Alan Tripp tore a few layers of skin away from his hand and reopened the wounds under his stitches, but he finally managed to get free of the restraint. After the first one, the rest were easy, if painful. He rummaged in the supply drawer until he found gauze and tape, and then awkwardly applied a pressure bandage.

Now all he had to do was get out of the psychiatric ward.

They were calling to him every night, just as soon as the sun set, and this time around, he intended to answer his family when they called.

They needed him, damn it, and he wasn't going to let down Avery or Meghan again.

He leaned against the wall near the only entrance into the room and closed his eyes, letting himself drift for a while. The pain was just enough to stop him from going to sleep, and when he feared that he would actually start counting sheep, he just slapped his hand against the wall. One quick explosion of pain and he was good to go again, a trick that worked every time.

Some time later, he heard the wheels on the meal cart squeaking down the long hallway. It was a distinctive noise far different from the other tables and carts the interns were rolling around. Best of all, it was usually manned by only one person.

That was important; he didn't know if he could bring himself to kill more than one.

It hadn't taken long to figure out the routine; every few hours the cafeteria worker would bring food, normally something that could be eaten with just fingers, and set it down on the ReadyServe rolling table at the foot of the bed. The table was put into position and locked in place at the height of the patient's chest, and the meal was left behind. The straps had just enough give that a patient who was limber enough could eat, even if they couldn't quite get the cloth covering their wrists to the right level for chewing through their restraints.

The less fortunate ones got spoon-fed or, in extreme cases, forced to choke down their liquefied meals with a tube down through the nose.

Alan had made sure to avoid that particular experience.

He wasn't really in the full-scale loony bin. He was "under observation" because he'd assaulted two police officers. He supposed he was lucky he hadn't gotten himself killed. But because the rooms were all full at the inn, he got put in the manger: the rooms he and four others were occupying were technically being renovated. That was okay. He could handle that.

In all honesty, it was kind of a bonus, because at least these rooms weren't equipped with cameras. He didn't know for sure, but he figured the really serious cases were kept in rubber rooms with several cameras taping their every move.

So he had a chance, at last. He could maybe get himself free from this place and get out to Meghan and Avery. He was willing to try; he was willing to die trying.

They needed him.

The wheels rolled closer and came to a stop outside his door. He waited as patiently as he could for the door to swing inward.

And when the man with the food tray stepped inside, he was ready. He was a big man, six feet, two inches tall and somewhere around two hundred and fifty pounds; most of it was muscle. The guy had shaved his head, presumably to stop patients from ripping it out by the roots. So his large, shiny skull made a perfect target. Alan pushed away from the wall and slammed his forehead into the back of the man's skull. It hurt, but it worked. The tray the man carried—paper, of course—fell from his hands and he reached back to check what had happened. As he did, Alan moved forward, too, bringing both of his fists into play and punching the poor bastard in the face and in the neck.

The bruiser hit the tile and grunted. Alan reached for him, ready to slam his face into the ground as many times as he had to in order to get free.

He never made it. The man spun on one hip and cocked back his leg. An instant later Alan had a size twelve loafer buried in his stomach and knocking him back against the wall.

"You outta your fucking head?" The man didn't talk, he growled. He also stood back up, a look of absolute rage on his face. Alan managed to duck the fist that tried to separate his face from his skull.

Alan didn't have time for any of this. He'd expected to be on his way by now and instead the damned fool was fighting him. Alan swung his left hand in a wide arc and the guy ducked under it, just in time to meet Alan's knee at the apex of its rise from the ground. Alan felt the nose give out against his kneecap and heard the man grunt, then sigh. He landed like a sack of potatoes when he fell to the ground. This time he didn't get back up or suddenly pull a Bruce Lee maneuver. Just to make sure, Alan kicked him four times in his stomach.

Then he left the room, pausing only long enough to pull the keys from the man's belt loop.

His hand was bitching and moaning about its mistreatment, and his knee was singing a similar song. Alan didn't care. He didn't have time to care.

He hopped down the hallway as best he could and looked for an exit sign. It was a hospital; they were always nice enough to have exit signs all over the place. When he found one and tried the door under it, the door was locked. The fourth key opened it. He took the key ring with him and went down the stairs as nimbly as he could manage. Graceful he was not. The knee he'd used as a battering ram was swelling, and he could actually see it happening. The sad side effect of wearing a hospital gown was that it didn't let you lie to yourself about how bad the injury was. He got to see the bruising colors as they formed.

It took him ten minutes to reach the second floor of the hospital. He let himself breathe for a minute when he got there and then he pulled the fire alarm right next to the secured door to the second floor.

Alarms started screaming shrilly and he nodded to himself. In a minute or so, the entire staff would be busy trying to find the source of the fire and while they were busy he would make his escape. He hobbled down the rest of the stairs and pushed the door open. It led to a garage just filled with cars.

He started trying handles.

VII

"I can see the headlines now," Boyd held his hands up to show the imaginary paper to Danny. "Escaped ball-buster seeks revenge against cop that did him wrong."

"Bite me."

"I figure he should be after you in no time. You're the one that got away with only one cracked nut."

"It was both, Boyd. And if he shows, I'm using you as my shield."

"You would, too. Wouldn't you?"

"Damn straight. It's why I keep you around."

"I thought that was why I kept *you* around, Danny."

"See? I always get confused about that part."

They sat down at the booth farthest back in the diner and waited for Sally to come serve them. She knew who they were and what they wanted, so she just waved and indicated she'd be there soon.

"I don't get it." Danny slipped his napkin into his lap and placed his flatware just so.

"Get what?"

"Why the guy would go all postal and break out of his room when they were planning on letting him go?"

"Because they didn't fucken tell him is why."

"How many times do I have to tell you to watch that nasty fucking language in my restaurant, Boyd?" Sally set down his burger—rare, extra onions—and Danny's fried shrimp as she spoke. The third plate, a double order of onion rings, she placed between them.

"Sally, I love you. Marry me."

"In your dreams and my nightmares, hon." She smiled as she said it.

They waited until Sally had put down the coffees and the large pot on the side before they started talking again.

"What did you find out about Jason Soulis?"

"Not much. Lived in Ohio before this, and off in California before that. Guy gets around. Mostly he likes to travel. In the last few years alone, he's hit almost every continent."

Boyd looked at him and chewed his burger slowly. "What? There was a really hot tamale at the information center?"

"What do you mean?"

"You were gone four hours and all you can find out is that he liked to travel?"

"There's nothing else to find out, Richie."

"My ass! How about where he's from? What about his date of birth? What does he do for a living? Why the fuck did he move here?"

Danny eyed him and popped a shrimp into his mouth before answering. He chewed nice and slow, too. "Oh, that stuff."

"Last nerve, Danny Boy, you're stepping on it."

"Don't get your panties in a wad." He took a sip of coffee. "Soulis was born in Europe, the records were destroyed in some bombing or other, but he lived in Scotland, Ireland, and Wales when he was a kid. He doesn't do anything for a living, because he's fuckin' rich as hell. His date of birth is among the missing, but he's supposed to be forty-five. He likes to move around because he's rich and easily bored. He bought his house from Albert Miles, who I also can't find out much about."

"Four hours of my life wasted so you could find out jack and shit."

"They weren't wasted. You had your own work to do. Tell me what you learned while I was breaking my balls for you."

"I learned that 'rush job' don't mean shit to the losers who do DNA tests. They won't have anything solid for at least another forty-eight hours." Unlike Danny, he spoke with his mouth full. He was capable of doing two things at once. "I learned that Captain O'Neill is a real hardass when he wants a problem solved and it ain't happening fast enough. I learned from a phone call that we have a lot of crows in town."

"Golly."

"Yeah, no shit, right?"

"Any new developments?"

"No. I think that's enough for one day."

"This is fuckin' stupid. What? We have a white slave ring in town now?"

"Maybe. Stranger shit than that happens all the time."

"Yeah? Like what?"

"Loch Ness Monster."

"There is no Loch Ness Monster."

"Sure, instead there are just rocks that turn people into jelly and we have a race of human lemmings sneaking out every night."

"I'm telling you, Richie, there's something about those rocks in the bay. They don't look right, they don't feel right."

"Anyway, so guess who got bailed out?"

Danny stared at him with a half-chewed shrimp in his mouth and forgot to finish chewing. His handsome model's face went red around the edges.

"You better not fuckin' say Freemont."

"So I won't say it." Boyd shrugged.

"What kind of asshole would bail that prick out of jail?"

Boyd finished attacking an onion ring before he answered. He liked to make Danny sweat. It was a cheap and easy thrill, but he would take them where he could get them.

"Does the name Tom Pardue mean anything to you?"

"You were right, Richie. We should have shot the bastard when we had the chance."

"Which bastard, Pardue or Freemont?"

"Yes."

"There's always tomorrow, Danny."

"We could go looking today."

"No, we're on the shit list. No way is O'Neill gonna approve the overtime."

"Fuck it. I ain't poppin' them for free."

"Not what you said about those stewardesses."

"Believe me, there was nothing to pop."

"Spoken like a sexist pig."

"Takes one to know one."

"Screw this. We've been running around town all damned day. I say we call it a night." Boyd covered his mouth with his napkin and belched as softly as he could. He loved onions, but they seldom loved him back.

"Yeah, that's great." Danny murdered another fried shrimp and washed it down with a gulp of coffee. "We can go on home and wake up to twice as many disappearances tomorrow. That'd be like the third night in a row."

Boyd dropped his napkin and stared hard at Danny. "I wish that was a joke, Danny."

"What?"

"That's scary shit there."

"What do you mean?"

Boyd held up a finger and thought hard. "You aren't right, but you're close. It's getting bigger. Whatever these disappearances are, it's getting bigger."

Danny looked back at him and scowled. "Well, screw this. I want a raise."

VIII

Maggie met Tom at his place, a large Cape Cod that had more class than he would ever be able to manage. It looked damned good. He still looked like a monkey.

"So what's up, Tom?"

"Not even a hello kiss?"

"Don't hold your breath."

He held the door for her, a regular gentleman. She managed not to roll her eyes and instead nodded her thanks. She was feeling better as the day grew long. That was a plus.

She'd just realized that turning her back on Monkey Boy was a mistake when she felt the needle slip into her hip.

"What the hell?"

Tom pulled back a syringe and smiled. "Just something to calm you down, baby. You've been too tense lately."

Her skin felt tender, but aside from that she didn't feel any different. "I told you when we started this that I don't do shit like that!"

Tom smiled and nodded. "This one is a surprise. Believe me, you'll thank me later."

"Fuck you. I'm out of here."

He stood back and raised his arms in surrender. She didn't like that very much either, because it meant he thought he had the upper hand. Maggie dug into her jeans pocket and pulled out her pepper spray. If this was going to get ugly, she intended to make sure she could get away.

She stormed the door and walked outside. Tom let her pass without a word.

"It's done, Tom. I'm sick of this shit and I'm sick of you. I quit."

"Maggie, don't be that way, baby. We have a long history together."

"It's done! I don't want anything more from you and you're not getting anything more from me. Over. Done. Finished."

"Well, it was fun, Maggie." He was smiling and that got her deeply worried.

"What did you do to me, Tom?"

"Nothing you won't live through."

Her knees buckled and the pepper spray fell from her numbed fingers. Before she could hit the ground, Tom was there catching her.

"See? Nothing deadly. It'll wear off in a little while." His tone was as falsely sweet as she had ever heard. "And by then, all the fun and games will be ready."

The feeling started coming back to her legs and arms, but only because the numbness was going elsewhere. It was creeping into her head, seeping through her senses like smoke through a screen door.

When Tom urged her to stand, Maggie did so without hesitation. She couldn't think of a reason not to.

She heard his words, but they didn't register clearly. They were words she would remember later, after it was too late. "You know I get a lot of my shit from Haitians, Maggie. What you just got is a mild dose of the shit they use to make zombies. Nothing permanent, but it'll keep you feeling nice and agreeable for about . . ." He looked at his watch. "Three hours."

He slid his hand under her arm and fondled her breast. Deep in the darkness, far away from her body, she wanted to scream. She was pretty sure the last thing she ever wanted to have happen to her again would involve sex with Tom Pardue.

She needn't have worried. Tom never went beyond the quick groping stage. Had she been able to think coherently on the surface of her mind, she would have realized that was because she was too compliant for his tastes right then, he preferred his sex toys struggling and crying.

Tom pressed up against her from behind and kissed the side of her face.

"We're going to a party, Maggie. And guess what? You get to be the main course."

Later, much later, she'd think about those words. When the drugs were all finished working through her system and the blood and violence of the night was done, she'd think about those words again and again.

And she would have reason to hate Tom more than she ever knew was possible.

But before then, she had a fraternity to meet.

IX

Children had a special place in Jason Soulis's mind. They always had. There was something fascinating about their youth and vitality. They were often sweet, sometimes vicious, and always so eager to explore new things. He loved those traits in the people around him.

Ideally he would have had only children, but he had to take what he could get. All of them were young, none much older than their late teens, and all of them were doing their very best to get wasted on alcohol. Their best was quite sufficient. The group had gathered in a clearing not too distant from his home and his birds had told him exactly where they were. He couldn't have been more pleased.

They'd been imbibing for quite a while, and there was little struggle as a result. The hardest part was getting them back to his house without being seen, and he had learned many tricks to cover that department over the years.

An hour after sunset, they were where he wanted them, and surrounded by his children.

"Can we go out tonight?"

"No. I have brought you your food."

"Please? It's always dark here."

"It's for the best. You won't much like the light anymore."

One of them tried. One of them almost always felt they had to try. He let the fool cover a few dozen feet and then moved to intercept the escape effort.

She cried when he struck her, and whimpered along the cold stone floor.

"I said no, my child. Not tonight."

"But why?" She was so sweet in her innocence.

"Because tonight is special. Tonight you will earn a new master."

They hissed, uncomprehending.

"Enough. I've brought you your feast. Eat and be happy with what you have. All will be explained in time."

They fell upon the teenagers he'd found for them, ravenous with the needs of their still-changing bodies. Most of them were still too new to hunt on their own.

Jason left them, walking back to his home and listening to the sounds of the youngsters as the alcohol failed to completely numb their senses.

Now he had to wait.

It was time, and Maggie was due to come into her own.

He had heard the conversation between the detectives in town—his birds had ears as well as eyes—and was surprised that they caught on as quickly as they did. That was the real reason that his children were not allowed out of their home.

The detectives were closer to thinking things through than he wanted them to be, and he wanted to throw them off.

Besides, Maggie would likely do more than double the numbers if everything went the way he suspected it would.

Maggie was suffering in darkness at the moment, her mind numbed by that fool who sold her services.

But the drug would wear off, and when it did, she would come into her own. She would be a magnificent animal and she would awaken to a radically different world.

And she would awaken hungry.

Soulis smiled as he heard a distant siren wail; it mingled well with the screams from below.

CHAPTER 15

I

There are only a few days until Halloween, and I couldn't care less about a costume. How sad is that? The thought crept into Ben's head while he was supposed to be working on more homework.

Damned near everything was depressing him tonight. What wasn't depressing him was leaving him agitated and annoyed. It was one of those days; he was restless and he was lonely and he wanted to have a life beyond his apartment.

A part of it was frustration. A big part. Sometimes being a decent human being sucked raw eggs. There was no way in hell that he would ever take advantage of an unconscious woman, but the reptilian part of his brain was kicking the crap out of his morals and had been since the early morning when he answered the door to find Maggie outside.

He was not a big man and accepted that he never would be, but carrying Maggie into his apartment had been easy enough. She couldn't weigh much more than a hundred and fifteen tops. He was guessing, of course, because he had no clue about how much a girl her height should weigh. At any rate, he'd managed to get her inside without killing himself or even straining any muscles.

Maggie put her arms around his neck and held on to him when he carried her back to his bedroom. Her pulse was fast and her skin was pale enough that she looked like porcelain. He set her down on his bed and fretted, unsure about whether or not he should call for an ambulance.

"Maggie? Should I call someone? A doctor maybe?"

"No. No, I just need to rest." She had barely even moved her lips. He nodded, looking at her closed eyes and knowing that she couldn't see the gesture. Somehow it failed to register. Common sense had flown out the window and didn't seem inclined to come back home.

He watched her fall into a deep sleep, and caught himself looking at her body as she lay prone on his bed.

For just a minute, he gave serious thought to taking advantage of the situation.

He left the room before he could act on any impulses.

Then he went outside to gather her purse and her shoes. He spotted her car keys halfway across the courtyard and got those, too.

Her possessions were almost worse than seeing her on his bed. That obnoxious little voice kept telling him it was okay to look through her personal possessions, that she wouldn't mind at all. It told him that there might be indications of a medical condition, or possibly signs that she had taken something illegal that she was having a bad reaction to. It whispered a hundred different reasons why it would be perfectly fine with Maggie if he violated her privacy.

Just to distract himself, he went back to check on her in his bed. She did not sleep peacefully. She moaned from time to time and she whined, and damned near every sound that came out of her mouth could have been taken as something sexual.

And damned near every thought that went through his head involved taking advantage of the situation.

When he couldn't take it anymore, he left his own apartment and paced out in the courtyard for close to two hours. He kept himself busy until physical exhaustion finally got the better of him and then he went back inside and dropped on the couch. The next thing he knew, Maggie was waking him up.

That had been torture. She was smiling and he wanted so much just to kiss her, to touch her. Any contact at all. So she made it worse by sitting next to him.

After she'd left his apartment, he went back to his bedroom and passed out on the covers, surrounded by her scent. When he woke up, the sun was on its way down for the night. His entire body seemed ready to explode.

So, yes, part of his dilemma was frustration; he'd had what could have potentially been a perfect situation for taking advantage of her, and had let it slip away.

Fifteen minutes of fun would never ease the guilt. That was what it came down to. She was more than a physical desire. She was someone he wanted to know and be friends with. She was someone he loved to see and to talk to, when his fucking emotions weren't going into overdrive.

So he'd done the right thing and that was how he would always look at it. But there was something else, too. Something about the situation he'd been in had triggered a response in him that had nothing to do with love, or sex, or even wanting to be her friend.

Deep inside his chest there was a burning, gnawing dread growing: something was going to happen to Maggie, and there was nothing at all he could do about it.

Shit, what could I do? I don't even know her cell phone number.

So instead of worrying about Maggie, a process that would surely drive him half insane if he let it, he thought about his childhood and how much he'd enjoyed Halloween as a kid.

Everything was simpler back then: his mother and father were still in the picture when he was still young enough to trick or treat. It wasn't until later that his family had fallen to pieces. He hadn't had to worry about anyone but himself, and even that burden had been shouldered by his parents.

Ben got off his couch and went back to his room and dressed himself in presentable clothes. He had no idea where he planned to go; only that he had to get there.

Something bad was going to happen. He could feel it. The thing that mattered to him was making sure that whatever happened, Maggie was still safe.

Ben left the apartment at ten minutes before eight. The sun had already set and the world seemed darker as a result of the heavy fog.

Ben started walking, trusting his instincts to tell him where he needed to be.

II

The girls were in the back of his van, all nice and cozy. Just thinking about what they were in for made Tom feel good about life. He wished he could stay around and film it, but there just wasn't enough time in the day.

Lenny had finally called him back, and it was time to get down to business. First though, he had a delivery to make.

He pulled up in front of the fraternity house and shut off the van. Doug Clark was waiting with a few other guys. They were practically dancing from foot to foot.

"Boys . . . nice night for a party, isn't it?" Tom climbed out of his seat and smiled at them. It was always best to smile for the paying customers. Especially when he considered what they were paying.

Clark handed him a heavy wad of cash. There is polite and then there is stupid: Tom decided to be rude and count it in front of the boys. "Looks like everything's here." He smiled at Doug. "I want to go over the ground rules."

"There are rules?" He sounded disappointed.

"Oh, yes. Definitely. Follow them, and I won't have to get all nasty about anything." He stepped closer to Doug and the college boy got a little nervous. It was best to make certain points in advance. "They're simple rules and they won't stop your fun. But obey them."

"First rule: Condoms. Use them. They're for your own safety." He looked at the gathered guys. "You all know where your buddies have been dipping their wicks. Do you really want to catch what they've probably got?" A few of them laughed. "That rule is so-so. If you break it, I'll forgive you."

"Next rule: Do not break the merchandise. Have fun, guys, but remember these girls belong to me. If I can't use them when you're done, I'm going to have to find new girls. I don't like finding new girls. So no cutting, no beatings, no hot wax or nipple clamps."

"That all?" Doug seemed okay with the rules.

Tom opened the back door of the van and urged the girls out. They were still in a stupor. "Almost. This is the last rule and don't think I'm kidding when I say this, because I'm not. Top quality is what I promised and top quality is what I deliver." He paused as Lizzie, Maggie, and one of his new girls, easily recognized by the boys in the frat house, stepped out and stared wherever their heads were turned.

Doug stepped forward and whispered in his ear, "Dude, these girls are hot, but they're all fucked up."

"Relax, it'll wear off soon. Just wanted to make sure they were in the mood to play."

"They won't call the cops or anything, will they?"

"No. Now shut up and let me finish my speech." Tom spoke louder when Doug nodded. "You probably know every one of these fine ladies." The boys were nodding and very, very pleased. "You get to have your fun tonight. They're yours. You guys want to talk about this later, that's great." Some of them looked like they wanted to go tell a few tall tales about what they'd done when it was all over; most looked like they'd already started having second thoughts. They'd still go through with it, they were guys and they wanted what the girls had to offer, but they weren't ever going to tell anyone about what happened tonight; shame would stop the majority of them. He made sure he looked at the ones who wanted to sing in the choir when he finished his speech. "I have a few snitches just about everywhere, guys. They're paid well to keep me informed of what's going on. If I ever hear that any one of you has ever mentioned what happens here tonight and used the names of one of my girls in the same sentence, I'll kill you." He spoke calmly, but clearly and if he had to guess, he was getting his message across. The one who looked like he was still having troubles with the idea was the one he focused on next. He walked over to the kid. He was skinny as a rail and looked like the only way he was ever going to get laid was by paying for it. "I'll do it slow, too. My girls have to go to this school, too, and you never talk about what happens here and you never mention their names. That's part of the deal I made with them." He jabbed his finger into the kid's sternum and watched him wince. "You never even look at them funny in class. You want to talk to them, you're as polite as you would be in church. You like what you get tonight and want to do it again, you call me and we make arrangements."

The kid was flinching a bit, and that was good, but he still wasn't quite scared enough, so Tom got in his face. He was close enough that he could count the eyelashes on his reflection in the kid's eyes. "You understand me?" His voice was an arctic breeze when he spoke again.

"Yeah. I mean, yes sir." Now he believed the kid would follow the rules.

"Good. They're all yours. I'll be back around one in the morning to pick them up. Make sure they have all of their clothes."

Tom climbed back into the van and started the engine as Doug took Maggie by the arm and started leading her toward the house. "Oh, and Doug?"

"Yeah?" The man looked back at him, a little worried.

"Have a good time. Don't worry if they scream, just turn the music a little louder." He smiled and Doug smiled back.

Then Tom was driving away. Oh yes, they would learn their lessons. It had been easily three years since he'd worked out a frat party like this one, but the girls came back with a lot less attitude and worked just fine when it was all said and done.

Except for Sarah. Sarah had been a little too roughed up by the time the boys were done with her. Not physically, because the frat had played by the rules. Emotionally. Something about her fiancé being one of the frat brothers had just ruined her.

She'd killed herself a few days later. When they found her, she'd been sitting in a dried pool of her own blood. She'd written the word WHORE across her chest with a razor and then slit both wrists.

Sometimes he still missed her. She was feisty and liked to try to slap back when he started in on her.

He wondered idly if one of the girls from this party would crack that badly. "Maybe Liz. She's close to burning out anyway."

He turned on the radio and drove on autopilot. He had to get home. Lenny was supposed to be waiting for him. So was Lenny's little girl.

III

Danny had just climbed into bed when the phone rang. "Better be good," he answered as he lifted the receiver. The digital alarm clock reminded him in bright, cheery letters that it was just after nine P.M.

"It's better than good."

"Jesus, Richie, I was actually gonna sleep tonight."

"Not anymore. Get your ass out of bed."

"Are you serious?"

"Danny, you're whining. You sound like a baby when you do that."

"You sound too happy. What happened?" He sat up in the bed and reached for his pants. They were already dirty, but he didn't care.

"My buddy made a mistake." Oh yes, Boyd was sounding far too happy.

"Who? Tommy?"

"Who else? Get dressed. We're gonna go bust his ass."

"You're lucky. I've been wanting a good reason to slap him around. He *is* gonna resist, right?"

"Hell yes, he's gonna resist. Danny Boy, I can bet he'll resist all over the place."

"Good, 'cause as much as I love you like a brother, I ain't getting dressed if he isn't resisting."

"You can arrest him just as good in your pajamas."

"Joke's on you. I don't wear pajamas."

"Please tell me you wear something."

"I could, but I'd be lying." He slipped the pants over his bare skin. He didn't have time for underwear.

"Next time, lie to me."

"You say the sweetest things."

"Fuck you. Get dressed. I'm at your door in ten minutes, Danny."

Boyd hung up on him.

Danny met him outside seven minutes later. Boyd had brought coffee. Lots of coffee.

"So what's the scoop?"

"You ready for this?" Boyd was smiling a lot. It was a smile of pure piss and vinegar joy.

"Yeah, shoot."

"So I get home, take care of the esses." *Esses* was Boydese for shit, shower, and shave; along with sleep and sex, he figured they were all Boyd needed for true happiness. The sex part and the sleep part were rarities. "And I get a phone call from Newton over at the precinct. He knows I've got a hard-on for Pardue."

"Richie, everyone knows you've got it bad for Pardue."

"Whatever. Shut up and let me finish. Okay, so he calls me up and tells me he's got some interesting stuff for me. Seems our buddy went looking to find out about who might have stolen all of his money."

"Getouttatown." Danny's face split into a gigantic grin. "Somebody stole his money?"

"Not just somebody, Danny Boy." Boyd was nodding his head like a bobble head Taco Bell mascot. "Seems somebody with a few computer tricks hacked into all of his accounts and made his life savings go away."

Danny slapped the dashboard as he laughed, narrowly missing spilling hot caffeine all over his lap. "Oh, that little fucker. I gotta send him roses."

"Yeah, you know he was pissed the other day. I guess he got his revenge. And roses? Screw roses, I'm gonna buy him a night with your sister."

"He did look like he needed to get laid."

"Yeah. Anyway, there's a college boy named Ryan Harper. Seems he's done stuff for Pardue in the past."

"Yeah, I know the name. Small change, trying to keep his nose clean since he did six months."

"Yeah, that one. Whatever he did for Tommy, it was the sort of thing that made Pardue figure he might have stolen from him or know how to get in contact with the thief. So Pardue threatened him and his girlfriend."

"And?"

"He carried out his threats. Pardue didn't think he'd go to the cops, what with him being involved in criminal activities himself. I guess he doesn't get that some things are more important than being outside a jail cell."

"Pardue wouldn't." Danny shook his head. "How bad is the girlfriend?"

"Bad enough, but she'll recover." The smile had left Richie's face. He took poorly to people getting hurt. "Anyway, Harper pressed charges and so did the girl."

"And we get to make the bust?"

"Oh yeah, baby. We're the ones."

"I'm glad you woke me up after all. Now I'm all tingly and excited."

"Don't go there. I don't need to think about you that way."

"My sister's number is area code—"

"Shut up. Dickhead."

"Oh, now you're just being bitchy."

IV

The boys were beyond excited. They were also discreet. There was a party going on and a lot of girls had already been invited to attend, but tonight was a special occasion, because Ray Lima, one of their own, was twenty-one today. Ray was the pet bookworm; he was also a confirmed virgin and needed to be placated from time to time. So it was party time and they decided to send Ray off in a big way. Three women, all class, and as a bonus, they got to have fun when he was done with his business. In the meantime, there were girls downstairs to talk to and enough booze to make even the ugly ones seem interesting for a few hours.

Doug Clark was done setting everything up. Three rooms had been prepared and each of them had little but a bed in it. They were normally guest rooms for when the partying got too rough. Tonight, anyone passing out had to stay elsewhere.

Tom Pardue was a god. He wanted to be just like the supplier when he got older, only not so ugly. The erection he was sporting felt like it might go away sometime next week and he wanted to score hard with all three of the girls. Hell, he'd tried to score with each of them in the past and had been shot down. Now he would get his wish and that was just gravy.

But Ray got to go first. That was the rule. After tonight, Ray would be a little less awkward around the girls.

He slapped Ray on the shoulder and smiled. "Go get some, Ray."

The way the kid was acting, you'd think he'd asked him to suck off a shotgun. "Dude, it's all good. They're paid and they're yours. Go have fun and no one will ever hear about it. Okay?"

"You sure, Doug?"

"Yeah, man. Go have fun."

He walked to the first room like a condemned man, while several of the guys made sure no one came up and ruined the surprise.

Ray spent a good fifteen minutes in the room with Liz Montclair. When he came out he was grinning like a baboon. Doug winked to him while several of the guys made comments and cheered him on. Next up was Maggie Preston. The original ice queen and now he knew why she was always so distant.

The second Ray entered Maggie's room, Doug went for Liz's. He made it first and closed the door. Liz was looking a little sleepy, but she was willing and he was definitely able.

He took his time and went for the trifecta. When he was done, he'd forgiven Liz for dissing him all those times.

Lloyd Tanner was after him and left the door open. Lloyd

liked to put on a show; before much time had passed, half the guys were in there with him and they probably weren't waiting.

Someone was moaning long and loud in Maggie's room, and it sounded like it was Ray.

He was just starting to grin at the thought of what she was probably doing to him when the screams started.

V

Maggie came to full consciousness with a complete stranger groping her left breast and trying to shove his hand into her panties. Whoever he was, he'd already rolled her jeans down to her mid-thigh level.

"What the hell?" She grabbed his hand and pulled it away from her underwear. He flinched as if he'd been slapped, but his other hand was still kneading away at her breast.

"Get away from me!" She slapped his other paw aside and started pulling her jeans back up.

Then the pain hit. Deep, dark pain that started in her skull and ran through her entire body. It wasn't incapacitating, just annoying.

So was the guy standing in front of her with his mouth open and his pants around his ankles.

"You, you're bought and paid for. I can do what I want to do."

"You come near me and I'll hurt you. I shit you not."

He wasn't looking like all of the circuits in his head were working. The erection in front of him had probably taken too much of his blood. He came for her again and tried to cop a feel.

There was no thought in the action, merely reflex. Maggie backhanded him and watched in shock as he spun a half circle and fell down on the ground.

The pain flared again, growing in strength. With each wave of rising discomfort, her anger grew as well.

Monkey Boy had done this. Tom had gone too far. The

twerp got back up and stared, shocked at her. "You hit me."
His eyes were wide and outraged and she could tell he was on
something. Every time some asshole around her decided to
start frying brain cells, he seemed to want to come after her.

"I told you to stay away."

"Fuck you. You're my birthday present." He seemed to
think that made everything all right. What he didn't understand was that she wasn't in the mood for him or anyone else
to touch her. The pain was annoying now and getting worse.

"You stay away from me and we'll get along fine. You can
go get a refund, loser."

"No. I want you."

"I. Don't. Care."

He didn't listen and came for her again. The anger bloomed
inside of her, dwarfing the pain that gnawed at her. Her hand
reached out and caught him by the neck, blocking his attempts.
He slapped her across the face in an attempt to make her let go.

Maggie saw red; deep, dark red that washed the rest of the
colors from her vision. Perhaps it was whatever Tom had
slipped her, or maybe it was something else, but whatever it
was, it felt good.

The kid slapped at her again, and she caught the hand,
squeezing until she felt his fingers snap like twigs under her
grip. He let out a moan of pain, and Maggie smiled.

"Never touch me again." She leaned in close and whispered the words in his ear. He smelled of sex and lust and
sweat and fear.

The pain inside her reacted to the smell, surging and driving the rage to an even higher level.

The kid tried to break away and she squeezed hard, his neck
almost collapsing and his hand shattering under the pressure.
This time, the sound he made was a scream of pure agony.

She liked it.

The red took over then. The red became everything. The
door to the room opened and she saw faces looking in. She
knew them. They went to school with her. They were faces in
the crowd, men who had tried and failed to woo her in the

past. Men who, in the long run, wanted only what the broken boy she was holding wanted.

Blood ran from the boy's ruined hand and she caught the scent of it. The pain became a gnawing thing that devoured nerve endings and ripped across her mind and body alike.

She acted without thought and licked at the stain of deepest, richest red in her field of vision. That taste, so like what she had tasted the night before on the body of Jason Soulis, entered her mouth and invigorated her.

The trickle from her boy's hand wasn't enough: it didn't whet her appetite as much as ignite it.

She bit his throat and felt his skin break, felt the hot flow of ecstasy run into her mouth and across her chest and face. The others were looking at her and screaming now, making noises that she hated, that distracted her from her pleasures.

There was a part of her that watched all of what happened with complete detachment. It observed on a nearly clinical level as she dropped the skinny boy and moved toward the door.

She was really much faster than she should have been. The people around her moved like they were suspended in amber, trying to swim through solid matter to get away from her.

Doug Clark was the first one. He had always looked at her as if she was nothing but an object, always talking nice and smooth while staring at her chest.

Yes, she knew his kind. "You want something, Doug?"

He backed away, his eyes wide and horrified. She knew she must be a mess; the blood that covered her face and front was probably leaving a trail down to the floor.

Doug looked at her hard, his expression a blend of terror, lust, and confusion. She pulled him close and kissed him, smearing the remains of his friend over his face as well as her own. Damnedest thing, she could tell he was terrified, but she could feel his erection pressing against her. On a whim, she reached down and gave him a squeeze. Something wet and red happened in his pants.

She kissed harder as he pushed against her, beating at her

shoulders and chest with closed fists. Maggie bit into his face, ripping through flesh and tongue, knocking teeth aside as she drew the blood into her mouth.

That detached part of her was horrified by the carnage, but it kept watching. It saw her drop Doug Clark's remains on the ground and turned with her as she eyed the rest of the boys standing around.

Maggie grinned and moved; the taste of red filling her and driving her on harder. She had a sense of urgency, a certainty that things needed to happen faster.

She also had an appointment to keep with Monkey Boy. Even as she cut through the people around her, even as the boys ran from her and tried to escape, she knew she had to leave soon.

Five naked men came out of the room on her right. She could see a girl in there curled up on the bed and crying softly. Liz. Her name was Liz. She was one of Tom's girls, too. The rage grew hotter, the world grew redder.

They backed up and tried to stop her by slamming the door in her face. She pushed the door aside with ease and knocked three of them across the room with the same push of her arm.

Liz screamed.

The boys in the room screamed.

Maggie screamed too, but hers was a bellow of hatred.

The screams went on inside the fraternity house for quite some time, masked by the sound of a loud stereo blaring.

Several people got out of the house and tried to reach safety.

Jason Soulis, waiting in the darkness, made sure that none of them got away.

Her sounds were a symphony to him. She walked through the building in a wave of blood and fury, leaving bodies wherever she went.

So many bodies.

Young and fresh and his now.

Maggie came out of the fraternity house drenched in crimson stains. Her chest heaved in great gasping breaths and her eyes were nearly insane.

She did not see him. She had eyes only for one man, one purpose at the moment.

She hissed the name like a curse and moved away from the charnel house she'd created. "Tom . . ."

She was perfect, a creature of pure instinct. He guided her, letting her see what she could do with simple mental pushes. Maggie took four steps forward, from a run to a walk, and lifted into the night air. She was gone in moments, leaving Soulis behind in the shadows. He worked quickly, gathering the bodies and moving them to a safe spot.

CHAPTER 16

I

Brian Freemont paced around his house like a caged animal. He could leave, he could go anywhere he wanted to inside the town limits, but he wasn't exactly sure that he was willing to risk it.

There were too many things in the woods. He didn't want to run across any of them.

He looked around his house and shivered. Those pricks, Boyd and Holdstedter, had laughed when they found him. They'd looked down and laughed while he was crying. That was after they got done looking disgusted.

He didn't get it. He'd made a very small mistake, okay, he could see them being pissed off about the whole drawing his gun thing. He would have been, too, but they were still all cops and he was still one of them.

They wouldn't have treated anyone else that way, like a common criminal.

Then again, not everyone was under suspicion for murder.

No, that can't be right. If they had any real evidence they'd have already booked him, and the chance of him getting out on bail for murder was none around these parts. There might be some places where it happened, but Black Stone Bay was not one of them.

So it was all just them being pricks.

He hated Boyd and Holdstedter with all the passion of an infant getting hurt for the first time. The pain came more from the sense of betrayal than from the actual deed.

All that, and the nightmares he'd been having every time he tried to sleep, was making him positively cranky.

The nightmares; he shivered just thinking about them. They were a repeat of what had happened in the woods, but worse, because he saw what was after him.

In the darkness, when he was all alone, they came from everywhere. They were young, mostly, the women he'd taken advantage of, the ones he'd forced to have sex with him. And they were always beautiful or at least cute. He had his standards, after all.

But when they came back for him in the darkness, they were less than lovely. Moving like nothing human could move, crawling along the trees and slithering through long grass in ways that shouldn't have been possible. They looked human enough, but their eyes were rolled back in their heads and the whites glowed with a silvery light. Their faces were pale and dead and almost completely incapable of expression, but he could still sense their hunger.

The dream always ended with them crawling toward him and touching his body while he was frozen and unable to help himself. Oh, he'd beg, he'd cry and whine and ask for mercy a hundred times. They didn't care, didn't react, save to flash lascivious grins and lick their lips with cold, dead tongues.

They would open their mouths to feed, and he would wake up, his heart ready to explode inside his chest and his breaths coming in ragged gasps.

It wasn't once or twice. It was every fucking time he closed his eyes. The thought wouldn't leave him alone.

He'd never seen what was coming for him in the woods. Boyd and Holdstedter had come back before they ever came into view clearly enough for him to see them.

He was grateful for that at least; he still would have loved to watch the two men suffer. He'd seen pictures of Danny's sister. She looked like a supermodel. He smiled at the thought of ever getting his hands on her. *Bet Danny would be pissed. Bet he'd go crazy. Man, I might have to see about finding her address.*

Boyd was different though. If Rich Boyd had any family, he hid them away well. Still, he knew how he could hurt the man. Nancy Whalen would do in place of a family member.

I don't get it. Why hasn't he bagged her yet? I know he wants to. I know she wants him to, so why not? I mean, it can't just be because she's married, can it?

He didn't have time to answer the question. The noises started up before he could give Boyd and Whalen another thought.

They started near the roof. The sounds were soft and chaotic, slow scratching noises that could almost have been a squirrel stuck in the eaves, but he knew better. They were too even and paced for that. The chaos came from the fact that it was more than one set of claws scratching at the shingles above his head.

Like they're digging for something.

Like they're digging for me.

The scraping noises moved, shifting, sliding down the sides of the house. He ran to the front door, to the light switches there, and flipped them all on. Light splashed across the lawn and woods. White, fearsomely bright Halogen lights sprayed the world in vibrant colors and drove away the darkness.

Brian heard a feminine giggle above his head.

"You shut up! Shut the fuck up and go away!" His throat felt strained from the shriek, hot and scratchy in an instant.

The giggling continued and spread out. There were at least four of the damned things on his roof now, and the noises became more frantic.

He paced, trying to decide what he should do. He couldn't call the police, because he was the police. How would it look to the guys if he couldn't even handle a few scary noises?

But he couldn't. Not really. The fucking sounds were driving him crazy.

"I've got a gun! I've got three of them! I'll shoot if I have to!" Epiphany. He did have guns, and he had ammo. He went to the closet in the master bedroom and quickly unlocked his gun safe. Inside he had one .44 Magnum revolver, one .357 Magnum pistol, and one 12-gauge shotgun.

He was just starting to put the bullets in the revolver when the power went out. From outside he could hear a loud, crackling buzz for a moment and then he saw a brilliant flash of sparks cascade down past the bedroom window an instant before the power died.

"Oh fuck me . . ."

"Briiiiannnnnn . . ." He recognized the voice, of course. He'd been married to her for a few years and had dated her for almost four years before they were married.

Brian turned to the window and saw a blur of a pale white face and long, dark blond hair outside. A second later a hand slapped the glass hard enough to make it vibrate and slowly dragged across it, leaving behind a heavy trail of wetness that smeared through the dirt on the exterior of the window panes. A moment later, it too was gone.

"Briiiaannnn . . . come out and play with me, baby . . . I'm lonely . . ."

"Angie? Is that really you?"

"Brian . . . baby . . . where were you? I was waiting for you outside. I was waiting and you didn't show up . . ."

"Angie, you're scaring me . . ." His voice broke. God, to hear her talking to him caused a war of emotions. He missed her, deeply and dearly, but she sounded so cold, so mocking, and the hand he saw was too pale to ever be hers.

While he was looking at the window, he saw thick streamers of hair slide down from above. There was no light to see clearly; he couldn't make out the face that slid into view, save for the eyes and their odd, silvery reflection. Whoever was out there had to be hanging above the window to look in from that angle. Dead white hands touched the glass again, pressing against it until the fingerprints flattened slightly and the face came lower, revealing little more than a shadow.

Angie's voice came from the shape, calm and sweet and teasing. "Remember when we met, baby? The dirty things you used to whisper to me when we were fucking?"

Brian expelled the air from his lungs and sucked in a breath, his entire body sweating.

"Angie, baby, you have to go away. I can't deal with you right now."

"Ssshhhhhhh. Don't go being mean now, baby. I miss you." That little pout she'd put in her voice when she wanted him was there, teasing and taunting as she slid still lower, her full breasts hanging down. She wore no clothes, and he remembered finding them on the porch. Whoever had taken her had torn the clothing from her body. He remembered that, too.

"Angie, please . . . go away. I don't want to hurt you. Come back tomorrow, okay? I can be brave by then, I know I can. I can be brave for you." He was crying silent tears that ran down his face and spilled across his chin.

"Can't you love me like you used to, baby?" She sounded so sexy, she always sounded sexy when she was in the mood.

"Angie, I'll shoot if I have to." He snorted back the drips from his nose and shook his head to get the tears out of his way. His fingers fumbled the last of the bullets into the .44.

Brian looked through burning eyes and studied his wife where she hung suspended above the bedroom window.

He didn't know if he could pull the trigger. After all the arguments and the disappointments, all the times she'd said she had a fucking headache and all the times he'd cheated on her, he still wasn't sure. He loved her. He did. He just couldn't always show it the way she wanted him to.

He took aim at her shadowy form. "Go away, Angie, I mean it. I'm sorry if I hurt you, baby, but you have to go away now."

"I know you're sorry, baby . . ." That sultry, pouting tone was still there.

"Please go away." He was crying again and his hands were trying to shake.

"But Brian . . . this time it's not enough. This time 'sorry' won't cut it."

Her hands pushed and the glass from the window exploded into the bedroom, raining down in jagged blades. Brian pulled the trigger six times, his wrists bucking from the recoil. Thunder ripped apart the night and blasts of fire lit the room in lightning flashes.

He saw the first bullet hit, saw the way her head slammed backward as the lead punched through her skull.

The second shot ripped through her collarbone and blew out a chunk of her back.

The third hit her right breast.

The fourth shattered two ribs on its way through her body.

Then she was falling, and the fifth struck the swell of her stomach where their unborn child rested.

The sixth bullet missed her completely.

She fell out of his sight and he heard her hit the boards of the wraparound porch.

"Oh fuck, Angie, baby, why did you make me do it?"

He got up and moved toward the ruined window, trying to swallow his heart and to get back his hearing. The gun trembled wildly in his hands and he moved as quickly as he could, weapon held at the ready. It was empty, but that didn't register.

He had to climb onto the bed and move to the headboard to look out the window.

Angie stood up and looked at him from inches away. Shadows blurred her face, but he recognized her just the same. He would know her face anywhere, even with the hole that was dripping blackness all over her white features.

Angie smiled, her faintly blue lips peeled away from her teeth, baring them in a leering, savage expression. "Sorry's not enough, Brian. Never again."

Her hand lunged through the window and slapped him across the cheek. The impact made him see stars and knocked him completely off the bed.

He felt numb and dazed, and it took him almost a minute to recover.

When he was able to move again, Angie was gone. He

would have believed it was a nightmare, but the window was still broken and his cheek was bleeding from where she'd struck him.

Brian Freemont sat on the floor of his bedroom and looked at the darkness beyond his window. There was nothing to see but darkness. He rocked back and forth, moaning deep in his chest.

II

Ben had no idea where he was going, only that it was imperative that he get there. He ran a good portion of the way, homing in on the need that filled his body.

Maggie needed him. Nothing else mattered. When he could no longer reach his destination walking, he backtracked to the apartments and got into his car, the agitation blooming in his stomach, filling him with nervous energy.

"Maggie . . . Maggie . . . where the hell are you?" The radio was too loud so he shut it off, making himself listen for the sound of her voice. Instead he heard the crows, wild and raucous as they flew into the night air, hundreds of them cawing and cackling into the night.

They flew around his car, soaring in graceful arcs, gliding on currents and peering through his window, yet not one of them blocked his path. It took a while for him to understand, but they were guiding him, their mass of bodies shifting and focusing his direction with subtle shifts in the tunnel they formed around him.

He'd be afraid later. Right now, if the birds wanted to help him get where he needed to be, he would let them. He saw several people staring at the black cloud of birds around him. Many simply looked on, slack-jawed. Others backed away, shaking their heads.

Ben ignored them and so did the crows. For whatever reason, they were all on the same mission.

"I'm coming, Maggie. Just don't get yourself killed in the meantime."

III

Tom was getting bored now. Lenny broke too easily and cried like a fucking baby in need of a diaper change. Seeing as he'd shit himself almost fifteen minutes ago, that was fair.

"Lenny, where's my money?"

"Honest to God, Tom. I don't know." He was still capable of using his voice, so Tom knew he hadn't gone too far.

His little girl, Renee, was in the next room. She was watching TV, because Tom didn't want her screaming all the way through the torture session with her father.

"Shame if I have to do something to Renee, Lenny. She's a pretty girl." He shook his head and frowned for the bloodied man in front of him. "I'd hate to have to change that."

What was that? A little glimmer of anger in Lenny's eyes. Was there still a spark somewhere in there that wanted to fight? He hoped so. "Don't you touch her, Tom. I told you everything I know."

"How can I be sure of that, Lenny? I mean, where were you all day that I couldn't get a hold of you?"

"I told you, Maureen needed tests. There's something wrong with her heart."

"She's too young to have heart troubles, Lenny. Come up with a better excuse."

"She's got congenital heart disease! Let me go home and I'll bring you the motherfucking papers!"

"You're not going anywhere until I get back my money!"

"I don't have the money, Tom! How many times do you want me to say it!"

"Lenny, the walls are soundproofed, but let's not test that, okay?"

"You can't hurt my little girl, Tom. I'll find the money for you. I'll fucking steal it myself, but you can't hurt my little girl." He was starting to cry again. Pathetic.

"Lenny, I'm a good sport. I'll give you until midnight to find my money. You have it for me by then, Renee gets to have a nice, safe sleepover. You don't . . . do the math."

Lenny looked almost ready to kill him. The restraints might have slowed him down.

"It's your choice, man. I want my money back. There are only a few people who know the right information to steal it. I already checked with the other one." He smiled and shrugged his shoulders. "He didn't have a daughter, but his girlfriend was nice and tight."

Tom moved over closer, until he could look into Lenny's swollen eyes. "I'm gonna let you go now, Lenny. Don't be stupid. Just get it done and we can go back to being friends."

The man groaned when his wrists were unbound. His fingers looked like purple sausages. He'd have to be careful about that the next time. He could have ruined Lenny's typing skills; live and learn.

Someone started pounding on the front door. Tom scowled and looked at his newly freed victim. "You stay here, Lenny. Don't want you getting jumpy while I'm busy."

The stairs up to the ground-level floor were nicely padded, and he moved up them quickly. He didn't carry a weapon on him, but he had easy access, so he wasn't overly worried.

He should have been. By the time he reached the short hallway to the door, it was obvious that somebody was extremely unhappy with the current situation.

"Hold on to your ass! I'm coming!"

The front door came apart before his eyes and large pieces of the wood and beveled glass ripped through the air on a path for him.

Tom dropped to the ground and covered his head; only one piece of wood actually hit him, but it drew a red line of fire across his upper back. "Fuck!"

He scrambled, reaching for his stashed weapon. All he had to do was get into the vent next to the living room entrance and that was easy enough to do. He'd had the vent designed to lift up with ease.

His hand caught the lower edge of the vent cover. Maggie's bloodied hand caught his wrist.

He looked up and saw the shape she was in: Maggie was

covered from head to toe in drying blood that flaked away from her skin. She looked like she'd been dipped in the stuff and then hit with a hair dryer until her clothes were merely damp. Her hair was still pulled back in a ponytail, still had its usual thick curls, but it was rusty brown from the bath she'd taken. Her face, always enchanting, always so hot in that girl-next-door way, was twisted into a look of undiluted hatred. Her dark eyes glared down into his. Her nostrils flared and her full, welcoming mouth showed him nothing but bared teeth.

"Maggie? What the hell?"

Maggie yanked on his arm and lifted him into a standing position. Several tendons in his shoulder let out screams of protest that matched flawlessly with his yelp of pain. When the hell did Maggie start working out?

"Look what you did to my fucking door!" He was a little nervous, but only a little. He could handle a bitch hopped up on too much coke. He had several times in the past. "That's coming out of your take, Maggie."

"Shut your face, Monkey Boy." She had a smile starting. It was dark and dangerous and mischievous and sexy as all hell. He was going to enjoy breaking her, but he'd make her take a shower first. He preferred his blood fresh.

"What did you say?" Now she was calling him names? Definitely time to put her in her place. He figured a good rail-road by twenty men would have taken care of that, but she was still ready for more.

Tom was always glad to oblige. He brought his knee up and nailed her on the crotch. He'd learned a long time ago that hitting a girl there hurt her almost as much as it hurt a guy.

She winced in pain and let go of his wrist. He used his other hand to grab a thick wedge of her ponytail, fully intending to bust her pretty face all over his wall. He pushed hard and succeeded in shoving himself back when she didn't budge. She'd no more moved than if he'd been pushing against his own house.

"Asshole." She hit him. Not a little girly slap, either. She hauled her arm around and clocked him across the face hard enough to leave him seeing constellations.

"Bitch, that's the last mistake you're ever going to make." Tom stood back up and pumped his arm at her face. Screw her looks, she was about to become damaged goods.

She took the blow to the chin and didn't even blink. "I told you we were finished, Monkey Boy. I meant it." Her hand blurred and she caught his nose between her thumb and forefinger. "Did I ever tell you how ugly you are?" She yanked back hard, and Tom let loose a shriek as the cartilage in his nose separated.

He backed into the wall, his eyes tearing furiously, and felt the blood flow from his broken proboscis.

Maggie looked at her handiwork and frowned. "I was kind of hoping it would come completely off. Let me try again."

Tom ran. He forgot all about the gun in its hiding spot and all about the man he'd been torturing and the little girl he'd planned to rape half to death. He ran.

Maggie let him. She stood perfectly still and followed him with her eyes, a little half smile on her face. He knew the look: it was the one she got when she'd heard a joke that was only a little funny. He didn't like to think that he was the joke, but right now he had bigger matters to deal with, like staying alive.

Tom's Camaro was right where it should be and he fished into his jeans for the car keys, trying not to freak out about how much of his blood was coating his fingers.

Maggie followed, pausing long enough to pick up her pepper spray, which remained where she had dropped it earlier. He cursed himself for not picking the damned thing up himself; he could have used it about now.

He almost dropped the car keys while he was fumbling for the right one, but managed to keep them. He opened the door and climbed in at a record-breaking pace.

He closed the door just as Maggie was reaching for him and felt an unsettling jolt of relief.

Then she punched through the tempered glass. Her little hand—and she was practically delicate along those lines— shot through the glass and grabbed at the back of his long hair.

"Maggie! Jesus, girl, stop!"

"Not done quitting yet, Tom."

She slammed his head into the windshield and shattered the safety glass. Maggie let go of his hair and reached around with her other hand. He was still groaning and stunned when she yanked him across the steering wheel and pulled him across the hood of the car. The glass shattered into tiny diamond shapes, and he got a few scrapes, but nothing compared to what she had already done.

Maggie let him hit the ground in front of his car and looked down at him. "Come on, Tom. I was expecting you to put up a fight."

He started crawling, and she let him. She just walked a few paces behind him and let him do his thing. Crawling was the best he could manage for a while. After about fifty feet of slipping around on the damp asphalt and then the wet front lawn of his place, Tom stood up. It hurt like hell, but he did it.

"That's my Monkey Boy. I knew you could do it."

"Maggie, please . . . uh . . . unhhunnhhh . . . stop. Please . . ." Christ, he was crying! He couldn't stop himself. He was begging and it was humiliating.

"I bet that's what Liz was trying to say to the boys gang-raping her." She still looked plenty pissed off, but her voice was calmer. He had hoped that he could talk his way out of this, or maybe get a weapon of some kind; it was a small hope, true, but it was still there.

"Hey, that wasn't supposed to happen. I told them they had to play nice."

Maggie nodded and then slammed her right heel into the side of his knee. Muscles pulped under the impact; bones splintered and his leg bent in ways no human limb was ever designed to.

He hit the ground again, gasping for air and wishing that the pain would end.

Maggie crouched next to him, looking at his sweating, agonized face. "Funny thing about that, Monkey; I told myself to play nicely. I guess I can't take orders, either."

She reached out and caught one of his hands in hers. He tried to pull away, but her strength was too great.

"I thought about taking a stick and fucking you with it, Tom. All the way over here I thought about it. I was thinking maybe it would be nice to give you a taste of your own medicine. A little payback for every time you forced me to take that little prick of yours."

She held his hand tightly with her left hand and with the right, she caught his little finger.

Her eyes looked at his again, reflective in a way that didn't seem possible. If he hadn't known better, he would have thought she had lights burning deep in the back of her skull. Her expression was calmer now, but he was finally beginning to understand that even if he lived through this night, he would never be whole again.

"Thing is, if I did that, I'd have to see parts of your body that disgust me even more than your face."

Her fingers pinched down and ripped at Tom's little finger. His nail came free in a sudden, brilliant lance of pain.

Tom writhed, pulling with all of his strength in an effort to free himself from her grip. She reached out again and tore off the nail on his ring finger, even as he was thrashing around and howling out broken obscenities.

"You're a sick bastard, Tom. You could have let me go and I would have left it all alone." He wanted to puke his guts out and the bitch was still talking. "You were going to let them pull a train on me? What was I supposed to do, be grateful?"

He swore he wouldn't give her the satisfaction of hearing him scream again. By the time she pulled the thumbnail away from his hand, he was begging for mercy and praying to God that she would let him just die.

When she was done with his right hand, she let it go and he rolled away from her, weeping silently. In all his life he'd never expected it was possible to feel that much pain.

"Okay. That was for Liz." Maggie looked him over and smiled. "Everything else is for me."

Then she got inventive.

Tom learned more about pain. Oh, so very much more.

IV

Maggie came out of her fury like a deep sea diver rising to the surface: it was a slow process and, while she could see the air high above her, it was distorted by waves of anger. The pain she'd been feeling was gone, but the memory of it lingered.

What was left of Tom wasn't very appealing. What made it worse was that he was still alive. His fingers looked like they'd been attacked by rabid pliers. His face was a mess. She could remember pulling at his nose as if she'd been dreaming; but she hadn't fully realized how hard she'd caught him. One nostril hung by a tiny shred of meat; the rest of it flapped loosely. His mouth was the worst. Somewhere along the way, she'd started breaking off his teeth.

Tom was alive, and he was conscious. His eyes reflected nothing of sanity, but he was there, awake and in agony.

The anger was gone. All that was left was a vague sense of pity. In the end, she punched him hard in his throat and watched him choke to death on his own blood.

His death was a loss to no one. He would not be mourned.

A car pulled into Tom's driveway. It was a Crown Victoria, and the crappy shade of brown made her think cop car as surely as wailing sirens and flashing lights would have.

She backed away as the two men got out of the car.

Maggie shook her head, trying to figure out exactly what had just happened to her. She knew what she had done, knew why she had done it, and now, for the life of her, she couldn't remember how she had done it.

The two men had cop written all over them. They looked around for only a moment before heading toward Tom's Camaro.

It wouldn't take them long to find the trail of blood he'd left behind and from there they could easily spot Tom's body.

She didn't have a mirror, but she didn't need one to see the blood all over her clothes.

The two men were looking over the car and talking, but she couldn't make out the words. She just knew she had to move, and fast, if she wanted to get the hell away from the scene of her crime.

Just as the cops would have been looking her way, she heard the racket. There are few birds that can make as much noise as crows, and the ones coming her way seemed intent on deafening the entire planet. They cawed and heckled and screamed as they flew, a seething mass of feathers that spread out over the entire area, flying low and circling around the two policemen. Her car was still in Tom's driveway, and if she was careful she might be able to get to it.

Even as that thought occurred to her, she heard the familiar sound of her Ford Focus starting up. The two men were surrounded by the crows and dodging desperately, but they weren't so stupid that they stood still when the car started forward and trenched Tom's yard in an effort to get around them. They got out of the way and damned fast. Neither of them drew a weapon, and she was very glad for that.

Her car stopped two feet away from her and the passenger's side door opened. One look inside and Maggie could have sobbed with relief.

Ben had never looked more handsome. Or more desperate. "Come on! Let's go!" Even with him yelling, she could barely hear him over the crows. She climbed in as quickly as she could, and he gunned the engine as soon as her door was closed. He steered off of the lawn and back out onto the driveway, narrowly missing the cop car.

Maggie shivered, the chill of the night suddenly overwhelming, as Ben drove toward the apartments.

He didn't look at her, didn't say a word. He just steered and kept his eyes focused on the road in front of him.

"Ben?"

"Please tell me you're not hurt."

She had to think about it. "No, I think I'm okay."

"Good. Great. Now let's get home."

"Ben, how did you know to find me?"

"I don't know and I don't care. I'll care later, maybe, but right now I just need to get you home and safe."

She nodded her head, drained.

"Thank you, Ben."

She closed her eyes until he parked her car.

The next thing she knew, she was in his bathroom and he was testing the water coming out of the shower. "Okay. It's about ready. There's shampoo and conditioner, and there're some towels. Soap's already in there."

"What?"

"You need to bathe, Maggie. Get clean. You're . . . covered." His face was pale, too pasty by far, and his eyes looked like the marbles placed in a mounted deer's head.

Maggie nodded and began taking off her clothes. Ben beat a hasty retreat as she peeled away the stiff, bloodied fabrics. She ran on autopilot, dropping the ruined outfit on the floor and stepping into the warm stream of water. She stayed there for a long while, until her fingertips resembled wrinkled prunes and she had scrubbed herself raw.

V

"Okay. What the fuck was that?"

Danny looked over at him and shook his head. "That was a lot of fuckin' birds. You should have listened to that call of yours earlier."

"Oh don't even fucken start."

"Okay. So what's that?" Danny pointed to a motionless ruin on the front lawn of Tom Pardue's house.

Boyd looked at the trail of blood that ran from the trashed Camaro to the mess in the grass. It wasn't a clean trail. The crows had shat over almost the whole area. His jacket was covered in droppings.

He ignored the slicks of crow crap on his clothes and walked over to the human body that was currently cooling down.

"You know what?"

"Tell me, Richie." Danny's voice wasn't its calmest. He could dig that. He was feeling a little jumpy himself. He'd always hated birds. They were messy and they were loud. He liked clean and quiet.

"I think that's Tom Pardue."

"Yeah? How can you tell?" There wasn't much of Tom that hadn't been beaten, broken, or crapped on.

"The shirt, the shorts, and the greasy blond hair. That's Pardue or there's someone else out there with shitty taste in clothes."

"Shit."

"Yeah. Sorry, Danny. I know you really wanted him to resist."

Danny shrugged. "You know what? Somebody did it better than I could have."

Anyone listening would have thought they'd both lost their minds. Joking was how they dealt with it. Joking kept them from screaming on days like this.

"You know, technically, this is a homicide. It ain't our department." Boyd lit a cigar.

"You thinking of giving this to Whalen and Longwood?"

"Damn right."

"So what did you see?"

"I saw a car driving away. And I saw a lot of birds."

"That all you saw?" Danny sounded doubtful.

Boyd shrugged. "I might have seen a really hot girl with a huge rack standing over Pardue's body. She might have been covered in blood and looking a little like she wouldn't mind finding some more. But I am not about to say that to the homicide kids."

Danny nodded. "I might have seen that, too. But I'm gonna pretend I didn't."

"Yeah?"

"Yeah. Because I don't know about you, Richie, but I don't wanna hear a bunch of fuckin' jokes about how I saw a ghost."

"Ghost?"

"What? You think some girl painted herself in blood and beat Pardue to death?"

Boyd gnawed on the end of his cigar and rolled it around his mouth a few times. Fuck Freud. He didn't care about the possible symbolism of his actions. Besides, Freud was a pervert.

"You know what I think, Danny?"

"What?"

"I think it's time to go check out his house. I think we saw birds and we saw a car."

"What kind of car?"

"I was a little busy ducking the fucken birds, Danny Boy. I didn't see and I don't care."

"Think those two will catch whoever did this?"

Boyd spat away from the corpse, despite the temptation to aim for an eye. "I sure as shit hope not."

CHAPTER 17

I

Sometime during the wee hours of the morning, the Phi Chi fraternity house caught fire. The fire investigation team ascertained that the blaze started in the main living room area near a substantial collection of single malt scotch whiskeys. From there, the blaze spread at a frightening pace, devouring the ancient wooden walls and igniting more fire hazards than should have been possible in any one dwelling. Of course the average dwelling wasn't inhabited by a small army of college kids who failed to clean more than absolutely necessary for appearances.

The fire was helped out by faulty wiring and several cases of overloaded electrical fixtures.

The blaze required all three fire stations in Black Stone Bay to put it out. By the time they managed to get it under control, the building was little more than a burned-out foundation.

No one came out of the fraternity house while it was burning, and the fire was actually reported by a police car that was doing regular rounds to make sure the party hadn't gotten out of control.

No bodies were found inside the structure, either.

The campus was abuzz with news the following day and there were plenty of students who were stunned into staying away from school; the students who lived in the Phi Chi fraternity were very popular and mostly they were well liked.

But a few held out hope. After all, if no bodies were found, it was possible that they'd escaped the blaze.

The truth was simpler than that. The bodies had been removed. Jason Soulis was not ready for anyone to know what was happening in the town, and that many corpses would have set off far too many warning bells.

II

Kelli didn't regret not going to the party. She kept telling herself that until she finally fell asleep. She didn't quite believe it, but she tried to.

She was in bed by ten o'clock and unconscious fifteen minutes later. She would have deeply loved to stay asleep, too. But the dreams came again. This time it was different. This time it was Bill, not Teddy, who came to the window.

The room was dark, but he was out there, calling to her softly. He looked at her with those warm, loving eyes of his and called to her softly. "Kelli, let me in. It's cold out here and I want to see you." His words were innocent enough, but the tone he used to speak them made promises of what she had dreamt of on a few occasions.

"Bill, you're married."

"Kelli, I want to see you, I want to hold you."

She sat up in the bed and stared at him. He was so handsome. But there was something wrong with the way he looked, something minor that was enough to make her wait. His hair was as perfect as ever, his mouth sweet and kind, his nose unchanged: it was his eyes. They seemed . . . bleached. The deep rich blue they had always been was missing, and there was a strange light in them that was unsettling. Dream or no, his eyes were completely wrong.

Kelli knew one thing for certain at that moment: dreams can become nightmares. She stayed away from the window. When the voice from outside became insistent, she left her bedroom and walked down the stairs to the living room. In her dream, she turned on the TV and watched reruns of old sitcoms she remembered from her childhood. Bill kept calling to her, asking her to let him in, so she cranked up the volume. Now and then she looked out the back window and saw him standing on the patio.

It was when *Who's the Boss* came on that she realized she wasn't dreaming at all. There was just no way she could willingly dream about that show.

Kelli stared at Bill standing outside and he stared back.

"Let me in, Kelli."

"No."

He grimaced. "Why not?"

"You're scaring me, Bill."

"What do you have to be afraid of?"

She looked at him, looked at his shirt with the torn buttons, his pants with several spots that looked almost like mold staining the fabric and finally, she looked at his feet. He had one shoe on. The other was missing.

"I think you're dead, Bill. I think you're a ghost." Her voice was a tiny thing, frail and broken.

"I'm not a ghost, Kelli. I'm right here. All you have to do is let me in and I can prove it to you."

"Why can't you just come inside?"

He looked at her for several heartbeats, his face working as he tried to come up with a proper explanation. "Just let me in. Please, Kelli, I'm cold and I need to get warm."

"Go away, Bill."

"Kelli . . ."

"I mean it. I'll call the police. They'll be here damned fast, too, with all of the people who've been vanishing from this house."

"Kelli, come on now, we're friends."

She shook her head and looked away from him. When she

looked too closely, she wanted to believe he was real and that
he was there to be with her in a way she knew was wrong. The
worst part was she knew he would be with her that way if she
wanted. The desire to be with her was in his gaze.

"I can't let you in, Bill. I don't want to die."

"I would never hurt you, Kelli. I just want to be with you."

She shook her head again and tried not to cry. Bill slapped
the sliding glass door hard enough to make her jump. "Let me
in the fucking house, you bitch!"

She looked at him and blinked. He wasn't handsome anymore. His face was dead white and slack, almost expressionless. His hair was plastered wetly to his skull, and she thought
she saw something crawling through it, like a small crab. His
eyelids were sagging, partially hiding that sickening glow
from his pupils, and his teeth . . . his teeth were all wrong,
grown obscenely long and sharp within the confines of his
mouth. A dark, black tongue licked across those teeth as he
suddenly snarled at her.

"You let me into the house before I have to get nasty with
you!"

"Get away from me, Bill! I mean it!"

"You can't stay in there forever, Kelli! And when you finally come out, I'll be waiting for you!" His threat held more
than merely the promise of violence. She shuddered and
stepped away from the window.

Kelli looked around for something, anything that she could
use to defend herself. Finally she settled on a letter opener and
grabbed it.

When she looked up again, Bill was gone.

When she woke up, she was in her bedroom and the alarm
was blaring at her.

"I can't take these dreams anymore. Fuck, I just can't."

She slipped out of bed and stood, chilled by the early
morning air and by the memory of Bill's fury.

She didn't even notice the letter opener near her feet. It had
bounced when she dropped it earlier and was now mostly obscured by the covers.

III

Ben finally made it to his car just after sunrise. He had plenty of company along the way; a gathering of crows kept an eye on him as he walked the three miles toward Tom's house.

He'd parked a block away from the place. Not by choice, mind you, but because the crows decided to land on his car and obscure his view until he did.

There was something very unsettling about having big black birds with wickedly sharp beaks telling you what to do. Still, he did it. He knew that Maggie needed him then and there, and he wasn't going to let having to walk stop him.

Thinking back on the night that had just passed made his mind want to run and hide. He was fine with the whole thing, except for Maggie covered in blood. He could live with the demented intuition telling him he had to find her. He was dealing pretty damned well with the whole birds-hijacked-my-car-and-made-me-drive-here thing; it was really, really creepy, but he could manage to swallow it.

What was bugging him most was the sight of Maggie when he finally saw her. Damn near anyone else would have had trouble recognizing her right then. Most people didn't know every feature of her face well enough to identify them through a caul of drying blood. The curve of her jawline and the teeth he knew so well were what gave her away. The way her hair fell, even when thick with crud, told him her identity. And her eyes as she came out of whatever spell had seized her; that was what really told him everything he needed to know.

She'd looked so confused, so dismayed . . .

Maggie didn't really let a lot show on her face all the time. She was not an open book by any stretch of the imagination. When she was at school, she was studying; when she was in public, she kept a careful guard on her emotions. It was when she was alone that she showed the most emotion. Sometimes, she let herself relax around him, too, and he had learned to understand her expressions.

She'd been horrified by what she had done. He knew that.

There were other emotions that warred with her fear in that moment before the crows swept through and blocked everything else, but he'd seen her repulsion at what lay before her on the ground.

He'd been horrified, too. There was a moment, very brief and fleeting, when he'd been afraid of her. She hadn't looked human when he saw her; she'd looked more like a demon or a goddess or something that went beyond Ben's definition of human. He'd been scared, and maybe he still was a little. But it was Maggie. Whatever else she might have become, no matter how frightening, he was in love with her.

And yes, he had recognized the remains of Tom Pardue, as well. Despite the vast mutilations, he had known the face of his enemy in an instant.

One look at the corpse and he knew he had to get her out of there. He also knew her car well enough by sight and knew a few other things that most people wouldn't have known, like where her spare key was. She had a little magnetic box that was hidden in the well of her front bumper. Watching her dig for it one time had kept him focused on the shape of her derriere for almost a week. She was definitely as lovely from the back as she was from the front.

Ben shook that thought away. He was here to get his car.

She'd been quiet on the way back home, exhausted by whatever had overcome her. He'd been quiet, too, while his mind tried to take in the sight of her covered in blood and the fact that he'd come only inches away from running down two men who were too close to where she stood when he arrived.

Boyd and Holdstedter were decent enough guys, and he knew they had no love for Tom Pardue. But he still didn't think they'd have let her walk away from the murder scene, and Ben knew he couldn't allow them to arrest her. If they came after anyone, he preferred they come after him.

He was at least as guilty as Maggie: he'd killed Pardue a hundred times in his mind.

So far there had been no knock at his door. They seemed to have gotten away without incident.

Now he just had to get his car back where it belonged and avoid getting himself caught this late in the game.

Even from a block away, he could see the flashing lights of the emergency vehicles that surrounded the man's house. That could be a problem, too. There might be an investigation into Pardue's past. That investigation might bring up Maggie's name.

He'd have to do something about that.

Ben was still thinking about how to handle the situation when he arrived back at his apartment. He entered quietly and crept back to his bedroom to find that she was still under the covers, only her thick curly hair in sight. He was closing the door when she spoke to him.

"Ben?"

"Hi, Maggie. I'm sorry. I didn't mean to wake you."

"Ben, I'm cold. Come sleep with me."

He climbed into the bed fully clothed. At first he lay on his back next to her and tried not to move. Eventually, she reached behind her own body and caught his arm. She pulled him closer until he was spooned against her back.

The feel of her body against his was an agony he willingly endured. Eventually, he managed to join her in her slumber.

IV

O'Neill was in a mood. Boyd wasn't in the right mood to put up with it. He stood with his arms crossed and scowled throughout the entire peppy conversation about how he and Danny needed to get their acts in gear.

"The thing is, Boyd, that you two are good cops. I know that. But if this situation doesn't get any better, I might have to look into outside help. I have to say I'm disappointed." O'Neill was one of those bastards that was aging gracefully. Boyd wanted to slap him on general principles but he was normally okay as captains went.

"All due respect, Captain. Fuck off."

"Excuse me?"

"I said fuck off." He uncrossed his arms and moved toward O'Neill's desk. "We normally deal with maybe ten cases. Right now we got over thirty. You want to go ahead and bring on a few extra people, you go right ahead. But don't you dare accuse me of sloppy work. I'll turn in my notice and take the time in jail for kicking your ass."

"That is uncalled for, Rich."

"The hell it is. You just said you're 'disappointed.'" He snorted. "What? You think I'm having orgasms over the way my week has been? Get a fucken clue. I got thirty fucken cases to handle here and not all of them are easily solved. You want my badge? Go for it. Wanna write me up? Do your shit. But you can shove your disappointment straight up your ass, you stupid bitch."

He left the captain's office and headed for the door, his expression murderous enough that everyone but Danny decided to look elsewhere in case his gaze might turn them into stone.

Danny took it in stride. He'd been there for the reaming. "So, what're we doing first, Richie?"

"First I'm keying the fucker's car."

"He'll know you did it."

"Not if I write 'Freemont was here.'"

"Maybe later. Right now I think you hurt him enough when you called him a bitch." He paused. "I thought only women could be bitches."

"Did you see balls anywhere on that piece of shit? 'Cause I sure as shit didn't."

"You're being a baby."

"Yeah? And?"

"Nothing. Just an observation."

"Any news on the ballbuster?"

"Alan Tripp? No. He vanished."

"I don't think so. He's just really good at not looking like a maniac in a hospital nightie."

"Think he's still hanging around?"

"According to him, his dead son kidnapped his dead wife. My guess is he's looking for dead people."

"Maybe we should let him know about the Red Lady."

"We aren't letting anyone know about her."

"Oh, come on. They might give us vacation time."

"No. But be on the lookout for red ladies with nice racks."

"I'm always on the lookout for nice racks."

"Do we have anything at all on the girls working for Tom?"

"No. Besides, you dropped this case."

"No I didn't."

"Yeah, you did. Just last night you handed it over to Whalen and Longwood."

"Only on paper."

"What? We're gonna bust her now?"

"Shit no. I wanna thank her for the public service."

"Seriously, Richie."

"Seriously? Anyone could do that, maybe they know something about the Falcone car accident. Maybe they know a lot and they got caught before they could get rid of another body."

"Shit."

"Covering our bases is all. Far as I'm concerned, Tommy being dead is just a plus."

"You heard about the fire?"

"Yeah. Fucken tragedy."

"They didn't find any bodies."

"Yeah, that's the tragedy. O'Neill is gonna shit a house when he hears."

"Fuck the bitch, Richie. I ain't wiping his ass."

"That's what I like about you, Danny Boy. You learn fast."

"So, we're going to the frat house?"

" 'Course we are."

"I knew you'd say that."

"Then why did you ask?"

"I just love to hear your voice, Richie."

"You need help."

"I need that vacation. Sure we can't mention the Red Lady?"

"Very sure."

"Bitch."

V

Alan Tripp crawled out of his cubbyhole and shivered. The woods were not a good place for sleeping, especially without any shelter aside from a few trees. His body felt feverish. The bandages on his hand were soaked again. He didn't have any more pads or even cloth, and he decided he'd have to risk a trip to his house.

Besides, he was tired of freezing his balls off. He had perfectly good clothes waiting for him at the house, and he had other things, like money.

And he wanted to go home. Screw everything else; he wanted to go home for a while. Even if home was empty of everything good but a few stale memories.

Alan winced and realized that he'd been clenching his fists. A steady stream of crimson ran from the web between his thumb and forefinger. The physical wound hurt, but the memory of how he'd been injured was a thousand times worse.

"That wasn't my boy. They don't understand that. But I know my son, and Avery would never . . ." He couldn't finish the words. They stuck in his throat like barbed hooks and he gagged on them.

Alan Tripp started for his house, ignoring the worst of the scrapes and cuts that adorned his bare feet. The ground was rough, covered with a thick layer of autumn leaves that hid a hundred different traps. His feet were suffering for every move he made.

He let himself go numb for the majority of his trek. It was easier on him when he wasn't lingering on memories of Avery's laugh or Meghan's sweet smile. The pain wasn't as great when he pushed away the scent of his son's hair as he came inside from playing, or the taste of Meghan's lips pressed against his own.

A blink of the eyes was all it took to have him recalling a thousand things he didn't want to remember anymore. Christmas morning, the first year after he and Meghan were married; their first celebration of the holiday on their own. Meghan holding on to his hand with crushing force, her eyes open and her mouth a beautiful scrawl of pain as she gave birth to their baby boy. Her not-completely-joking promise to kill him if he ever let her opt for natural childbirth again. The first time he had to change one of Avery's diapers by himself. The look on Meghan's face when she saw the end result and her laughter, sweet as honey, that took the sting from the exasperated look she cast his way. Avery's first step, his first word, his first time falling down and bruising himself: they were all beautiful, painful mementos of the life he'd had until just a few days ago. They were his life, his reason for living, his sole purpose for drawing in another breath.

Alan drew in a ragged breath and pushed those wonderful agonies aside. He sucked in another gasp of air and held it like a treasure as he thought of the look on Avery's sweet, blood-stained face as he looked up from feasting on Meghan's neck.

He could survive a little longer if he just let everything go but the anger. That was the most important element. Without his rage, he would have stayed in that room and eaten the pills they kept giving him for as long as they wanted him to.

But if he held it close, fueled it with tiny scraps of the pain that overwhelmed him, he could make his anger grow big enough to do what he had to do.

No creatures on this planet were going to steal his wife and son without suffering for it.

A branch punched into the sole of his left foot and drove a hot lance of pain into him. He stopped exactly long enough to yank out the irritation and continue on. He fingered the stick, felt the blood slick across his hand, and let that add more fuel to his anger.

Anger was his weapon. It was his shield.

There was something else that he would use, too: knowledge.

He wasn't one hundred percent sure, but he thought he knew what he was facing. There were only a few things he'd ever heard of that came out at night and drank blood. Maybe the thing wearing Avery's face had actually been eating the flesh of his mother, but if so, he took small bites.

*No, it was the blood. Her neck was torn, not chewed away.
At least I think it was. So damned hard to focus on anything.*

Were vampires real? Was it even a possibility? He didn't
know, but he was going to find out.

*He looked at the bloody stick in his hand and smiled
tightly. Either way, a bit of stick through the heart will stop the
thing that stole my boy.*

Alan had a wood shop in the garage and plenty of wood he
hadn't quite gotten around to doing anything with.

That was about to change.

He had nothing left that mattered, but it was possible to
find a substitute, at least for a while. He could fake a reason to
live; he could make one up and use it for as long as possible.

His reason to live was that he had something to kill; something that looked like his son.

                              VI

Brian Freemont slipped out of his house a little after noon,
and kept a cautious eye on the houses around him. He carried
two bags of clothing and a third that held all of his weapons
and enough ammunition to let him hold off a small army. He
checked under his car, and inside it, too, before he finally
threw his luggage into the backseat and slid behind the driver's seat and started the engine.

His face was bruised and stinging from the blow he'd taken
in the wee hours of the previous night. The lacerations were
not deep, but they burned. He needed to get something he
could use to clean the wounds, because there was nothing in
the house.

He also needed supplies. He wouldn't try to leave town yet,
but it was on his agenda. He wanted to be gone before night-
fall. He wanted to be far away from Black Stone Bay before
Angie could come haunt him again. She'd be back, too. He
knew it.

Maybe a hotel would be best, a place where he could hide

and not risk being screwed over by his ex-associates in the police force. Because he knew, sure as the sun rose every day, that if he left town, he would be hunted down like a dog.

One week ago, his life had been good. He'd had a life. Now he was reduced to this. Running from his home and from the ghost of his wife.

She has to be a ghost. No one living could take a bullet in her head and get back up like that. No one! Not ever! If she is a ghost, who killed her?

Who else? The voice on the phone. The voice that called and taunted and then stole his life away in the first place. Oh, it was fixed now, but he knew the voice could do it again, just reach out and take everything he'd worked for, everything he'd made with Angie and everything he'd wanted to have for his child.

Oh God, I shot her. I shot Angie in the head and I killed our baby.

It took him almost ten minutes to recover from his crying jag. He sobbed and shivered in the slight warmth of the afternoon and let all of the fear creep slowly from his body in the form of bitter tears.

I wish I still had my uniform. If I still had my uniform, I could find a girl and get my life back. Make her put out for me and get control of everything again. I need that! I need the control and I need the sex. It's all I have. All I've ever had.

No. No that's a lie. I had Angie. I just wish that she'd been enough.

"Angie, baby, I'm sorry. I wish you'd been enough."

He was just getting ready to pull out of the driveway when the detectives showed up.

"You gotta be kidding me." He groaned and rested his head on the steering wheel.

Boyd walked up to the side of his car and stared in the window at him. Holdstedter came up and stood at the back of the car, his arms crossed. Neither man looked like talking to him was something they really wanted to do.

Boyd looked him over for a second and then looked into the

back of his car and saw the bags. "You weren't thinking of going somewhere, were you, Freemont? Because the conditions of your bail say you have to stay where we can keep an eye on you."

"I was going to a hotel."

"Yeah? Why's that?" Boyd lit one of his cigars and looked him over, one eye squinted against the sunlight. Holdstedter was still in the same place, his face expressionless and his eyes unreadable behind reflective sunglasses.

"Someone tried to break in last night. Broke the window in my bedroom." It wasn't exactly a lie, so he managed to say it with a clear conscience.

"You recognize the perp?" Boyd had a cloud of smoke around his face. He looked like a demon to Brian.

"Looked like Angie."

"Yeah? Did she say anything to you?"

"It doesn't matter."

"Sure it does. What did she say?"

"I said it doesn't matter."

"You really want me to drag your ass down to the boys' club so we can talk in depth about this, Freemont? Or do you just want to go over it here? Because, I gotta tell you, your neighbors weren't happy with all the gunfire last night. Had two of them call us a little while ago to piss and moan about it."

Shit. He hadn't thought about that. If he had, he would have left hours ago.

"What I'm trying to figure out here is why a fucken cop, of all people, would want to go and break a bunch of ordinances about firing weapons inside the town limits, and then load up his car and get ready to head out with still more guns in the backseat." Boyd leaned in closer, the thick smoke from the cigar wafting into Brian's car in a nauseating wave. "How do you think I should react here, Freemont? Oh, and don't think of reaching for your backseat. Danny'll take the top of your head off. He's been itching for a reason ever since you pointed your piece at us."

"I didn't do anything wrong!"

"You murdered a young girl, you sick motherfucker!" Boyd's face was close enough that the cigar tip waved an inch from his nose. "I'm looking at your face and I'm seeing new cuts that look like somebody scratched your face and there were gunshots here! So you tell me why I shouldn't just bust your fucken ass right now or I swear to God I'll back Danny up and say you were going for the guns in your fucken backseat!"

Brian was ready to go insane right then and there. That was the first time Boyd had accused him of committing a murder. He didn't need this, he needed to get out of town before Angie came back for him again and brought her friends.

"I DIDN'T DO ANYTHING!"

"I got a fucken DNA test that says otherwise. When it comes back, I'm gonna drop you like a sack of shit." Boyd was calmer now, or at least he wasn't screaming.

"And when it comes back negative, I'll have your badge." It was the best bluff he could manage.

"It ain't coming back negative, Freemont. You know it and I know it." Boyd stepped back a bit and glared. "How many girls did you make suck that limp dick of yours to get out of tickets, Freemont?"

That one made him jump. That one made him want to shit himself. No one was ever supposed to know!

Boyd nodded. "Yeah. I thought so. Guilty as shit."

"You just leave me alone, or book me."

"Try to leave town, Freemont. Please. We've been looking for a reason." Boyd opened his back door and pulled out the bundle of weapons. "Gonna hold this for you, so you can't get too stupid."

"No! I need those!" He started to reach and flinched back fast and hard when he saw the pistol appear in Holdstedter's hand.

"You can't be that stupid, asswipe." Boyd shook his head.

"I need those!"

"Yeah?" Boyd was staring hard at him. "Why do you need these if you're all innocent and sweet like you say you are?"

"Because Angie's trying to kill me!"

"Really? Your missing wife is trying to kill you now?"

Brian shut his mouth. He'd already said too much.

"You don't wanna talk to me anymore, Freemont?"

Brian shook his head.

"That's okay. I got what I need for now." He pulled the cigar out of his mouth and slipped it into his left hand. Boyd was right-handed. Brian figured he wanted a clear path to his piece. "Don't even think about crossing the city limits. You do, I'll have you busted so fast you'll think your mommy was watching out for you."

"Look, why are you doing this to me?"

"Why do you think, asshole? Because you've been raping young girls and you murdered one, too. That makes you shit in my book."

Boyd walked back to his car. Holdstedter waited until his partner was seated and comfortable before he looked away from Brian. When he was sure, he went to the passenger's side of the Crown Victoria and joined his partner.

Brian waited until they had backed out of the long driveway and the dust had cleared before he let himself start crying again.

VII

"Are we there yet? . . . Are we there yet? . . . Are we there yet?" Danny sat in the seat next to him and kept going like that pink bunny with the drum in the battery commercial.

Boyd was in too good a mood to be goaded. "I got a lit cigar, Danny. Don't make me put it out on your forehead."

"You know, I think he was crying when we left."

"I love when little boys like him cry. Makes me feel all manly."

"Probably why he did all the girls the way he did."

"Yeah, he'd need that sort of shit to feel like a man." Boyd thought about the crew cut and the hawk nose and the thin lips on Freemont and shook his head in disgust. "That's what all the shrinks say, anyway."

"What? That rape is about power?"

"Yeah, or anger."

"I don't think that's always true, Richie."

"No?"

"No. Maybe violent rape, but I think with Freemont it was just about getting laid and feeling like a man."

"You don't think what he did to Veronica Miller was violent?"

"She's the exception." Danny shrugged. "Mostly I think he's just a horny prick on a power trip."

"Fair enough." He pulled the car up to open the gate of the sprawling black house, and then moved slowly past it and up the driveway.

"Ever wish you were this rich?"

"Isn't your family this rich?"

"Yeah, but your family isn't."

"Thanks for the reminder, dickhead."

"Hey, it's what friends do."

"Just put on your polite face. We don't need any rich pricks giving O'Neill a reason."

"Well, hell, Richie. You already gave him one, didn't you?"

"Yeah, smart-ass, so he doesn't need another."

"Oh, yeah. Good point."

"What's his name again?"

"Jason Soulis."

"You gotta wonder if that name is real, don't you?"

"It's real. The FBI checks that sort of shit, too."

"Lah-dee-dah."

"Hey. Don't you go picking on the feds, now. They're very important to the pursuit of justice."

"Bite me."

"Nah, you probably taste like you smell."

"You saying I smell bad, Danny Boy?"

"I'm saying you should maybe buy better cigars."

"You're the one with money, dickhead."

"Okay, am I dickhead or am I smart-ass? Because I'm starting to get confused here."

"Drink more coffee. You definitely need to drink more coffee."

"Maybe Soulis will have some."

Boyd climbed out of his car and walked toward the front of the place. "Maybe he'll even let you have some."

"I can hope."

Naturally, there was a big damned brass knocker on the door. Boyd used it. When no one answered, he used it again. After the third time, Jason Soulis appeared at the doorway, squinting against the bright sunlight.

"Yes?" The man's voice was cold but polite.

Boyd flashed his badge and Danny did the same. "Really sorry to bother you. Are you Jason Soulis?"

"Yes I am, Detective Boyd. How can I help you?" He stepped back and gestured for the men to enter the house.

Boyd nodded his thanks and stepped inside, followed by his oversized blond shadow. "We just need to ask you a few questions."

"By all means. I was just making coffee. Would either of you like a cup?"

"You're a god." Danny nodded as he said the words.

Soulis's lips curved slightly into a smile and he led them into a large, tastefully decorated room. He left and came back a few minutes later with a large silver tray loaded down with fresh coffee and a few cookies.

When everyone had been served—by the man of the house, no less—Soulis leaned back in an antique chair and nodded. "Ask your questions, please."

"We just needed to know if you've seen or heard anything unusual in the last week or so."

"This is in regards to the missing people around town?"

"You know about that, huh?"

"I read the paper every morning."

"There've been fifteen disappearances from this neighborhood." Boyd shrugged and sipped at his coffee. It was disgustingly good. He could get used to coffee like that.

"Well, I know about the Listers, of course. And about the Tripp family."

"Did you know any of them personally?"

"I met both of the boys from the families and I tried to offer help when the Lister boy took ill."

The man was calm and cool. He was exactly the sort of person that Boyd distrusted on sight.

"Have you seen anyone strange hanging around these parts?"

"My good man, I'm sure you're aware that I have only recently moved here. Everyone is still strange to me."

"Okay. Have you seen anyone stranger than you?"

Soulis gave that little smile of his and nodded his head. "Nicely put, Detective. I had a man visit me the other day, asking if I was interested in purchasing sexual favors. His name was Tom Pardue, I believe. He struck me as rather unsavory."

"That was the only reason Pardue came to see you?"

"Indeed. I declined his offer."

"He was here for a long while."

"Was he? I wasn't aware. I was out looking at the ocean." Soulis shifted slightly in his seat and rested one hand under his chin.

"Like the ocean, do you?"

"It's why I moved here. The view is spectacular."

"Where did you move here from, Mr. Soulis?"

"Ohio."

"Why did you move?"

"My house was broken into and I no longer felt safe."

"Did they take anything?"

"There wasn't much worth taking. Most of my valuables were in holding."

"Did you know that Tom Pardue was dead?"

"Yes. I am also aware of the tragedy at the university. Something about a fraternity house fire."

"It's been a busy week."

"I suspect so, yes."

Boyd couldn't get a thing from the man in front of him. He might as well have been speaking about the weather.

"If I leave you my card, will you call me if you see anything suspicious?"

"Naturally. Has the police force considered a curfew?"

"There's already a curfew in place for kids around here, high school and under. They have to be off the streets by ten P.M."

"How's that been working out?"

"Not so good. We have around fourteen or fifteen missing right now."

He read a list of names to the man, and asked if he'd met or knew anyone on the list. The only ones he claimed to know were the kids he'd already mentioned.

"We'll be in touch if that's all right, Mr. Soulis?"

"Please, call me Jason and of course, if I can help in any way, you have but to ask."

Boyd shook his hand as they were leaving and winced. The man had a grip that was intimidating.

On the way out to the car, Danny was grinning like a runway model.

"What are you smiling about?"

"You don't like him."

"No, I don't."

"You think he did something, don't you?"

"Yeah. I just haven't figured out what."

"You're getting jumpy, Richie."

Boyd shrugged. "It's a hobby."

"You think he took those kids?"

"I think he knows something is all."

"Why do you say that?"

"Because he looks like he knows something."

Before Danny could come up with an appropriate answer they were called back to the station. O'Neill wanted to bitch them out again. He'd recovered from being called a bitch.

He hadn't driven twenty feet before Danny started in again. "Are we there yet? . . . Are we there yet? . . ."

"I've still got the cigar, Danny. I can light it right up."

"You're no fun when you're pissy, Richie."

"That ain't what your mother said."

"Gave up on Whalen, did ya?"

"Again with the damned Whalen comments!"

"Somebody's getting oversensitive."

Boyd lit his cigar. Danny shut his mouth.

CHAPTER 18

I

Soulis walked down into the basement of his house, smiling to himself. They were pleasant enough men, the detectives. Annoying, but pleasant.

It was easy enough to slide between the stones in the floor and move through the darkness until he reached the cave far below the house. There were a lot of tricks he'd learned over the years, and becoming a shadow was one of the simplest.

When he stepped into the cave, they were all waiting, most of them in a stupor, a few conscious and ready to escape if they could. The new ones were still dead. They would be until the sun had set. That was still a few hours away.

The cavern lay below sea level, a deep, dank secret place that only two living people knew about. It was one of the main reasons he had chosen Albert Miles's house as the proper location for his experiments.

The problem had always been the same as far as he could figure: the newly risen were always rather stupid. It was hard to rise from the dead and come out of the entire situation feeling alert and perky. Not only did they lack any substantial strength, but they also looked like they'd just recently been killed. The average life expectancy of a recently reborn vampire was not very long. The ones that didn't get killed by whomever they were attacking in the first few nights of their new lives usually didn't make it past the first sunrise. They were delicate creatures, really, and the sun could destroy them in very little time.

So Jason had decided to experiment. He'd done well enough in Ohio, before Jonathan Crowley showed up and killed off his new prizes. After that, he decided it was time to get a little bolder in his tests.

He hid the bodies away and let them fester for a while; let them stew in their own death with just enough blood to keep them coherent and recovering from their journey back to the world. That was how they all explained it to him, the ones that had actually died: they said it was like coming back from a far darker place.

They also said they came back without their souls in a lot of cases. He wondered about that and whether or not there was any truth to the notion. Most of the time he didn't give any consideration to the idea of a soul or a life force; it was something he'd never had to deal with.

There were different types of vampires; he knew that much for certain. There were the ones like what he had been leaving in this cave—killed as food, they would rise within a few days and continue the cycle of feeding and killing—and there were the ones who were created through the exchange of blood and other bodily secretions. The latter were far rarer to encounter. It wasn't often that one of his kind decided to make a new Undead. He wondered if others thought of the distinction or if it was only him. Oh well, live and learn.

He knew a few others who had created Undead as opposed to merely vampires, but they seemed to find the entire affair some sort of secret, best left locked away. Jason couldn't understand that notion. He had no shame regarding what he had created. The rest seemed to look on what they had done as a mistake of epic proportions.

Still, he supposed if he was going to experiment, he needed to cover all of the possibilities. Besides, it was only a rare few he had ever found who he felt could handle the changes in their lives.

Maggie Preston, for example, was virtually ideal for the part. What a lovely young woman. He wondered idly how angry she would be when she found out what he had done to her.

Back to business. He looked at the sickly things crawling or sleeping in the cave and smiled. Some of the braver ones had figured out how to escape around the same time they realized that breathing was not a necessity any longer. Most of them hadn't come along that far in their thought processes.

Waking up, it seemed, took a while.

"Please, let us go." Her name was Danielle Hopkins. He'd taken her from the campus of the university right after she'd dealt with the boy Maggie had befriended.

"Not yet, Danni. It's not time." He spoke as patiently as he could. That one tended to whine. She wasn't doing well; her skin was sloughing off.

"When? Can you tell me that?"

"Maybe tomorrow night."

"So long?" Her voice was miserable.

"Not so long, my child. Barely any time at all."

"I'm so hungry."

"I know. Soon, Danni. Soon."

She slipped across the ground, her eyes wide and casting their faint silvery light. "Please, just for a short time? Just for a few hours?" Danni suddenly got a crafty look on her face. "I can tell you who has been sneaking out . . ."

Jason looked from her to where the Lister family was sleeping, pale, yes, but far better nourished than she was. They had barely decayed at all. "Oh, Danni." He patted her pale blond hair and felt a few strands fall out at the light touch. "I already know who's been escaping."

He did, too. He knew by how healthy they looked. The children normally managed to figure it out first. Sometimes they even caught on to the limitations of their abilities and got back before the sun incinerated them.

Yes, he was very pleased with how this was going. There were more of them surviving and getting stronger. He rubbed the hairs off his fingertips and smiled. Danielle was crying again. She cried a great deal of the time.

"Danielle, my dear, only until tomorrow night and then you will be free."

"Do you really mean it?" Suddenly another day or two in the ground seemed like a small price to pay to her, and she was smiling.

"Of course, child. I would never lie to you. Tomorrow night, and then the world will be yours for the picking."

She wept again, this time they were tears of joy.

II

It was almost four in the afternoon when Maggie woke up. She stretched and realized that Ben's bed was empty, except for her.

With just a moment's concentration she realized that he was in the kitchen, cooking something that smelled absolutely heavenly. The scent of coffee coming into the room didn't hurt either.

She was wearing a pair of his pajamas. Mostly they fit, but she had to hold up the waistband with one hand and her chest was straining a few buttons.

She walked down the hall and into the kitchen where he was just finishing with his preparations. Grilled cheese sandwiches on rye bread and a pot of cream of tomato soup.

The room was bright, but not uncomfortably so. She sat down at the table and watched him while he finished up the last of the sandwiches.

"Good morning, Ben."

"Afternoon, sleepy head."

"Thank you." She looked into his eyes and he quickly looked away. He was cute. She'd never known a college-aged boy who was so shy around her.

"You haven't tasted it yet."

"That's not what I mean."

He finally looked back at her and flashed a tentative smile. "I know. You're welcome."

They ate in almost complete silence. The food was good and she was ravenous.

When they were finished, he cleaned the dishes, waving off her offer to help.

Parts of his apartment were messy and looked lived in. The kitchen and the bedroom were the exceptions. In those two places he was a bit of a neat freak.

"So, what happened last night, Maggie?"

She had to think about that, because, honestly, she didn't really understand it all herself. "I don't know. I have a few suspicions."

"You don't know what happened to Tom?"

"That I do know." She looked him in the eyes and this time he didn't look away. "I killed him, Ben. He went too far and I killed him." She looked away from him for the first time, suddenly worried. "Do you hate me for that?"

"I don't think I could ever hate you, Maggie. No, I think he got what he deserved."

"He did. He definitely did."

"Then why would you think I would hate you?"

"I killed a man." She'd killed several, actually, but he didn't know about them and she wasn't sure she wanted to tell him.

"Well, no, I don't hate you. I'm just a little worried about you."

"So am I."

"I didn't know if I should take you to the hospital or what, Maggie." He was starting to get a look of panic on his face. "I was afraid the blood was all yours and I was afraid you were going to get sick and die on me."

"I didn't, though."

He nodded his head and closed his eyes for a second. "I know. I just . . . I don't normally get close to people. I'm not used to it. So when I do, I get a little weird."

"Well I don't really go out of my way to meet new people either. My profession doesn't really encourage it."

He nodded again. "Yeah, what are you gonna do now? I mean, you don't have Tom there to help you set things up or whatever he did."

She smiled. He was very diplomatic when he wanted to be. "I'll figure something out. I've got some cash stowed away."

"Yeah, well, about Tom . . ."

"Yeah?"

"I sort of stole his money. All of it."

"You're shitting me."

"No. No, I stole it and put it in a safe place. Not easy to access, but I figured if you wanted to check into it, I can give you the account numbers."

"What the hell made you do a thing like that, Ben? That's just dangerous."

"Yeah, well, him kicking my ass the other day sort of made me angry."

"So you robbed his accounts?"

"Yeah."

"Why are you telling me this?"

"Well, I don't know if it maybe caused whatever had you so pissed off at him."

She had to think about it. Yes, it probably had been an influence, but not the biggest one. "No. He was just a dick."

"Good, because I would hate myself if I did something that hurt you."

"Don't hate yourself. There's enough of that going around already."

"You hating yourself for what happened?"

"Which part?"

"Don't. You're a good person." He got really bold and touched her hand.

"Don't count on it." She shook her head, remembering the blood from the night before. It didn't seem completely real, but she could remember it in vivid detail.

The thing was she really didn't feel badly about it. She should have, that was the part that bothered her. She was actually very surprised that Ben wasn't ready to head for the hills instead of being anywhere around her.

"So what's next?"

"I think I have to talk to a man I met. I think he might have done this to me."

"What? Did he hide you in a secret lab?"

"Something like that." She smiled. He probably wouldn't want to hear the details and she really didn't want to share them anyway.

"You need someone to cover your back?"

"I don't know. Maybe."

"Well, if you want help, I'm not really planning on doing anything special right now."

"Okay. So it's a date."

"Might want to go by your place first. I mean, I like the pajama look on you, but it's going to be hard for him to focus on answering questions with you in that."

She punched him lightly on the shoulder and laughed. "Goof."

III

Kelli went into town and started shopping. She had to go trick-or-treating tomorrow and there was no time for being picky. She needed a costume ASAP.

Of course she'd heard about the fire. She was just not going to think about it. She was starting to get very good at avoidance. Having people dying all around you did that to a girl. At least that was what Erika said and she should know; she was a psych major, after all.

Erika Addison was a svelte redhead with big baby blue eyes, a devastating pout, and a passionate love of parties and the morbid. Halloween was her kind of gig and she insisted that Kelli have a good time. She was also right, so Kelli was listening.

"What do you think?" Erika was holding up a witch outfit that would get most girls thrown in jail for public indecency. She could not only get away with it, she would probably get a marriage proposal or two.

"I think you might need one of those for each boob."

"Prude."

"I am not."

"Not a total prude, but you're working on it."

"Family values do not make me a prude, Erika."

"They don't make you any friends with guys, though."

"Not all of us need a 'Now Serving number' sign on our doors."

"Meow, Kelli. And I don't need the sign, I just like it."

She rolled her eyes and shook her hair out. Erika wasn't happy if she wasn't being scandalous. Kelli caught a costume that struck her fancy. It was a zombie costume and it wouldn't take a lot of work. Also, not so scary the kids would freak out.

"God, you cannot be serious." Erika looked at her like she'd lost her mind as she examined the costume.

"Why not?"

"Because zombie chicks do not get laid at frat parties and you definitely need to get laid, girl."

"So . . . maybe I'll get a second costume for afterwards." It wasn't in the plans and it sure wasn't in her budget, but she wouldn't mind looking a little sexy for a change of pace.

Erika waved the devil outfit at her. "I'm buying this for you."

"Okay, Erika, you might have the body for that, but I do not." Kelli shook her head good and hard to make her point.

"Fine." She reached out and grabbed an outfit that was just a bit less revealing than Elvira's usual black ensemble. Erika raised one eyebrow in question and challenge alike as she held out the package for Kelli to see. "Try this one. And yes, you have the tits for it."

A woman hauling two shell-shocked kids around the store looked over with a frown of disapproval at the language and Erika stuck out her tongue in response.

"I can't wear that, Erika."

"Of course you can." Erika smiled brightly. "I'm glad we agree."

"No, seriously, Erika . . ."

"Honey, it comes with a mask. You're wearing it."

"But—"

"It's settled. We can even dye your hair if you want."

"Are you spoiling me?"

"Yes. Deal with it."

She nodded and smiled. It was nice to get spoiled now and then. Besides, the number of times she'd spoiled Erika, she figured she had one coming.

One full section of the wall was completely emptied of costumes. An illustration on the wall showed a black-hooded affair with tattered sleeves. "Popular costume . . ."

"Ever since that *Scream* movie came out." Erika shook her head. "No originality."

"Well, it was kind of a neat costume . . ." Kelli had seen it a week ago and toyed with it. She was shocked to see them all gone.

"No, it was kind of a neat movie. The costume shows no cleavage, so how good can it be?"

"You have no shame."

"Shame is for the weak and the virgins."

"Well, I guess I'm weak."

"Yeah, but at least you're not a virgin."

"Could you announce that a little louder?"

"Nah. I'll just tell the guys you're easy at the parties tomorrow night."

"Don't you dare!"

"Watch me," she smirked. "You'll have a wig and a mask. Keep the mask on and have a party, I say."

"You would." Kelli started to laugh and stopped when Erika looked at her funny.

"Who are you kidding? I already did. Try it some time."

"Thanks for doing this." She felt like crying but hid it well.

"For what? Going out and partying? Any time!"

Kelli nodded and tried to hold in her feelings, but it was harder to do all the time. Erika moved over and pulled her close, offering a shoulder that Kelli did not want to use. She used it anyway. She needed it. The days were driving her crazy and the nights were a hundred times worse.

"We need to get you out of that house, Kelli. Even if it's only for a few nights."

"I don't have anywhere to go."

"Shit. You can come stay with me, okay?" All the usual caustic charm was gone and Erika was just herself; a warm, wonderful person who hid it well sometimes.

"I don't want to be a bother."

"Screw you. You're staying with me tonight."

Kelli nodded, grateful. She needed to rest, and she hadn't had a good night's sleep since Teddy disappeared.

IV

"It's pissing me off. Something Soulis said was wrong. I just don't know what it was."

"You're obsessing, Richie."

"I do not obsess. I get results."

"Save it for O'Neill."

"O'Neill can kiss my hairy ass."

"Better be careful. He might if we actually figure out what's going on around here."

"You're starting to whine again."

"I got a headache."

"Suck it up." Boyd reached for the coffee again. If he kept drinking it this fast, he'd be pissing all night.

"Don't go getting all grumpy bear on me, Richie. Only one of us can be bitchy at a time and it's my turn."

"Okay. Good point." He stole one of Danny's shrimp. "So here's the deal. I think Soulis is dirty."

"We already discussed that."

"I know, but I want to talk about it again."

"Well, he gave a good excuse for dealing with Tommy, didn't he?"

"Yeah, but it was almost too good."

"How do you figure?"

Danny stole a French fry from his plate. Then the bastard went and took a bite of his burger.

"He didn't say how he knew about Tommy's death."

"Yeah? It's a small town."

"Yes, it is. But that doesn't mean everything that happens is spread around town to a stranger."

"Maybe he gets the paper."

"Maybe we need to look at this morning's paper . . ."

They both called for Sally at the same time. She sighed and moved their way.

"Yeah, guys?"

"Sally, love of my life, flame of my heart."

"Don't make me sick, Boyd."

"Hmmph. Okay then, you got any copies of this morning's paper lying around?"

"I knew you wanted something." She shook her head and walked toward the kitchen door.

"I love you, baby, honest."

"You tip like we're already married, Boyd."

"You gotta start tipping her better. She's gonna start spitting in your coffee or something." Danny took another bite of his burger and Boyd scowled. One shrimp was not worth that much of his burger.

Sally came back out with a slightly wet newspaper. "It's all yours. It's been in the trash, so have fun."

"Yeah?" Boyd smiled at her. "Want to order me another burger?"

"Sure, hon."

"And Sally, my love?"

"Yeah?"

"Wash your hands for me, okay?" He stole another shrimp and opened the paper.

"Boyd, I'm bored."

"Stop whining or I'll make you read, Danny Boy."

When Danny didn't comment, he looked up to see why. Ben Kirby was walking into the diner with a bombshell on his arm.

"When the hell did he get popular?"

"Maybe he's spending some of Tommy's money." Boyd watched the two sit down and saw Sally move over to them in a hurry, a smile on her face.

"More power."

"Amen, brother. On the other hand, if he's giving out loans, I could use a new car."

"You could use a car that doesn't belong to the department, you cheap bastard."

"I ain't cheap and my parents were married."

"Not according to Sally."

"Yeah? What would she know about my parents?"

"You're a funny man, Richie."

Boyd went back to reading. He scanned every headline and then threw the paper into Danny's lap just as his partner was finishing off his burger. "See if you can find any mention of a dead pimp bastard in there, Danny."

"Nothing?"

"Not a damn thing. And that's the other thing that bugged me. Why did Soulis talk to us about the frat fire? Far as that article says, it started and it burned; the article didn't say anything about who died or missing bodies."

"That might be stretching it, Richie."

"The fuck it might be. We're gonna go pay our new friend another visit."

"What? You're getting my second burger to go?"

"Touch that burger, Danny Boy, and I'll bust your head open."

Danny waved until Sally looked his way. Ben looked over, too, and the girl next to him smiled tentatively. Sally walked over and put her hands on her hips. "What?"

"Sally? If I make Boyd give you a good tip, can I have another burger, and maybe they could both be to go?" He was putting on his pretty-boy pouty face with the big baby eyes. Sally fell for it the same as all the women did.

"Sure, hon. But I'm not letting you off the hook for crappy tips, either. I dug into trash for you boys."

"But, Boyd loves you . . ."

"Yeah, love like that I can get on the radio." Boyd wasn't quite sure what that meant, but he laughed anyway. Five minutes later Sally put the burgers in a bag and handed Danny the check. Danny put down enough cash to pay for five times that much food. Seeing as she only charged them for around half of their orders, she earned a fat tip now and then.

On their way out, Boyd smiled at Ben and stopped. "How's things, Ben?" He noticed the bruises on the kid's face, but most of his attention was stuck in his peripheral vision, where the girl was sitting and watching him. Danny didn't even pretend to notice Ben. He was almost drooling.

"Good, Officer Boyd. How did things go with our mutual acquaintance?"

"Which one? Tommy or Freemont?"

"Freemont."

"He's out on bail for now. But not for long. Waiting for a few test results to come in."

"Do you think he'll go away?"

"Oh, hell yeah, kid. He's already gone, he just don't know it."

"Good." It dawned on him that the girl might be a material witness in the case. He made a note to ask Ben. He'd wait until the kid was alone, however, just in case something had happened to her that would be embarrassing. He wasn't into embarrassing kids like Ben or their dates. Christ knew he probably didn't get out that much.

"Funny thing happened to Tommy."

Both Ben and the girl looked ready to rabbit when he mentioned the name. Danny noticed it too.

"Yeah?"

"Yeah. He wound up dead. He also wound up with his bank accounts drained."

Ben was looking a little green, and Boyd smiled at him.

"I don't think the two are connected or anything like that, and it's not my case anyway." Danny snorted and Boyd resisted the urge to hit him over the head with the burger sack. "I just thought it was interesting."

"I guess it is."

Boyd leaned in much closer and looked Ben in the eyes long and hard. "If I was the sort of person that would take that sort of money from someone like that, Ben, I think I would make very sure my tracks were covered. Because I can't promise the detectives on the case will notice anything, but I wouldn't be surprised by it, either. I know them both. They're very good. We'll see you around, Ben. Nice to meet you miss . . . ?"

The girl with the devastating smile looked his way and gave her name. "I'm Maggie. Ben and I are study buddies."

"I'm Boyd and this is Danny. He and I are detectives." He smiled and went on his way.

When they were outside of the diner, Danny looked at him and shook his head. "She look familiar to you?"

"Not really." He shrugged and kept walking. "Could be I'm used to seeing her in red."

It was worth the casual act for the stupid look on Danny's face. "You're fuckin' kidding me."

"No, I am not fucken kidding you. But we already agreed not to discuss red ladies."

Danny looked back into the diner. His eyes searching until he found the right booth. "Fuck me, Richie. You're good."

"Not with O'Neill's dick, Danny Boy. And I'm better than good."

"Gotta watch that ego, sunshine."

"Not in this lifetime."

"Soulis's place?"

"Yep. But we're just gonna watch for now."

"Yeah? Why?"

"Call it a hunch. Something about that girl in there and something about Soulis."

"Yeah? Like what?"

"Something about their eyes . . ."

"Let's go, Richie. I'm bored."

"Yeah, now that you ain't staring at that girl's tits."

"Man's gotta have hobbies, Richie."

"Man should learn subtlety, Danny Boy."

"Where's the fun in that?"

V

Alan Tripp was feeling much better after a shower and a meal. So far no one had noticed that he was home. Well, no police cars at least. His closest neighbor, a man he still did not know by name after twelve years, waved when he saw him. Happily, that was after the shower and a set of real clothes.

The shower was wonderful. The meal he barely tasted. Part of him just wanted to get comfortable, but he couldn't let that happen. So he cleaned the wound on his hand, scrubbing with soap and then rinsing with hydrogen peroxide seemed to take care of any possibility of comfort. The flesh around the wound was angry, red and swollen.

He wrapped it tightly and forgot about it almost as soon as he was done.

He'd planned on getting busy with his weapons, but instead he sat down at his home office and signed onto the Internet. There had to be a few sites about vampires out there.

There were over seven and a half million sites that listed vampires. He sighed and searched through the first fifty or so before his eyes started closing on him.

The sound of glass breaking was what woke him up. It wasn't a small pane of glass being cracked by a rock; it was more like somebody had swatted at the sliding glass door with a hammer. He'd gone to sleep in front of the computer screen and had rested his weight on both arms. His hands were sound asleep and not at all happy about being awakened.

Groggy and dazed, he listened for any further sounds. At first there was only silence, but he heard the whispers. They were sibilant sounds, not that different from the leaves blowing down the street, but with a pattern hidden inside. Alan stood up and swayed, a bit of the room shifting rudely around him. He hadn't counted on an infection to begin with, but now it seemed his hand had decided to share the wealth of bacteria with the rest of his body.

Or maybe he'd get lucky and it was just a cold.

Either way, he had to see what was going on; not checking went against everything he believed in. This was his home and he couldn't sit idly by and do nothing if someone was breaking in. He walked as best he could to the doorway, and leaned against the wall for support.

He listened for the whispers and heard them again. Something about the sound sent shivers across his spine. He listened closer and finally understood what it was. He knew the voices. He couldn't make out the words, true enough, but he knew the voices.

Meghan was whispering to Avery and he was whispering back.

Hearing them, knowing they were right outside the house and talking, took all of the strength from Alan's limbs. He made himself slide along the wall until he could look toward the broken window he knew was close by.

Vampires can't get in unless they're invited, right? That's what it says in all the movies. They've got to know more than I do. Okay. So how did Avery get in? Damned fool. You invited him.

What else was supposed to work on vampires? He thought fast and hard and finally decided to move into the living room. There, on the end table where she always kept it, was Meghan's family Bible. The bookmark that held her place in the book was a crucifix on a leather strap. He pulled the book to him and carried it in his left, wounded hand, the bookmark in his right. He felt heat surging through the wound and clenched his teeth.

Avery stood in front of him, trying to coax his mother through the window and having no success.

"Come on, Mom, you can do it."

She reached again then backed away, her expression showing her frustration. "I can't. Something is stopping me."

Alan watched her try again and fail. The sweet face he'd fallen in love with back in their senior year of high school—long before they dated, but it was love—grew ugly with anger and she snarled. He'd never seen her with that look on her face. He wasn't sure her face had ever been designed for that sort of rage. She was like an almost perfect copy of the woman he married. He hated the thing outside his back door for that reason; hated it easily as much as he had ever loved his wife.

"Meghan." His voice broke when he said her name and he

felt the sting of tears threatening to escape. God, how he'd loved her; how she had completed him.

Avery turned to face him and so did his wife. "Alan? Can I come in?"

She had to ask. That much was true at least. They couldn't come in unless they were invited; he wondered if all of the evil things in the world had that limitation. *Maybe*, he thought. *Otherwise how could there be anything left?*

"Yeah, hon. Come on in."

Her sweet, sweet smile was his reward as she gracefully stepped past the window that the two things had shattered. *Broke that fucker apart, Meghan*; he looked at the fragments of glass on the ground and was surprised to see that they cast reflections in the shards. The reflections showed a different Meghan, one who'd been dead for two days and an Avery who'd been dead most of a week. *Same as you did my heart and soul.*

"Alan, we've missed you, baby." Yes, oh that one hurt. That perfect smile on that perfect face as she came toward him with her arms opened, ready to hug him and to love him again.

He wished he could believe it for a moment. A thousand times he wished he could believe it as Meghan and Avery came closer.

Alan held out the crucifix, showed it to them and let them see what he carried. Avery flinched, but Meghan kept coming. Alan waved it around to make sure she saw it.

"Silly man," she smiled and grabbed the cross in her hand, drawing the cord from between his numbed fingers. She held it up for him to see and then kissed it with her full lips. Her eyes lit up with amusement. "It's just a pretty little trinket if you don't believe in it."

Avery bit him on his wrist, sharp teeth cutting through his flesh with the greatest of ease. The Bible fell to the ground as he tried to shake his son free.

Meghan dropped the necklace and reached for his face with her hands. Her strength was amazing. Avery had been powerful, but Meghan was so much bigger than a ten-year-old boy.

Alan kneed his son in the chest and, as Avery staggered back from him, spitting blood and profanities, he brought his left hand around to punch the monster with Meghan's features as hard as he could in her face. His right hand came into play too, groping along the bookshelf that held most of the family's mementos.

Meghan barely flinched from his fist, which flared into a lightning blast of pain as he tore the stitches from the infected wound. His right hand caught a picture frame that held their favorite wedding photo. He brought the edge of the frame around and slammed it into her right temple hard enough to bend the polished chrome corner and drive slivers of breaking glass into his fingertips.

She let out a small gasp of pain as the flesh on her temple dented inward, and then Meghan caught his hand in her grip and squeezed until his bones broke and the Kodachrome memory was sliced apart by glass and bathed in his blood.

Avery lunged forward and sank his teeth into Alan's crotch, gnashing and savaging even as his tiny hands sank into Alan's thigh with enough force to tear the denim covering his flesh.

Alan did not go gently into the darkness. His family made sure of it.

VI

Boyd woke up to the sound of Danny whistling "It's a Small World," and started into consciousness as his partner tapped his shoulder. Before he could tell his friend to shut the fuck up, Danny was pointing.

Ben Kirby and the bombshell were approaching Soulis's front door.

"You fucken kidding me?" He sat up, fully awake, and looked as the door opened without the two bothering to knock. Jason Soulis smiled familiarly at Maggie Preston. He gave a polite bow of his head to Ben. For only a second, he looked toward their car and, even from a distance, Boyd would swear the man looked right at him through the glass.

A moment later the three were inside and the door closed.

"Did he just wink at us?" Danny chuckled as he asked the words and then shook his head. "I think that prick just winked at us."

Thirty seconds after that, the crows started landing all over the Crown Victoria. They dropped from nearby trees and from the darkness overhead and landed, making themselves comfortable. There were enough of the damned things settling down that Boyd could feel the car's shock absorbers compensating.

"What do you think the chances are we'll get shit on if we climb out?"

Danny laughed out loud. "I'm thinking we get out of this car and we're gonna be pecked to death."

"Yeah?"

"You ever see a crow go at roadkill, Richie? They can use them beaks to cut meat like a steak knife."

"So screw it." He started the car and activated the wipers. The birds on the windows hopped out of the way, cawing in protest. Boyd started driving.

"We're just quitting?"

"No, we're going to do something else instead." Boyd lit his cigar, filling the car with thick white smoke. When he was done with that, he shifted into drive and they pulled away from the curb.

"You're getting fickle, Richie."

"I don't want to get my eyes plucked out of my head, Danny. Do you?"

He pretended to think about it. "Not really on my list of things to do, you know what I mean?"

"You want coffee?"

"Duh."

"Yeah, I thought so." The birds started flying away. He was surprised they'd stayed on a moving vehicle for that long.

"Where are we going?"

"I'll think of something."

"We could go to bed."

"With you? You're a sick bastard, Danny."

"So where are we going?"

"The morgue. I wanna check on a few things. Then I think we'll check on our old pal, Brian Freemont."

"Yay. I love field trips."

VII

"I was wondering how long it would be before you came to see me, Maggie." Jason led them into his house. "I didn't expect you to bring a friend." The notion seemed to amuse him.

"He's a very good friend to have, Jason. We were both wondering what the hell you did to me."

"I made you better." He led them into the dining room. "Sit, be comfortable. I'll bring refreshments."

They waited for a few minutes. Ben looked around the place with a nervous eye.

"Nice place."

"I think Jason does all right for himself." She'd been with a lot of men who managed to make money hand over fist. Jason was just the first to make her into something that wasn't human. She rubbed her arms.

Jason came back in, carrying a tray with coffee and an array of small sandwiches. "I believe you would like answers."

"Yes, please."

He looked toward Ben, with that amused smile back in place. "Do you want them with Ben in the room?"

Ben made no comment and kept his face perfectly neutral.

"Yes. You can tell me in front of Ben."

"You trust him that far?"

She nodded.

"Good. Excellent. That's a rare thing, a trust like that."

"What did you do to me?"

"I gave you power and the ability to defend yourself from almost anything."

"Don't play with me, Jason, please. Tell it to me straight."

Jason shrugged. "I made you into a vampire."

Ben looked at him as if he'd lost his mind. "You're serious."

"Of course. It's a serious subject, Mr. Kirby."

"A vampire?" Maggie sat very still as she tried to absorb that. "As in coffins, sunlight, and drinking blood?"

"You can forgo the coffin, actually. They're hardly necessary." Jason looked from one to the other and let that little smile play around his dark eyes. The worst part was that she wanted him. She wanted to politely ask Ben to stay here and then she wanted to take Jason up to his room and do everything they'd done before all over again. Damn, he was a sexy man.

She shook the thought away. "Okay, why did you make me a vampire and what does that mean, exactly, because I saw my reflection in the mirror not ten minutes ago."

"There's a lot to explain, so I'm going to hit the high notes and we'll go from there."

They both nodded.

"First, you do not need a coffin. That's just one of those little things the fiction writers came up with. You also do not need the soil you were buried in. You were not buried. You are not dead. You are very much alive." He smiled. "That makes you an exception."

"How so?" Ben asked the question. Jason got an irritated look for a second. He recovered quickly.

"Most vampires are created when you feed and kill." He shrugged. "They are a different breed. They die, they rise from the grave. They need to worry more about coffins and soil than you do."

Ben opened his mouth again and Jason waved him silent before he could speak. "I'll get to it, Ben. Please save the questions for later."

Ben nodded apologetically and Jason went on.

"There are other ways to make a vampire. Maggie, I suspect you already know what acts we did together that caused this." Ben closed his eyes. Other than that simple action, he remained perfectly calm.

"But why me, Jason?"

"Because you fit the needs I was looking for."

"How so?"

"Well, for starters, you're a very independent woman. You

have no strong connections to the world around you, and you fascinate me." He shrugged. "All three were important to my criteria."

"What? I'm an experiment?"

Jason laughed softly and shook his head. "No. And yes."

She felt herself growing agitated and tried to follow Ben's example.

"I am experimenting, but not on you. I'm experimenting on the other type of vampires because I'm curious. But that's not really important. I did what I did because I wanted to, and because I think certain types of beauty should be saved. Maggie, you will never grow old and you will never have to die as long as you are smart."

"How do you fix it?"

"There's nothing to fix, Maggie. It's done. You are what you are from now until the end of your existence."

Her ears were ringing. Ben was looking from her to Jason and he was looking very unhappy. She'd have to talk to him about that. Not to chastise him, but to make sure he was okay with everything. She needed him to be okay, much as that unsettled her.

"Now, listen carefully, because there's a lot to say. Sunlight will not kill you, but it will make you weaker. It will kill the ones that are made from your bite—"

That one took her off guard and she jumped a bit. "Oh shit."

"They have been taken care of."

Ben was looking very puzzled. She couldn't take the time to explain and she didn't want to either.

"How often do I need to drink blood?"

"When you hunger for it," Jason shrugged. "There has never been any rhyme or reason that I have discovered. Sometimes I don't need to feed for a couple of weeks and other times I cannot get enough without going on a killing spree."

"Do you have to kill them?"

"No. But it's convenient."

Ben was shaking his head from side to side very slowly.

"Why?"

"If you bleed them and do not kill them, you can create more like yourself. It might take a while but it will happen if you feed from the same ones too often." He placed his hand under his chin and looked at her intently. "Sex can cause the same problem."

"So why is that bad?"

"Because too many predators can cause harm." He smiled and shook his head, the dark hair moving in a soft wave. "We can be bad for the human population."

"If you don't kill someone, they don't come back as a vampire?"

"Not often, and not unless you share with them."

Maggie's mind kept focusing on the fact that she would never grow old. "What about children? Can I have children?"

The answer was not what she expected.

VIII

Brian Freemont thought he was safe at the hotel. He'd chosen one in the center of town and stayed there with the lights on and the TV playing drivel in the background. He slept peacefully for a few hours.

Then the pounding started at his door. The blows were loud enough to scare him into consciousness, gasping and clutching at his chest. In his dream, Angie had been giving him a blow job—something she seldom did—and her teeth had been tearing his flesh away. He was glad the nightmare was gone, but terrified by what might be on the other side of the door.

"Who's there?"

"Housekeeping, numb nuts." The voice belonged to Richard Boyd. "Open the door before I kick it down."

Brian opened the door, almost glad to see the little bastard.

"What do you want now?" He was wearing jeans but had taken off his shirt. The chill from outside was like walking into a gigantic refrigerator.

Boyd walked into the room, his face set in a shit-eating grin that chilled Brian far worse than the cold did. "Brian Freemont, you are under arrest. You have the right to remain silent, if you give up the right to remain silent anything you say can and will be used against you in a court of law . . ." He kept reciting the Miranda while Holdstedter pulled out his cuffs and smiled a promise of lethal force if Brian even considered resisting.

Brian had the good sense not to resist. He wanted his shoes and his shirt. They wouldn't let him have them.

"So what are you charging me with?"

"The rape and murder of Veronica Miller."

"I didn't do anything."

"Evidence found inside the condom left at the scene places her DNA on the exterior of the condom and yours on the interior. Oh, yeah, and aggravated sodomy. Can't forget that one, can we, Danny?"

Holdstedter looked murder at Brian. "No, Richie, I don't think we can forget that, either."

"Guys, I've been set up." He knew how lame it sounded, but it was all he had.

"Hey, Richie."

"Yeah, Danny?"

"Look, he resisted." Holdstedter backhanded Brian with an open hand. He hit the ground and groaned, his entire face feeling like it had been slapped. Holdstedter had big hands.

"That was the only one, Danny Boy. We don't want this dick walking on a technicality."

Holdstedter picked him up, lifted him completely off the ground with frightening ease and set him on his feet. He smiled into Brian's face. "He wouldn't think of trying that sort of shit. He's got to know I've got weapons of his with his greasy fingerprints all over them. I mean, it'd be easy to put one in his dead hand and say he tried to shoot first, if he did something really stupid like trying to weasel out on a technicality."

Boyd walked over. "You got weapons of his, Danny? 'Cause I thought we'd confiscated his shotgun."

"Yeah, we did. It's in evidence lockup. One firearm."

They let that sink in. They still had his pistols. Brian nodded his head to make clear that he understood.

"Let's get this asshole to the lockup."

Brian sat in the back of the car without saying a word, numb to any sort of thinking or actions.

Holdstedter yawned in the passenger's seat.

"I need coffee, Richie."

"I need food, Danny."

"Diner?"

"Diner."

"We dropping shithead off first?"

"Nope. He can sit and savor the sweet smell of freedom for a while."

"More like the smell of your cigars."

Boyd turned his head and blew a heavy cloud of cigar smoke into Brian's face. "Whatever makes him happy. Gonna smell better than sitting in a lockup room with Dirk Lockley."

"Richie, are we that lucky?"

"Oh, yeah. Dirk is in for the night. He tried to hit a convenience store and Coswell nabbed his stupid ass."

"What is it Dirk is always saying he'd do to a cop if he ever had a chance?"

"Fuck 'im up the ass and make 'im lick his cock clean."

Danny laughed. Brian closed his eyes and prayed he wouldn't have to deal with Lockley. The man was a giant mountain of fat and muscle. His bowels seemed ready to leave his body any way they could.

The detectives pulled up in front of the Silver Dollar Diner. They made sure to lock the doors when they got out.

Brian watched them walk away until he saw the figures on the roof of the brick and chrome building. In the neon light, he saw Angela and five college girls that he knew intimately.

"Boyd! Boyd! Fuck's sake! Boyd let me out of here!" He screamed as loudly as he could, trying to break the cuffs that held his wrists together in the small of his back. All he got for his trouble were a few lacerations.

Boyd and Holdstedter probably heard him, but they didn't respond.

He looked up as the six women on the roof dropped down to the parking lot and walked his way. Every one of them was smiling, baring wickedly sharp teeth.

He was still screaming when they peeled the roof of the car away and reached for him.

CHAPTER 19

Boyd drew his weapon and ran for the door when he heard the sounds of metal bending and glass shattering. They were enough to get him to turn, but it was the bloody shriek that came out of Freemont that made him draw his pistol.

Sounds like that weren't supposed to come out of people.

Danny was right behind him and as soon as he was out the door, Danny had his back covered and was shifting to the right.

"What the fuck?" Six women, some clothed and some naked, were pulling Brian Freemont out of what was left of the Crown Victoria. Freemont was screaming like there was no tomorrow. Maybe for him there wasn't. In the glow of the parking lights, he recognized each and every one of the girls. One of them was Freemont's wife. She was nude, her body glistening it was so pale, her belly distended with the unborn baby she was carrying.

The others were all younger, mostly pretty, and all of them had files on his desk. He'd dealt with the families and friends of all of them in the last few days. They were all among the missing persons he was investigating. He took all of that in instantly.

He also took in the fact that they were going to kill Brian Freemont if he didn't do something about it.

"FREEZE!" He lowered the pistol to just over their heads.

Danny was already waiting for them to do something stupid.

Freemont's wife looked over her shoulder at Boyd and shook her head. "He's my husband, I'll kill him if I want to."

One of the others laughed: Danielle Hopkins, if he was remembering names as well as he usually did. She looked like she'd covered herself in white clay and let it dry and flake off. Her lips were blue and if he hadn't known better, he would have thought a corpse was laughing at him. His skin suddenly felt too tight. Her face barely moved, even when she moved her mouth, like some of the muscles wouldn't work. Her eyes were staring at him and he thought he could see something moving in her hair.

"Put him down and back away, ladies. I don't want to hurt any of you."

Brian was making all sorts of noises, but none of them were coherent. Danny was as still as a statue, his eyes looked half-glazed, but Boyd knew it was just how he got ready to fire a weapon.

"No, I don't think so." Freemont's wife shook her head. "We have unfinished business with Brian."

"I'm not kidding here, lady. Put him down."

He took the time to aim at her shoulder. He didn't want to shoot a pregnant woman, but if he had to, he would.

"You can have him when we're done." She rose straight up into the air, and the other women followed her example. Boyd forgot all about the pistol in his hand as they rose higher and higher, taking a screaming Brian Freemont into the air with them. Boyd just kept watching until they were almost gone.

He put his piece away.

"This is one of those Red Lady moments, Richie."

Boyd looked over at Danny and nodded. "Yeah. I'm gonna have to give a big ten-four on that."

"You get to call it in."

"Call what in?"

"The disappearance of Brian Freemont and the wrecking of the car."

"This wasn't a disappearance."

"No?"

"Fuck no. This was kidnapping."

"Were they wearing Halloween makeup?"

"I hope so. I really fucken hope so."

Several people had come out of the diner and were looking at the remains of the car. Boyd shot one of them a murderous look when he started walking over to investigate. "Get the hell away from there!" The kid backed up fast, his eyes wide. "Do you really need the fucken yellow crime scene tape, bright boy? Go back inside and eat your food. All of you!" A few comments came from the crowd, but they listened.

Danny shook his head. "You gotta worry about some of these assholes."

"I gotta worry about filling out the fucken reports. You worry about the assholes." He pulled out his cell phone and started dialing. "I'm calling Whalen and Longwood. We can't do a damned thing until we get gloves."

"What do you think they're gonna do to him?"

"Same thing we were hoping Lockley was gonna do."

"That's not gonna be pretty."

"Neither was he."

"Should I feel bad for him, Richie?"

Boyd shook his head and grinned as Whalen answered her phone. "Nancy? Hi, Boyd here. We got a situation you might want to know about."

"Boyd? What are you doing calling my house at . . . twelve-fifteen at night?"

Somewhere in the background he heard the grumbling noises of Nancy's husband. "I'm calling you to an investigation."

"You know, you have crappy timing."

"What? You were about to get lucky?"

"No, asshole, I was getting lucky."

"Yeah? I'll send your husband a dozen roses and an apology note." He supposed it was wrong to be happy about interfering in their love lives, but he took his petty little victories where he could.

"Better get to the store, Boyd. He says he's coming with me."

He was glad she was only teasing. "Would he take donuts instead?"

"If it's got a hole he can fuck, probably."

Boyd laughed out loud until his face was red. When he was calmer and Nancy was done calling him names on the phone, he told her where they were and explained a little about the situation.

She told him she'd be there in twenty minutes.

"You live five minutes away."

"Can't leave the poor bastard suffering, Boyd."

"I was gonna give him donuts . . ."

"There would be that waiting time. He isn't really a patient soul."

"Okay, I don't need to think about what you're doing to make him groan, so I'm getting off the phone, Whalen." That was true. She frustrated him enough without extra help.

"You sure? I was gonna let you listen. It's kind of kinky that way."

He hung up the phone, not one hundred percent sure she was joking and very bothered by that notion.

Danny was looking at him and grinning like a chimpanzee again.

"Not a fucken word, Danny."

"Who, me?" He managed the innocent look for all of two seconds before he cracked up.

Boyd shook his head and tried to get the idea of Nancy Whalen naked out of his skull. He threw the phone to Danny. "You call Longwood, dickhead."

He was still trying to figure out how to explain the flying-away part of the kidnapping when the other detectives showed up. Nancy was wearing tight jeans. He hated her a little for that. The worst part was, she knew it and reveled in his discomfort.

II

Kelli woke up from a deep sleep feeling invigorated. She hadn't enjoyed a good night's sleep in over a week. Her body desperately needed it and so did her mind, so it was like heaven when she awoke fully rested.

Erika was on the phone when she stepped into the kitchen. Breakfast was ready; cereal and milk, and not just any cereal but generic corn flakes. They tasted like paradise.

No coffee made, so she hit the Mountain Dew stash she'd picked up on the way over. Erika had helped herself to two already.

While her temporary roomie stayed occupied, she went off and showered. Erika had all the sorts of shampoos and soaps that were advertised on TV and Kelli tried everything that was outrageously expensive. Erika was a wonderful girlfriend, but she'd stolen Mountain Dews and therefore had to suffer. When she was done, Erika helped her dye her hair a brilliant flaming red. It was a temporary dye but it looked a lot better than she had expected it to when it was done and dried and styled.

They were supposed to go to school, but played hooky instead. Marie and Rita showed up later in the afternoon and they all reclined in silent luxury while eating too much comfort food and watching a stack of rented horror movies to get them in the mood for the night to come.

Kelli put on the Elvira costume and looked at herself in the full-length mirror. She barely recognized herself. Normally it was sweaters and jeans or a skirt. This showed a lot more flesh than she was comfortable baring. On the other hand, it showed off her cleavage nicely.

"Screw it. You only live once."

After that, she put on the tattered robes of the zombie costume and successfully managed to hide the scandalous black outfit beneath it. She still preferred the zombie look, it was safer, but for once she would let herself go a little. What the hell? It hadn't killed Erika yet.

Soon enough they were all ready to go and it was just a matter of waiting patiently. School wasn't even out yet and they weren't supposed to get started until five.

It was going to be a busy day. But she hoped it would be an exciting one.

She had no idea.

III

Ben drove, looking at Maggie out of the corner of his eye. She was staring out the front windshield and from time to time chewing on her lower lip.

He went back to paying attention to the road when a tractor trailer honked at him. He'd been drifting.

"You okay?"

"No. Okay isn't on the menu right now, Ben."

He nodded and took a right onto Van Buren Avenue.

It was the priest thing that was bothering her. He was certain of it. When he realized that most of what they were saying was going over his head and that a lot of it was stuff he shouldn't even hear, Ben had pulled his invisible stunt and left the two of them to talk.

"Why the churches?" Maggie had asked. "Why the priests and ministers?"

Ben wasn't stupid. He could figure out what she meant. He doubted sincerely that she'd gone to synagogue to study for a comparative religion course she wasn't even taking, and he knew good and damned well that Tom had to have had reasons for questioning her being inside for too long.

Soulis had merely smiled. "Because faith causes us troubles. I don't really know that I believe in God, Maggie, but I know that those with a powerful belief in him can inconvenience me. If their faith is broken, they are no longer a threat."

"So you had me . . . cause a crisis of faith?"

"They sinned in the houses they raised to their god and they did it willingly. Most men do not like to admit their sins. Most hide them and keep doing what they've always done, even if they know they should seek absolution."

"You've put too much thought into this."

"More than you know."

He pushed his thoughts away from the conversation.

"You're not a monster, Maggie." Ben spoke the words softly, knowing she would hear them.

She laughed. "Don't be so sure."

"So, okay, you have to drink blood now and then. There's ways to work that out."

"I don't want to think about it."

They drove in silence for a while. Maggie's face reflected her warring feelings. He wanted to make it better, but had no idea how to do it. He was still a little off balance about the whole thing himself.

"He made me a freak."

"He's a freak."

"Yeah, the same kind."

"Maggie, you're still the same person. There's got to be ways around this."

"Yeah, when I eat them I can leave their bodies in the sunlight and hope no one finds them." She was justifiably bitter. Her hands clenched and relaxed, clenched and relaxed as she thought about the situation.

He was about to answer when they pulled up to the front of the complex. Detective Boyd was standing in front of his apartment. Holdstedter was near him.

"Shit!" Maggie hit the dashboard with her open palm. She left a very small dent.

"Calm down. Get some sleep. I'll handle these guys."

"Hi, Ben. Maggie." Boyd was looking tired.

"I didn't see your car."

"We had a little mechanical trouble." He pointed to a Mercedes Benz. "So we have to take Danny's piece of shit."

"He's just jealous, because I have a car." Holdstedter was looking at Maggie. She was looking at the ground.

"Was there something I could help you with?"

"Well, actually, yeah. We wanted to ask what you know about Jason Soulis."

Maggie wasn't looking at the ground anymore. She was looking at Ben and then at Boyd.

"What would you like to know?"

"Mostly, I want to know what he's doing here in town and whether or not he's got anything to do with the disappearances."

"I just met him last night."

He looked over at Maggie. "Do you know him very well, Maggie?"

"Not very well at all." Her voice was tiny and hurt.

"Well, we figured we had to give it a try. Saw you go by his place last night."

Maggie looked up at Boyd and studied him very carefully. He looked back with the same intensity. Ben couldn't decide who to stare at, and it seemed Holdstedter was in the same boat.

"You might want to look into him." That was all she said before she went to her apartment.

The two detectives stared at Ben after she had vanished from sight.

"Was it something we said?" Holdstedter was looking perplexed and tired.

"She's having a bad day."

"Sympathies on that. If you think of anything, please let us know, okay?"

"Will do."

"Ben?"

"Yeah?" He looked back at Boyd.

"She's someone special to you?"

"Yeah. Sort of."

"Watch out for her. She looks like she could use a vacation."

He nodded and waved as the two cops walked off.

IV

Black Stone Bay was at odds with itself. There were a lot of parents who actually paid enough attention to consider keeping their children inside on Halloween.

There were people who had vanished of late, a lot of them, and the fire at the fraternity house was another thing to consider. There had been no talk of arson, but there had been rumors spreading in only one day. There were people talking about Satanism and cults, orgies (which was partially true), and human sacrifices. Naturally any fraternity that had a reputation as blackened as the Phi Chi house must surely have been up to something bad.

People look for excuses sometimes.

Still, it was Halloween. Despite the fears or even because they added a certain thrill to the day, no one decided to keep their children locked away. There were several groups planning on taking the children around town and keeping them safe.

Throughout the town, the stores made sure they were properly decked out, and the run on pumpkins continued. School let out and the children did what they do every year and ran home to spend the next hour making sure they looked just so in whatever they had to wear.

Kelli Entwhistle and her friends were in place by a quarter before five in the afternoon. There was no need to drive anywhere, because they'd been given the Cliff Walk homes to handle. The kids in the area were likely to get some exceedingly large amounts of candy, if the previous year was any example.

The other girls were dressed in baggier clothes, with their party outfits concealed or not worn at all. Erika had painted herself white and was going with the ghost motif; she had enough white clothes and wasn't afraid to layer herself against the cold. Maria was done up as a witch and wore the same costume she'd have on later, with a shawl and black pants. Rita was dressed as a black cat, complete with painted nose and ears.

The kids were a little bit of everything. There was Sponge-Bob SquarePants, Superman, Spider-Man, a fairy princess, a homemade devil costume, and a ghost—who latched on to Erika like iron onto a magnet.

She checked off the names and kept her mouth shut when it came to reading Avery's and Teddy's off the list. What was supposed to be ten kids was actually seventeen. She didn't mind.

Everyone had flashlights, and there were plenty of bags for goodies. By a quarter after five, they were ready to start knocking on doors.

V

Maggie woke up to the sound of someone knocking on her door. She didn't want to get up, but it was very insistent knocking.

She opened the door, took one look at Ben and felt her mood lighten. He was painted up as a clown, complete with a psychedelic wig. His red nose flashed off and on, and the hobo pants were preposterous.

He was holding out a costume for her, too. She would have expected him to be offering her a fairy princess outfit with the way he looked at her sometimes, but no, it was a clown costume. This one sported baggy pants and oversized shoes. There was also a bright blue wig.

They stood silently for almost a minute before she finally stepped aside and let him in. "Why are you doing this?"

"You need to smile."

"No, I don't."

"Yes, you do. No Maggie the student. No Maggie the vampire or anything else tonight. You get to be . . ." He read the label on the outfit "Chuckles the Clown."

"Okay, so where are we supposed to go?"

"Bar hopping."

"I don't really do the bar scene, Ben."

"Yeah, because, really, I'm there all day and every night, looking to get drunk and get laid."

"I don't know about this."

"Just get dressed. You can worry about it later."

She took the costume and walked back toward her room. "Fine, but I want the rainbow wig."

"I dunno . . . that's a pretty cool wig."

"No rainbow wig, I stay home."

"Rainbow wig it is."

She was ready twenty minutes later, complete with enough pancake on her face to completely hide every feature she had except for her eyes.

They hit the first bar, O'Malley's Irish Pub, at ten minutes until six.

VI

Boyd woke up from his nap at six fifteen. When neither of them could keep their eyes open anymore, they crashed. Just to save time, and because his place was nicer, they both passed out at Danny's place. Danny had a comfortable couch.

He woke his partner by throwing a sofa cushion at him and telling him to get his lazy ass out of bed. Danny was good enough not to shoot him with the pistol Boyd knew good and damned well he kept under his pillow. It was nice to have a partner he could trust.

Danny forgot about the shower he normally liked to take and got dressed.

They were on the road by six twenty-five.

VII

At six-eighteen in the evening, the last rays of the sun were completely gone from the sky.

At six twenty-three, Jason Soulis looked around the vast cavern under his home and smiled.

"Go," he said softly. "Go and feed."

In two weeks' time, he had brought his experiment to the end of its first stage. Now he would see how well the second progressed.

They rustled in their new clothes, a sarcastic gift presented by him to his children. Black costumes that trailed dark streamers and shredded capes.

The sounds were crushed by the weight of the ocean as they found the entrance to the cave and swam deep into the bay.

Black Stone Bay was awake and the night was young. On street corners and in bars, down long stretches of roads littered with homes, the people who loved to celebrate Halloween walked and played and partied.

At the edge of the Cliff Walk, the waters seethed against the thrusting black teeth that ate the waves as they came in.

One old couple was walking along the side of the Cliff Walk when the vampires made their way out of the cave.

Lionel Woodruff and his wife Cecelia were not fond of Halloween. They'd enjoyed it when they were younger and when their children were still living at home, but that had been a long time ago.

These days they only wanted to be left alone to enjoy their remaining years in relative comfort. Between his arthritis and her angina, it was always a challenge to stay happy, but they managed well enough. The night was young but it was dark, and the fog that seemed to spring from the very edge of the cliffs made it darker still. They were the first to see the black shapes that came out of the water and crawled up the side of the cliff as effortlessly as smoke.

The wet, pale faces and dead eyes of the vampires were the last things either of them saw.

CHAPTER 20

I

The fog came first, in a thick wet wave that swept over the shore of the bay and into the town proper at a maddening speed. There was nothing subtle about the stuff; it was over-whelming.

The houses along the Cliff Walk were works of art, every one of them an architectural accomplishment that had cost preposterous amounts of money even when they had been built, and were now so expensive that the taxes alone would have ruined a lot of lower-income families. The fog buried them completely as it rose and moved ashore.

Kelli lost track of her friends almost immediately. She was taking care of a little girl named Jayce Thornton. Jayce had planned to dress as a witch for the event and had lost her hat when the wind picked up. So the two of them stayed behind to look for it, and by the time they discovered the black, pointy affair, it had wedged itself in a tree. Kelli did her thing and climbed up the elm while the little girl watched her. The air had been misty when she started up, but the fog had struck and done its damage by the time she finally climbed down with the hat's brim caught between her teeth.

In thirty seconds the visibility was down to nothing.

In a minute, she and Jayce couldn't even see the sidewalk under their feet and all the damned flashlights did nothing but make the air glow brightly.

"Where are we?" Jayce was laughing, but she sounded a little nervous. Kelli couldn't blame her. It was crazy dark out.

"Hey, perfect weather for Halloween. Let's go find some goblins."

She took the little girl's hand in her own and they started walking, listening for the sounds of the others. Happily, the noises were still there, because it didn't take them too long to find the rest of the group.

Erika was just about completely gone in the fog, and she used it to her advantage to scare the shit out of Kelli. One second, everything was just dandy and the next, the whiteness came alive and shot a flashlight beam in her face. The little ghost next to Erika did the exact same thing to Jayce. It could have gone south fast, but she managed to stop the witch from beating the bejesus out of the little ghost. If she'd been a little slower on recovering, she would have never stopped the fist Jayce swung at the ghost kid in time and there would have been a lot more boohooing and a bloody nose.

A minute later both of the kids seemed fine again and all was well, give or take the fog. They finished with the last house on the seaside of the street and were getting ready to head for the other side when things really did go wrong.

The little boy dressed as Spider-Man let out a very sincere shriek. As Kelli looked around for him in the fog, calling out his name—her list told her it was Nicky dressed that way— she realized he wasn't anything because he wasn't answering.

"Nicky? Hey, Nicky? Where are you?" she called, and soon her friends were joining in. They kept the kids gathered in a little island between them and called out, waited, called out again.

The fourth time they called out, Rita didn't add to the cacophony. Kelli got a chill down her spine and when she called out again, she also called for Rita.

Rita didn't answer, either.

"Okay, this is sooo not funny, guys." Erika didn't sound amused. There were parties to be hit and she wanted to be there already. She was only doing this for Kelli's sake.

"Rita! If you're joking, you can stop it!"

No answer.

Kelli moved in closer to the kids, quickly doing a head count. There were still sixteen. Only one had vanished.

Only one. And Rita hadn't answered her.

"Okay guys, let's all go."

Several children started protesting at the same time and she waved her flashlight and her hands. "Calm down. We're just going to move over to my place and then you can all check out what you already have, but Rita and Nicky might be lost and we have to find them."

"Man, this sucks . . ." Barry Winston was a brat and there was no reason for that to suddenly change. Superman had never looked more pouty. His bottom lip was stuck out like a diving board.

"Barry, it's just for a few minutes."

"No it's not! You're just trying to ruin Halloween!" Eight years old and he was already a major-league drama queen.

"Barry, we're going, *now*."

Something came out of the heavy fog and grabbed Barry before he could respond. It was big and black and had the boy in its arms before he could even catch a breath to scream with.

They all saw what happened next. Damned near every flashlight in the group turned to Barry as he was grabbed. The dark shape that caught him stood revealed. Bill Lister had looked better before. His skin was loose on his face, and bloated with water. He was deathly pale, save where some kind of black fungus was growing on his features. His eyes shot back a silvery glare into the beams from the flashlights, and his teeth, the teeth she had always thought looked perfect in his handsome face, were bared, made longer by the way his gums had receded.

Bill looked directly into Kelli's eyes as he leaned over and bit down, his mouth covering the wound he made, but not before she saw Barry's blood leaking from behind the moldy lips.

Not a single person there thought for even a second that it was a fake-out.

Erika reached for the man and clubbed him over the back of his head with her flashlight. She didn't recognize Bill; she'd never met him. Bill didn't recognize her, either, but he attacked her for her efforts. His hand reached out and grabbed Erika's face. He caught her pretty skin in the grip and it tore as easily as tissue paper. Erika's scream was cut short by her jaw and nose breaking under the force he applied.

After that, everyone started running. Kelli managed to catch Jayce's hand and the little boy in the devil outfit's wrist before she turned and started hauling ass. Neither of the kids had a chance in hell of keeping up with her so she wrestled them both into her arms and ran faster. Jayce wrapped her legs around Kelli's waist and the little devil did his best to monkey crawl over her back as they moved.

She had no plans, but spent most of her time looking at the ground to make sure her feet didn't hit the curb and take all three of them down.

"They're coming, Kelli! They're coming!" Jayce's voice was so loud and her speech so fast she could barely make out the words. She nodded instead of answering and pushed herself as fast as she could. She didn't even have time to wonder what had happened to Bill. She was fixed on the dead look of him and the way his teeth disappeared into Barry's flesh. Adrenaline kicked into her system at the thought and she groaned.

The little devil boy was pulled from her arm with enough force to strain her muscles. His screams vanished, rising higher into the air until Kelli had to turn and look. She saw him reaching for her, his toddler hand stretched out and his eyes grown frightfully wide. He kept rising, a black, fluttering form going with him until they were both lost in the fog. She kept running, breathing hard and suffering a stitch that started burning in her left side. Jayce's legs around her waist were cutting off half of her air and she needed to put her down where she would be safe.

Jayce was screaming. So was Kelli. She made herself snap out of it and set the girl down. Somewhere along the way she'd stopped running on the road and wound up in uneven dirt and mulch.

"No! Don't leave me, don't leave me!" The girl clung to her with desperate strength.

"Hush, honey, I'm not leaving you." She pulled off her jacket and wrapped it around Jayce's shoulders. "You're going to hide, okay?"

"Where are you going?" Jayce's wide, dark eyes were filled with tears.

"I'm going to get help, and I want you to hide."

Kelli was looking all around them. She'd screwed up. She had no idea where she was, but there were trees all around them in the fog and she couldn't see the road anymore. One of the larger trees was close enough that she could make out the details. She moved with Jayce and pointed to a rotted-out hole in the center, what her grandfather had called a faerie door. "You see that hole, Jayce?"

"Y-yeah . . ." The little girl sounded dubious.

"Can you hide in there?"

"I don't know." She was starting to cry more, starting to get nervous and Kelli couldn't blame her.

"Try for me, baby girl, okay?" Kelli took off her coat.

Jayce backed into the spot carefully and managed to crawl completely in. Kelli smiled.

"There you go. I'm gonna give you my coat and you use it to cover the hole up, okay?"

The poor kid was crying, but quietly, and she nodded her head. Kelli tucked her jacket in around her and tried not to cry herself.

"Okay. You stay right here. I'll be back as soon as I can."

Finding her way wasn't as hard as she expected. She just had to listen to the sounds of the screams. She said a silent prayer and jogged back the way she had come, searching for lights. Something above her dropped a plastic Spider-Man mask to the ground. The mask was broken in three places.

Kelli stopped and looked up, her heart thudding into overdrive.

Her baby boy looked back down at her. Teddy was crouched

on a limb, Nicky draped across the heavy branch a good ten feet above her head. Nicky wasn't moving at all. Teddy was licking his lips.

"Hi, Kelli!"

"Oh God, Teddy."

"Miss me?" He sounded amused.

The worst part was, even with the blood on his face, even with a dead boy pinned under his weight, she was happy to see him. Some part of her was rejoicing.

"Oh, Teddy, honey, what did they do to you?"

Teddy stood up and Nicky's body rocked threateningly as he moved across the branch to look directly down at her. "I'm coming for you, Kelli. And we can be together again."

"Teddy, no . . ."

He didn't listen. He dropped out of the tree, his preposterous black costume fluttering around him like batwings. He landed in a crouch and stood up. By all rights, his knees should have been driven through his shoulders from that height.

"You wouldn't let me in, Kelli. I should be mad at you." He was pouting, but it was a playful, mocking pout that she knew well from when bedtime came and he didn't really want to go to sleep. Unlike Bill, Teddy's skin was soft and fresh and firm. He was just very pale.

"Teddy . . . what happened?" God, she wanted to hug him to her. She knew better and had no intention, but he was so perfect to her and so alive.

Then she looked into his eyes and saw how perfect he really was. His sweet face and his crazy messy hair and his goofy costume and she knew she was being stupid. He would never hurt her, and every other sin was forgivable. She could take him to a doctor and get him patched up. "Oh, come here, baby boy."

He moved closer, smiling. His eyes glowing with a light as bright as what she felt for him inside her heart. Such a wonderful boy and always so sweet.

The sound of his foot breaking the plastic Spider-Man mask made her look down. The instant she did, she knew she'd been played.

Kelli backed away fast, looking at his water-logged tennis shoe instead of at his face. The skin wasn't pale; it was gray and filthy.

"Oh Teddy . . ."

She turned and ran again and heard his anger when he spoke again. "Get back here you BITCH!"

The words shocked her so much she looked over her shoulder and saw him as he started moving, gaining speed and coming up so fast he almost blurred. Kelli caught her foot on a root and dropped like a rock, barely covering her own face before she hit.

Teddy was fast, true, but he seemed to lack reaction time. He overshot and had to come back around.

Kelli was up and running again, this time with a rock in her hand. She'd brain him if she had to.

II

They came out of the fog in droves, some of them wearing the black costumes and some of them wearing the remains of whatever they'd died in. All of them stank of stagnant salt water and darker things, and they were hungry. The worst of it for the babysitters was being recognized by some of the frat boys. They got creative with where they bit and how long they could make the suffering last.

The children died quickly for the most part.

Jason Soulis watched it all, standing on the top of his roof as the attack took place. He willed the winds to gather stronger and summoned the fog to go further inland, and the elements obeyed.

The night was only just starting and he wanted to savor all of it.

One of the children ran away and he let him. The boy cowered against the side of his house and cried soft music into Jason's ears.

He loved to hear children cry.

Soon enough it was done and the bodies were left behind.

Jason had expected nothing else. The new ones were too hungry to care and the older ones had awakened enough to want to settle a few scores or just to be with their families.

It was going to be a long night.

Off to the left, he heard the girl from across the street struggling in the woods. He wasn't alone. The rest of the new ones heard as well, and a few of them seemed to take particular interest: Lister and his wife, her previous employers, as well as a large one from the fraternity.

He watched as they moved toward the woods and the sounds of the struggle.

III

Kelli felt Teddy's hand grab her shoulder and, as he spun her toward him, she brought the rock into play and cracked him across his face as hard as she could. Teddy's face broke. So did the rock and two of her fingers.

He staggered back, teeth bared in a feral snarl, and he covered the left side of his face with his hands. She kicked him in the knee as hard as she could and felt the bones of the joint give out and break under the impact.

Teddy fell down and spewed obscenities at her.

Somewhere along the way, her rational thoughts were submerged in white noise. She couldn't let it get away. This thing, this nasty, vile creature that had been Teddy Lister was a mockery of everything she'd loved about the boy and she would not let it live. She couldn't, just in case it looked at her again and made her come close enough to think Teddy was still alive.

She took the largest piece of rock and hit it again and again, her fingers throbbing with each strike. He fought back, of course. He pushed at her with his arms and he hit her and clawed her, but she wouldn't let it go.

"Elli . . . shtob . . . heb me." *Kelli, stop. Help me.* She meant to. She intended to help Teddy the only way she could, by ending his misery.

She drew back her arm and hit him again. Again. Again. The motions were almost mechanical. When she finally stopped, there was nothing left of Teddy's head that she could recognize.

She stood up and shook violently, repulsion washing away the madness that had taken her and grief bringing back her sanity. Her eyes burned from the tears she'd already cried, and she knew that things were only going to get worse. Bill was out there and so was Michelle. She loved them, too, if not in the same way or as intensely.

She would do it for them as well if she could.

Kelli tilted her head and realized that the screams were all gone. She looked at her bloodied hands and shivered as the first of the exquisite pains made themselves known. Her ring finger and her pinky were broken and hung slackly. Both digits were swelling and almost black already.

Her skin was sliced and diced from the rock cutting into her palm and her wrist was aching.

Kelli groaned deep in her chest and shivered as the pain and the grief met and danced across her mind and nerve endings.

She heard noises in the trees behind her and looked just in time to see them coming. The dark shapes did impossible things that left her feeling disoriented. They hopped from tree to tree, suspended sideways, as they landed in complete defiance of gravity's laws. Some of them once again came out of the sky, dropping like stones only to land gracefully on the heavy branches. Others moved on the ground, a few of them crawled in predatory stances that shouldn't have been possible for anything that looked human.

All of them looked her way, their eyes burning with cold light and their faces dead, slack things. When they moved again, it was solely for the purpose of hunting her down for killing one of their own.

The mind is an amazing thing; somewhere in the reptilian part of Kelli's brain, messages were sent off and the body listened to the commands issued. Adrenaline fired into her system again, increasing her alertness and shutting down pain receptors even as she started to run. Her ruined hand became a minor inconvenience and the painful flare that was going off in her side calmed and became a faint whisper.

Kelli Entwhistle ran again, and as never before in her life. Her legs lifted gracefully, her feet falling with a feather's touch and her eyes alert to every sight around her. She saw the monsters as they came for her, moving through the trees and then dropping to the ground, or soaring into the air as the woods fell away and were replaced by the immense houses of the Cliff Walk. The wind across her face felt like a perfect kiss; her heart surged with blood and her lungs drew in sweet breaths of oxygen that fueled and invigorated. The salty scent of the ocean cleared her senses even more and brought her world into perfect focus. She could see Jason Soulis atop his house, his handsome face bearing his elusive smile. She could taste the fog, the heavy brine of the ocean, and a dull metallic hint of iron from the blood that seemed to be everywhere.

She moved with a grace known only to a few creatures ever, none of them awkward and human, and despite her fear, despite the desperation and grief that wanted to crush her down, she felt fully, wonderfully alive.

Then the houses were past, and Kelli was running harder still, faster, fast enough to leave the dead things behind. She could have laughed she felt so good.

Alas, she could not fly. As the ground dropped away beneath her and she saw the ocean stretching across the horizon—her vision so perfect that even the thick fog failed to stop her from seeing—she came to the simple understanding that all things must end. Her flight from the monsters was done, and that too was a fine thing.

Kelli arched her body out as gracefully as she could and turned her drop toward the teeth of the bay into a dive. Her death was mercifully quick.

Far above her, above even the horde of shadowy forms that stumbled to a stop at the edge of the cliffs, Jason Soulis looked down upon the waters where the pretty girl from across the street had ended her grief, ensuring that she would never be his.

He brought his hands together three times in sharp applause and then spread his arms wide as he bowed low before her remains. With no weapons and no time to prepare for the threat he had presented her, she had drawn blood and killed one of his own. In the end she had won, and he always respected a worthy adversary.

IV

Around the same time that Kelli Entwhistle was making her final curtain call, Boyd and Danny were listening to O'Neill finally lose his temper. He could, he admitted, have possibly been out of line when he made his comments the other day about being disappointed in their performance. Nancy Whalen and Bob Longwood had been in earlier and had gone on and on about how well they had handled themselves and how, without them, Brian Freemont would still be making fools of the police force and having his way with the young ladies at the local universities.

That part had all been good and, doubtless, was planned to make them feel all warm and fuzzy inside, so when he came down like the wrath of God, they would be ill prepared.

Yeah, like they didn't know they were in deep shit for losing the cop who had been raping the local girls.

And yeah, like Boyd wasn't prepared for that part.

What he wasn't prepared for was that Brian's remains had been found in his house. And outside of it. And in the neighbor's yard. And in the trees.

There was no way in hell there could ever be an open casket ceremony for Brian Freemont.

And O'Neill was letting them know he wasn't happy. He let them know for almost an hour before he was done. Boyd was thinking he might need hearing aids in the near future.

O'Neill gave them written warnings and told them to get the fuck out of his face for the next month or so.

"What I should do is have your sorry asses booked on suspicion just to make you sweat." He must have been practicing his mean face in the mirror. It was almost working like he wanted it to.

"Are we done here?" Boyd sat in his chair like a good boy, his arms crossed over his chest to avoid giving the captain a proper ass-kicking.

"No, Boyd, we're not done by half."

"Are you firing us, Captain O'Neill?"

"No."

"Are you arresting us?"

"No." The man didn't like where the questions were going. Boyd could tell.

"Are you giving us formal reprimands?"

"Yes."

"Fine. Give them over and shut the fuck up. I got work to do and I'm already behind."

"How dare you?"

"It's easy, you're a bitch. You wanna fire me, I'll always find another job. You wanna have me arrested? Go ahead. I'll own your little ass for an ashtray by the time the lawyers are done. You wanna reprimand me, do your stuff. It's within your rights. You wanna yell at someone? Go marry a weak-willed little woman, because I ain't got the time for you or any of your bullshit."

Boyd stood there with his hand out waiting for the reprimand until the captain handed it over. He signed where he was supposed to, made a rude comment where he was asked for his side of the situation on paper, and then took his copy. Danny took his and did the same thing, but without as many foul words.

Boyd waited until they were out of the building before he called his partner a suck-up.

"I think he'd have fired us if he had anyone lined up to take over the cases." Danny was sounding all philosophical now.

"I think he needs to fuck off and die slowly."

"We did lose a perp . . ."

"No, Danny, he was stolen."

"Yeah. By flying girls."

"How is it our fault if some missing persons show up and start flying around?"

"Well, we were supposed to find them."

"And we did. We saw them. They're found. Six fucken cases closed, just like that."

"What did you write on your reply?"

"That if O'Neill could lick his own dick he'd have a marketable skill."

"You're lying." Danny was grinning again.

"I only lie to suspects, Danny. Otherwise it's just an omission of the facts as they may or may not pertain to the case."

"Your girlfriend stuck up for you."

"She's not my girlfriend and so did Longwood."

"He's your ex-partner. He's supposed to."

"Fuck off."

"You only curse when I'm right, Richie."

"What a load of shit! I'm always cursing!"

"That's because I'm always right."

"I think I know how to resolve this."

"What 'this'?"

"You and your Whalen fixation."

"Oh? I'm fixated?"

"Yeah, you are." Boyd shot Danny a murderous look.

"Okay, so what if I am. How are you going to resolve this?"

"I'm either gonna sleep with her—which is doubtful—or more likely I'm gonna tell her all the things you've been saying."

"You think she'll kick my ass?"

"Her, or her husband."

"Is he really that big?"

"No. He's bigger. Scariest motherfucker I've ever met in my life."

"No shit?"

"Completely serious."

"Where are we going?"

"We're gonna play it by ear this time, Danny. We're gonna listen to the radio, and see what happens."

"Are you serious?"

"Of course not, dickhead." He rolled his eyes.

"Well, I thought maybe because it was Halloween you were getting all soft and sentimental."

"Never gonna happen. No, we're off to see Jason Soulis."

"Again, Bullwinkle? That trick never works." Danny did a pretty good Rocky the Flying Squirrel. Sometimes it was unsettling.

The radio was blaring nice and loud as soon as they started the Mercedes. Something was going wrong at the Cliff Walks.

Boyd put on the flashers and pulled on his seatbelt. He had to let Danny drive, because it was Danny's car. Unfortunately, Danny drove at speeds that were just this side of physically impossible.

"Slow down, Danny."

"Quit being such a sissy."

Boyd lit another cigar, and Danny got the message.

He slowed down to under the speed of sound when they reached the fog. The headlights were damned near useless, but the car came with all sorts of extras, including a set of fog lights that turned the road yellow. It stopped them from running into the first of the bodies.

Danny slammed on the brakes and Boyd got out of the car. "What the fuck is this . . ." His voice was strained.

Danny stood right next to him and looked at the little kid's corpse. He was maybe five, dressed as a devil, and some sick fuck had cut his throat apart.

Boyd crouched, careful not to touch anything, and looked closer.

"Somebody bit him in the neck." He didn't recognize his voice anymore. He sounded completely alien to himself.

"Call it in, Danny. Do it now."

Boyd drew his piece and looked around. The fog was heavy and the silence was ruined only by the gentle idling of the Mercedes's engine.

Danny talked quickly and sedately into the radio. He came back a minute later with his usual smile gone. "Every fuckin' car is busy and no one has heard from Whalen and Longwood. They aren't answering their radio."

Boyd held up a hand and motioned Danny to be quiet. Both of them listened. Closer to the Cliff Walk, they could hear screams echoing.

"Open the trunk, Danny."

"You got it."

Rules and regulations made it clear that officers had to carry their service firearms. Technically, there was nothing about not carrying a few extras with you for emergency situations.

Danny liked his guns. He got out the spares. Nothing illegal, technically, just bigger than the usual .38. The shotgun was a big comfort sometimes.

They left the boy where he was and kept the flashers going. Later they could feel guilty. For now, they had other things to worry about.

CHAPTER 21

I

Maggie enjoyed herself. She didn't think she would, but she was having a blast. There was definitely something to be said for anonymity and wearing the sort of clothes where no one was trying to see down her shirt or up her skirt. At least for tonight.

The dance floor was crowded and, with his costume on, Ben was more relaxed than usual. He was dancing, and she figured under most circumstances that was about as likely as him working as call girl.

No, that was *her* job.

She pushed the ugly thought away and grabbed Ben's arm as a slower song started up. That was when he started getting antsy.

She should have expected it. He wasn't exactly an aggressive man. Maggie leaned in closer and put her arms around his neck. It was a little awkward due to the wardrobes, but she managed to pull him in tightly and smile at him.

"Thank you, Ben Kirby."

"What for?"

"Making me go out."

He smiled and shook his head. "You needed a day off."

"Yeah, I did. Thanks for noticing."

He looked her over and a grin split the makeup on his face. "Hard not to. Your hair's a fright and your makeup isn't up to your normal standards."

She turned her head as they swayed to the soft music, and managed to kiss his mouth without either of them getting their clown noses knocked off.

It was not a passionate kiss, but it was heartfelt. He closed his eyes and she watched the shiver run through him. She might have been worried about it being a tremor of fear, after all she had done and he had seen, but his lips kissed back and his hands slid to her waist.

And when the kiss was done, he released a trembling breath and looked into her eyes and saw something there that he liked.

He amazed her.

The door to O'Malley's slammed open before she could say so.

Ben turned his head sharply and Maggie looked over his shoulder as ten figures in black costumes entered the place. A few people were making appreciative comments about their makeup. Maggie was not among them. While she had never seen a vampire—as opposed to an Undead, according to Jason—she knew immediately what they were. How could she not? They were all boys from the frat house.

And they had all looked better. To the very last, they had wounds that she had inflicted on them. Fatal wounds in some cases, disfiguring in others. According to Jason, they would heal given enough time.

Todd, a big jock she'd taken downstairs, reached out and grabbed a man in a Dracula outfit by his arm and hauled him closer, his mouth opening wide to bite down on the screaming icon's neck. Several of the patrons standing nearest the incident tried to scramble away from the carnage with only moderate success.

The rest of the vampires moved into the room, grabbing indiscriminately. Maggie stepped back, drawing Ben with her.

Ben looked on, almost mesmerized. "Maggie, what the hell?"

"We have to leave, Ben. Right now. I think Jason let his vampires out of their cages."

People were reaching full panic now, and pushing toward the far side of the bar out of desperation. One of them almost knocked Ben down and she shoved the man without thinking, as shocked as anyone else when he went airborne and slammed into three others trying to escape. Ben watched with wide eyes.

"Run, Ben!" She pushed a few more out of the way as the vampires came further into the bar, grabbing and biting like rabid dogs. One of them reached for her and she turned to stare it in the eyes. It was the birthday boy from the frat house. He didn't recognize her, he was just hungry.

She stared into his eyes and he looked at her with absolute terror, backing away and hissing mindlessly. That was unexpected, but a good thing just the same.

Somebody got fed up with watching people get chewed on and broke a pool cue over the head of one of the frat boys. The good thing about mob rules was that a lot of people tended to follow the leader. That was also the bad thing.

Several of the people in the room tried to fight back. All they got for their troubles was a little more pain and a lot more bloodshed. The man with the pool cue struck Doug Clark across the back of his head. Clark turned on him fast and hit him so hard that his head exploded. The vampire's fist went clean through the skull and into the wall behind him. Another man tried the pool-cue trick and wound up with both of his arms broken before he was killed.

A third got a little craftier and threw vodka on the dead thing coming his way. The vampire didn't take the crowd into consideration, or the decorative candles that were still burning on several tables. He stumbled back into a person who shoved him sideways into a table, where he promptly caught fire.

Maggie lifted Ben completely off the ground and pushed. Ben worked better as a battering ram than she would have expected. People were knocked left and right and down to the ground as she pushed through the people in her way.

Somebody broke under her foot. She didn't have time to think about it. The fire ran across the spilled vodka and caused even more panic. She hit the back door and the fire alarm went off. Maggie ran while Ben made an interesting array of sounds.

Right after they exited, one of the vampires grabbed and pulled the door shut. They didn't wait around to see if anyone else got out alive.

II

The night had gone completely insane.

Boyd and Holdstedter walked through the fog at a fast jog, listening for the sounds of people dying. Most of what was going on seemed to be silence.

"You see where we are?"

"Yeah, the Cliff Walk." Danny wasn't throwing banter. He was all business. That was maybe the worst part.

"I'm seeing blood and I'm seeing candy bags. What I am not seeing is bodies."

"This is fucked up, Richie."

He scanned the area carefully. Not a single body to be found and not a person on the street, but there was enough scattered candy to keep a small army of kids hyperactive for a month.

"You ever see kids leave their candy behind?"

"Not without a good fuckin' reason."

They heard the footsteps coming down the street. They couldn't help but hear them; the only other sound was the distant sigh of the waves.

The steps started slowly and then increased. Not one person, but several. Grown men in black costumes were coming at them. Maybe a few women, too, it was hard to tell.

"You're fuckin' kidding me, right? Do these assholes actually have blood on their faces?"

"Matter of fact, Danny Boy, they do."

They spared one quick look at each other and then started shooting.

Boyd tried it by the book for the first three rounds. He shot one of the creeps in the shoulder and then in the elbow and then in the other shoulder. He saw the bullets connect, saw them punch through the meat and send spray flying from the perp's back. When the guy kept coming, he changed the rules. The fourth shot blew out the freak's kneecap. He fell down wailing and crying and then started to get back up. His one leg was useless and both arms were flopping around a bit. He switched targets and aimed for the legs again. Two shots and another one was down.

The third one got all *Exorcist* on him and rose into the air, screaming like a monkey on crack cocaine. That one just kept coming, making all sorts of barking noises every time another bullet went through him.

Seventeen bullets, including the one in the chamber, and he unloaded most of them into the sick fuck coming down at him. "Fucken die when I kill you, you stupid bitch!" It didn't listen. "Danny! Shotgun!"

Danny was standing off to the side, methodically blowing heads open. He didn't play by the rules. He knew why, of course. One or more of these sick bastards had killed at least one little boy, and if the blood was a good sign, maybe a whole lot more of them.

Danny aimed, fired, and moved on; leaving the first one he shot at without much of a head. The second one almost got away. The bullet blasted into his throat, but he kept coming. Danny took out his left eye with the third bullet.

Before he could aim at his fourth target, Boyd was calling for the shotgun. Rather than handing it over, his partner pulled the sort of stunt that gave Boyd an occasional nightmare and took aim about a foot in front of the moving target. The flying nun turned his head to see what was pointing his way, and Danny pulled the trigger even as Boyd was dropping backward toward the ground. If he'd kept standing, there was a good chance he would have lost his nose at the very least. The thing's head vanished in a wet cloud of black and red.

Danny turned back and fired again, hitting one of the things in the nuts. It kept coming, and that scared Boyd more than anything else he'd seen.

He drew the next weapon from the four he had strapped to his body. This one was the type that made Dirty Harry Callahan famous. It was filled with glazer bullets and did lovely things to the targets. Glazers are filled with pellets suspended in gel: so it was sort of like putting the barrel of the shotgun into the target and then pulling the trigger. One of the things that was getting far too close to Danny took the first shot and was cut in half.

It was over in roughly thirty seconds. He hadn't actually been timing it.

Danny was looking down at the remains with that weird-ass look he got whenever he was ready to shoot something. Danny was a good-looking guy, but sometimes he could be a cold bastard. Not that Boyd was complaining.

"Well. That was different." Boyd looked at the things on the ground. Not a one of them looked much like it was planning on getting up and attacking.

"No, Richie," Danny pointed with his pistol, and Boyd looked to where the first one he'd been using as a clay pigeon was still moving around. "That's different."

Danny walked closer to the pasty thing and looked at its face. It lunged and tried to bite him. He stepped back. "You notice anything weird here, Richie?"

Boyd laughed. "You mean aside from everything?"

"Well, yeah, but this is really weird."

"What?"

"Ain't a damn one of them that's dead."

"My ass."

"No, really, look."

Boyd looked. Danny was right. Even the ones with most of their heads gone were still twitching, still trying to do something. "That's just fucked up."

"Yeah. What do we do with them?" As Danny asked, the one that had been Boyd's first target tried for his leg again. Danny aimed the shotgun and pressed it into the thing's back before pulling the trigger.

"Wanna tell me how it is that you're firing a shotgun one-handed and not getting your hand blown off for your troubles?"

Danny smiled. "I work out."

"Yeah?"

"Yeah."

"I didn't know jacking off built muscles like that."

"You learn something new every day, Richie." He shrugged. "So . . . Soulis?"

"Yeah, I'm thinking it's about time we talked with that boy."

"Backup?"

"From where?"

"Just checking. You never know."

"We could call O'Neill."

"Think he'd show?"

"Probably. He's a cop first and a bitch second."

"True enough."

They walked toward the dark stone house they had visited before. "We going in like gentlemen?"

"When the fuck were you ever a gentleman?"

"That's what the ladies call me, Richie."

"Your momma doesn't count as a lady."

"Oh, then it hasn't happened yet. Never mind."

They knocked nice and polite but didn't get an answer.

"Richie, I want to kill the bad man."

"No bad man here, Danny. We're gonna have to look for him."

"That sucks."

III

The police were definitely staying busy. Every time they turned around there was another report of a violent crime, and most of those were calls about murders.

Someone must have slipped something into the water when no one was looking, because either there were a lot of false alarms, or the murder victims were getting up and walking away.

At least that was the way it seemed to be going until Alan

Coswell saw the guy taking the bodies from one crime scene. He was driving up to what was supposed to be another massacre and for a change of pace, he saw corpses. There were five people inside the 7-Eleven and every last one of them was dead. It looked like they'd been slapped around and dragged across half of the store in the process, too.

He called it in and asked for backup. Whatever the hell was going on, he didn't much like the idea of trying to handle it by himself. Maybe he was being a little weak-kneed today, but he'd seen what had been done to that sick fuck Freemont, and he didn't feel any special desire to get himself ripped limb from limb. Looking at the carnage inside the store convinced him that whoever had done it was exactly the sort who could scatter Freemont across the map.

As Coswell was stepping out of the car, he saw the man. He seemed to come out of nowhere, to just appear all of a sudden, walking out of the shadows.

Coswell froze, more than merely startled by the appearance. He was scared. Something about the guy just gave off an air of menace. Everything about him was dark: dark hair, dark clothes, dark eyes, and a dark demeanor. This was not a man he wanted to play with.

He knew it for certain when the man in question picked up the first body and laid it over his arm. The corpse had to weigh somewhere near two hundred pounds, and the man carried the bulk like he was holding a small purse.

I'm supposed to go in there and stop him. I know that, but I don't want to.

Why?

Because any man that can swing that much on one arm is going to knock my head off my shoulders if I try to stop him.

And there was the gun to consider, of course. The man didn't look armed.

The man doesn't look like he can pick up a corpse and swing it like a baseball bat, either.

As if to prove his point that guns didn't automatically make everything superspecial, the dark-haired stranger lifted a second body and started to carry them away from the crime scene.

"Screw this acting-like-a-pussy shit."

Coswell climbed out of the squad car after calling one more time for backup and pulled his pistol at the same time.

"Stop where you are." He did his best to sound like he was in control of the situation. The man looked his way and let a very tiny smile curl the edges of his mouth before he kept going.

"Mister! Are you crazy? I said stop where you are. Now!" He'd been holding his firearm to the side of his body but now lifted it and got into a proper firing stance.

The fucker kept going. "One more step and I'll be forced to restrain you."

Tall, dark, and creepy looked his way and took two more steps. Coswell fired a warning shot five feet ahead of him. The bullet hit the brick wall, rebounded, and passed through the body in the man's grip.

He dropped the body and looked at Coswell. "Was that entirely necessary?"

So he could speak after all. "I told you to stop moving, and I meant it."

"Well, here I am. What seems to be the problem?"

"Murder? Bodysnatching?"

"Oh, I didn't murder anyone." He was smiling again. The sick fuck was having a good time with all of this. "I'm just moving the bodies."

"Well, that's called tampering with a crime scene. It's against the law."

"You just fired at an unarmed man. What? You don't have handcuffs?"

"Put down the bodies and get against the damned wall, smartass."

The man dropped the other body unceremoniously to the ground. It flopped down like a rag doll. He crossed his arms and leaned against the wall. There was blood all over his sweater and the dark jeans he was wearing.

"What's your name, mister?"

"Jason Soulis."

"Why were you taking the bodies from a crime scene?"

"I wanted them."

Coswell was starting to get the idea that the man was teasing him and he didn't much like the notion. "Turn, face the wall, and place your hands above your head."

"No. You can have the bodies, but I really have other things to do right now."

"Mister, I wasn't asking." Soulis was an arrogant little prick. A minute ago he'd been worried because the man was obviously stronger than an ox. Now he didn't give a damn.

"I'm trying to be a good sport, Officer . . ." He was far enough away that reading the name on Coswell's tag should have been impossible. "Coswell, but I really do not have time to deal with any more of this. I have things I need to get done and you're becoming an inconvenience."

"Face the wall, spread your legs, and put your hands over your head."

"No."

"Excuse me?"

"No. I'm leaving."

"Mister, stay where you are!"

He heard the sound of sirens and smiled. He was about to get backup and that helped with the nerves that wanted to twitch.

Soulis looked past him and shook his head. "Now you've made things complicated."

Soulis looked at him and scowled as two more cars came up from behind him.

Murphy and Torrance got out of their cars. "What's the problem, Sarge?" Torrance was a burly man with enough attitude to scare the average perp into the back of a car without ever lifting a finger.

"The guy over there has been getting pissy about behaving."

Torrance nodded and started toward Soulis, his face set in grim, unforgiving lines. "Get your ass against the wall and put your hands above your head, mister. Right now!"

He was just fine until he touched Soulis. Torrance grabbed Soulis by the shoulder and tried to spin him against the wall. Normally, that meant the person he was pushing got spun.

Soulis didn't budge. "Don't touch me." The man's face grew positively murderous.

Torrance pushed a second time.

Soulis grabbed Matthew Torrance by his arm and pivoted at the waist, sending the policeman into the wall. Torrance dropped as hard as the corpse the man had been carrying earlier. A large red smear ran where his face had struck the bricks.

"You stop right fucking there or I'll shoot!" Murphy drew his firearm and took aim. Coswell did the same thing, both of them completely serious. Murphy pressed the talk button on his radio and called the words every cop loathed the idea of hearing. "Officer down! Repeat, officer down!" He continued on, giving their exact location.

"Torrance? You all right?" Coswell knew the answer even as he asked. There was no way the man was all right; half of his face looked like it had been pressed into an industrial steam iron.

Jason Soulis stepped toward the two of them and Coswell decided not to take any chances. He pulled the trigger and fired three shots. None of them were meant to be warnings.

The first bullet caught Jason Soulis in the center of his stomach. He didn't even flinch. The second bullet passed through the spot where Soulis had been, which was currently filled with a thick black cloud of shadows.

The cloud dispersed in a matter of seconds, and when it was gone, so was Soulis.

"What the fuck was that?" Murphy was looking at the spot and shaking his head. "Where did he go?"

Coswell was about to answer when he saw the blackness creeping around his sides. He turned just as the cloud re-formed behind him, and Jason Soulis reached for his throat.

Coswell screamed and backed away, firing his weapon again and again. His nerves were shot, and he was definitely feeling a little jumpy. The bullets slammed into Soulis and staggered him this time. Whatever weird-ass protection he was using didn't seem so perfect at point-blank range. Soulis backpedaled madly, but his feet weren't touching the ground. He ran into the front of Coswell's squad car and flipped onto the hood. The windshield was a splattered ruin where the bullets that passed through the man found another target afterward.

Both men looked at Soulis's body and fell silent.

"How the fuck did he do that?" Murphy was staring hard, his face pasty and white.

Coswell shook his head, at a loss for words. Then he remembered Torrance and moved over to see if the man was still alive. The perp could wait.

Up close he could see that Torrance's skull had been pulped. There wasn't enough solid bone left to even give a hint of its previous shape. "Jesus Christ." He practically threw himself to the side before he lost his dinner. Unfortunately, one of the corpses from inside was directly in his way and he wound up vomiting on the mortal remains of the heavyset man he'd seen Soulis lift so easily. Dead eyes stared accusingly back at him as he finished with a series of dry heaves.

It was while he was blowing his meal that Jason Soulis got back up.

Lee Murphy was a good cop. He'd been with the department for ten years and planned on staying there for the rest of his life. He kept his plans. Jason Soulis grabbed for him as he started firing into what should have been a dead man.

The bullets knocked him back again, but this time he kept his footing and started walking forward, his lips peeled back to reveal hard white fangs where his teeth should have been. From under the shadows of his brow, the man's eyes were burning, and Murphy stared into them as he kept pulling the trigger.

Jason Soulis caught Murphy's wrists and pulled them apart, sending the now empty pistol falling to the ground. He kept staring hard and Murphy kept staring back, frozen with fear and then with pain as the man yanked savagely and dislocated both of his shoulders.

Murphy passed out. Coswell couldn't blame him. The sound of more sirens coming didn't even make the madman blink.

Coswell made himself crawl over to Torrance's body and grab his weapon. He hadn't thought to reload his own as yet.

"You're beginning to piss me off, Officer."

Coswell laughed, the fear sending him over the edge a little further than he was comfortable going, and started firing. He aimed for the head. His hands were shaking, but his aim didn't completely suck and he got the man in the neck, the shoulder, and the chin. He saw the wounds as they were formed, and saw them as they healed, too. One instant there was a hole in the man's jaw and the next it was gone, just . . . gone. The skin was unmarred; the bones he knew should have been shattered were intact.

"That's enough out of you, I think." He took two steps forward. Coswell threw the weapon and stood up, his knees shaking violently and his head feeling far too light.

The squad car that came toward them came in hard and fast, not slowing down in the least. Coswell had enough time to see the driver—Logan Walker, and the passenger who was busily chewing on his face.

Then the car was ramming into the rest of the parked police cars and starting a chain reaction. Metal screamed in protest and the car Murphy had pulled up in rolled forward like a rocket, bashing in the rear end of his cruiser. His cruiser, faithful to the end, jumped forward and hit Soulis in the back.

Jason Soulis went down, pinned under the black and white, and Coswell looked on, stunned. A few feet in front of him, Jason Soulis lay pinned under a vehicle and twenty feet further away, the newest addition to the police car pileup kept revving its engine sporadically.

He started toward Soulis and changed his mind, remembering that Walker was in deep shit of his own. He stepped past the dead perp and moved toward Walker's car. Before he could even call out the officer's name, the door came open and Walker flopped to the ground.

A naked, pregnant woman climbed out of the car, wearing only a crimson stain across her full breasts and her swollen belly. She looked right at Coswell and licked the smear of red from her lips.

Angie Freemont stepped toward him with a look of unadulterated hunger on her face.

And as he stepped back, he heard the sound of metal groaning.

Angie looked over his shoulder and her deathly white face grew a shade or two whiter. She backed away from him as fast as she could, her breasts swaying and her eyes wide and terrified.

Coswell looked over his shoulder just in time to see Jason Soulis finish lifting the car off of his back. His cruiser was well over a thousand pounds, maybe even a ton, and the man was standing up, the whole of the fucking car supported by his arms. He looked like a modernist's demented sculpture of Atlas.

"I've had enough of you."

Soulis threw the car at him. Coswell was too shocked to duck.

CHAPTER 22

I

Four more policemen tried their luck with Jason Soulis. He broke the back of the first and shattered the rib cage of the second. The third and fourth, he bled dry. The wounds he'd sustained drained him and he needed to feed.

By the time it was done, a substantial crowd had gathered to see what was happening. Most of them became food.

After that, he rose into the air and let himself drift away from the carnage. He hadn't intended to participate at all. This was the night for his children and his experiments.

He had theories to test, and the police were not a part of what he wanted to examine.

Once he was high enough in the air, he spread his senses out, reaching for his creations and seeing through the eyes of his crows. The results were interesting enough to keep him distracted.

II

The town had lost its mind. That was the only possible answer as far as O'Neill was concerned. First he had to deal with Boyd and Holdstedter, which was like dealing with rabid pit bulls as far as he was concerned, and now half of the town was making insane phone calls. Somehow in the last twenty-four hours his little corner of the world had gone off the deep end.

Brian Freemont had been torn apart. He had a drug dealer who had been tortured to death in an ugly scene, a man who had been tortured by the drug dealer, and the man's daughter who was supposed to be the next new victim of the drug dealer, over forty missing people in the last week, a frat house that had burned to the ground, and now his cops were screaming about officers being killed near the 7-Eleven.

It wasn't the least bit funny, but he felt like he should be waiting for the punchline to a joke.

He also felt like he was going to have a stroke in about five minutes. Every single car was out, and the dispatcher was getting more calls and fewer responses all the time.

He didn't have a choice. He called the State Patrol out of Newport and climbed into his bulletproof vest.

"Where are you going?" Mike was on dispatch and he was looking a bit shell-shocked.

"I've got officers down. Where the hell do you think I'm going?"

"You can't leave me here alone."

"Watch me. Call if you need me."

He left the building and climbed into his car. In the distance he heard the wail of fire engines taking off. "This fucking night is never going to end."

It ended sooner than he expected. The vampires came down hard on the police captain. He never even had a chance to draw his weapon.

III

The Black Stone Bay High School Tigers were stuck playing a game in Newport. After that, the plan was to get together and party for a few hours. They had won the game and were ready for a little celebration.

The deep fog that had settled over the area made getting where they wanted to go a lot slower than they would have liked, but there were a few pleasant distractions and everyone was feeling pretty good about the victory. They only grumbled when the bus came to a stop nearly a mile from the school.

"Come on, Jonesy!" Mitch Larson was fed up with the delays. He had a promise from Leanne that he was going to get some action if he scored more than half the points in the game and he'd done it, "What's the holdup?"

Oscar Jones, the bus driver, was a mellow old man who never complained about how the kids called him Jonesy, They loved him for that; but sometimes he was a little slow on the driving speeds.

Jonesy looked over his shoulder and shrugged. "We got four cars here that ain't moving, Mitch. They're blocking both sides of the road."

Mitch stood up and shook his head. "They're gonna move; believe it." Leanne chuckled at his attitude. He'd make her pay later.

Mitch and two of the others got out of the bus and headed for the cars. All of them were empty, but it looked like whoever had been in them had left in a hurry.

Mitch was just climbing into the first of them when the frat boys from the college came for the fresh meat. A few of the guys coming their way had badly burned flesh. One of them was missing most of his arm. If it was makeup, it was fucking realistic. He couldn't see where there were any smears of stage paint, and the sagging of their faces didn't seem like it could have been done without heavy latex applications.

It wasn't makeup.

The varsity football team put up a good fight. They didn't last very long, but they tried.

Go Tigers!

IV

Sol Marcone was not a very good sailor, but he loved to fish. He was anchored out in the middle of the bay and decided he was just fine staying there until the damned fog lifted. He had cereal, milk, and enough coffee and beer to keep him going for several hours.

He liked fishing on Halloween. It kept the kids from being annoying. They could knock to their heart's content and never ever manage to disturb him.

He had a reputation for not liking children very much and it was well earned. He'd never actually drop-kicked one of the little shits, but he thought about it all the time. Kids were noisy, smelly, and only slightly less offensive than their parents these days. Used to be that parents knew how to use a belt for discipline; these days they tried to reason with their pups, which was just stupid.

He really didn't expect to have a young teenager come swimming across the bay toward him. The girl couldn't have been more than twelve or so, a pretty little thing who was stuck in the bay.

Sol frowned and wondered if some idiot had wrecked their boat against the rocks. It would be easy to do in this fog.

"Hey! You okay, kid?"

She swam closer and he put down his fishing pole. He didn't like kids, but he wasn't an asshole about it. She obviously needed help and he wasn't about to let her drown.

He reached out a hand and she took it. When he pulled, she came out of the water, her clothes stuck to her developing body like a second skin. He was embarrassed to notice that she had breasts.

While he was looking, she bit into his weathered neck and pulled him closer. He tried to fight, but she was too strong for him. Their struggles wound up knocking them both into the water.

She took her food with her and went back to the cave. It was scary in the waters and she had always been a poor swimmer, but it was easier now that she didn't have to breathe.

V

The fire at O'Malley's brought three engines worth of firefighters. They worked hard to put out the blaze and in the end they succeeded. The Tripp family thanked them for their efforts by killing them. The hunger had grown overwhelming and they needed sustenance.

Alan Tripp was the one that suggested taking them back to the cave. Meghan agreed and Avery too, just as soon as Alan told him he could drive one of the fire trucks.

The resulting accident left several cars mutilated beyond repair and caused another fire. No engines responded to the frantic phone calls.

VI

Maggie and Ben got back to the apartment complex as quickly as they could. Ben had held up pretty well, all things considered, but he was having a little trouble handling the frat boys from hell.

"I can't believe this shit. I knew those guys." He was a little obsessive about it. He didn't say much, but he said it several times. Jason had told her they were taken care of, and she thought that meant he'd destroyed the bodies.

Her mistake; she'd trusted him. It would not happen again.

Ben was looking a little off, his face was almost too loose for his skull and he was staring a lot. Staring at nothing, but definitely looking at it intently.

"Ben?"

"Hmm?" He shook himself out of it. "Yeah?"

"I think we should stay in tonight."

He chuckled. "I'm not going out there again."

She pulled off her wig and looked him over. He was still in the clown outfit, and he looked lost inside of it.

"Good." He wanted to drift again she could tell and so she kissed him. It wasn't long before he was fully focused on her. When she broke the kiss, he was looking into her eyes again, seeing whatever it was inside of her that fascinated him.

"Remember what you said before about us working everything out?"

"Yeah, of course I do." He shrugged.

"Did you mean it?"

"Yeah, of course. I'm being goofy, I know that, Maggie. It's just a lot to take in." He stepped back from her, suddenly self-conscious again.

"Why do you do that?"

"Do what?"

"You always back away from me."

"I don't . . ."

"Yeah, you do."

He shook his head. "No. I don't know how to say it."

"Say what? Tell me."

She reached out and took the nose off his face. Then she pulled the wig away. His short hair was plastered to his scalp.

"It's stupid."

"What is, Ben?"

"I love you, Maggie. Okay? Satisfied? Ready to have your laugh?" He was bitter, expecting her to knock him down and kick him once he had fallen.

"Am I laughing?"

Ben shook his head, refusing to look at her again. She took his hand and brought it up to her lips, kissing his fingers. "I like you, Ben. I like you a lot. But I've been having a few complications in my life."

That brought a small laugh from him.

"Doesn't mean I don't think of you as a friend, okay?

Maybe my only friend in the world. I don't think I could have made it through the last few days without you."

He nodded slowly, still not looking at her. She moved closer and kissed the side of his face. "Stay with me tonight, Ben? Just be here and stay with me?"

"Yeah, of course." Like it was the easiest thing in the world dealing with what he knew was a monster that had killed before and would again. She still couldn't believe that part of it. He trusted her even with all that had happened.

She took off the oversized shoes still on her feet and Ben laughed suddenly. "Oh my God, you carried me halfway here wearing those stupid things . . . we must have made one hell of a sight."

"Two-headed clown monster from hell." She nodded her agreement. It was funny, but nothing seemed worth laughing at anymore. "How do you know you love me, Ben?"

"I just do." He shrugged as he pulled off his shoes. Then he sat down to peel off the ridiculous pants he'd been wearing for the entire night. He had jeans on under them. Of course he would, it was the way he was.

"Well, try to explain it because I can't quite get that part."

"I'm happier when you're around. Even with all the weirdness, I would rather be with you than have you gone."

"Are you sure about that? Really sure?"

"Yeah, of course." He said it like there was no doubt in his mind. "Maggie, I know all about the fangs and the people you killed and all about what you do for a living and what you did with Jason and Tom and everything, and I don't care about any of it. I can fix whatever goes wrong whenever I can and I can cover for you and help you work out all of the shit that's coming down around us, and it doesn't bother me." He stared hard at her, his eyes still looking into hers for whatever it was. "I can do all of that and I'm fine. But I can't stand the idea of not having you around in my life. If that isn't love then it's close enough for me."

She moved to where he sat and settled in next to him. Did she feel the same way? She didn't know. She'd have to think about it, because just lately she wasn't feeling much of anything. She'd been putting everything on hold for so long she didn't know if the lack of emotions was just a natural reflex or something else that Jason had done to her.

Maggie pulled his head closer to her, and rested his head on her shoulder. He wrapped his arms around her waist and rested; his breathing soft and rhythmic against her skin.

"Yeah," she said. "It's close enough for me, too."

VII

The fog was a joke. They couldn't see ten feet in front of them when they hit the woods, but they kept walking. Danny was back to his normal self, which meant he wasn't looking like he wanted to puke anymore. Boyd was sort of feeling like himself now, but only sort of. He was still trying to wrap his mind around the whole dead-people-who-weren't-dead thing, but at least he knew they could be hurt. They could be stopped. He'd worry about how to dispose of the crawling body parts later.

"You hear something, Richie?"

"I hear you breathing like you're gonna take a crap in your pants."

"Yeah? Smells like you already did."

"That would explain the wet all over my ass."

"Seriously, though, I can hear something."

"So check it out." He took the shotgun and aimed it. "You got something ugly, I'll blow its head off."

"Yeah? What if it's something pretty?"

"Then we can take pictures and maybe get an autograph."

Danny crouched lower to the ground and craned his head, listening intently. Finally he reached out and grabbed at a tree base, pulling out a heavy coat. From behind it a little girl let out a squeal and tried to crawl deeper into the knothole she'd been hiding in.

Danny looked at the girl. She flinched, and shivered in her hole. "Come on, sweetie, come on out of there, we're here to help."

She made a sound that let him know she trusted him as far she trusted a big, fat spider sitting on her nose.

"Come on now, do I look like a bad person to you?"

Boyd shook his head and grinned as the little girl stared at Danny and let out a very small smile. He doubted there was a girl in the world that would think Danny looked like a bad person. At least until he didn't call them back after a night of gnarly sex. As the girl was way too young for Danny, she was probably thinking he looked just swell.

She crawled out of the tree and looked at him with wild rabbit eyes. Danny leaned back a bit and waited, making no sudden moves. Finally the girl came all the way over to him.

"Did anyone hurt you, honey?"

"No. I wanna go home." She was petulant. He felt the same way, but couldn't really do anything about it and didn't think Danny's arms around his shoulders would make him feel any better.

"Well, we're gonna try to get you there."

"What's your name, honey?" She almost jumped. She hadn't seen Boyd and was looking at him like he was a very large frog. Next to Danny he was, but so were half the guys on the planet.

"Jayce."

"Well, Jayce, why don't we get you home?"

She put her hand in Danny's when he offered it up, and they started back toward the main road. They'd have to look for Soulis in a little while. The idea of dealing with him while they were dragging around a little girl didn't sit too well.

"Where's Kelli? Did she send you for me?"

Boyd ground his teeth together and reached for a cigar. Kelli was probably the cute girl who'd lost her entire extended family. He hadn't seen her and doubted that he would.

"Yeah, honey, she did. Said she had to leave a real cutie out here and go for help."

"She's okay?"

"She was the last time we saw her."

"Good. I like Kelli. She's nice."

Something was moving out in the woods, moving up in the trees. It didn't sound like a cat or a raccoon.

"Hey, Jayce?"

"Yes sir?"

"Did you see any of the creeps running around in black suits?"

"Un hunh." She didn't sound really keen on them.

"Want to see any more?"

"No."

He walked over to the coat Danny had pulled away from the tree and picked it up. "Why don't you put this over your head for a minute, okay?"

She looked at him like he'd spoken in ancient Aramaic. "Why?"

"Because things are about to get loud and messy, honey, and you don't want to see it."

She put the coat over her head and stood perfectly still. Boyd looked up into the trees and pulled his Dirty Harry piece.

"Gimme my shotgun, Richie."

He threw the weapon and Danny had to reach but he caught it.

Three of the damned things dropped out of the trees like they were on bungee cords and not at all worried.

Danny got a smile on his face and yelled "Pull!" like he was at the skeet range. He nailed the first one to the tree, blowing its head clean off.

Boyd caught the second one in the groin with a glazer. Most of its legs slapped the ground on either side where the rest of the torso landed. It let out a scream. Once it had been a reporter that Boyd had never much liked. He'd have let it sit there and look at its legs, just out of easy reach, but it started screaming obscenities and there was a kid present. He took off its head.

Jayce was wearing her coat, so she didn't get covered in its blood. She let out a scream anyway.

The third one jumped at Danny like a cat pouncing at a

mouse. Not a very smart cat, mind you: Danny still had the shotgun. Danny pulled the trigger just as its mouth was coming to bite his face off.

It did a great back flip and fell down, twitching, the stump where its neck and left shoulder had been was dark and oozing, and it was still trying to crawl away. Danny blew its back all over the mulch.

"Well, that was fuckin' disgusting."

"Language, Danny Boy, we got a little kid here."

"I heard my daddy say it. It's okay." The girl's voice was muffled by the coat.

"Yeah?"

"Yeah."

"Then let's fucken go."

"You said it too!"

"Honey, you can even say it if you want."

"I can?"

"Yep." Boyd rolled his cigar around.

"Then can I fucking go home?"

Danny laughed and so did Boyd. They led her a distance from the carnage before they let her take off the coat. By then, they had both reloaded.

VIII

The people of Black Stone Bay never knew what hit them, and Jason Soulis smiled at that thought.

Throughout the streets, the corpses of the recently murdered lay spilled like garbage from a torn Hefty bag. If he had his way, they would not stay dead for too long. They would come back and he would hide them away and try again to make a stronger, smarter vampire. Some of the ones he had hidden away had already proven themselves; they were more able to think and the survival rate for the first few days was promising.

There was something about coming back from the dead

that left them dazed, as evidenced by the boys from the fraternity house. Only one day back from the dead and not a one of them seemed capable of even remembering his name.

Then again, he had doubts they could have remembered their names even if they were still alive. They had more money than brain cells.

He moved back toward his home. He had enough bodies for the caves and he would soon discover if the town of Black Stone Bay would know how to keep the newly dead from rising. For now, he was finished with the night and wanted to recover.

He spotted the detectives and their young charge as he was descending and decided to wait. They were aggravated, and they were determined to see him.

He wondered if they would die well and decided that it didn't matter. He would kill them and they would rise and he would be fine with that.

In the distance he saw fire engines rolling toward the Cliff Walk. He knew who was driving them. He knew that they carried a lot of bodies. All the better.

He scanned the horizon as he descended and saw that three police cars were heading toward the finer homes as well.

"All right then. One last dance before I sleep."

He waited for the players to be where he wanted them, and then he dropped from the sky and landed on the roof of his black home.

This would be interesting and, in the end, he knew how it would play out.

He'd been here before.

But it was always a fascinating place to be.

CHAPTER 23

I

The fire engines hauled ass down the road, their lights and sirens going full tilt. Boyd figured there might be something wrong when he couldn't see the head of the driver in the first one. He knew for certain there was a little of the crazy stuff happening when the massive vehicle ran over the curb and clipped a fire hydrant. The resulting geyser shot up at an angle and started watering the closest lawn with a torrential downpour.

"You seeing this shit?" Boyd stepped back as the next engine came around the corner and skidded to a halt.

"What the hell?" Danny was looking at the first of the giant red trucks. It rolled to a stop and the driver's side door opened.

A dead kid climbed out, grinning ear to ear. "That was so cool!" He looked at the new water fountain and jumped up and down, waving his hands like a monkey on fire.

A woman climbed out of the second vehicle, dressed only in a nightgown. The third driver climbed out without putting the fire engine in park and watched as the red truck rolled into a tree. He had a small frown on his face. "I was sort of hoping it would hit the house. Never liked that house . . ."

Boyd recognized all of the Tripp family when he saw them. "You fucken kidding me or what?"

The kid turned and looked at the detectives, but didn't seem very impressed until he saw the girl with them. "Jayce!"

"Avery?" Her voice was very small.

Avery Tripp started toward her with an eager smile, his eyes flaring with their own light. Aside from the fangs, the glowing eyes, and the pasty white skin, the kid looked healthy and happy.

"Happy Halloween!" He started walking toward the little girl and Boyd took careful aim at the boy's head.

Avery Tripp ignored him completely, heading straight for Jayce. For her part, Jayce slid in closer to Danny, who was eyeing the Tripp boy suspiciously.

"Oh, come on now, Richie. He's a kid! What the hell am I supposed to do here?"

"You could try non-lethal force, I guess . . ."

Danny nodded and flipped the shotgun in his hand around so that the butt was held in front of him. "Stop, kid. I don't want to hurt you."

Both of the Tripp parents were smiling, amused by their son's dilemma. "Come on, Detective. He just wants to say hello to Jayce, isn't that right, Avery?"

Jayce was shaking her head, her dark eyes as round as plates. "You stay away from me, Avery."

"Why wouldn't you open the window when I knocked, Jayce? I wanted to see you." His voice was light and sweet and his face was pure venom. He didn't walk toward her anymore; he stalked her instead.

"Danny . . ."

"I mean it, kid. One more step and I'm gonna clock you." Danny hefted the weapon and set himself up for taking a game-winning swing with his makeshift bat.

Boyd saw the motion before anything could go wrong. Alan Tripp came at him like a runaway train, moving with the deadly speed and precision of a guided missile.

He took aim and fired, and missed: the sonuvabitch dodged to the side and the bullet blew a hole in the yard behind where he had been a second earlier. Before he could try to get a bead a second time, Alan Tripp ran into him.

The impact lifted him off his feet and the yuppie fuck kept going, his teeth far too close to Boyd's face for comfort. Powerful hands reached out and grabbed at his face and his neck. Boyd did the only thing he could think of and pulled the trigger on his pistol again. This time he hit well enough to blow half of the bastard's back away.

Alan Tripp took it poorly. He shoved himself away and used Boyd as his brace. Boyd rolled with it, which meant that he didn't break any bones. He hit the ground and felt the pistol escape his hand and slide toward the gutter.

When it hit the curb, the pistol fired and a bullet punched through the side of the closest fire engine, hitting something deep inside the engine that let out a hiss.

When Boyd stopped rolling, he too was along the curb. He didn't explode or hiss, he just moaned. The back of his head and his left hand both felt freshly sanded.

He looked around to see Tripp coming his way, his previously almost human face suddenly dead and slack, even if the eyes in his skull were still doing the inner-light thing.

Before he could do anything else, Tripp had him by his ankle and was lifting him off the ground. There aren't many advantages to being a short man, and if he'd ever needed proof he had it. The dead man tried to play crack the whip with him, shaking his entire body roughly. Boyd decided enough was enough and grabbed his regular service piece. He pulled the trigger after being tossed around enough to make him seasick.

The first bullet passed through gray meat and flesh and exited on the other side of Tripp's neck. Tripp dropped him and, as he fell, Boyd tried for a second shot. He'd have missed it, because the angle was all wrong, but just as he was firing, he hit the ground and was jostled well enough that the second shot put a bullet through the dead man's backlit eye.

Alan Tripp fell back as if pole axed and hit the ground hard. Boyd could see through the hole in his head to the curb beyond it.

That was around the same time that Danny broke the stock

of his shotgun off against little Avery's head. The heavy piece of oak shattered into so many toothpicks, and the Tripp boy fell on his face with a dent in the side of his skull that would have served well as a cup holder.

Little Avery came back up roaring like a midget lion on steroids. He fought like a kid, with flailing limbs and gnashing teeth. Unfortunately, as Danny was finally realizing, Avery Tripp was not an average little boy.

His fingers ripped the jacket on Danny's back into confetti and his foot kicked into the detective's stomach hard enough to double him over.

"You hurt me! Bad man! Bad man!" He was screaming, his voice that of a child, but the tone was completely wrong. He was going postal all over Danny and sounding an awful lot like he was just toying with the man.

Avery grabbed Danny by his hair and wrenched the man backward. He bared his teeth and prepared to chew half of Danny's face off. He would have done it, too, but Jayce Thornton interfered. At only ten years of age, she'd seen enough movies to know which end of a shotgun meant business. She grabbed the ruined weapon by the remains of the stock and swung it around on her hip like a gunfighter in an old Western flick. When she aimed, she pushed the barrel into Avery's side and then pulled the trigger.

Avery Tripp was cut clean in half by the shell. Jayce was knocked off her feet and landed on her ass a couple of yards from where she'd started. None of the Westerns her father liked to watch showed how much kick a 12-gauge delivers and she was completely unprepared.

The upper half of Avery growled and crawled in her direction while she sat on the ground and did a mental repeat of the action to see where she had gone wrong. He was dragging a heavy collection of organs with him as he went, and Danny stomped on what he thought was a lung as he tried to stop the rabid little fucker from reaching his destination. It was the sound of dead meat popping under his shoe that snapped Jayce out of her daze.

For the most part, the little girl had held herself together pretty well in Danny's eyes, but she cut loose with a scream worthy of all three fire engines when she saw the thing that had been her classmate crawling across the ground and aiming to rip her limb from limb.

Danny didn't figure one more trauma could do too much more damage; she got to watch while he blew Avery's head into mincemeat.

Boyd sat up and very carefully backed away from the dead man he'd killed. It was wise of him. The dead man got back up, one large portion of his brain sliding out of the ruined head as he did it.

Alan Tripp took a tentative step forward, his legs twitching, and then he took another more confident step. By the fourth pace toward Boyd, he was doing just fine. And smiling with what was left of his face.

Boyd unloaded every bullet in his pistol into the remains of that head and only stopped when there was nothing left above the shoulders to fire on.

"Okay, that one was harder to kill."

Danny looked at him and nodded. He was looking a little like he wanted to wake up from this bad dream. On the ground nearby, the little girl was staring at the ruin of Avery Tripp with horrified fascination.

Boyd looked around. The third member of the Tripp family was missing.

He walked across the street to pick up his other pistol. It still had a few rounds left and he was growing very fond of the holes the glazer bullets made in whatever they hit.

In the distance but coming their way at high speed, they heard the sound of police cruisers. Boyd had never been very fond of the sirens before, but they were sounding like sweet music as he started to reload his weapons.

"He broke my shotgun, Richie."

"Be fair, Danny. You did that yourself."

"I didn't think his fuckin' head would be so hard."

"Well, we'll buy you a new one."

"Promise?"

"Have I ever lied to you about a thing like that?"

Danny looked at him and grinned. "You lie to me all the time, Richie."

"I wanna go home!" Their new friend, the little lost kid, was starting to freak out. He made a silent prayer that her home was still there and occupied by loving parents.

"Where did the little missus get off to?" Danny was frowning.

"Back off, Danny Boy, she's married." He knew he'd made a mistake as soon as he said the words.

"And how has that stopped you and Whalen?"

"Again with the damned Whalen comments!"

Danny grinned and the three of them looked around as the first of the state troopers pulled up.

Boyd and Danny pulled their badges. Jayce just sat where she was and crossed her arms petulantly. She didn't have a badge, so Boyd couldn't really blame her.

The trooper climbed out of his vehicle. He was a tall drink of water with a face made for intimidation. "What in the name of God has been going on in this town?" His voice was better suited to Pee Wee Herman, but Boyd was glad to have another cop or fifty show up. He really wasn't that picky at this point.

"Wish I could tell you. So far we got a bunch of dead people that won't stay dead and a lot more people dying." Boyd shook his head.

The trooper looked at the headless body of Alan Tripp, which was currently twitching and clenching its hands again and again. "The fog out here has been causing a lot of troubles. We've got a ten-car pileup on the interstate and more reports coming in. Jesus on a pogo stick, half the roads in this town are shut down."

The other two state troopers were climbing out of their vehicles now and looking around with shocked expressions on their faces. One of them walked over to the closest fire truck and climbed into the driver's seat to turn off the flashing lights. Boyd was grateful. The damned things kept his eyes from adjusting to the darkness.

"So." Pee Wee Herman looked around and scratched at the back of his neck. "What can we do?"

"We're looking for a man named Jason Soulis. He's supposed to have the skinny on what the fuck is going on."

"I'm right here, Detective Boyd. What can I do for you?"

Soulis came walking out of the fog behind the last of the trooper cars, a smile playing at his lips. Boyd did an admirable job of not pissing his pants if he did say so himself.

The trooper closest to him reached for cuffs.

Soulis walked past him as if he weren't even there and headed for Boyd.

"Speak up, man. What is it you want from me?"

"Answers would be a good starting place."

"Fine. They're vampires. There are a lot of them." He shrugged. "Is there anything else I can help you with? If not, I have business to attend to."

"Did you make this happen?"

"Yes, actually, I did."

Boyd didn't like the way the conversation was going. He shook his head. "Why don't you come along with us, Mister Soulis? We need to figure out a way to stop this shit and right now."

"I really don't have the time or the inclination." He looked bored with the entire thing and Boyd ground his teeth together.

"I don't fucken care what you have time for, you sick fuck. Make this stop."

"No."

"Then you give me one good reason not to blow your goddamned head off."

Soulis looked over his shoulder just as the troopers were coming toward him. One look and all three men stopped in their tracks, their faces showing uncertainty.

"I like you, Detective Boyd. Why don't you go home and get some rest?"

"Say what?"

"Go home. Get a good night's sleep. Things will look better in the morning."

"I have dead kids in the streets, you sick fucken bastard. Nothing's gonna look better in the morning." He felt the hairs on his neck starting to rise, not with a fear reaction—something he knew very well—but with a charge of static.

"Detective, I'm tired and I have no desire to hurt you or anyone else at the current time, but I will." Soulis looked at him, pinned him with his gaze, that half smile still on his lips.

"This isn't going to go the way you want it to, Soulis."

"No?" Soulis closed his eyes and the sky opened up. Rain came down in heavy sheets. From nowhere the devastating downpour soaked everyone in an instant.

Boyd looked around, surprised by the ferocity of the weather's assault, but he was looking at Soulis when the man opened his eyes. He was looking at the black pools of shadow where his eyes should have been and he was fully aware that at exactly the same time the man looked back at him the downpour stopped.

"What the fuck?"

"Precisely, Detective. That was just a little water. Imagine what I could do if I decided to get creative."

Pee Wee made an inquisitive gesture, wanting to know if he should attempt an arrest. Boyd nodded slightly and the man grabbed Soulis by the arm, wrenching backward.

Soulis let him, his smile getting a touch more pronounced.

"Must we, Detective Boyd?"

"Yeah, I'm afraid so. I don't know what the hell you're doing or how, but it stops now."

"No." Blackness crept from the man's skin, spilling from him like heat from a fire, engulfing his entire body. Boyd took aim, uncertain what to do. He couldn't just fire; he'd hit a trooper. The darkness expanded outward until Soulis was completely hidden. A heartbeat later it began to contract, collapsing inward until it simply vanished. Soulis was gone with it, leaving Pee Wee holding the cuffs he'd already wrapped around the man's wrists. The cuffs were still closed.

"Shit on this!" Boyd looked around and saw Danny doing the same thing. He had a migraine starting and he was not amused by the disappearing trick.

"Where the hell did he go?" Pee Wee was having a little trouble with the notion that his perp had just vanished.

"Well you're the one that had his hands on the guy, you tell me!" Boyd glared.

"Screw you! You saw it too! He just disappeared." The trooper didn't look at all happy about the turn of events. He looked scared (maybe) and pissed off (definitely) but happy wasn't a part of his expression.

"Let's just all stop freaking out here." Leave it to Danny to try placating the troopers.

"Dennison, call HQ and tell them we need backup. This is fucked up beyond all repair," Pee Wee called out and one of the troopers with him headed back for his car.

The lightning bolt stopped him. The world turned brilliantly white and Boyd covered his eyes as the flash went off. The explosion of thunder shook the bones in his body and half deafened him, leaving his ears ringing even as his eyes tried to adjust.

When he could see again, Trooper Dennison was a burnt ruin on the ground. His badge was glowing white hot and his pistol looked like it had melted into its holster.

Most of Boyd's body felt like he'd been fried alive. He knew he wasn't deeply injured, but the current had carried far enough to send his nervous system into a frenzy. He could barely get any part of his body to respond to the simplest commands.

The little girl was crying her eyes out. He couldn't blame her. Danny reached over and pulled the girl into his arm, settling her on his hip. She wrapped herself around him like a constrictor, her legs and hand pulling him as close as physically possible.

"You're okay, sweetie. It's all going to be okay." He could just hear Danny's words over the reverberations still bouncing around in his skull.

What the fuck are we dealing with here? This guy can't be for real. He had no doubt that somehow Soulis had caused the lightning.

The two state troopers ran to their fallen friend. He was dead; Boyd knew it as sure as he knew his name.

"Danny?"

"Yeah, Richie?"

"You hand Jayce over to the troopers." He looked at Pee Wee. "Hey! You need to get this little girl home for me, all right?"

"What?" Pee Wee had been even closer to the blast and he was having a little trouble hearing anything.

Jayce was clinging to Danny, and when she heard the plan she started crying again. The kid couldn't make up her mind.

Before another word was spoken, both of the troopers ran for their cars. He couldn't blame them; this was the weirdest shit he'd ever encountered.

Jason Soulis was standing in his front yard, staring down at them. His smile was darker than before and even through the heavy fog, he could tell the man was looking right at him. He hadn't been there two seconds before, Boyd would have bet on it.

"Are we finishing this, Detective Boyd? Or are you going to leave this alone?"

Boyd looked at Danny and Danny looked back.

Both of them looked toward Soulis and pointed their pistols.

"Jason Soulis, you are under arrest." To make his point very clear, Richard Boyd opened fire and so did his partner.

II

Hunter Williamson had been a state trooper for almost two decades. He liked the job and he loved the people he worked with. Stewart Dennison had been with the force for eight years, and he had been a good man.

So he was a little upset by the notion that a man who could disappear at will and cause rain storms just by thinking about it had just killed a good friend.

There was no denying what he had seen with his own eyes. The man he'd had in cuffs was responsible for what had just happened; he had no doubt of that at all.

The only question was what to do about it.

He looked to Martinez and saw that the other man felt exactly the same way.

"I don't think we're going to stop this guy with bullets."

"I don't think we're gonna stop him at all, but I'm not letting him get away with that shit." Martinez was practically screaming, but Williamson could just make out the words.

"I'm gonna run his ass down."

Martinez nodded.

The local cop said something, but he couldn't make out the words. Williamson called out for him to repeat himself, but the man looked away to where the murdering fuck he'd tried to cuff was standing on the lawn and looking like he was having the best time he'd ever had outside of sex.

Fuck 'em. Maybe they can keep the piece of shit distracted.

He climbed over the remains of his friend and back into his car. The engine had stalled thanks to the lightning, but it started up just fine. He didn't bother with seatbelts or any of his usual precautions; he just aimed the cruiser and gunned the engine. The engine roared and the tires screamed and the car just barely missed hitting a fire engine as he drove over the curb and through the stream of the fire hydrant that was spraying down the neighborhood.

Behind him, Martinez was already rolling, gathering speed. The grass was soaked through and the car slewed sideways, sending up a thick wave of ruined lawn and mud before the tires caught properly.

Then he was moving and fast, gathering a proper head of steam as he aimed the cruiser at the sick bastard who claimed he'd caused all of the devastation.

The two local cops fired repeatedly at their target and Jason Soulis took a staggering step backward as his chest exploded. The smile was gone from his face, and he was falling to the ground. All the better.

Williamson compensated for the change in position and ran over the man. The car shuddered and jumped as it hit the prone form, and Williamson made sure to gun the engine even more. He felt the tires sliding through bone and gristle as he rocketed over the body.

Martinez was next and he aimed well and true, the front tires rolling straight for the man's head and legs.

He was watching in the rearview mirror when the other trooper's car slammed to a complete halt. He was still watching, stupefied, as the vehicle was thrown through the air, rolling end over end until it crashed into the closest fire engine.

The crushed, bloodied body of Jason Soulis stood up. His ribs were caved in and he still had a massive hole in his chest, but the freak was standing up.

Williamson hit the brakes, switched into reverse and started backing toward the thing that was now looking at the two local cops. He gained speed, swerving slightly as he adjusted to backward driving, and made sure his aim was as perfect as possible.

Soulis turned his way and braced his body. The car hit, the rear end crumpling inward and the rear window exploding on impact. Williamson was flung backward and then forward in his seat. His head slammed into the steering wheel and the air bag deployed, punching him in the face at high velocity.

As soon as it had done its job, the cushion began to deflate and Williamson helped it along, terrified. Nothing should have been able to stop a fucking car like that! Nothing!

He climbed out as the thing behind him lunged, driving hands through the roof of the car in an effort to reach him.

Soulis snarled, his face as far from human as it could be while sharing the same basic features. He looked at the man in absolute terror, his mind taking in the details and then refusing to acknowledge what he was seeing. The wounds were gone. The man's clothing had been blasted apart, and tire tracks were clearly visible, but the white skin underneath was perfectly fine, unmarred and supported by what was obviously a whole ribcage.

He was still trying to work that out in his head when Soulis grabbed hold of him.

III

Pee Wee was screaming, and Danny was, too. Jayce was crying, and Boyd was pretty sure he had a few tears coming from his own eyes, but he couldn't tell anymore. There was too much going on and no time to take it all in.

Jason Soulis held the state trooper up by one hand and climbed off the wreckage of the police car. He was grinning ear to ear now, and walking toward Boyd and Danny with absolute confidence in his abilities.

Williamson was thrashing like a freshly hooked carp and making faces that came pretty close to matching a fish's expressions at that moment. Soulis walked closer and stopped five feet away.

"How much is he worth to you, Detective?"

"What do you mean?"

"I mean he can live or die depending on what you say."

Boyd had his weapon aimed at the man. He wasn't stupid.

"What? I'm supposed to trade you for him?"

"Something like that."

"He's a cop. He knew the risks."

Williamson was still looking ready to jump out of his own skin, but he was also reaching for his service revolver. God love him.

"You can still walk away from this. I genuinely like you."

"You can't. I bet if I hit you in the head enough times you won't go getting all better."

Danny was doing his thing again, looking far away and keeping his aim on Soulis.

"It's possible. Are you willing to take that risk?"

"Danny over there is ready. So am I."

"What about your little friend?" He looked over to where Jayce was protected against Danny's side. "If we call this done, I will let her live."

"For all I know, she's already an orphan. Maybe she'd want to be with her family."

"I don't think I've ever met a man as stubborn as you." He

had more to say, but just at that moment, Pee Wee opened up and started firing bullets into his chest and head. Six bullets at point-blank range blew holes into the monster with the human face, and Boyd and Danny took that as their cue. Danny moved his hand ever so slightly and pulled the trigger. Jason Soulis's left eye exploded. An instant later his right eye followed suit. The next bullet took off the top of his skull and the one after that blew his jaw away.

Boyd focused on his chest. He had four glazer shells left and he used every last one of them aiming for where the heart should be.

Jason Soulis took enough lead to blow his body into pieces. What remained of him fell down and stayed down.

Pee Wee fell too, screaming again and crab-walking backward away from the remains.

Boyd loaded his weapon again and stepped closer. He fired every round into the body. Danny stayed where he was trying to calm down the hysterical girl in his arm. Williamson scooted a bit further away and started vomiting.

Boyd stared down at the corpse and waited for something to happen. He wanted to see if what was left would grow back again. Finally, convinced that nothing was going to happen, he moved toward the squad car leaning against the fire engine. Maybe if he was lucky there would be a can of gas he could use to burn the remains.

"Richie!" Danny's voice got his attention and he spun, ready to fire again. The fog was lifting, fading away, and as it did he saw them coming. The crows. He couldn't begin to count how many there were. They filled the air around them, and Boyd did the only sensible thing and backed away. Danny was ahead of him in that department and Pee Wee was leaving the area as fast as he could while still puking.

The birds circled briefly and then landed on the remains of Jason Soulis. They attacked what was there violently, plucking and ripping at the flesh and cloth, tearing away cold pieces of flesh and eating them.

Danny held the little girl in his arms and made sure she didn't see what was happening.

There were a lot of the black birds and they were hungry. By the time they were finished there was little to look at except for the ruined clothes Soulis had been wearing.

"Well. That was disgusting." Danny's voice was weak.

"Yeah."

"Red Lady?"

"What the fuck do you think?"

"Red Lady."

"Let's get out of here."

They left, not a one of them having any desire to stay for another moment.

CHAPTER 24

I

The sun rose at the usual time, but it rose on a very different town than the one it had set on the night before.

Bodies littered the streets and lay scattered through several buildings as well. When they could finally get there, the state patrol vehicles rolled into Black Stone Bay and began cataloguing the damage.

The bodies of three priests were found at the Sacred Hearts Cathedral. They were found badly beaten, with their throats torn open. Someone had taken the time to write "Forgive them, Lord, they were only human" on the walls in the blood of the three men. Similar epitaphs were found in every single house of God in the town.

While the crimes were added to the list of damages inflicted, the details of the bloody notes were not made public. The matter of finding replacements for the priests, rabbis, ministers, and administrators of the various religious establishments was handled quietly and carefully. There might have been more scandal added to the issue, but with everything else that occurred that particular Halloween night and a few carefully worded comments from higher ups in the churches, the matter was left alone.

Over half of the police force was dead or missing. All four detectives were still alive, though two of them had been holed up in a bank vault overnight. They were found when the bank opened in the morning, both of them disheveled and very, very angry. Though they were vague about details, it seemed that an informant had gotten the drop on them. Sadly for him, he didn't realize that there was proper circulation in the vault and that, in fact, being locked inside would not cause suffocation. He was arrested as he was packing his bags for an extended vacation.

Jayce Thornton was returned to her parents just before sunrise. They had actually been expecting her to spend the night with one of her friends, and were shocked to hear that she had been lost in the woods. It would be four years before she was given permission to sleep over anywhere again. It would be two years before she could go to sleep with the lights off in her bedroom.

The Silver Dollar Diner was in ruins. Something very bad occurred inside the building and the line cook was found cooking on the grill. Sally Harmon, who was a staple at the place, was never found.

Seven Halloween parties on the campuses of Winslow Harper and Sacred Dominion ended in disaster. The details remained blurry, but most everyone agreed in their descriptions of people dressed in black who came in and attacked at random and with unexpected violence. With all of the confusion, it was difficult to establish just how many people were killed. There were more people reported missing than actually murdered. It's hard to prove murder when there is no body. Several corpses were found, but most of the students who disappeared were listed simply as missing. Detectives Boyd and Holdstedter were not amused.

II

"So we get to look like assholes, and those two get to come out of this with a better track record?" Danny was whining.

"Yeah, but on the bright side, we always look like assholes."

"Oh, yeah. Never mind then."

They were standing on the Cliff Walk, looking down at the waters where they crashed against the jagged rocks. They'd been there for over three hours. A good portion of that time they were supervising the divers who had to pull Kelli Entwhistle's remains from the spot. She'd been found by a jogger early on. Her body was stuck between two rocks and her arm pointed toward Soulis's place like an accusation.

Danny had looked down at the remains and shaken his head. "Sometimes," he said, "I hate being right."

He had been right, too. Most of her had been pulped into jelly by the waves. Boyd didn't respond; he was too busy looking at the way her arm moved in the current. There was something there. He just couldn't figure it out.

He caught it when the tide changed. The undertow was all wrong. When he thought about how the girl's hand had moved, he looked to the spot and finally understood that there was something there, a cave or a well or something.

He and Danny spent a long time looking at it.

A big enough cave could hide a lot of bodies.

It could hide a lot of bodies that weren't as dead as maybe they should be. It took a little work, and he had to pull some favors, but after Boyd explained it, Danny got a few things they would need.

III

Maggie got the letter from Jason Soulis in the mail the next day. It had been sent overnight express.

She opened it while Ben was sleeping and read it carefully. It read:

Dear Maggie,

It was a pleasure to make your acquaintance. I suspect you remain confused by what has happened to you, and I can most certainly understand that. Know this: You will endure.

If all goes as I have planned it, you will be reading this after I have left Black Stone Bay. I have to ask a favor of you. Please watch over my house. It is empty of all that was mine, and for the present time I have no need of it. I would consider it a kindness if you could move in and make yourself at home. You will find all of the appropriate paperwork has been filed and that you can move in at your convenience.

I will leave you with the following thoughts: First, know that there was a reason for everything I did. We may well discuss it some day. Second, keep your secret well. I have met the boy you trust and he should do well for you, but do not spread the secrets of your condition to others. Believe me, they will not understand.

May your life be less complex than it has been and may your nights and days be peaceful.

> *Until we meet again,*
> *Jason Soulis*

She folded the letter up and placed it back into its envelope. The thick sheaf of papers she also found inside included a lifetime lease for the property and the understanding that the structure could not be altered or sold.

Maggie and Ben moved in a few months later, after their leases at the apartment complex expired.

IV

"Hello?" The voice that answered was familiar and comforting.

"Mom?"

"Angie! Oh my God! Are you okay, honey? Your father and I have been worried sick, just sick! We kept calling, but no one answered, and when we talked to the police, they told us about poor Brian."

"I'm okay, Mom. But I have to get away from here; there are too many memories . . ."

"Oh, honey, of course there are. You could come home if you wanted. You could stay with us."

"Would it really be okay if I did, Mom?"

"Oh, honey, of course it would be. We haven't seen you in almost a year."

"I have a few things to take care of, but I can be there in a couple of days."

"We can't wait to see you, honey. Oh, thank God you're all right."

She flinched a bit. Even the mention of God seemed to cause discomfort, but she was almost certain she could endure. There were things she didn't understand about what she had become, but she was learning.

"I love you, Mom. I can't wait to see you again."

"Honey, all you ever have to do is come on by. The door will always be open for you."

"I'll see you soon and I have a surprise for you."

"Really? Is it a good surprise?"

"I think you'll like it."

They said their good-byes and Angie Freemont carefully packed her bags.

She felt a twinge and the baby kicked. He was feeling stronger too, recovering from all that had been done to the both of them. She ran her hand over her swollen belly and smiled, even as the first hunger pangs hit.

She was always hungry. How could she be anything else? She was eating for two.

V

The bodies were gathered through the course of the day. They were more than anyone wanted to consider, and a surprising number of them seemed to be at least a week old. Though it took time, eventually they were identified.

Witnesses claimed that several of the corpses gathered had been alive and well until the sun hit them. No one really believed the accounts. The bodies that had most of those claims had obviously been dead for several hours or days.

VI

Boyd smoked his cigar and watched Danny as he maneuvered the radio-controlled boat.

"Fuck's sake, Danny! It's a big goddamn hole in the side of a cliff! How hard can it be?"

"About as hard as it is for you to get into Whalen's pants."

"What? Now you're changing your mind about me and Whalen?"

"Hardly. I think you could get in her pants if you really wanted to."

"She's a married woman, Danny Boy."

"So? She wants you!"

"So maybe if she was single, okay?"

"Being a dumbass about it."

"You go around banging married women?"

That shut him up.

"So get the fucken thing in there already!"

"Relax, Richie. The best things take time." He couldn't decide if Danny was talking about Whalen or the damned boat, so he kept his mouth shut.

Finally the waves pulled back in just the right way and the water from the cave's entrance spilled out. As the next wave came in, the boat was sucked into the underwater entrance.

"The SS Kelli has breached the defenses."

"Good."

"You wanna do the honors, Richie?"

"Yeah, if you don't mind."

"Knock yourself out."

Boyd picked up the detonator and waited for one full minute as Danny kept urging the small motor further along. He waited until they could no longer hear the whining toy engine's noises.

"Come on, Richie. Damn, I need coffee!"

"Fuck you and your coffee. It was my idea." He pressed the detonator and the four sticks of dynamite let out a dull thump that was hidden by the waters.

They couldn't see much at first, but after watching for a while they saw that the undertow wasn't doing as many weird things anymore. There wasn't a delay or a sudden gulping of the ocean.

"Did that close it off?"

"I guess we'll know tonight, Danny Boy."

"Yeah. I guess we will."

"Ready to go?"

"Yeah. I'm bored, Richie."

"Ain't you always."

VII

He was miles away, but he could still hear them as they screamed. How could he ever not hear them? They were his children.

Jason Soulis stared out at the waters and looked at the dull gray clouds that hid the sun away. In the distance, he could hear the crows cawing and chatting to each other. Maggie could have her human and he wished her the best.

He preferred the crows. He knew where he stood with them and never once worried about their duplicity.

He really hadn't expected the detectives to find the caves and supposed that was his fault for not realizing just how perceptive they were.

"I'm glad I let you live." He smiled and stretched, stifling a yawn. "I suspect you will prove interesting to have around."

Deep beneath the house he'd left behind, the vampires were trying to find a way out of their newly sealed prison. Far too much rock had fallen to allow them to simply swim out as they had before.

He wondered if they would die a second time, starved of blood and unable to feed. Or if they would change and evolve, become something better than what they were meant to be.

A few days in the cave had made several of them stronger than they had ever been before. Most often they were too weak and stupid to live for more than a single night. But the ones he'd created in Black Stone Bay? There were at least four he knew of that had survived their first night of freedom, and they were coming along nicely.

None of them stayed in the area. They were too smart for that. If that wasn't proof of improvement, what was?

"We shall see, my children. We shall see what you can become."

He listened to their frustrated screams and allowed himself a small smile.

Time would tell if the second phase was successful.

And Jason Soulis had all the time in the world.

AFTERWORD

BY JAMES A. MOORE

If you'd asked me even eighteen months ago if I had any desire to write a vampire novel, the answer would have been a resounding "HELL NO!" It's not that I have anything against vampires, per se, it's just that damn, people, they've been done a few times. They've also been done a few times by me. My first published novel was a collaborative work-for-hire vampire novel written for White Wolf Publishing. I wrote it a long, long time ago. Long enough ago, in fact, that sometimes I forget the details. That's probably for the best.

So, no. No desire whatsoever to pick up a pen and write about vampires. Better writers than me have already done it and been imitated a thousand times over. Bram Stoker's *Dracula* remains a powerful piece, strong enough to almost guarantee a hundred imitators alone. Anne Rice's writing style and more "humanized" approach to vampires hasn't just been imitated, it's generated a full-blown subgenre. She did to vampiric erotica what McDonald's did to hamburgers. And I could go on for a page or two about the number of vampire detectives/vampire monster hunters out there in the literary markets.

So, again, no desire whatsoever to touch on the subject of vampires.

But then I thought about the other writers, the ones who always manage to make the subject interesting for me all over again. Brian Lumley did it with his excellent *Necroscope* series of books. Simon Clark—yes, the very one who was gracious enough to give this book a read and throw some nice words in my direction—did it with *Vampyrrhic*. Christopher Golden did it with his unique twists on the concept of vampires and where they come from in *The Shadow Saga*, and there have been others as well. Richard Matheson's excellent *I Am Legend*, Stephen King's timeless *'Salem's Lot*. Dan Simmons did it, Ray Garton managed very well indeed, F. Paul Wilson has done it. Robert R. McCammon not only did it, but took it to all new extremes. Fred Saberhagen's *The Dracula Tapes* and several sequels are all fascinating reads and well thought out. He makes changes in the legends of Dracula and he also adds depth to the villainous Count. Dick Laymon's *The Traveling Vampire Show* was a fabulous tale with a nice twist or twelve. The same for *The Stake*; what a glorious excursion into familiar territory! Nancy Collins with her Sonja Blue novels took a few nice spins into the extreme and handled them beautifully. For every one of the books I've run across that seems to be nothing but a derivative, there's a gem out there, a little nugget of a book that makes it worth the time to delve back into the vampire myths and have a little fun. Of course, all of the authors who wrote these gems have talent in spades, and I'm never quite sure if I'm up to that sort of challenge.

It didn't take much time for my mind to start playing What If with me. Every writer knows the game. What If I DID write a vampire novel? What would I do to make it different?

Sometimes that little game can get you into trouble. The What If Game was helped along by Paul Miller, who introduced himself to me last year and asked if I'd be interested in working with him. Well, duh, yes. Of course!

And he said he might like to see a "big, fat, juicy vampire

novel" out of me. That took some serious thinking on my part. A nanosecond later, we agreed to talk about it.

And my mind kept playing that What If Game with me.

Did I want to write a vampire novel? No. Not really. The idea was a little intimidating. How in the name of God would I possibly hope to do one original enough to make anyone at all give a damn about it? Not bragging here, but I've had a lot of comparisons to Stephen King come along. I thought about that a lot.

Because, if I was going to do a vampire story, I had to make it stand out against some very fine examples of the genre. So many in fact, that the task quickly became daunting.

I pulled out my extensive collection of vampire movies and watched a lot of them before I wrote the very first word of *Blood Red*. I also pulled out roughly twenty novels and did the same thing. Not because I wanted new ideas. I'm happy to say that ideas are the easy part for me. I normally have a plethora of stories bouncing around in the cesspool of my mind and practically screaming to get out. No, I did it because I wanted to make sure that the ideas were mine as much as possible. There are certain inevitabilities in the vampire genre. Blood sucking or life draining is going to happen, otherwise it's hardly a vampire tale. I didn't try to get away from that. I didn't want to reinvent the vampire from the ground up. I am perfectly happy with putting a few spins on the old fanged menace and leaving most of what shows up intact, but there are certain aspects of the myth that change from writer to writer and certain parts that have been done, pardon the pun, to death. I didn't want to consciously or unconsciously imitate the writers I found the most outstanding. It's always a risk, especially when you're not only a writer but also a fan of the genre.

So, yes, I immersed myself in Hollywood renditions of vampires and then rolled around in the blood and viscera of a number of books, many of which are mentioned above.

And then I spent a few months thinking about vampires and what it is that makes them fascinating. First, there's the sex appeal. Then there's the danger. Somewhere along the line, there's the mystique and the notion of living forever.

I decided to go with a more monstrous vampire. I wanted a bad guy who is actually, truly a nasty thing to wake up to in the middle of the night. I wanted a different reason for a vampire to come to town and set up shop. To be fair, I wanted to write something that was uniquely mine in a field that has been paved over and reseeded a million times in the last century.

When it was finally time, I sat down and I wrote. I broke my own personal record for writing speed on *Blood Red*. Happily, I had an excellent editor to push me along and help me over the rough spots. I also had a second excellent editor come along afterward and give me a fresh perspective on what I had written because, I have to tell you in all honesty, as a writer I tend to stay too close to the subject I've been writing about for at least a year. I see forests, not trees, and I see the devil, not the details. It's hard to be impartial about something that consumes you for a month or so and won't let you bother with little things like sleep. Kelly Perry and Paul Miller are amazing people, and they did so much to make this book come out the way I wanted. I could thank them every day for a decade and still not feel like I've made it clear how indebted I am to them for their hard work.

The end result of that work is in your hands and, unless you've cheated and read this first, you've finished the tale. I truly, truly hope you enjoyed the ride. I know I did. I've heard praise from a few sources that has left me grinning for a few hours and I've heard a few comments (some not meant to be seen by me) that have left me scratching my head and wondering where I went wrong. Either way, this is my vampire story. Either way, it is done. For now.

Did I answer every question I posed in the book? No. I almost never do. I like leaving possibilities and loose ends out there. As a writer, I like the idea that maybe people will think about the unfinished business of the book and try to find their own answers. As a reader, I've seldom been satisfied by a story that leaves all of the questions answered and wrapped up in a nice, neat little package. Life does not leave things settled and done, once and for all. If I am to imitate life as much as possible, I can't overlook that sort of thing and be comfortable.

So yes, there are a few unanswered questions. If they grate too much on your nerves, I do apologize. If they left you wondering about what happens next, then I'm very pleased indeed.

Either way, I hope you enjoyed the ride.

James A. Moore
Marietta, Georgia
August 18, 2005
www.jimshorror.com
http://redredrage.livejournal.com